THE
HEALER

THE
HEALER

a novel

GREGG LUKE

Covenant Communications, Inc.

Cover images: *Norwegian Viking Runes, Traena Island* © Cloud Mine Amsterdam, coutesy shutterstock.com; *Roman wall background in sepia, Rome Italy* © ROMAOSLO, courtesy istockphoto.com

Cover design copyright © 2015 by Covenant Communications, Inc.

Published by Covenant Communications, Inc.
American Fork, Utah

Printed in the United States of America
First Printing: February 2015

21 20 19 18 17 16 15   10 9 8 7 6 5 4 3 2 1
ISBN 978-1-62108-826-4

To Traci Levinson Luke and Jared Luke, sister-in-law and nephew. Two people who have endured so much and who still believe.

ACKNOWLEDGMENTS

THIS BOOK IS THE BRAINCHILD of my good friend, author Daron Fraley. A while back he came up with the idea to novelize the Jewish legend of the Lamed Vovniks. He began the series by recruiting fellow authors to write stories that linked a relic from the Old Testament with one of the gifts of the Spirit. His pilot book, *Thirty-Six*, was released in 2012. He asked me to tackle the gift of healing (go figure), and the story quickly came to life from there. To find out more about the series, go to www.lamed-vav.com.

My heartfelt thanks also goes out to fellow author Sian Ann Bessey, a native Welshwoman who aided in correcting the dialect, scenery, and accents in this book. Her contributions were invaluable. If there are errors as to anything Welsh, they are the result of brandishing my artistic license with mindless abandon.

I would also like to thank my beta readers Melissa Duce, Brooke Ballard, Dawn Bergeson, David Dickson, and Daron Fraley, and Dr. Janelle Wells and Ben Boyer, FNP, who gave great medical information and suggestions along the way.

Finally, I would sincerely like to thank my editor, Stacey Owen, and everyone at Covenant Communications who believed this book was not too speculative to produce.

To the reader: Although I am a man of science, I truly believe in the gifts of the Spirit. I hope this tale helps you believe too.

CHAPTER 1

IT WAS ONE OF THOSE surreal moments when everything moved in slow-motion. Christian Pendragon was driving along A484 through the Welsh countryside, just outside Cardigan, when he felt a curious sense of premonition. He slowed his speed, just to be on the safe side. After a week in Wales, he was used to driving on the left side of the narrow roads, but the drizzly weather wasn't making navigation any easier.

The ubiquitous, midmorning haze was low and disorienting. As he passed through a particularly dense veil of mist, an old four-door sedan zipped recklessly by. His breath caught as the sedan skidded past a sharp bend and flipped several times on the moor. Time slowed as he watched the car's windshield crack and explode from its casing. The driver—a woman in a skirt—was tossed out of the opening like a discarded rag doll. The car finally came to rest upside down, some thirty yards off the road. Thick smoke hissed from the engine compartment, churning with the mist in spectral apparitions of gray and white.

A small flock of woolly sheep fled, bleating in panic. Chris pulled onto the shoulder where the sedan's skid marks left the road and sprinted to the woman. She lay face-up with one arm pinned behind her and both legs folded unnaturally to one side. She looked about thirty-something. Her short, dark hair was matted with blood; her eyes drooped half-open.

"Ma'am, can you hear me? Are you okay?" Chris asked urgently, fearing the worst.

The woman did not reply, did not move or blink.

"Ma'am, I'm going to check your vital signs." Pressing his fingertips against her carotid artery, he watched for the rise and fall of her chest. Neither reference indicated any sign of life.

Stay calm, Chris, he thought as his heart thumped forcefully in his chest.

He looked up when he heard tires crunching on the gravel shoulder. A car stopped behind his rental, and a man and a woman stepped out, looking in his direction.

"She's not breathing," Chris yelled. "I can't feel a pulse! Call for help! I'm starting CPR."

He began a series of thirty chest compressions, followed by two breaths into her mouth, then repeated.

"Come—on—lady," he huffed in sync with his thrusts. "Don't—die—on—me."

The other man joined him. "Is she responding?"

"No. Did you—call for—help?"

"My wife is on the horn with 999 presently," the British man said. "Would you like me to have a go?"

Chris nodded, remembering the UK's emergency services code differed from the US's 911. He moved to her head to perform resuscitation while the British man began compressions.

Before long, two more cars had stopped. One contained elderly motorists, who stayed by their car, watching from the shoulder. The other couple joined the effort to revive the woman.

Chris stepped back to catch his breath. Flames now flickered from the inverted sedan's engine, adding thick black smoke to the sorcerous dance above. A siren wailed mournfully across the moor.

Without warning, a woman standing near the back of the sedan screamed. She stood with her hands pressed against the sides of her head. Chris jogged over to her as another man—probably her husband—put an arm around her, trying to console her. Trembling, she buried her face against the man's chest. Chris assumed she was in shock from the hopelessness of the scene.

"Is she all right?" Chris asked.

The man kissed the top of her head. "She's jus' upset is all."

"Is there anything I can do to help?"

With her face still pressed against her husband's chest, the woman pointed to the rear of the upside-down vehicle. The roof was partially collapsed; the safety glass was fractured but intact. Chris moved to the back of the car—and drew a sharp breath. With all the attention on the engine fire and the unresponsive driver, no one had noticed the small hand pressed against the cracked rear window.

Dropping to his belly, Chris peered inside. The hand and arm disappeared behind the seat, and they weren't moving. It looked like they belonged to a child about seven or eight years old. Chris quickly scooted to a missing side window. A gap of about twelve inches allowed minimal vision into the backseat. He could barely see a pair of sneakers boasting Captain America graphics. The child's body and head were hidden by the crumpled seat.

Putting his face to the opening, Chris smelled gasoline. "Hey, buddy. Can you hear me?" he said, trying to keep his tone light.

There was a muffled whimper in reply. It sounded like a boy.

"My name is Chris. I'm gonna help you, okay? Can you breathe in there?"

"I want me mum," was the boy's plaintive answer.

"Your mom can't help right now, so it's up to you and me. We need to get you out of the car right away. Are you hurt?"

"I want me mum," the boy repeated with more urgency.

"I know, buddy. There are some good people taking care of her right now. You'll see her soon. Is there anyone else in there with you?"

A muted *unh-unh* was the answer. The boy's legs fidgeted a bit, and he cried out. It was then Chris noticed that both ankles were twisted at extreme angles—undoubtedly broken.

To keep the boy distracted, Chris said, "Hey, I see you like Captain America, is that right?"

"Yeah." The reply was weak and laced with fear. Even so, Chris sensed the boy was trying to be brave.

"Well, I'm not Captain America, but I *am* from the United States. Listen, buddy, I can see you're pretty squished in there. I can try and shift your car, but you're gonna have to help get yourself free, okay?"

A stuttering breath. "Okay."

"Before I try, I need to ask you two things. First, what's your name?"

"Nigel. Nigel Madsen."

"Wow, that's a cool name. Okay, Nigel, can you tell me if you're in any pain?"

"My ankles hurt something terrible, but I . . . I can't feel me feet."

Probably the initial numbness that comes from severe trauma, Chris reasoned. "I see. Well, that's okay for now. Can you move your arms?"

"Yeah."

"Excellent. Now listen, when you feel the car move, you try wriggling backwards, okay? Hold on a sec." Chris stood and pushed against the car. It rocked only slightly. It was a small car; he was sure if someone helped they could right it.

"I need a few men to help me here," he called to the people helping the driver.

Most of them averted their eyes; some shook their heads. Chris couldn't believe it. Their hesitation caused anger to surge within him.

The engine flames grew, hissing and spitting into the air. He turned his back to the heat and pushed against the car a second time, trying to get it into a rocking motion.

The two-toned wail of a siren died as a police car pulled off the road.

"Let the constable handle it, mate," one man said.

"Back away before you get hurt, ay?" another added.

Two more sirens now droned in the distance. Chris hoped at least one was an ambulance.

He watched the constable kneel beside the mother. No one was continuing CPR. Someone had draped a coat over her face. Chris's heart sank.

Dropping to his knees, he took a steadying breath and stuck his face in the window. The smell of gasoline was stronger now; it stung his nostrils. "Sorry, sport. I can't seem to budge the car. I guess I'm not very strong."

"Is me mum all right?"

Chris swallowed hard. "I don't know. But there's an ambulance on the way just in case." He scrunched his eyes against the caustic fumes concentrating in the confined space.

"My nose burns," the boy complained. "It smells like petrol."

"I know. I smell it too. Listen, Nigel, a moment ago I saw you move your legs. Maybe I can pull you out of there. Can you shift your feet to your right?"

The boy's legs squirmed a few inches, but his feet dragged behind. He cried out loudly.

Just then, a loud *pop* came from the engine compartment. The smell of gas intensified. Chris felt strong hands grab his legs and pull him away from the car.

"Move away from there, sir. This thing's likely to blow."

Chris looked up at the hard face of the constable. "Wait! There's a small boy in there," he gasped. "He's still alive."

As the officer bent to look inside, a fierce explosion rocked the vehicle. Several women screamed. The engine was fully ablaze now, belching acrid smoke into the murky air. The flames quickly spread across the bottom of the car, igniting freshly leaked oil and gas.

"No," Chris yelled. He tried to crawl back to the car, but the constable grabbed his feet, stopping him.

"It's no use, sir. That fire's already at the boot. It's done for."

"That's why we have to get him out now!"

When he tried crawling again, the officer once more grabbed his feet. Chris rolled, dislodging the man's grip, and kicked him in the chest, dropping him flat on his rump with a grunt of shock. Chris then soldier-crawled back to the missing window. Forcing an arm and shoulder in, he said, "Nigel, can you hear me?"

"What's happening? It's hot in here."

"The car's in trouble, buddy. We have to get you out in a hurry. Scoot backward as much as you can."

The young boy complied, again crying loudly as he did. His ankles folded at grotesque angles.

Reaching for Nigel's legs, Chris's arm scraped across a jagged shard of glass. It cut deeply into his flesh. He hissed in pain. Another crackling *pop* sounded directly above him. Searing heat and flaming drops of oil rained down.

Nigel yelled, "Get me out of here!"

Chris grabbed the boy's legs and pulled with all his might, praying he wasn't further damaging the ruined ankles. Nigel slid a fraction toward him—then caught.

"Nigel. Can you push with your arms?"

"I want me mum!" the boy sobbed.

"You've gotta help me, buddy. Now, you push when I pull, okay?"

Chris pulled again, but the awkward angle made it impossible to gain any leverage. The hiss of a punctured line erupted to his right; a burning glob of oil landed inches from his face.

He cocked his head and yelled, "Help, please! I need some help here."

This boy is too young to die, he silently pleaded, as if in prayer. *Please, God. Help me help him!*

At that moment, someone gripped Chris's ankles, two men, perhaps. Someone tugged at his coat, helping pull him away from the car. One of the men said something: "*Rwy'n pasio i chi y pŵer i gwella.*" Maybe it was Gaelic or Welsh. It probably meant "hold on tight" or "try again." Chris knew a little Welsh but not enough to translate—especially in this situation.

He again grabbed both of Nigel's ankles. It would hurt the boy, but it was his best grappling point. When he felt a tug from the men behind him, he shouted, "Push, Nigel. Push with all your might!"

Chris felt like he was being stretched by some medieval torture device. There was no way he *wasn't* causing further injury—he could feel Nigel's flimsy ankle bones shifting unnaturally. But he had to get him out of the blazing car. Any injury was better than burning to death. He heard Nigel scream over the roar of the flames; the panicked shrieks of spectators filled the air. Chris's prayers went from fervent to pleading to commanding. Finally, he felt something give from within the vehicle. He was dragged backward, bringing Nigel out with him.

As Chris clambered to pick up the boy, the gas tank exploded, rocking the scene. The concussive wave blew past, knocking him to the ground. The hot blast seared his neck and singed his hair. He hurriedly picked up Nigel, staggered a few more feet from the inferno, then collapsed, cradling the boy tightly.

Chris's eyes burned from the pungent smoke and gasoline fumes. Someone wrapped a blanket around Nigel and gently pulled him from Chris's arms. Although his vision was blurry, he could see people milling about on either side. Most were watching the burning car.

He then felt someone checking his vital signs. They were talking gently, asking him questions he couldn't decipher.

"I'm okay," he wheezed, surprised at the hoarseness of his voice.

Hands slid under his shoulders and carefully strapped him onto a litter. He felt himself carried away from the wreckage; then, for a moment, he was motionless. The sounds of the accident echoed in the back of his head. His body ached from stress and angst; he must have twisted his ankles because they were very sore.

Before long he heard someone addressing him. The voice was very close. He looked up, forcing his eyes to focus. Expecting an EMT or the constable, he was surprised to instead see an elderly man with a closely trimmed, gray beard.

The old man bent low and placed his face next to Chris's ear. "*Rydych dim ond un o triginta secs.*"

Chris was still in a state of shock; he could swear the old man said something about ridding diamonds of trying sex. That couldn't be right. "I don't understand," he croaked.

The old man switched to English. "I've been waiting a long time for you, young man. A lot of folk have."

CHAPTER 2

Two emergency vehicles had shown up. Chris had some minor burns, but nothing serious. The EMTs suggested the gash on his arm be stitched, but they didn't deem it worthy of an ambulance trip. They sealed the wound with Steri-strips and wrapped it in gauze and Coban. Chris's ankles were still incredibly sore, but that would pass.

Finished with his triage, Chris sat on a collapsible camp chair in the lee of one ambulance to escape the numbing breeze. The drizzle had stopped, but chilled moisture still thickened the air. With a blanket wrapped around his shoulders, he watched a fire truck drive onto the moor and quickly extinguish the blazing sedan. It was a total loss.

Nigel's mother was an even bigger loss. Draped in a shroud, she'd been loaded onto the ambulance behind him. No one attended to her; she was already gone. Nigel was being treated inside the second ambulance. Chris wondered how they would break the terrible news to him.

Penetrating cold set in upon Chris—a mix of the biting, damp air and the deep remorse that follows human loss. He tried to fight it but knew it was a hopeless cause. So many things in his life felt like hopeless causes . . .

"You did your best, son," a voice said, startling him.

He looked up at the old man with the gray beard. Standing slightly bent, he favored his weight on a sturdy wooden cane. The man was not tall—maybe five seven when standing erect—but what he lacked in height he made up for in breadth. He was stocky, with wide shoulders, a solid torso, and thick, stout legs. His woolen trousers were secured at his waist with a length of chord. A patchwork tam sat low on his brow. He wore a natty sweater-vest over an Oxford-cloth shirt missing both collar buttons. His tweed sport coat bore work-worn, suede elbow patches with matching lapel points. Chris guessed the man was close to eighty.

"Wasn't enough though, was it," Chris mumbled bitterly, looking back at the scene of grief. "Two broken ankles, one death."

"Takes a special kind of faith to raise someone from the dead," the man said with a heavy Welsh accent and a trace of remorse. "Only man I know can do it died on a cross 2,000 years since."

Continuing to gaze out across the lonely moor, Chris grumbled a soft acknowledgement. The black smoke had dissipated, but the patchy haze continued to scrabble across the bunch grass in ever-morphing patterns of white on white—as if nothing untoward had even happened.

"Mind if I sit a spell?"

Chris shrugged.

The old man tipped an empty plastic box on end and groaned to a seat. He removed his patchwork cap and ran gnarled fingers across his scalp. He had an impressive head of closely cropped hair for one so old; and although it was fully gray, his hair and beard did not bear any of the thinning associated with men of advanced years.

"How are *you* fairing, lad?" the man asked. His voice was not particularly deep, but it resonated with the confidence of many years.

Chris raked his fingers through his own hair, surprised at the lack of burnt ends. "Surprisingly well, considering what I just went through. Man, I feel like all my energy's been sapped."

"And your ankles?"

He must have seen me limping, Chris reasoned. "They're sore . . . but that's nothing compared to the boy's."

The old man grunted. "It were a brave thing you did there, son, no mistake," he said, gesturing toward the charred vehicle. "Very noble. Very compassionate."

"Like I said, it wasn't enough," he groused, more harshly than he intended.

"Aye. Life can feel that way sometimes. We do the best we can, don't we. But when we look back, it always falls short of what we could have done, ay?" The man paused, forcefully rubbing his deep-set eyes.

Chris felt a surge of umbrage. "You're saying I could have done more? I'd sure like to know how." He didn't try to check his affronted tone. "You saw what happened. I was almost killed. If it weren't for you, the boy and I would be as dead as his mother."

"Oh, you did everything you could, lad; no one's saying to the contrary. It's the other folk—the ones who stood by and watched you risk your life for a complete stranger. Them's the ones should be ashamed. You showed unselfish compassion, didn't you. That's the true measure of a man. The other folk won't think on it again, except when inflating their trifling contribution at a pub."

Chris snorted harshly. "You're probably right." He rubbed his forehead, willing his frustrations to subside. "So . . . why did *you* help?"

"It's what I do, or rather, what I did."

Chris's brow furrowed. "You . . . *help* people? What—are you a psychiatrist or something?"

"Good heavens, no, lad. I haven't brains for the like. But I do try to heal . . . when it's appropriate."

Chris continued to rub his forehead. He wasn't sure if it was the shock from his brush with death or the man's heavy, Welsh accent, but it sounded like he was talking in circles. "You're just a Good Samaritan then?"

"Aye," the old guy chuckled warmly. "As are you, son. As are you."

Chris smiled at the way the man had turned the point of conversation back to him. "So what do you mean, it *was* what you did? Have you decided to retire from Samaritanism?"

The man slowly rotated his cane in his fingertips. Secured at the crown was a smoothly polished chunk of milky-white stone, roughly the size of a tennis ball. The man stared at it intently, as if seeking the answer to Chris's question within its translucent depths. When he spoke, his voice was soft but sure. "I am ready to meet my Creator, and gladly. I accepted my calling and fought the good fight, ay? Now it's the call of the next in line."

Chris just stared at him. *The next in line?* What in the world was he talking about? "Are you . . . Well, do you have a terminal illness or something?"

He shook his head. "No, no. Quite to the contrary."

"Then what makes you think you're going to die?"

A mischievous smile creased his beard. "Who said anything about dying? I merely said that I'm ready to meet my Creator, didn't I."

"O-kay . . ." Chris's head tilted to one side. The man's logic made no sense, but Chris couldn't tell whether it was intentional or not. "What was that you said to me when you pulled me from the wreck? It sounded foreign. Was it Gaelic?"

"Old Welsh. My native tongue."

"What did it mean?"

"Just some words of encouragement, now, weren't they, lad."

Chris shrugged and stretched. "Well, in any case, I haven't yet thanked you for helping—and for quite possibly saving my life." He extended his hand to the stranger. "I'm Christian Pendragon, from America. Call me Chris."

The man's hands were surprisingly soft for looking so knobby and work-worn. "Nicholas Tewdrig. A pleasure to make your acquaintance, I'm sure. Here on business then, are you, Mr. Pendragon?"

"Oh no. No, I'm here on vacation. And it's *Chris*."

"Have you a trade, Christian? A particular vocation?"

Giving up on having his name used informally, he said, "I teach history at Gonzaga University in the States. Why?"

Nicholas grunted softly while continuing to stare into the opaque stone atop his cane. "Oh, no reason, lad. Just curious, is all." After a long moment, he continued in a tone of reverence, as if asking something so deeply personal he didn't want anyone else to hear. "Have you ever wondered if you might have a higher calling in this life, Christian?"

The whole conversation had seemed strange; now it was downright creepy. The old man had just unearthed a concern Chris kept buried deep in his soul, one he was hesitant to share with anyone. *Did* he have a higher calling in life? Something more significant than teaching? A true *destiny*? He believed he did, but it had never progressed further than something gnawing deep in his soul. And that bothered him.

Chris had always viewed teaching as perhaps the highest calling a person could have. What other profession held the future of civilization in its palm? But for the longest time, he felt as if it wasn't quite enough, as if he was meant to do more—although he didn't know what or even why he felt that way. It was one of the reasons he'd come to Wales. He'd told everyone it was simply a present to himself for successfully finishing his first year of teaching at Gonzaga. While that was partly true, it actually went deeper than that. Much deeper.

When Chris didn't answer, the old man continued solemnly: "You have a gift, Christian Pendragon. It's in your blood, lad, whether you know it or don't. And it's about to have a profound influence on the rest of your life."

Chris's eyebrows peaked. "Excuse me?"

"Compassion, son. Healing."

He stared at the old guy a moment before chuckling. "Look, Nick, I don't want to burst your bubble, but you're mistaken. I make my living as a history teacher not a physician." He wasn't about to open up more than that to this stranger.

"Ay. My livelihood was ministering to the Master's flock. Always has been, ay? But that was not my *calling*, now was it?" He stood slowly and stretched his lower back with a pronounced groan. "By gaw. I didn't think it would come on this quickly. I'm going to miss the mantle, no mistake. But . . . these things happen. It's up to you now, my friend."

Up to me? Chris felt truly lost. He had no clue what the old guy was talking about, nor did he want to. He was cold, sore, and depressed. This whole incident had only unearthed concerns he'd chosen to suppress. He simply wanted to get back on the road and get his mind on something else.

Chris stood and extended his hand to say good-bye but paused when he heard a young boy calling in their direction. "Ho, Mr. Yankeeman! Wait a tick, ay?"

A young boy jogged toward him. He was short and lean, with dark hair and blue eyes. He wore a ratty sweater, jeans, and Captain America sneakers. Chris couldn't believe his eyes.

"Nigel? You're—you're running?"

"Ay, thanks to you, I am." The boy didn't stop until he had his arms wrapped around Chris's waist.

In shock, Chris held him away and dropped to his knees. "But your ankles, your feet."

Nigel looked down. "You mean me tennies? They're a wee bit mucked up, aye, but at least I can feel me feet again, ay?"

Chris numbly took in the perfectly healthy young boy in front of him. He knew the child's ankles had been broken—there was no doubt. And yet, here he was, walking and running, without any pain.

"Have you seen me mum?" Nigel asked in a tone that revealed he suspected something was amiss.

Chris's stomach lurched. "You mean no one's told you yet?"

Nigel frowned. "Told me what?"

Chris looked around for help. The EMTs were chatting with the firemen and the constable. The other bystanders had all left. Even Nicholas Tewdrig was no longer there. Chris had no idea where the old man had gone.

Grasping the boy's shoulders, Chris swallowed a lump of sorrow before speaking. "Your mother is gone, son."

Nigel's frown deepened. "Gone? Gone where?"

Again Chris looked for help, but everyone was headed back to the wreckage, laughing and slapping each other on the back. He couldn't see anything remotely funny about the situation. "Nigel. Your mother was killed in the accident. I'm very sorry."

Stunned refusal lashed the eight-year-old's face. Tears welled and spilled as he shook his head in denial. Chris sensed the boy wanted to put on a brave demeanor, but the shock was too great. When his emotions gave way, Chris drew Nigel into his arms and held him tightly. Wrenching anguish tore at Chris's heart as the boy's sobs went from whimpering to convulsive. The sorrow of the moment—along with sequestered memories of his own childhood—mixed in a tortured blend of heartache and emptiness. Tears filled Chris's eyes.

"But why?" Nigel's voice was thick with grief.

"I don't know, son. Perhaps God had need of her." His reply was tenuous, unsure. It seemed like such a pat answer, a cop-out really, but it was all he had.

"No. Why couldn't you save me mum?"

Chris felt an unfair sting of accusation in the question. He hadn't caused the accident . . . directly. Yes, he was driving slowly, perhaps a bit overcautiously, but the hazardous conditions warranted it. The mother's recklessness had led to her death, not Chris's conservative driving. He couldn't change the fact that she was already dead by the time he got to her. But . . . he couldn't really tell Nigel that.

"I don't know, buddy. I tried to save her. Honestly, I tried." His tone was filled with remorse, his throat pinched with shame.

Nigel continued to cry into Chris's shoulder. His tiny arms clung tightly to Chris's torso, as if letting go would cause him to lose his mother all over again. After an unbearable silence, he again asked in a small voice, "But why, mister? I don't understand."

"I don't know, Nigel. I wish I had an answer for you, but I don't."

It seemed forever before the constable came over to lend a hand. He explained that he'd called for a social worker to assist with the boy. "She just pulled up and will be here presently," he said in a concise tone.

"Thank you," Chris replied.

The officer held an aluminum clipboard and a pen at the ready. "Witnesses say you were first on the scene. Can you tell me about it, sir?

Was the woman dead when you got here?" His voice was businesslike, without emotion.

Chris scowled at the man. Indicating young Nigel with a quick tip of his head, he said, "Can we talk about this later?"

The constable rolled his eyes. "Fine. But don't leave these premises without talking to me first. Understand, sir?"

"Sure."

After a time, Nigel's crying lessened but did not totally abate. "I still don't understand, mister," he said through short sniffles.

"I don't either, buddy. I wish I did," Chris consoled him. "I really do. Sometimes bad things happen to me too. And I can't do anything to change them."

"Yes, you *can*. My ankles were hurt—I know they were. But then you touched them and healed them. So why couldn't you heal me mum?"

CHAPTER 3

CHRIS HAD NO REASONABLE RESPONSE for the boy. It was an astute question, heartfelt and sincere, but one he couldn't answer. He hadn't done anything to heal Nigel's broken ankles. In fact, he'd been worried about damaging them further. And yet, they were obviously now healed. The EMTs had checked him over thoroughly. Perhaps . . . perhaps they hadn't been broken. Just severely twisted.

"I'm very sorry, Nigel. I wish I could've done more for your mom."

Not only were the boy's eyes red and swollen from crying, they also had a desperate, lost look in them, a terror-filled blend of not understanding mixed with chilling realization. Chris wondered how he could explain when he didn't fully comprehend it himself.

"I couldn't move my ankles 'cause they hurt. But after you touched them—"

"Look, I didn't heal anything," Chris interrupted, feeling his frustration growing. "Please stop saying—"

"Hello, Nigel," a kind, female voice cut in. "I am deeply sorry for what happened to your mum. Truly I am."

Nigel and Chris looked up at the woman standing next to them. Chris had no idea how long she'd been there. She looked to be about forty and had a face that radiated kindness. She wore a photo-ID nametag from the lapel of her woolen overcoat. Kneeling, she slowly held out her hand, palm up, not in anticipation of a handshake but in an offering of solace. "My name is Mrs. Mary McKenzie. I'm from the Department of Social Services out of Carmarthen. I got here quick as I could, and I'm glad I did, because you know what, Nigel? You remind me of *my* son. He's a bright, handsome boy, just like you." Her smile was genuine, sincere.

Nigel clung to Chris but did not turn away from the McKenzie woman. She kept her hand extended, her palm open.

Chris cleared his throat. "I'm Chris Pendragon, Mrs. McKenzie."

Her smile expanded. "Yes, a pleasure to meet you, Mr. Pendragon. You bear a Welsh name but not the accent?"

"I'm visiting from the States and happened upon the accident in time to help Nigel."

"Ah, yes, and we're so glad you did. We cannot thank you enough. They say you saved young Nigel's life."

Chris dropped his gaze. "I did what I could. Wish I could've done more."

"I know you do, Mr. Pendragon. You're a good man. I've been doing this job for thirteen years, and I can sense a compassionate soul when I meet one. That's undoubtedly why Nigel has taken a fondness to you."

"Thank you," he said, touched by her kindness.

Her hand remained extended. If it caused her discomfort, she didn't show it. "Nigel? Would you like to come with me now? I know the fire captain personally, and he said he'll let you sit in the hose lorry and even blow the air horn if you like. How's that sound? After that, I know a brilliant ice cream shop in Carmarthen we could visit."

The young boy looked up at Chris with questioning eyes.

"Are you kidding me?" Chris said with a huge grin. "A fire truck *and* ice cream? I'd take her up on it in a heartbeat. And if I recall, Captain America *loves* ice cream."

After a moment's hesitation, Nigel reached out and took Mrs. McKenzie's proffered hand. She stood and led him toward the fire truck, talking incessantly, asking him question after question—probably to keep his mind off the tragedy.

Chris assumed Nigel would eventually be taken to the hospital for a comprehensive examination while the next-of-kin was contacted. He hoped the best for the young boy.

As per his promise, he spent the next half hour detailing exactly what he'd witnessed to the gruff constable. Clearly, the officer was still unhappy about the kick to his chest, but he said he was not going to press the issue—or charges—seeing as how Chris was a Yank and would be leaving the country soon. Chris thanked him and rehearsed how Nigel's feet had gone numb and that he'd grabbed the boy's ankles when he felt his own legs being pulled from behind. The only hitch was when he mentioned Nigel's previously broken ankles.

"You must be mistaken there, sir," the constable said. "The boy's been walking about, right as rain. Maybe his ankles were just twisted a bit, ay?"

"I've never seen ankles twisted at such extreme angles without being severely damaged. Even if they weren't broken, I'm surprised he can walk on them."

"And yet we both know he's doing quite well," he countered, scribbling on his clipboard. "Let's just put that you *thought* they looked injured, shall we?"

Chris didn't want to argue the point. For now, he simply wanted to be on his way. The overcast sky was darkening quickly, and he still had several miles to go before he reached his next scheduled stop.

"That's fine, officer. Put whatever you like."

"Right. Splendid. Now, I have your address in the States and your mobile number. You may get a ring from my superior about this, just to confirm everything in my report is up to snuff like. Not to worry, though. It all seems on the up and up. I've got statements from the three couples who lent a hand. Terrible misfortune about lad's mother though. Well, you enjoy the rest of your holiday, Mr. Pendragon."

"Wait," Chris said, confused. "There was one other man, an older gentleman: plaid cap, close-trimmed beard, carried a walking stick. His name was Nicholas Tewdrig. He was the one who helped me pull Nigel from the car. Did you talk to him?"

"Nicholas Tewdrig?" the constable asked, flipping through his notes. "Nicholas Tewdrig? I got statements from a number of folk, but I don't believe I talked with him. Ah, one couple did mention a gentleman in a tweed sport coat, but they didn't catch his name. You say he witnessed the accident too?"

Chris rubbed his neck. "I don't know. He was there right after you tried pulling me away from the car. You don't remember seeing him?"

A dark shadow passed behind the officer's narrowed eyes. "I remember being kicked to the ground. The next thing I knew, the car exploded and you had the lad in your arms."

"Yeah—that part I remember. And I apologized about the kick already. But without Mr. Tewdrig, I wouldn't be here talking with you. And Nigel certainly wouldn't be alive. You *had* to have seen him."

"I'm sorry, sir," he said with zero apology in his voice. "I don't recall seeing anyone of that description about the scene." He paused and shot Chris a look of mistrust. "Are you sure you're okay, sir? Maybe that explosion gave you a slight concussion like. I could have EMTs take you to hospital for a quick once over, eh?"

Chris was too tired to argue. He declined the assistance, signed the report, and bid the constable good-bye.

Continuing along A484 toward Newcastle Emlyn, Chris felt completely drained, as if he'd just finished a fifty-mile hike. He figured it was the stress from the accident and rescue. Anxiety can do that to you. His always did.

Consulting his map, he decided to stop at the Gwesty'r Emlyn Hotel in the center of Newcastle Emlyn. Normally he didn't opt for fancy hotels or touristy venues; but it was late, and the three-hundred-year-old building looked inviting. He simply wanted to get there, check in, go to sleep, and forget this ever happened.

By the time he arrived at the hotel, the night had brought a light rain. Not enough to wash away the haze but sufficient to add a biting chill to the darkness. He grabbed his suitcase and satchel, and entered the lobby.

Chris checked into a ground-floor room, grabbing some cookies and a soda from a vending machine. The room was cozy and quaint, but the DVD player and flat-screen TV detracted from the old-world charm. No matter. He was only staying one night.

While slipping off his outerwear, he felt something small and hard inside his coat pocket. Reaching in, he discovered a rectangular piece of stone, roughly the dimensions of a domino tile, only slightly longer and severed at an angle on one end. The back was pitted and scored, as if the small section had broken off a larger mosaic of some kind. The obverse side was polished smooth and bore markings, ancient script of some sort, not Roman or Asian characters, something more akin to . . . what? Perhaps Middle Eastern? He wasn't sure, nor did he have any idea where the stone had come from. He hadn't picked it up off the road. He hadn't purchased it at a souvenir shop. He sensed it was somehow connected with the strange events of that afternoon. The tile's off-white, marbled hues reminded him of the stone atop Nicholas Tewdrig's walking staff.

Shrugging, he placed the odd stone on the dresser with his keys and cell phone, and prepared for bed. After brushing his teeth, he unwound the Coban from his forearm and gawked at the wound—or lack of one. He rubbed his eyes and looked again. He distinctly remembered receiving a deep laceration. His torn, bloodstained shirtsleeve attested to that. The EMTs had even suggested that it needed stitching. But in the light of the bathroom, all Chris saw was a thin white line underneath the Steri-strips. It looked like nothing more than an old scratch. There was no redness, no swelling, no indication of infection. Nothing. He touched the area, pushing against the wound he knew should still be tender but wasn't. It was pain-free. No heat, no soreness or discomfort of any kind. Perhaps his perceptions had been exacerbated by angst—just like his misjudgment of Nigel's ankles. There was no way a substantial wound like that could've healed so quickly.

Chris shrugged again, deciding not to worry about it until morning. He removed the sticky strips from his forearm and washed off the residue. Then, finishing his nighttime routine, he knelt by his bed and offered a quick prayer. He was grateful for being able to help save Nigel's life. He hoped the best for the boy. He didn't know if Nigel had a father or other siblings, but Chris suspected he didn't. Nigel hadn't said a thing about having family.

He also prayed for resolution to his inner struggles. He prayed for peace and validation, for direction and happiness. His past plagued him. Just as he hadn't caused Nigel's accident, he knew he wasn't responsible for the death of his father. His pastor had told him so on numerous occasions. Yet, he couldn't deny feeling like he'd played a key part in his father's passing . . . and in the death of Nigel's mother.

Pushing that aside, Chris ended his entreaty and crawled into bed.

He mentally rehearsed his itinerary for the following day—a day filled with roaming the ultra-green countryside, taking in spectacular vistas and ancient ruins. But try as he might, he couldn't stay focused on the planned agenda. His mind ran rampant with unbidden images: broken ankles, a lacerated forearm, a mysterious old man spouting cryptic messages, and an off-white stone engraved with archaic markings that somehow connected it all.

CHAPTER 4

CHRIS WAS JOLTED FROM SLEEP by a loud peal of thunder. It didn't matter. He'd had a fitful night up to that point anyway.

Sitting on the edge of his bed, he rubbed his puffy eyes, sensing that his well-laid itinerary of bucolic repose was now a thing of the past.

Chris had come to Wales with three tasks in mind: the first *was* to reward himself for having finished his first year at Gonzaga. He'd taught general world history, European history, and a course in his specialty— historic corollaries in Welsh mythology. All three had finished exceptionally well. Now it was time to relax and enjoy the scenery. He'd visited Wales once before for research, but he'd been so caught up in the details, he'd missed seeing the country.

The second task was to unearth a bit of family history, to get to know who he really was. Perhaps a bit of self-discovery. He hated applying the old cliché, but he was really hoping to "find himself." He'd always liked his surname of Pendragon. He knew the moniker was coined by Uther Pendragon, father of the legendary King Arthur, at the time of his brother's death. When Ambrosius died, Uther saw a portentous, dragon-shaped comet, which the magician Merlin interpreted as presaging Uther's glorious future. It inspired the king to use dragons on his military standards and armor. *Pendragon* roughly translated to mean "Chief Dragon."

The final reason Chris came was to be alone. No family, no friends or colleagues. No pressure to enter medical school as his brother and sister had, following in their father's footsteps. No explaining to anyone— including himself—why, despite his successful first year, he was still having doubts about the path he'd chosen. And why it had yet to bring him lasting happiness.

He closed his eyes and massaged his forehead. How could he *find* himself without *explaining* himself? Teaching history was the path he'd chosen, but was it the right one? He loved history. He loved everything about his vocation: the sharing of facts and legends, chronicles and mysteries. But in the end, it was just a job. He'd always felt there was more to life than simply earning money and spending it. And yet, that is exactly where he found himself. Deep inside, it gnawed at his sense of worth. He wondered if teaching was truly his *calling*—just as old Nick had inferred. Was teaching his destiny? Perhaps he *was* meant for bigger things.

Thunder grumbled again. It sounded distant, lonely. He walked to the window and took in the restless, brooding night. It matched his mood perfectly.

As he reviewed his first week in Wales, a barrage of fresh uncertainties assaulted his mind. Other than a little sightseeing, he'd yet to delve into his true plans. And now this, an event that threatened to derail his itinerary. He could handle the accident and the miraculous rescue of Nigel Madsen. It was the appearance and disappearance of Nicholas Tewdrig and the old man's bizarre questions and comments that plagued him. Perhaps it was the similarity of the stone on Nick's walking staff to the one on the hotel dresser that brought it all to mind. Was there a connection? Or was it all mere coincidence?

"Coincidence is just God's way of remaining anonymous," he mumbled to the night. He couldn't remember where he'd heard that, but it seemed poignantly true at that moment.

Chris wasn't an overly religious man. He believed in God. He tried to attend his local parish at least once a month. Were these events some kind of heavenly intervention to get him to increase his piety? Or was the accident mere happenstance and Nick Tewdrig just a kooky old man spouting nonsense?

I've been waiting a long time for you.

I accepted my calling and fought the good fight. Now it's the task of the next in line.

Have you ever wondered if you had a higher calling in life?

You have a gift, Christian Pendragon. It's in your blood, lad, whether you know it or not. And it's about to have a profound influence on the rest of your life.

What gift? What higher calling? What was in his blood? What the heck was the old guy talking about?

Such forced indoctrination was what Chris's mother had preached ever since his father's death. "Being a physician is what your father wanted for you. I know he'd smile down on you if you went back to medical school. You can always study history and chase your legends as a hobby."

And now, still trying to escape the guilt, Chris was being told by a total stranger that healing was in his blood. That it was his true calling in life. That many people had been awaiting his arrival, like some presaged miracle worker appearing from the west. He wanted to deny it, to laugh it off as absurdity. But for some reason, he found it more portentous than humorous.

Staring out the window into the cold, wet night, he felt overwhelmed by moral responsibility. Suddenly, strangely, in fact quite exquisitely, something inside him was sanctioning this course of aiding his fellow man.

It's in your blood, lad.

"Yeah, like a virus," he scoffed.

He went to the sink for a glass of water. In the mirror he saw the items on the bureau behind him: his keys, his wallet, and the stone he'd found in his pocket. No longer able to ignore the curious artifact, he returned to the dresser and flipped on the light.

Turning the stone in his fingers, he watched its translucent, pastel colors flow and ebb just under its milky surface. As he held it closer to the lamp, the strange characters seemed to speak to him. They weren't mere decoration; they signified something important, something powerful.

Frowning, Chris knew it was a guide to the maze in which he now wandered. And while part of him wanted to simply chuck the stone into the nearest trash can, another part urged him to move forward. More importantly, he somehow knew that discarding the stone would have serious, potentially deadly consequences.

CHAPTER 5

Chris left the Gwesty'r Emlyn early in the morning. A breakfast of scones, coffee, and tea was offered, but he had no appetite. All he wanted to do was get back on the road and leave this area in his past. He figured if he focused on his vacation, he could push yesterday's mysteries behind him. He had better things to do.

A few miles south of Carmarthen stood Kidwelly Castle. The impressive structure had great historical significance but little to do with his personal research. Chris wanted to go simply because it'd been used in the opening of one of his favorite movies, *Monty Python and the Holy Grail*. The movie overflowed with historical, social, and political satire and hyperbole. He loved it.

Yet, for some reason, he felt compelled to head east instead. It didn't really matter. There were other points of interest he could visit; he didn't really care which he saw first.

Meandering through endless vales of pastoral countryside, Chris passed countless hamlets whose names most tourists could only guess how to pronounce. When his stomach began to grumble, he pulled up to an old pub called the Black Boar in the small town of Cwmllynfell.

The public house seemed not to have aged since its establishment in 1850. A crackling, open-hearth fire took the damp from the air and added a cheery warmth to the rustic interior. The smells of spirits, yeast, and malt permeated the atmosphere. A few old men puffed on pipes, adding a smoky sweetness to the room. Chris didn't smoke or drink alcohol, but he loved the ambience of this old Welsh tavern. He placed an order with the old barkeep and sat at a small table near a window.

Savoring a plate of hearty bangers and mash, the British term for sausages and mashed potatoes, he took in the public house with a historian's eye. Old photographs adorned the walls: black-and-white shots of prize Friesian and Hereford bulls, enormous Belgium draft horses, huge barns, and sundry events at county fairs. Coats of arms lined the lintel above the bar. He recognized most of them as Welsh family names: Argall, Llewellyn, Goodwyn, Rhydderch, Maddox, Bythell, and Pendragon. Tongue-and-groove mortising in hand-hewed oak beams bespoke architecture of decades past. Electrical conduit running across the ceiling and down the walls revealed the post-construction advent of modern power and lighting. And the time-worn, cobblestone flooring was gently troughed, having borne the tread of patrons for nearly two centuries.

"Can I bring you anythin' else, lad?" the pub matron asked in a lilting accent. She was a stout woman with a hard, no-nonsense face, but with cheery, bright hazel eyes. She wore a pinafore stained with years of food and ale, and a blouse whose buttons strained at her ample bosom.

Chris held up his empty mug. "May I have another one of these, please?"

She accepted the mug, sniffed it, and scowled. "What the heck? What're drinkin' here, mister?"

"Dry ginger ale?" he replied, confused at her revulsion.

"By gaw, that's not what you're supposed to be suppin' with bangers 'n mash, you daft beggar. The Black Boar's best brown bitter's the ticket. Brings out the flavor right nice like. Let me fetch you a proper pint, ay lad?"

Before Chris could argue with the large woman—or comment on her five-word alliteration—she was halfway to the bar.

"Hey, Angus. What the heck are ye doin'—givin' our guests sissy drinks with our bangers 'n mash? Fetch me a pint of brown ale, and be quick about it, ay?"

The barkeep was a few years older than the woman and much smaller in size. He bore a work-worn, henpecked demeanor brightened by an accommodating smile. "But that's not what lad ordered, Gwendolyn, love."

"He's an American, Angus. He knows naught about proper Welsh bitter."

With a closed-lip chuckle, Chris reached into his pocket for some change, but his fingers brushed the stone relic. He closed his eyes. He'd already forgotten about the artifact and all it represented.

Withdrawing the stone, he held it to the light. The pearlescent white exterior glowed with inner hues of pink, ivory, and amber. The engraved markings were clear and sharp, but they still held no meaning. He'd seen examples of Celtic, Gaelic, Welsh, and even some Cumbric lettering, but none of those resembled the scrawl on this piece.

Barmaid Gwendolyn returned, setting down a large pewter tankard brimming with froth. "There now. Take a sup of that and see if I don't know me ale," she said saucily.

A strong odor of yeasty fermentation wafted toward Chris. "That's very kind of you, but actually, I don't drink," he said with his best apologetic smile.

Gwendolyn gawked openly. "Don't drink? Don't drink?" Her expression quickly turned to one of contempt. "Say, you're not one of them religious types who go about pesterin' poor folk into givin' away all their brass for a better queue at the Pearly Gates, are you?"

He laughed. "Good heavens, no. I'm a history teacher. Not drinking alcohol is more of a health choice."

"More of a health—?" She stopped abruptly, eyes wide. "Our brown bitter has been known to cure many an affliction, I tell you. Weaned my own kids on this, I did. No better sedative when they won't go to bed, ay? And it'll knock any headache right proper like, quick as you please."

"I don't doubt—"

"You could do a lot worse than supping on a mug of this, by gaw. 'More of a health choice'? Rubbish. Healthiest stuff around is that."

"Look, I'm sure that's all true," he said, setting the small stone aside to fish in his pocket for change. "But really, I—"

"Ay, what have you got there, lad?" the barmaid interrupted, bending toward the small artifact.

He shrugged. "No idea."

"May I?" she asked, indicating the stone.

Chris nodded.

Holding it to the light, the woman drew in a long, backward whistle. "By gaw, I ain't seen one of these since I were a lass. Ay, Angus, come take a look at this," she shouted over her shoulder.

"You know what it is?" Chris asked.

"Ay, maybe I do. Long ago, when I were naught but a wee thing livin' up north, my uncle used to collect these from old pagan gatherin' sites— Druid and Nordic, I think. Secret places only he knew about."

"What's amiss, love?" barkeep Angus asked, eyeing the stone in her fingers. He also took a sharp intake of air. "Bless my soul; it's a rune stone."

"A rune stone? You mean like a burial marker?" Chris asked.

"Aye, that's one use for them," said Angus. "Some of the first history books, they were. Tells the life of the chap planted there. Only, many of them tell some pretty tall tales like. Don't know as you can trust them more'n you can toss them, ay?"

"Oh, I agree," Chris said, impressed at the barkeep's knowledge. "But small rune stones are very rare. Most are quite large, bigger than modern headstones. I don't believe they've found many pocket-size ones."

"Poppycock and balderdash," the barmaid spat.

"Now, Gwendolyn, love. No need for harsh language," Angus admonished.

Chris gave a crooked smile. "Well, I know of only one or two small stones that've been *confirmed* as rune stones."

"That's where you're wrong, lad," Gwendolyn said with a raised eyebrow. "They exist aplenty, I dare say; if you know where to look."

Chris thought for a moment. "Well, there are scores of artifacts like this that were used as money. Polished stones and gems predate metal and paper currency by thousands of years. But they were never used as *rune* stones as far as I know. As you said, rune stones are history books. You can't carve much history on something this size."

"Aye, but that's not all they're used for, now is it," Gwendolyn countered.

Chris raised his eyebrows in expectation. "Like . . . ?"

She hesitated, turning the stone in her fingers.

"Go on, then. Tell him, love," Angus prompted.

She drew a steadying breath. "Not all, mind, but some were used for . . . magic."

"Magic? Like a talisman?"

"Aye, that's right. A talisman," Angus eagerly agreed.

Chris cleared his throat, hoping he wasn't about to sound flippant. "I see. And you think this one has magical properties?"

The tavern owners exchanged a glance.

"No telling, lad. But it's som'et you ought not be mucking about with, ay? Better to bury it right where you dug it up."

"But I didn't dig it up," Chris explained. "It just showed up in my pocket yesterday afternoon."

The tavern keepers' eyes simultaneously widened.

"Saints protect us," Gwendolyn breathed, dropping the stone on the table and vigorously wiping her hands on her apron. Then, sniffing her fingertips, she spit on them, dipped them in the tankard of ale she'd just brought Chris, and wiped them a second time on her apron.

Another reason not to sample the drink, he mused.

Angus put his arm around Gwendolyn to comfort her. "There, there, love. Don't be vexed."

Chris tried not to smirk at how paranoid the two Welshfolk had become over the small artifact. They looked utterly terrified.

Picking up the stone, he asked, "Do you know what these inscriptions mean?"

"No," Gwendolyn snapped, shoving her hands deep in her pockets. "And you'd best be leavin' our house now, sir."

Chris blinked.

"Now Gwendolyn, dear. Don't be the shunning poor lad like that. He's done nothing amiss. Let him finish his mash first. Here," Angus continued, handing the tankard of bitter to his wife. "Go and fetch lad a fresh mug of ginger punch now; there's a good lass."

The stout barmaid took the pewter mug and marched back behind the bar.

"I'm terribly sorry," Chris said. "I didn't mean to offend anyone."

"Nay, nay, sir. Our Gwendolyn is a bit touchy about such stuff, is all. You'd best be putting that bauble back in your pocket afore she returns though."

He did as instructed. "You wouldn't happen to know where I could find out what the inscriptions mean?"

Angus thought for a moment, scratching the stubble on his jaw. "Aye. Aye, I just might. There's an old church past Brecon Fell a piece, over in Trellech. Used to be part of an abbey where monks and vicars used to study like. The church is popular with tourists and such. I seem to recall seeing such things there a time or two."

Gwendolyn returned with the ginger ale, slammed it on the tabletop, and returned to the bar without a word.

"Thank you," Chris said to her back. Deciding he was already full, he took a sip of the ginger ale and laid his fare plus a healthy tip on the table. "Thanks, Angus," he said, standing.

"Thank you, sir," the barman beamed.

As Chris was exiting, a black-and-white photo hanging on the wall caught his eye. It showed six men standing next to each other dressed in priestly robes. Each held a small rectangle of cloth at their waists; each cloth had been embroidered with a unique pattern. Kept in a glass frame, the photo was ancient but clear. And there was something in the shot that looked familiar to Chris. Deeply familiar.

Leaning closer, he focused on their attire. The embroidery was exquisite: Druidic symbols, Celtic knots, Tree of Life motifs, all ubiquitous patterns in Wales. But there was something else . . . something he couldn't put his finger on.

Then he saw it: a *who*, not a *what*.

"Excuse me, Angus?"

The barkeep was still wiping down his table. He looked up. "Yes, sir?"

"Do you know who this is?" he asked, pointing to the picture.

The old barman whipped his towel over his shoulder. "Let's have a looksee."

"The last man on the right."

Peering at the photo, he snorted. "Him? Oh, aye. That's our beloved St. Nicholas the Healer, isn't it? Not old Father Christmas, mind—your Yankee Santa Claus," he said, grinning, "but the vicar who blessed St. Anne's Well, near yon abbey."

"What abbey?"

"The one I told you about in Trellech: the Church of St. Nicholas."

"But . . . well I thought you said it was a tourist spot. You mean it's still functioning as a monastery?"

"Nay, lad, nay. Don't be twp. They still hold service there, but the abbey closed its doors hundreds of years ago."

"But—" Chris stopped and examined the photo again. "But that can't be. I met him just yesterday, just outside of Cardigan. That's Nicholas Tewdrig."

The barkeep scoffed. "Bah. Can't be."

Chris looked again. "He's got the same features, same hair and beard; he's about the same size. He looks *exactly* like the man I met yesterday."

Angus's eyes narrowed. He leaned in close to Chris and sniffed the air. "You sure you haven't been supping our best bitter, lad?"

"Of course. I told you I don't drink."

"Maybe he's a relation then," Angus said as he slid the framed photo off the wall peg and turned it over. "Look here, lad."

On the back was a faded, handwritten photographer's insignia, indicating the picture's content and the date it was taken. Chris blinked hard and looked again. It read: *Clergy of St. Nicholas Church. April, 1880.*

Chris scratched his head and smiled sheepishly. "Huh. I guess you're right. But . . . well, he looks just like him."

"Aye, no surprise. Lots of family from the old days have kin hereabouts. Could be a relation." The barkeep used his towel to dust the glass front of the frame then handed it to Chris. Chuckling warmly, he continued, "If it were him, he'd be nigh on two hundred years old or more, give or take. If you see him again, ask him his secret, eh? We'll bottle it and sell it, ay?"

Chris stared at the picture, dumbfounded. It was surprisingly clear. He was certain it was the same man—but at the same time, knew it couldn't be. Maybe it's just a coincidence, he thought, then chuffed. There's that word again.

As he seated the frame on the wall peg, one more detail caught his eye—and his breath. Nestled in the crook of St. Nicholas's arm was a walking staff topped with an opaque, off-white stone.

CHAPTER 6

CHRIS REHUNG THE PHOTO AND exited the pub. He now felt he *had* to travel to Trellech to see the old abbey. Nothing else seemed to matter anymore. The mysterious rune stone—if that's what it was—now bothered him almost as much as it had bothered barmaid Gwendolyn. Plus, there was the old photo of Nick Tewdrig's doppelganger. With steadfast resolve, Chris determined that once he got some answers, he'd leave the small stone in the abbey and finish his vacation.

The distance to the old church was roughly seventy miles, but the drive took almost four hours. Instead of following major roadways, Chris traveled the lesser highways, skirting the base of Brecon Beacons, the tallest mountain range in South Wales. Stark and rugged, the mountaintops were shrouded in misty clouds. Below, the hilly countryside was sectioned into large paddocks with rock walls and hedgerows of shrubbery and trees. Random patches of old growth forest meandered throughout the ultra-green vista. It had a medieval feel, as if Chris had traveled back in time to an era unpolluted with the selfish apportioning-down-to-the-last-inch of the modern world.

In spite of his fitful night, Chris felt incredibly rested, and he caught himself singing and laughing for no apparent reason. He had no aches or residual soreness from his exploits of the previous day. Even his hair, which he knew had been scorched by the car fire, felt full and healthy, with no indication of ever having been burnt. Must be the humidity, he reasoned.

* * *

Chris arrived at Trellech around six o'clock. A weather-worn sign indicated a turnoff to St. Anne's Well—the same one Angus had mentioned. What was it he said? That St. Nicholas had *blessed* the well? Did that give it special powers of some kind? Chris knew that wells and springs played an important role in Welsh mythology. Many people believed they were portals to and from the afterlife. Legends often told of faeries and elves coming from the ever-flowing depths.

Taking the exit, Chris drove to the turnout, which boasted a placard telling a short history of the site, as well as some of its unique features. Presently, the place was vacant. Chris was grateful for that.

St. Anne's Well—also known as the Virtuous Well, according to the placard—was surrounded by a semicircular, three-foot stone wall, with a notch in one side for an entrance. A bushy tree just outside the enclosure had multiple strips of cloth and ribbon hanging from its branches. The placard explained that the cloth strips were left by people who'd come to the well for a particular blessing, usually one of health. It was a practice that dated back to the fourteenth century.

Entering the surround, Chris peered into the dark depths of the well and saw . . . nothing but water. He smirked, unsure of what he was *expecting* to find. Certainly not any mythological creature staring back at him. It looked just like many of the other wells he'd seen throughout the Welsh countryside.

Chris shone a penlight into the small ensconced opening; the water appeared dense with particulate. He dipped a finger in and brought it to his lips. It was cool and fresh, with a slight metallic aftertaste. Sweeping his light along the interior of the stone revealed engravings that looked Druidic in origin. But his tiny penlight could be distorting the images; there wasn't enough natural light to be sure.

Sitting on the rim, Chris reached into his pocket for his mystery stone. With a curious twinge of disappointment, he compared its markings to those on the wall. They were nothing alike.

He jumped when his cell phone rang. The caller ID read Carmarthen Hospital. "Hello?"

"Hello, Mr. Pendragon? This is Mrs. Mary McKenzie from Carmarthen Social Services. Sorry to bother you so late in the day, but I really need to double-check something if you have the time, please."

"Sure, Mrs. McKenzie. What is it?"

"You told the officer at the scene that you were certain Nigel Madsen's ankles were severely damaged—perhaps even broken—when you first saw him in the car, is that correct?"

"Yes, they certainly *looked* broken, but apparently I was—"

"You were correct. We x-rayed his ankles, just to make sure, because there was some residual edema in that area."

"Edema? Like a hematoma?"

"Why, yes, as a matter of fact. Are you a physician, Mr. Pendragon?"

"Just a history teacher. But I come from a family of doctors, so I was raised on medical terminology," he said, almost apologetically.

"Brilliant. Then you also know a fracture hematoma looks different than a traumatic compression wound or contusion."

"You mean like a bruise."

"Precisely. And that's where we found something quite remarkable. The x-rays showed fully formed fibrocartilaginous calluses at the fracture sites of both ankles."

"Sorry, you just lost me." He chuckled.

"My apologies. As it was explained to me, there are basically four steps in bone healing. First, you develop a fracture hematoma, and small capillaries form to supply fresh blood to the wound site. After several days, the hematoma develops into a soft callus, from which collagen begins to build cartilage at the site. This cartilage is what creates the tougher, firmer fibrocartilaginous callus. It's what bridges the gap between the broken ends of bone. This callus lasts for about four weeks before becoming a hard-bone callus, under which the new bone is formed and knitted to the old."

Chris pinched the bridge of his nose and scrunched his eyes. "Okay. So why are you telling me this?"

"Because, Mr. Pendragon, it *only* happens when there's a break—and Nigel's x-rays showed fully formed calluses."

"Could they be from a previous fracture?"

"Yes, it's possible. But Nigel claims he's never broken a bone in his life. And his health records back that up. There's no history of him ever being treated for a fracture of any kind. In other words, Mr. Pendragon, his ankles *were* broken—quite severely, from what showed on the radiograph."

Chris frowned. "But . . . he was walking around just fine immediately after the accident. I don't understand."

"Neither do we. I just wanted to verify *your* story."

The way she said "*your* story" made him feel guilty for some reason. "So his ankles . . . I'm still confused. Are they broken?"

"Oh no. Like I said, they're almost completely healed. But because the x-rays show the callus formation, we know that they *were* broken. What's confusing is *when* they were broken. According to your testimony, it was at the time of the accident. His exam results indicate it happened weeks earlier, and yet we know that is not the case either. So the question arises: if they *were* fractured at the time of the accident, how did they heal so quickly?"

"I have no idea," he admitted.

"Are you sure nothing else happened from the time you pulled him from the wreckage until I collected him?"

"Pretty sure," Chris said. A headache was building at his temples, hindering his ability to concentrate. He still held the shard of stone in his other hand. Catching the last hues of evening sunlight, it smoldered with an intense, inner luster. *Did the stone have anything to do with Nigel?* As soon as the thought came to him, he laughed it away. "Let me think about it some more, okay Mrs. McKenzie?"

"Yes, of course. But please contact me if you remember anything of note."

"Okay. Sure."

"Very well. Thank you again, Mr. Pendragon. Good night, sir."

Chris pocketed his phone and the stone relic, and returned to his rental car. The lights of Trellech beckoned him. He drove to a hotel called the Lion Inn and booked a room for the night. After a mutton sandwich at the inn's café, he went to his room and collapsed on the bed. He wasn't physically tired; instead, he felt mentally exhausted, completely sapped of energy.

The confirmation that Nigel's ankles *had* fractured and instantly healed did not help his already beleaguered mind. The list of oddities kept growing: the car accident, a visit from a dead vicar, the strange rune stone, tales of magic, sacred wells, Druidic sites . . . and now miraculous healings. Harried images tormented his mind like a cat teases a mouse before killing it. He'd never before felt such angst from coincidental occurrences. Why was this happening?

He hoped and prayed tomorrow's visit to the ancient abbey would bring some resolution . . . and a strong measure of peace. And although he felt that peace *would* come, he also sensed he would not like *how* it came.

With a grunt of concession, Chris pulled off his shoes and socks. He had just loaded his toothbrush with toothpaste when a knock sounded. He opened the door, and his breath caught in his chest. Standing there, leaning heavily on his cane, was Nicholas Tewdrig.

CHAPTER 7

"Good evening, Christian. Mind if I come in and sit a spell?" the old man said in a voice rife with fatigue.

"Who are you?" Chris asked, not moving to allow entrance.

"Is your memory that addled, lad?" he said, grinning. "I'm Nicholas Tewdrig."

"No. I know your name—or at least what you *claim* it is. I want to know who you *are*."

Nicholas shifted, placing both hands atop his cane for support. He looked feebler than the last time Chris had seen him—less stout, less sure, almost frail. "If you let me come in and rest, I'll explain everything to you. I give you my oath."

Chris saw a tremor in Nick's legs and arms. He looked like he couldn't stay upright much longer. Chris nodded and gestured toward an armchair beside a small writing table. Respecting his elders had been ingrained in him for as long as he could remember, so Chris decided to give the old guy the benefit of the doubt.

"Thank'ee." The old Welshman hobbled over and fell into the chair with a pronounced expulsion of air. "This is the part I was not looking forward to."

Sitting on the bed, facing him, Chris asked, "What part?"

"Losing the mantle." He smacked his lips and patted them with the back of his hand. Clearing his throat, he pointed at a pitcher of water on the bureau. "May I?"

With a perturbed huff, Chris got up, poured a glass of water, then brought both the glass and pitcher to the table.

Nicholas drank it and smacked his lips again. "Thank you, Christian. You've taken a huge burden from this old man's shoulders."

"What burden? What mantle?"

A twinkle flashed in Nick's eyes. "Yours, my friend."

Chris sat hard on the bed. "No. No more of this cryptic talk. No more half-explanations. Who are you, and what do you want from me? Is it money?—because I don't have much."

Nicholas's brow furrowed. "I have no use for money, lad. My life's been rich in ways money cannot buy, now hasn't it."

"Well, hey, that's swell." Chris didn't try to conceal the frustration and sarcasm in his voice. "What does any of that have to do with me?"

Nicholas sighed. "Christian Pendragon. A noble name, that," he said, shakily pouring another glass of water. "Are you a descendant of Arthur Pendragon then? T'would make sense if you were."

Chris did not want to get distracted from finding out why this old man was pestering him. "Look, Nick. I don't mean to sound rude, but I want you to answer *my* questions for a change. To start with, who you *really* are."

The Welshman nodded and doffed his patchwork tam. "I suppose that's only fair," he said, drawing his hand across his head. "It's quite a tale, if I do say so myself. My name truly is Nicholas Tewdrig. I was born in Bridgend, the Vale of Glamorgan, South Wales, in the year of our Lord, 1799."

Chris scowled then snorted. "So that makes you, what?—more than a decade over two hundred years old?"

"Aye, thereabouts."

This was going nowhere fast. Chris stood and shoved his hands in his pockets. "Okay. Since you obviously aren't taking my questions seriously, I think you'd better leave. Thanks for the tall tale. It was riveting."

Nick did not meet Chris's angry glare. Instead, he gazed longingly at the stone atop his walking staff. "Christian Pendragon. Please sit down." When Chris didn't move, the old man looked up. His eyes were hard with resolution yet softened with an underlying aura of compassion. "You came to this land to find yourself, did you not?"

Chris wanted to deny the revelation, but he knew it was partly true. He nodded.

"You came here to discover the path you should pursue. The one you *need* to pursue, ay? Not the path your family wishes of you, but the one *you* have yet to confirm. And you seek for it in legends, do you not? It's what you teach in your American university, no doubt. Your whole life is based on legends and tall tales, am I right?"

Chris felt his knees falter, but his anger kept him on his feet. The old man was right on all accounts. It was frightening how much he knew, but it only increased Chris's mistrust of him. "How do you know such things? Have you been spying on me? Did my mother send you?"

Nicholas gestured toward the bed with his hand. "Please, sit. No need to get all aerated over a wee chat. I'll explain everything if you'll just give me an ear, won't I?"

Reluctantly, Chris sat. He felt rigid, on guard, suspecting he'd need to vehemently oppose everything the old man was about to share—even if it *was* the truth.

"Thank you, lad." He took another sip of water. "Right. Now, since you're an expert on legends, perhaps you'll recall the tale of the Physicians of Myddfai."

Chris thought for a moment. He was in no mood to play intellectual games, but he knew he'd get no rest until everything was clarified. Deciding to take Nicholas seriously for a moment, he said, "Um, yeah. They were famous Welsh doctors known for folk remedies."

Nicholas huffed lightly. "Come now, Christian, you can do better than that. You teach Welsh history. You know the legends inside and out, I should think."

Chris rubbed the back of his neck. "Yeah. I just wasn't expecting to spend my vacation taking an oral exam from a creepy old man in the middle of the night."

Nicholas recoiled. "Creepy old man?"

"Sorry," Chris returned. "I'm just a bit on edge right now."

A reassuring smile spread across the Welshman's face. "I know, son. Why don't you hold the Dial to your chest and be still a moment like. You'll feel better in no time, ay?"

"The Dial?"

Using his cane, Nicholas pointed to the bureau on which sat Chris's wallet, keys, and the curious stone artifact.

"The rune stone?" he asked.

"Rune stone? Nay, lad, 'tis nothing of the sort. The Dial is not one of those barbaric trinkets. That there bauble is a shard from *the* Dial of Ahaz."

More images filled Chris's mind, stories from ancient Babylon and the Old Testament. It didn't help his confusion or his nerves. "Whoa, wait a minute. One thing at a time, please."

Nicholas chuckled. It was rich and warm but edged with discomfort. "Fair enough, lad. The Physicians of Myddfai first. Many folk in these parts know this legend well." He took another sip of water and again stared into the opaqueness of the stone atop his cane. Fondness crinkled the corners of his eyes.

"There's a small lake in the heart of the Black Mountains called Llyn y Fan-Fach. It means *Lake of the Small Beacon-Hill*. It's the site of our own Lady of the Lake tale, isn't it. The legend goes that the son of a widow from Blaen Sawdde used to stare into the tranquil stillness of the lake when he was grazing his sheep like. One day, a beautiful lass appeared from the lake and promised he'd be wealthy beyond all his dreams if he'd marry her. He consented, of course, because she was so lovely to look upon, but she gave him a solemn warning not to strike her more than twice. He swore his oath, and they lived happily for years in a town called Myddfai. It was there she bore him three sons, wasn't it."

"Yeah, now I remember," Chris jumped in. "Everything was great until the man broke his promise and struck his wife three times; twice as gentle admonishments, once in a teasing jest. But that didn't matter. She instantly returned to the lake, according to the oath, taking all her livestock and wealth with her."

"Ay. The man was heartbroken and destitute, wasn't he. In due course, however, his sons went on to become famous doctors, known as the Physicians of Myddfai. They were compassionate men, very knowledge-able. The legend says they were taught ancient herbal remedies and other forms of healing from the Lady of the Lake herself."

"Yes. A number of their medicinal formulae are still in Welsh medical texts today."

"Ay, and so it is. But that's not where the legend ends, now is it," Nicholas said, seemingly gaining strength from the telling. "Do you remember anything about the *fourth* son?"

Chris cocked his head to one side, his eyes searching. "No. What about him?"

"He's where the legend continues, lad." Nicholas leaned back and gazed at Chris with an introspective eye. "Some say by learning the secrets of healing, he was adopted into the family Myddfai."

Chris waited for more. "And . . . ?"

"Some say the fourth son *continues* the legend . . . even to the present day." Nicholas again fixated on the stone atop his walking stick. His bushy eyebrows rose knowingly. "The truth of it is, son . . . he does."

Comprehension slowly crept into Chris's mind. He gave a skeptical chuff as all the subtle points in Nick's narrative came together. "Ah. So you're saying the fourth son . . . is you?"

Nicholas shook his head and again used his cane as a pointer. "No, my son. It's now you."

CHAPTER 8

THE REVELATION WAS SO ABSURD that Chris started laughing. Nicholas simply sat there, taking him in with a curious mix of disapproval, admonition, and deep admiration.

"Wow. Really?" Chris continued to chuckle. All his resolve to treat the old man seriously dissolved in an instant. "So I'm the next guy in line, huh? You're saying my Pendragon lineage comes directly from these doctors of Middle Earth? That I've always been part of the legend 'cause it's in my blood?"

"Nay, lad. Don't be twp. The Pendragons don't own into it. And it's naught som'et to jest nor joke about either, now is it," Nicholas chastened.

Maybe it was his overall fatigue, but Chris felt little remorse for mocking the old guy. Perhaps the man *was* delusional or mentally handicapped, perhaps even schizophrenic. More likely he was simply drunk. Whatever the reason, Chris wasn't about to believe such farfetched nonsense. In fact, it made him a little angry.

"Boy, I sure wish my crystal ball had warned me about this. I would've vacationed in Hawaii instead."

Nicholas sighed heavily. He looked as tired as Chris felt, perhaps more so. And suddenly very sad too. "As I said, your family line, while noble for sure, does not own into it. This is much more personal, yes? I am very serious, Christian. This mantle you now bear carries great responsibility."

Chris felt a twinge of guilt, seeing tears pool in the old man's eyes. He stood and moved to the window. The night still pressed against the glass, dark and oppressive. He had no idea what was going on here or where it was going, nor did he feel he was likely to get a straight answer anytime soon. Nicholas Tewdrig's wild claims certainly fell under the classification of tall tales—perhaps even psychoses. But Chris also could not deny the impressions of veracity pricking his soul.

"Listen to me, lad," Nick continued. "You're confused and tired, and this is a lot to burden you with. Perhaps I should just come back in a few hours when your mind is at ease, ay?" His voice took on a measure of reproach. "I've been around long enough to know when I'm talking to a stone fence."

Thunder grumbled outside, sounding closer than the previous night. Chris began to consider his assessment of his visitor. Maybe the old guy *was* mentally challenged. He shouldn't make light of something like that. Perhaps he should simply end the conversation and show him to the door before the storm hit.

Returning to his seat on the bed, Chris leaned forward with his elbows on his knees. He steepled his fingers to his lips and tried to look concerned. "Listen, Mr. Tewdrig. I don't mean to be disrespectful, but try to see all this from my point of view. An old guy shows up out of nowhere, claims to be more than two hundred years old, tells me I have a higher calling in life when he knows nothing about me, and says I'm not who I always thought I was—that now I'm part of an ancient line of magical physicians? I mean, come on, man. Seriously?"

Nicholas set his cane to one side and folded his arms. "You healed Nigel Madsen's broken ankles, didn't you? Exam at hospital proves it. How did you do that, being *only* a history professor?"

Chris sat up and gawked. "How did you get access to hospital rec—? Never mind. Look. I did *not* heal that boy's ankles. I merely pulled him from the car."

"And in doing so, you had to touch his wounds, didn't you? You grabbed him about his ankles and pulled him to safety, didn't you?"

"As I remember, *you* had a hand in that too."

"Aye. But *I* never touched him. You did that. And in doing so, you healed him. It's what you're meant to do, lad."

"I DID NOT HEAL HIM," Chris bellowed, leaping to his feet. "I am *not* a doctor. I am *not* a priest or a—a televangelist faith healer. I'm a tourist who happened upon an accident and helped pull a boy to safety. That's it. End of story!"

"No, Christian. It's just the beginning of the story. Your story."

Chris marched to the door and yanked it open. "You may leave now. Get out this instant, or I'll call the police."

Nick leaned forward and rubbed his face in his palms. "No need to get the constabulary involved, son. All of this will make sense if you just hear me out."

Chris stayed firmly planted at the door. Thunder grumbled again as rain began to tap against the window. He was frustrated by this whole ordeal—mostly because he didn't understand any of it—*and* because it had gotten way too personal. Yes, some of it was true. But there was no way he had healed a young boy by grabbing his ankles. There was no way Nicholas Tewdrig could know such personal information about him. And there was no way the elderly Welshman was over two hundred years old. And yet, strangely, Chris felt somehow that if he'd just listen to him, some of it *might* make sense. Even if Nicholas ended up being totally nuts, at least Chris would have a clue as to why the man had shown up at his hotel room.

"Please, Christian. Hear me out, son. There's so much you need to learn, ay? And I don't have much time."

"And just what is *that* supposed to mean?" Chris mumbled, knowing that asking a question would only delay the old man's departure.

"It means I need to teach you som'et before I go. It will happen soon," he sighed heavily, rubbing his face again. "As I said, I'm not afraid to meet my Creator, but I haven't finished my work yet, now have I. And to do that, by gaw, you have to listen to everything I have to say. Please, son."

Chris took a deep breath and let it out slowly through his nose. He closed the door and returned to the edge of the bed. His nightstand clock read eighteen minutes to twelve. Turning the clock so Nick could see it, Chris said, "I'll give you until midnight. I don't care if you're finished by then or not. At the top of the hour, you're out of here. Deal?"

"Agreed," Nicholas said, extending his hand.

Chris hesitated a moment before accepting the accord.

"I suppose I should start at the *very* beginning then, shouldn't I. Even before the Physicians of Myddfai," Nicholas said as if convincing himself. He groaned to his feet and retrieved the rune stone—or Dial, as he'd called it—from the bureau. "And it all starts with this."

CHAPTER 9

FALLING BACK INTO THE CHAIR, Nicholas held the small stone to the light. It seemed to glow with renewed pearlescence. Chris had to admit it really was quite pretty. If only he could figure out where it came from—

"Wait—*you* put that in my pocket, didn't you." It was an accusation, not a question. "How else would you know about it?"

"Of course," Nick answered, as if stating the obvious. "As a historian, I take it you're familiar with the Dial of Ahaz as referred to in the Second Book of Kings in the Old Testament?"

"A bit. It wasn't a dial with a circular face, as many people think," Chris explained. "The Hebrew word for *dial* can also be translated to mean *degrees* or *steps*. The Dial was actually a staircase built by King Ahaz as a special entrance to the upper chambers of Solomon's temple. Its alignment to the sun made it perfect for measuring time, hence a 'sun dial.'"

"By gaw, you *do* know your history. That's exactly right, lad," Nicholas said, smiling broadly. "And do you remember what miraculous event happened there?"

"Yeah. The sun appeared to move backward."

Nicholas looked surprisingly disappointed. "Nay, lad, not that. That was the *sign* of the miracle—not the miracle itself."

Chris scoffed. "Having the earth change rotation or shift on its axis so that the sun appears to go backward seems pretty darn miraculous to me."

"Aye, but what significance did it have to the king then?"

"Oh. Um, King Hezekiah was healed of his sickness."

"Aye. And not just any sickness. It was a leprous plague, now wasn't it. He was on his deathbed. He knew he wouldn't live to see the next day. But he was worried his people would fall to the Assyrians if he died, so he asked Isaiah the prophet to entreat God to heal him, didn't he. And because of the king's compassion for his people, the Lord did just that *and* blessed him with fifteen more years."

"Yes. The origin of the fifteen Songs of Degrees sung on the temple steps during the Feast of Tabernacles," Chris confirmed.

"Aye, and so it is. Those steps became a sacred spot to which people could gather to be healed," Nick went on. He leaned forward and passed Chris the stone. "This here bauble is a piece of those steps; a shard from *the* Dial of Ahaz."

Chris held the small tile with renewed respect . . . and a large measure of skepticism. "Really? I suppose it wouldn't do any good to point out that Solomon's temple *and* the palace *and* the staircase were all razed to the ground by Nebuzaraddan in 587 BCE?"

"Aye. Every building was destroyed, leveled to the ground as you say. But the riches were carried back to Babylon, were they not? Precious metals, gems, treasures, and the like. Do you suppose that included precious stones?"

"Well, yeah. But we're talking about a stone staircase, not some sacred altar," Chris argued.

"And what is the precious stone you hold in your hand?"

Chris held the artifact to the light. The pink and amber hues danced across its translucent surface. "Marble?"

"Nay, lad. You're the historian. What stone did they always make vessels out of to hold precious ointments and healing balms and such?" Nicholas asked, still leaning forward.

It suddenly came to him. But it didn't make sense. "Alabaster?"

"Now you're using your noggin, m'boy."

"But alabaster is used purely as a decorative stone. It's too soft to use architecturally. Building a staircase with it would be foolish because it'd wear down too quickly."

"Only if it were used on the treads, which it wasn't, now was it. Remember, Christian, the Dial of Ahaz was a marker; it was a way to measure time. Therefore, only the *face* of the stair would be covered with such precious stone, ay? Do you not recognize the characters on it?"

Chris rubbed his fatigued eyes and looked closely. "Is it Arabic?"

Nicholas shook his head. "It's Aramaic, son. The language of religion. The language of Solomon's temple. The voice of God."

Although it added up, it was almost too much for Chris to process. Everything Nick was telling him seemed so farfetched that it shouldn't make sense. And yet there was just enough truth that it *could* make sense. Alabaster was often used in religious motifs and sacred artwork because it symbolized purity. It was favored in sculpting religious statues and mosaics. Every time the Bible mentioned alabaster, it was as a vessel holding an ointment of great monetary value.

Modern archeologists were continually finding pieces of pottery, fragments of statues, and other evidences of ancient civilizations. Why couldn't a shard or two from ancient Israel be in existence today?

But was it magical? Did it hold mystic powers, like the owners of the Black Boar had claimed? He doubted it.

"Look, Nick. This is all very fascinating, and I'd be lying if I said I didn't enjoy this kind of discussion. But to say this piece of rock has healing powers—or that it gives *me* healing powers—is something I just can't accept."

He handed the relic back, but the old man pushed it away.

"Then you misunderstand me, son. And the Dial," he said, as if issuing a warning. "The Dial does not give *you* power; you give *it* power."

Great. More cryptic mumbo-jumbo. "*I* give it power?"

"Aye. Remember what the Apostle James said? Faith, if it hath not works, is dead. *Your* faith is what made the Dial work on young Nigel. It proves you and the stone have bonded."

This was completely nuts. What power was he talking about? What bond? Chris glanced at the clock. It read 11:59. He set the alabaster tile on the nightstand.

"I'm sorry, Nick. It's late and I'm tired. I gave you a fair shot at explaining yourself. It's been educational discussing history with you, seriously; but you have yet to convince me who you are—*convince* being the operative word. And as for this piece of rock . . . well, the jury is still out." He yawned and stretched. "Look, I'm exhausted. Perhaps we can take this up again in the morning, after we both get some sleep? I'd be happy to buy you breakfast tomorrow, say around eight?"

Nicholas looked deeply crestfallen. He trembled to his feet and stretched his lower back with an ill-disguised moan. Donning his tam, he said, "If that is what you wish."

"Yes, please."

The Welshman took a lengthy breath and sighed. "You disappoint me, Christian Pendragon, but I do not blame you. I too was reticent when the Dial was passed to me. But I had faith on my side and a firm belief in

God, didn't I. You have knowledge and a sharp mind. Do not make the mistake of using knowledge as a crutch, or worse, letting it blind you from the truth. It's a marvelous thing, knowledge, in its proper place. Just think on it, lad. Ponder it as the psalmist instructed: Be still and know God."

"Be still? So I just hold perfectly still and this will all make sense?"

"Spiritually speaking, yes. A still, small voice is how God spoke to Elijah the prophet. It's how He speaks to many souls on this earth. And it's how He'll speak to you . . . *if* you have the sense enough to listen."

Without awaiting a reply, he ambled toward the door. Chris fought a contradictory mix of desires. He wanted to stop the old man and offer him some consolation, but at the same time, he delighted in seeing the crazy senior citizen finally leave.

Nicholas placed his hand on the knob and turned to face Chris. "There is so much more yet to learn, Christian. It would be much easier if you let me help, ay? But . . . but some folk are more stubborn than others. Some are downright twp. At least you have a nose for knowing *where* to look." He paused and pointed a gnarled finger at him. "Listen to me closely: Do not use your gift for money or fame, son. It is not som'et to be trifled with, always remember that. Above all else, son, do not lose the Dial; for in the wrong hands, it is a powerful danger."

Chris was speechless. It was as if he'd felt the warning more than heard it.

"A long life to you," Nicholas said, opening the door, allowing a thick mist to flow into the entry. "Go with God, Christian Pendragon. He'll never lead you astray."

"Wait," Chris said, finding his voice. "So we're meeting tomorrow, right?"

The old man smiled softly, but his eyes were filled with sadness and remorse. "By the by, Christian, I'm glad your arm healed so quickly," he said, tipping his cap.

And with that, he left, closing the door behind him.

CHAPTER 10

CHRIS HAD FORGOTTEN ABOUT HIS arm. How *had* it healed so quickly? The EMTs had said it would require stitches. He examined it again; just a thin white line. According to the social worker, Nigel Madsen's ankles *had* been fractured. There was scientific proof. And yet they had healed as quickly and as miraculously as Chris's arm had.

What the heck was going on?

You give power to it. The power to heal? Is that what the old guy was saying?

Chris leapt to the door and yanked it open. Nicholas Tewdrig was nowhere in sight. The rain had passed, but it left the night murky with haze, dense enough to mask the old Welshman's retreat. Still, Chris couldn't believe Nicholas had vanished so quickly.

"Nick?" he called out, not too loudly. It was past midnight, after all. He didn't want to wake anyone.

The moisture-laden air encircled his body with penetrating cold. He stepped back into his room and rubbed his arms vigorously to dissipate the chill. Everything he'd discussed with Nick bounced around in his head, threatening to morph into a migraine. He swallowed two Excedrin and crawled into bed, hoping—but not believing—everything would make sense in the morning.

* * *

Chris awoke to a rooster crowing just outside his door. The wretched bird sounded like he was trying to herald in the apocalypse. Chris covered his head with his pillow, but it did no good. The rasping caws penetrated everything. Slowly, Chris peeled one eye open. The first thing he saw was the small alabaster relic on his nightstand. He closed the eye and groaned. Nope, it hadn't been a bad dream.

Sitting on the edge of the bed, Chris inhaled deeply through his nose, trying to dissipate the miasma in his brain. It did little good. His mounting headache from last night was still there—not yet painful but on the verge of crossing that threshold. He had to get moving. Stretching forcefully, Chris found his eyes drawn back to the shard of alabaster. The artifact made no noise, but it was just as loathsome as the rooster outside. According to the enigmatic Nicholas Tewdrig, the small chunk of stone was the nucleus of everything perplexing him. Ridiculous. It was just a stupid piece of rock!

He stomped to the bathroom to splash cold water on his face and across the back of his neck. Staring back from the mirror, his reflection didn't look happy . . . or very human.

You and the stone have bonded.

Well I certainly feel like my head is full of rocks, he scoffed inwardly. Then, remembering Nick's suggestion from the previous night, Chris returned to the bed and held the relic to his chest. *This is insane.* Sitting, he closed his eyes, breathed deeply, and freed his mind of worry, focusing only on feelings of serenity and peace. Surprisingly, his head began to clear. As much as he wanted to deny it, he could actually feel the pall drain from his skull, taking the discomfort with it.

Frightened, he quickly dropped the stone on the nightstand and wiped his fingers on his t-shirt. It had to be his imagination. It *had* to be!

Chris showered and dressed, trying to ignore the relic but without much success. He knew it was there. He knew it was nothing more than a pretty chunk of alabaster. So why, then, did he feel an overpowering urge to slip it back into his pocket?

Staring into the mirror, he scoffed loudly, "You're an idiot."

There was no logical reason for believing it held any kind of healing power. In fact, he shouldn't even allow himself to entertain such thoughts. He should just leave it on the nightstand and finish his vacation. Some mysteries are best left unsolved.

Brushing his teeth, he tried to focus on the places he still wanted to visit. Wales was a country steeped in history. Castles and ruins littered the landscape; petroglyphs and stone monuments abounded. He loved talking with the locals. The Welsh denizens often knew more history than any dozen textbooks could reveal. Even Nick Tewdrig had taught him a few facts he'd not known—

He closed his eyes and clenched his jaw. He'd promised to meet Nick this morning for breakfast. So much for ignoring anything to do with the Dial. Returning to his bedside, he felt compelled to pocket the relic, almost as if his life depended on it, almost as if it'd become part of him.

You and the stone have bonded.

As absurd as it sounded, Chris derived an inexplicable measure of peace from that thought, as if possessing the Dial cloaked him in a protective mantle.

I'm going to miss the mantle.

Was that what Nick was referring to?

Fixating on the stone artifact, Chris had to admit it was very pretty but . . . No. There was no way it contained magical healing powers. And yet, Chris sensed . . . *something* powerful. He picked it up, felt its weight. Was it real alabaster? Was it actually from Ahaz's staircase in Solomon's temple? Perhaps he could ask some experts—a geologist to identify the stone and a linguist to interpret the markings. He'd feel better about what it really was then. But how did a lowly minister like Nick know so much about history and legends and archeology?

Chris scoffed again. "Well if you were two hundred years old, you'd probably know a thing or two."

With a huff of defeat, Chris slipped the Dial in his pocket and headed out the door.

As he entered the lobby, the delicious smells of frying onions, potatoes, and meat did little to enliven him. Just meet with Nick, insist he take back the Dial, and leave. That was the plan.

"G'morning, my good man. I trust you slept well then?" The man behind the counter beamed. He was short, stout, and wore his thin hair combed forward to a peak. Chris tried unsuccessfully to ignore the image of a teapot.

"Fine, thank you," Chris lied politely.

"Splendid. Right then. Breakfast is ready when you are, sir. Jus' sit yourself down in the dining room, an' my missus will fix you up right nice like. I hope you're hungry."

"Not really, I'm afraid."

"What? A strapping young man like you, not hungry? Why, I never heard such nonsense. Jus' wait till you get a mouthful of my missus' sausages. Makes them herself, she does. And fresh too. Butchered a pig jus' last week, we did. Blimey, you've never tasted the like, I'll wager. As your southern Yanks say, 'It'll make you slap your mama.'"

Chris smiled. "How can I argue with that?"

"Right you are, sir. Come with me," the innkeeper said, leading the way.

The room held only a few tables, most occupied. The portly man directed him to a small one near the front window.

"Is it coffee or tea this morning, sir?"

"My stomach's a bit on edge for coffee. Do you have any peppermint tea?"

The man didn't blink an eye. "Ay, your stomach's fussy 'cause it's empty. Jus' you relax. I'll be back before you can say, 'Bob's your uncle.'"

Chris had to stop himself from repeating the phrase just to prove him wrong. The innkeeper soon returned with a plate piled high with fried potatoes, two sausages the size of bratwurst, scrambled eggs, poached apples, and a steaming mug of sweet tea. "There you are, sir. Get tucked in to that lot, and I'll be back with another plate right soon."

Chris looked at the plate and forced a smile. It's not that he didn't like such food, he simply was not used to eating so heavily first thing in the morning. There was enough grease on the plate to lube a bulldozer. There was little doubt how the man got his teapot physique.

"Som'et wrong, sir?" the innkeeper asked, still hanging over Chris.

"Wrong? No. It looks fabulous. I just usually don't eat this much breakfast."

"And that's why you're naught but skin and bones, sir."

Chris arched his back and patted his belly. "Not necessarily."

"Ha! You've a long way to go before you can best this," the man said, patting his own ample girth with pride. "Now get stuck in, or I'll send missus out here to give you what for." He winked and marched back to the kitchen.

It was all said in jest, but Chris could tell the man was close to being offended by his lack of appetite. He picked at the crisp edges of fried potatoes and got down half a sausage. Both were incredibly delicious but very heavy. The eggs tasted watery, and the apples were too mushy for his liking. Chris's normal breakfast consisted of a protein smoothie and a banana. But since he was on vacation, and since he'd recently experienced an undue amount of stress, he figured a few heavy calories wouldn't drag him to the grave.

He blew on his tea and gazed out the sizeable picture window. The haze had lifted and the sun was making an honest effort at breaking through the overcast. It might turn into a decent day after all.

Chris spent an hour, picking away at his breakfast while waiting for Nicholas Tewdrig. He again wondered if the man was a charlatan. Would the old guy return and demand money for the alabaster trinket? Or claim that Chris had stolen it? Chris sipped his tea and frowned at his last thought. The answer was no. Old Nick had honestly believed everything he'd shared last night. And he hadn't tried to sell Chris anything—except for the fact that he was now some kind of New Age healer. Well, not New Age, more like Old World. *Very* old world.

He withdrew the stone tile and ran his thumb lightly over the markings. Were they really Aramaic? And if so, what did they *really* say?

"Excuse me?" Chris hailed.

The innkeeper scurried to his side. "Yes, sir? What can I get you?"

"Where is the closest university to here?" he asked, slipping the stone back in his pocket.

"A university, is it? I knew it! I knew the minute I laid eyes on you that you were a man of letters. By heck, you have the look, and no mistake. You're a scholar visiting from the States, is it?"

"Yeah, more or less."

"Right you are, professor. The grandest school in the whole of Britain is the University of Wales in Cardiff, about forty miles south of here. Have you a map then?"

"Yes," he said, pushing away from the table. "I'll try there. Thank you very much."

"My pleasure, professor." The host then pointed to the half-full plate. "Why—you haven't tasted a bite, sir. Is there something wrong with your breakfast?"

"No, it's quite delicious, really. Like I said, I'm just not very hungry."

"I can make a packet for you, right quick like," he said without much jovialness.

Not wanting to disappoint the man, Chris agreed. "Sure."

"Right you are, sir."

The innkeeper scuttled away and returned with a sheaf of newspaper. He rolled it into a cone then unceremoniously plopped the contents of the plate inside. Chris had seen that done with fish and chips, but not with other food products.

"Um, thank you. Say, is it okay if I leave a note for someone in case he shows up after I leave? A local man was supposed to meet me here over an hour ago."

"Of course, professor. Happy to oblige a man of letters."

Chris pulled a notepad from his satchel and scribbled down some information, including his cell phone number.

The innkeeper read the note and frowned. "Are you having me on, sir?"

"Excuse me?"

The man fluttered the note. "Is this some kind of a lark?"

"Not at all. Why?"

"There isn't a soul I don't know in these parts, you see. There's no one around here goes by *this* name. Not anymore, anyroad."

"Really? I was certain he's a local. He visited me late last night. He's about five seven, broad shouldered, short gray hair, wears a closely trimmed beard. He carries a walking stick with an alabaster stone on top."

Clearly suspicious, the innkeeper's eyes narrowed. "You say he visited you last night? Nicholas Tewdrig did, ay?"

Chris nodded. "He said he'd meet me for breakfast."

"If you saw him last night, sir, you were talking to a ghost."

Chris chuckled uneasily. "No, he was real flesh and blood. I shook his hand."

The innkeeper leered for a moment before a sly smile split his face. He roared with laughter. "Oh, you Americans; always havin' a jest." He tapped the side of his nose and winked. "Okay, professor, you got me. The beloved St. Nicholas; shook his hand, did you? Ha! If you say so, sir. Oh, and if you see him again, send him here straight away. I've got a bad back the doctors have given up on trying to fix."

"And Nick Tewdrig can?" Chris asked with raised eyebrows.

"Faster than a jockey running the Gold Cup and Sandown Park, he can. Fix it right as rain, and no mistake," he said, folding the note into his pocket. "He's known as the Healing Saint, don't you know."

"The *healing* saint?" Chris echoed, seeking more information.

"Right you are. Cured many a soul, spiritually and physically, he did. He blessed St. Anne's Well so as to heal people, ay?"

"The Virtuous Well," Chris said, mostly to himself.

"Yes, that be the one. Have you been there then, professor?"

"Just yesterday. But . . . well, I didn't find anything remarkable about it." He didn't want to raise the man's ire, but he had to be honest. "Perhaps I wasn't looking close enough."

"The stuff of legends is that," the innkeeper said, brightening even more. "When a maiden wants to know how long it'll be before she marries, she tosses a pebble in yon well and counts bubbles that come up. Each bubble is one month until she's wed. Other folk tie ribbons to the praying tree at the well for special blessings. Many an ailing soul has been cured by them holy waters, they have. I swear to you."

"Yeah, I saw the ribbon tree," Chris said, absently fingering the stone in his pocket.

"Now, you listen to me, professor," the man said, narrowing his eyes again. "Such things are not to be trifled with, ay? You get my meaning, sir?"

Chris nodded. "Oh, I agree, I agree. I didn't mean to sound like I was making light of it. I'm just . . . curious about such things, I guess."

"Well, you know what curiosity did to the cat, don't you? And beware of highway men, sir. Even money says your visitor last night was nothing but a swindler. Did he ask you for money then?"

"No. We just talked."

"Were you missing any personal effects this morning?"

"No, not that I've noticed."

The innkeeper looked up and down the street through the large window. "Well, you just be cautious anyroad, ay professor?"

"I will." Chris removed his billfold and laid his fare plus a nice tip on the table. "Thank you for your wonderful service."

The innkeeper beamed. "Oh my. Thank *you*, sir. And come again anytime—especially if you're in company with St. Nicholas Tewdrig."

CHAPTER 11

CHRIS SAT IN HIS CAR waiting for the engine to warm so he could crank up the heater. The newspaper-wrapped food on the passenger seat filled the car with the thick odor of old grease. He figured he'd toss it in the first trash bin he could find.

The alabaster relic rested in his hand. As much as he wanted to toss it too, he knew he couldn't. Just thinking about doing so carried with it a foreboding portent. What frustrated him the most was that he couldn't explain why.

Presently, Chris was torn between traveling to the university in Cardiff to have the stone analyzed or driving to the Church of St. Nicholas to find out more about Nick Tewdrig. Since the old monastery was closer, he opted to start there.

It turned out that the large brownstone structure was no longer an abbey or a monastery; it'd long ago been recommissioned as a simple house of worship. The church had a tall, prominent spire and slate shingle roofing. Outside in the churchyard stood a baptismal font, an ancient sundial, and a preaching cross that dated back to the eighth century. The present building was adorned with Gothic stonework, which indicated fourteenth-century renovations. The heavy oak doors were open. Chris passed through with as much reverence as curiosity. He loved these old structures.

Although spacious and airy, the interior of the church was surprisingly austere. Tall, steeply pointed porticos were topped by clerestory windows along the flanking walls. The ceiling was flat and bare, no vaulting arches or cantilevered trusses. All interior colors were muted. The floor, plain fieldstone tile. The benches, close and unpadded. There were none of the gaudy gold-leaf embellishments, colorful frescoes, or opulent trappings often found in old cathedrals. About the only ornate feature was the stained-glass window high above the chancel.

"May I answer any questions, my friend?" asked a tall, well-dressed man coming up the aisle from the narthex. The middle-aged clergyman appeared out of place in such an antiquated building. He wore a dark, tailored suit and had a delicate gold cross hanging around his neck. He looked more like a businessman than a man of the cloth. Perhaps he simply felt more comfortable in a suit than in an evangelical collar or ecclesiastic robes.

In the vestibule, Chris had taken a pamphlet that described many aspects of the old church. He returned the man's smile. "Maybe. I'm surprised at the simplicity of this church, considering the prominence of St. Nicholas Tewdrig," he said.

The man visibly flinched. "May I ask your name, my son?"

Chris offered his hand. "Christian Pendragon, from America. Call me Chris."

"Reverend Collingswood," the man said, shaking Chris's hand. The reverend was roughly three or four inches taller than Chris and in good shape. His refined accent hinted at an upper-class English background rather than simple country Welsh. But the lighthearted gleam in his eyes bespoke more playfulness than piety. "Are you an historian, Mr. Pendragon?"

"As a matter of fact, I am. What gave it away?"

The man tapped the side of his head. "I'm clairvoyant."

Chris didn't know whether to smile or frown at the man's declaration. "Um . . ."

Collingswood burst out laughing. "Gotcha!" It seemed deeply disrespectful in such a humble setting. "Please forgive me," he continued to chuckle. "I'm a hopeless prankster, Mr. Pendragon. A life spent in solemnity can be tedious at times. Besides, I'm told you Americans love a good joke."

"I guess," Chris said, returning the man's chuckle with a measure of wariness. "But that doesn't explain how you knew I was a historian."

"Yes, of course. My apologies. I watched the way you took in the architecture and vestiges here. Most tourists are quickly bored with the simplicity of this edifice. You, on the other hand, seem to know precisely what you are looking at."

"Well, thank you, but I really don't. I'm actually looking for information on Nicholas Tewdrig, not architecture."

The reverend's smile never faltered. "I assumed as much. Point of fact, not many people know St. Nicholas's surname. It's not listed in the pamphlet you're holding. Those who do know are either lovers of wives' tales or are treasure hunters."

"Really? What treasure are they hunting?"

"Come, come, Mr. Pendragon. As an historian—and as someone bearing the family crest of Pendragon—surely you are familiar with Arthurian legends."

"As a matter of fact, I am, but the more I tour this area, the more I find stuff that didn't make it into the history books—which is great. I love discovering the echoes of what really happened. There's often more accuracy found in folklore than in history books."

Collingswood's head tilted knowingly. "So you *are* a true historian, much like myself. I find history comprises a great deal more than a few facts written by biased scribes. History comes from everywhere; it's seen in everything. The Tewdrig name, for example, goes back several centuries in this shire. A Tewdrig was one of the founding fathers of this area—did you know that? It was the Tewdrigs who dedicated this site in particular as a place of worship."

"Very interesting," Chris said, looking toward the altar at the front of the nave. "So did St. Nicholas design this chapel?"

"Yes, I believe he did. But it wasn't the first church on this location. The original structure was made of wood. The stonework you now see was erected by the people of Trellech after the township was reorganized in the eighth century. This edifice wasn't constructed until the thirteenth century. It's had many renovations since then, but I think they've maintained the flavor of the original building. That's where the influence of St. Nicholas comes in."

He began walking down the aisle, gesturing at many features in the chapel, taking on the mannerisms of a tour guide. "Notice the way everything in the nave points to the altar. It's one of the few Gothic churches where the bema encircles the altar on three sides. It was built that way to represent the table at the Last Supper of our Lord."

Chris knew some of this was listed in the tourist pamphlet, but the depth of information the cleric shared was encouraging. He guessed the old church didn't get many visitors. They were the only ones inside—and probably had been for some time. Everything seemed clean but seldom used.

Collingswood continued talking as he walked toward the bema. "You'll notice the pre-Raphaelite glass motif," he said, pointing to the large stained-glass window above the chancel. "The glazing shows the risen Christ acting as host, welcoming all those who kneel around Him at His altar table."

Chris slowly tagged along. He loved learning the history of the old building, but there was something peculiar about the man acting as his guide. True, he wasn't wearing a traditional religious frock, but it was more than that. Chris had said he wanted to know more about Nick Tewdrig than about the church. It was almost as if the cleric was avoiding the topic.

"Most of these features were commissioned by the beloved St. Nicholas during his administration," Collingswood continued, stepping onto the elevated bema.

"Look, Reverend, this is all very fascinating," Chris said respectfully, "but as I said, I was hoping you could tell me more about the man himself."

Collingswood folded his arms and looked down with an expression of fatherly admonition. The playful glimmer in his eyes was replaced with hooded caution. "Of course, my son. What is it you'd like to know?"

"Well, to start with, is there more than one St. Nicholas?"

An inkling of distrust crossed the man's face. "May I ask the reason behind your query?"

Chris slipped his hands in his pockets in an effort to look nonthreatening—not that he could ever pull off threatening. "Okay, here's the gist of it. You guessed correctly, Father. I *am* a history lover. In fact, I teach history at Gonzaga University in Washington State. I'm here doing some on-site research about Nicholas Tewdrig. Hopefully, the stuff *not* found in textbooks." It wasn't a complete lie.

"Do you have proof of credentials, Professor Pendragon?"

Chris blinked. "Proof of credentials?"

The vicar cleared his throat and raised an eyebrow. "No offense intended, I assure you. Every two or three years, we get a new rash of investigative reporters and the like wanting to dig into the tales of our beloved St. Nicholas. They want to know if he was the original Santa Claus, you see. Most 'investigators'"—he said the term scornfully, pantomiming quotation marks in the air—"are rude and insensitive. They take hundreds of photographs and fabricate an equal number of tales, few of which carry a modicum of substance or validity. Most are blatant sensationalism. I am merely judging if you are interested for the right reasons."

Chris pulled out his wallet and removed his university ID: Christian Pendragon, Faculty, Gonzaga University, Spokane, Washington.

"Thank you," the tall man said. "I too have found more history in folklore than in texts. Not all folklore is fiction. It should be treated with respect, Professor Pendragon, as I'm confident you do. Again, I assure you I meant no offense when I questioned your intent."

Chris wasn't offended, just dubious. "I appreciate that."

Collingswood's head tilted again. "So what *is* your intent, professor?"

"Well, while my research centers on Welsh folklore, my interest in Nicholas Tewdrig is more recently of a . . . a personal nature."

The vicar's eyebrows rose again.

"And it has nothing to do with Santa Claus," he added.

Collingswood gave a reserved smile, a long pause, then a nod. "I believe you. Do you have a specific question for me?"

Chris thought quickly. "Was he was one of the Physicians of Myddfai?"

The man's guarded expression morphed to one of admiration. The childlike gleam returned to his eyes. "I am impressed. Very impressed. Yes, as a matter of consequence, he was. Is that the crux of your interest?"

"I wouldn't say the *crux*—but a definite *link*."

"I see. You also said it's 'recently of a personal nature.' How recently, may I ask?"

Chris smiled, guessing what the man was hinting at. Deciding to cut to the chase, he removed the Dial from his pocket and held it out. "Ever since I got this."

The reverend's mouth dropped open. With a hand over his heart, he drew a long breath before asking in hushed, tremulous tones, "May I ask how you came by that?"

"Do you really want to know?"

Collingswood folded his arms then unfolded them. He stepped off the bema for a closer look. "Yes. More than you can imagine."

Chris held the relic to a shaft of light filtering through the time-yellowed side windows. "I'll make you a deal, Reverend. You help me learn what I need to know about Nicholas Tewdrig, and I'll tell you everything I know about this."

The man's eyes never left the stone. His mouth worked, but no sound came out.

"Look," Chris continued. "I'm not here to cause trouble or gather dirt to sell to some tabloid. I am honestly interested in the history behind St. Nicholas the *Healer*. Can you help me?"

Collingswood took only a moment to consider the proposal. "As you may have surmised, I too am a disciple of Nicholas Tewdrig lore." He nodded at the stone. "And if that's what I think it is, we have a lot to share with one another."

"Honestly, I'm not 100 percent sure what this is," Chris said, pocketing the stone. "But I'm going to find out."

The cleric's eyes slowly moved from Chris's pocket to the empty chapel before returning to Chris's face. "Keep your voice down, and follow me, Mr. Pendragon."

CHAPTER 12

Collingswood led Chris behind the chancel to a small door concealed in the wood paneling. Why they were supposed to stay quiet was not revealed, but Chris went along without asking. The cleric took another quick look around before pushing through the doorway. Both men had to duck to clear the transom.

The room beyond was just as tall but only half the width of the chapel, basically a private chamber that was used as a study. A shallow countertop lined one wall, and two dingy windows sat opposite each other some fifteen feet above. A muted shaft of sunlight illuminated timeworn cabinetry along the opposite wall. Dust motes drifted lazily through the beam, giving the narrow space an archaic, monkish feel. A long, black-oak table sat in the center of the room. A smattering of books, a wire box of pencils and markers, and two stout, pawn-shaped marble paperweights littered the timeworn surface.

The cleric walked around the table and pointed to an aged, handwritten roster hanging in a glass frame above the countertop. "This is the earliest record the church has on St. Nicholas."

Chris looked closely at the faded scrawl. Much of it was streaked and blotchy but still fairly legible. The roster contained the names of all the vicars and churchwardens of St. Nicholas Chapel, dating from 1359. Most of the Welsh names had dates beside them; Nicholas Tewdrig's name sat about one-third of the way down the list.

Rev. Nicholas Tewdrig, Vicar from 1878 to 1881*.

So my *Nick Tewdrig* isn't the *Nicholas Tewdrig.* "1878, huh?" Chris said. "Why is the church named after him if he wasn't its first cleric?"

"Because he played such a prominent role in the church's renovations and in the community—particularly in his blessing of St. Anne's Well."

"Ah. May I see his gravesite?"

Collingswood shrugged. "I do not know where it is."

Chris cocked his head. "I thought part of a vicar's remuneration was a burial plot reserved for him in the chapel cemetery, if he chooses."

"True. But he is not buried here."

The vicar removed a map of the cemetery from a cabinet and laid it on the desk. Each grave plot was marked with the name of the deceased and date of interment. A key to one side listed the names chronologically.

Placing both hands on the desk, Chris examined the map. No listing for Nicholas Tewdrig existed. "Did he officiate anywhere else?"

"No. This is the only parish in which he ministered."

"So . . . where is he buried?"

A mischievous smile pulled at one side of the reverend's mouth. "You are assuming St. Nicholas is dead."

Chris's confusion grew. "But the roster says he died in 1881."

"Did you notice the asterisk?" the reverend asked, still smiling.

Chris looked closer. Sure enough, there was an asterisk. "Okay. What's that mean?"

"It is an estimated date of death. In truth, no one knows."

Great. If he had proof of Nicholas Tewdrig's demise, it would validate his theory that last night's visitor was just a crazy old man. There was simply no way the Nicholas Tewdrig he'd met was the same guy listed on the church roster—even though he claimed to be roughly that old. "Are you suggesting he's still alive?"

Collingswood casually walked over to a cast-iron radiator at the far end of the room. Holding his hands over it, facing the wall, he said, "Do you believe in the Bible, Professor Pendragon?"

"Yes. I was raised a Methodist—though I don't attend as much as I should."

"I understand. But you accept everything in the Bible as factual, yes?"

He thought for a moment, wondering where this line of questioning was headed. "Well, there are obvious metaphors and animal simile in a lot of the revelations, but as far as the miracles and history, yes, I accept those as factual."

Collingswood nodded and turned back to Chris. "Yes, I thought you might. I feel you are being honest with me, and for that I thank you."

"You're welcome?" Chris said hesitantly, still not sure where the man was headed.

St. John the Beloved died, Professor?"

Trick question. Christ granted him immortality."

vior *did* promise that John would not taste of

cond Coming. So do you know where St. John

...nt?

Of course not. Do you?"

Looking past Chris's shoulder, Collingswood said, "He's right behind you." When Chris whipped around, the cleric chortled: "Gotcha."

Chris frowned, more irritated than amused.

"Sorry about that," the vicar offered, still smiling. "I simply wanted to see how much you trusted me."

"Frankly, I don't know who or what to trust anymore," Chris admitted.

"Do you trust that St. John the Beloved is still alive?"

"Well, yeah, but he was given the gift of immortality from Jesus himself and—" Chris stopped short. "Wait. You're saying St. Nicholas was also granted immortality?"

"It would add credence to the legends of Santa Claus, would it not?"

"Well yeah. But you're also saying that the Nicholas Tewdrig on that roster is the same one I met yesterday."

The cleric's eyebrows rose sharply, and for the second time, his jaw dropped. He anxiously returned to the table and sat. Leaning forward, he said, "So you *have* met him."

Chris sighed. "I met a man *claiming* to be Nicholas Tewdrig. But I never saw his driver's license or other identification, so I have no proof it was him." He intentionally did not mention the photo he'd seen in the Black Boar tavern, hoping the vicar would reproduce it or perhaps offer other visual references.

"And yet you have ample proof already," Collingswood said.

"I do?"

He pointed to Chris's pants. "The alabaster stone in your pocket. Nicholas the Healer gave that to you, did he not?"

"I . . . I'm not sure," Chris said, rubbing his neck. It wasn't a total lie. Nick had *claimed* to have put the relic in his pocket, but again, there was no proof. "Do you know what it is?"

"Of course." Collingswood nodded. "It is a shard from the Dial of Ahaz."

Chris sighed again. "Yeah. That's what Nick said too."

Placing both hands palm-down on the table, Collingswood asked, "May I see it again, please?"

Chris removed the stone and placed it on the table in front [ ] vicar.

Collingswood studied it intently. "I've only seen pictures of this— drawings and woodcuts, no photographs. It's . . . it's breathtaking."

"Yes, it is. But is it *magical?*"

"Magical?"

Chris shifted his weight. "Does it give a person immortality and the power to heal?"

Collingswood gasped. "You *have* met the beloved Nicholas Tewdrig! I knew it. He *is* real. I believed it all this time . . . and now I have proof. They were wrong, and I was right." The man's face fairly beamed like a child's at Christmastime. "I have so many questions to ask you, Professor. I—I recognize jealousy is a sin, but I envy you in more ways than you can possibly know."

Collingswood's reaction seemed over-the-top to Chris. If Collingswood was a scholar of all things Tewdrig, he'd certainly have come across people claiming to have seen the beloved saint before, perhaps even met people claiming they had a piece of the Dial of Ahaz. But Chris wasn't interested in becoming the idol of someone's fancy. He simply wanted to get to the bottom of this mystery and be done with it.

Returning none of Collingswood's enthusiasm, Chris said, "Look, Reverend, I don't know if that piece of stone really *is* from Ahaz's staircase or if it's just some trinket Nick slipped in my pocket. But there's no need to envy me. I didn't ask for this higher calling, nor do I want anything more to do with it. You promised to tell me what you know about Nicholas Tewdrig, but so far you've asked more questions than answered. If you're not going to give me straight answers, I'll just have to look elsewhere." Chris snatched up the Dial and shoved it back in his pocket. "Thank you for your time."

"No, wait. Please," Collingswood said in a rushed voice, beseeching with his hands. "I'll tell you what I know. I—I have no idea if Nicholas Tewdrig is immortal or not. The legend says whoever carries the Dial of Ahaz will be blessed with long life and immunity. Just how long that is, no one knows. This shire abounds with St. Nicholas stories. Some say he is the original Santa Claus, because he freely gave gifts of healing. Every now and then a new story surfaces, someone claiming to have been visited by the beloved saint. It's rather like your Big Foot sightings in America," he said in total seriousness.

would appreciate that comparison," Chris

ou, my friend, are the only one to ever offer

the Dial and turned it in his fingers. "Certainly there've
people claiming to have a shard from the Dial of Ahaz."

"Yes, yes, of course. I've seen several," the cleric admitted. "Most are just bits of local river rock or imitation ivory made in Taiwan." He stood and pointed at the Dial. "But this specimen looks unerringly like the illustrations I've seen. And the story of how you came by it matches the writings."

"What writings?"

"Mostly from the journal of St. Nicholas, of course."

Chris frowned. "I've never heard of that record."

"Not many people have. Only a random page or two has ever been discovered and authenticated."

"Dare I ask what's in it?"

Collingswood smiled again, only this time, to Chris's dismay, his eyes were filled with greed instead of glee. "It says whosoever possesses the Dial will have the power to stave off disease and heal all manner of illness."

"And Nick claims that's now me."

The reverend shrugged, his eyes still fixed on the alabaster tile. "The only way to know for certain is if you can heal someone."

Nigel Madsen. My arm. No, it can't be true. I don't want it to be true. Chris frowned, hoping he had a believable poker face. "Well, then he gave it to the wrong guy. I'm not a priest. I don't even go to church regularly."

"Oh, you don't have to be a priest," Collingswood explained. "You don't even have to be Christian or Jewish. When the gift is passed, the receiver is adopted into the family of Lamed Vovniks. You, sir, have become one of the Righteous Thirty-Six."

CHAPTER 13

THE NAMES SOUNDED FAMILIAR TO Chris, but he couldn't place them. "Nick didn't say anything about becoming one of the thirty-six lamed whatever."

"Lamed Vovniks," Collingswood continued anxiously. "I'll explain what that means in a moment. But first, you must tell me everything that happened from the instant you first met Nicholas Tewdrig to the present—everything he said to you, everything he did to you. I need to establish how much you already know. After that, I promise to answer every question you ask."

Chris considered the proposal while massaging his neck. "Something tells me I'm going to regret this . . . but okay. Here's what I know: Yesterday, I witnessed a single-car accident over by Cardigan. I helped pull a young boy from the wreckage, but I didn't do it alone. A man claiming to be Nicholas Tewdrig helped me. I say 'claiming' because the more I learn about this Tewdrig guy, the more I realize he shouldn't be alive. Or maybe this guy's name really *is* Nicholas Tewdrig, just not *the* Nicholas Tewdrig."

He paused and stared at the languid dust motes passing in front of the roster of vicars and churchwardens. "Anyway, he said his name was Nicholas Tewdrig, and . . . well, he seemed so sincere. The guy sure knew his history." He drew a short breath and aimlessly toyed with the relic. "So as I'm pulling this kid out of the wreckage, Nick slipped this into my pocket, said something in Welsh, then showed up later at my motel to explain what it was. He made all sorts of claims about it, about passing it on to the next in line and bestowing some sacred mantle. Then he left. I'm just following up on it because that's what I do: research legends and teach about them."

"And what claims did he make?"

Chris chewed his lip, mentally weighing the outcomes that could accompany the amount of information he shared. "He said he was one of the Physicians of Myddfai, a fourth son adopted into the family because of his compassion for his fellow man. That this stone is a shard from the Dial of Ahaz—the one mentioned in the Old Testament—and that whoever possesses the stone will have the power to heal almost any ailment short of death."

Collingswood didn't blink. His face still showed astonishment and awe, but behind the dazed glow was something stronger, something covetous and calculating. A fine sheen beaded across his forehead. "And have you had the chance to use it?" the cleric asked with eagerness.

Chris's brow knitted. "Why do you ask?"

"To see if the legends are true, of course," he said, grinning with what looked like forced innocence.

Chris knew he *had* used the Dial . . . inadvertently. Maybe. There was no proving *he* had actually healed Nigel Madsen's ankles. And he hadn't had the chance to test it on anyone else. Nor did he want to. "The young boy I mentioned was hurt. I was certain he'd broken both ankles. But after I pulled him out, he was just fine. He was walking around as if nothing had happened. Nick claims I healed him." Chris held up the stone. "As far as I know, this is just a piece of alabaster with some funky scrimshaw on it. I don't even know how old it is."

The cleric's bottom lip quivered. "But it *is* alabaster? You know for sure it *is* alabaster?"

"Well, no. I was going to the university in Cardiff to check it out. That, and the writing on this one side. If it *is* something from the fifth century, I figured they could check with an international registry to see if it's a stolen artifact."

Panic flashed across Collingswood's eyes. "NO! You can't! They'll defile it. They'll destroy it. They'll—" He went silent, but his mouth continued to move; his eyes remained wide. Then, quite abruptly, his demeanor changed. Where he had been as anxious as a child with an unopened birthday gift, Collingswood now acted strangely unconcerned, disinterested. He dropped his gaze and ran his fingertips aimlessly across the tabletop.

"They'll what?"

"Oh, nothing. You're probably right. It's probably just a fake. In fact, I'm certain it is. Marble trinkets are often touted as alabaster. There are hundreds of them about—just like these paperweights," he said, nudging one of the large pawns. "As I said, I've seen many myself."

"Perhaps," Chris said, his brows still furrowed. Collingswood's rapid change in disposition had raised a score of red flags.

"Point of fact, the more I think about it, the more I know it is. Trust me. I believe your trip to Cardiff will be a total waste of time, my son," the cleric said with an obsequious smile.

Chris shrugged.

"Good man. I'm glad we're agreed," he said, daubing his forehead with a handkerchief. "So, if your trinket has no true value . . . why don't you let me take it off your hands? I'll even pay you for your troubles. As I mentioned, I collect St. Nicholas oddities, even if they are forgeries."

"Actually, you *never* mentioned that," Chris corrected without apology. "And if you're certain it is a fake, then why offer to buy it?" He pocketed the Dial and took a step back. "No, I think I'll stick to my original plan and ask around—"

"But you can't!" Collingswood yelled, rising to his feet so fast he knocked over his chair.

Chris took another step back. "Why not?"

"Are you mad? You have no idea what power you wield. Nations would pay untold fortunes for that stone—"

Just then, the noise of the wood panel door opening caused both men to turn.

"What the devil is going on here?" blustered a short, older man as he entered the room. He wore a priestly frock with an ecclesiastical collar, and he was not smiling. "What are you two—oh, it's you, is it," the clergyman said with disdain, glaring at Collingswood.

"Good morrow, Father Llewellyn," Collingswood said in a greeting filled with mockery. He gave a greatly lampooned low bow. His countenance had changed again, this time to arrogant, haughty, even dangerous.

"I told you not to come in here anymore," the priest fumed, close to a growl. "That's trespassing in my book, pure and simple. I'm calling the police."

Slack-jawed, Chris gawked from one man to the other. "I, um . . . I'm not . . ." was all he could manage.

"And who are you—his new sidekick?"

Only then did Chris notice the priest's glare was fixed on him. "Me? No. I, um—I just met Reverend Collingswood an hour ago—"

"*Reverend* Collingswood?" the priest decried. "Reverend, indeed. He's no more a man of the cloth than I'm the queen of England, yes? Are you a false priest too or a thief trying to steal from the church, like him?"

Chris was flummoxed. "But I thought—" He turned to Collingswood. "You're not the vicar here?"

The false priest's smile oozed with smugness. "Gotcha."

Enraged, Chris spun on his heel and stepped toward the real vicar. "Look, Father, I don't know what's going on between you two, but I am *not* involved with him at all," he said, thrusting a finger in Collingswood's direction. "I apologize for trespassing. He brought me in here under false pretenses."

"An American, are you?" the priest asked.

"Yes. From Washington State."

"Aye. You sound like an Ameri—"

Both men turned when they heard the racking of a handgun slide.

Pointing a silver semiautomatic at them, Collingswood's smile exuded pure malevolence. Chris didn't know guns well enough to recognize the make or model; all he saw was a large bore muzzle pointing at his face.

"Now hold on there, son," the real vicar said evenly. "No need to get messy here, you know. Remember, this is the Lord's house—"

"Shut up!" Collingswood snapped. "I've finally found one of the items I've been searching for. He holds the Dial of Ahaz," he said, jamming the gun at Chris. "He's a Vovnik."

"Hey, if you want this piece of junk, take it," Chris said, holding out the Dial.

Collingswood laughed. "You fool. Do you really think it's a just piece of junk—when all the evidence points to its authenticity?"

"What evidence?" Chris argued. "I told you, I have no proof it does *anything.*"

The gunman's smile became calculating. "Oh, you want proof, do you?" Without awaiting an answer, he shifted his aim and shot the priest in the belly.

CHAPTER 14

THE GUN BLAST FRACTURED THE sanctity of the small study. The sound was deafening. Chris's ears rang to the point that he felt woozy, nauseated. The sharp smell of spent gunpowder assaulted his nostrils.

The priest lay on the floor, his hand gripping his robe over a dark, spreading stain. His eyes were wide with fear and shock.

"Are you okay?" Chris asked lamely, kneeling at the priest's side. It was obvious he wasn't, but Chris had to say something.

The vicar's mouth worked open and closed, but no words came out—just some gurgling, thin wheezes.

"Heal him, Vovnik," Collingswood demanded.

At first, Chris didn't realize the gunman was talking to him. "Heal him? How? I'm not a doctor."

"Don't give me that nonsense. You know what I'm talking about. Now heal him."

"I'm not a doctor!" Chris repeated. "I'm not one of your stupid magicians."

"Magician? You think this is just—just silly folk magic?"

"Yes. As a matter of fact I do." He then felt a wet hand grip his wrist. The wounded priest looked through his pain with an expression of . . . of what? Of trust? The man gave the slightest nod before coughing up a mouthful of foamy blood.

A bitter mix of anger and hopelessness closed off Chris's throat. He swallowed several times before being able to whisper, "I can't."

The old priest's grip tightened around his wrist. He nodded again.

"You're losing ground, Vovnik," Collingswood said with a snicker. He was now standing right next to them, still pointing his gun. "Once he's dead, you can't bring him back. I'm sure that's something Tewdrig explained to you."

Chris shook his head, unable to bring words to his mouth. *I can't do this! I am not a healer!*

The priest drew Chris's hand just below his ribcage, over the bullet hole. He nodded once more, mouthed the word *try*, then closed his eyes.

Chris felt blood pulsing from the wound. *I can't do this! I'm just a school teacher!*

"Say the words, healer," Collingswood pressed. "I want to witness the miracle."

Chris closed his eyes, wondering what to do, what to say.

"Say the words!" Collingswood yelled.

"I don't know the words!" Chris yelled back.

"You carry the Dial of Ahaz. Nicholas Tewdrig passed it on to you. He passed you the mantle. Now say the words and heal him!"

"HE DIDN'T TELL ME THE WORDS!" Chris bellowed, glaring at the gunman.

There was a suffocating pause as the two men glowered at each other. The old priest's wheezing grew lighter, softer. Chris placed both hands over the wound. *Compression. Stop the bleeding.* He pressed down—and the priest blanched, groaning in sharp agony.

"I'm sorry. I'm sorry," Chris said quickly, lifting his hands.

With his eyes half opened, the priest pulled Chris's hands back to the wound. Then, meeting his gaze, he whispered, "Believe," just before blacking out.

Trembling uncontrollably, Chris could not steady his hands. He didn't know why he *should* steady them; he just felt like it was the right thing to do.

The right thing to do is call an ambulance; he cursed to himself. He quickly pulled his cell phone from his pocket but stopped when he felt the barrel of Collingswood's gun against the back of his skull.

"Toss the mobile, Professor, and heal Father Llewellyn."

"I'm—not—a—doctor," he spat. "How many times do I have to—"

"How many times do I have to tell you what you are?" Collingswood spat back. "Now heal the priest, or join him in the grave. Your choice."

With zero confidence, Chris slid his phone to one side and placed his hands back on the gunshot wound. His mind whirled. How had he healed Nigel Madsen? He didn't! But his mind raced to the scene of the accident anyway. He hadn't done *anything*. He'd grabbed the boy's ankles and pulled. He didn't chant some mystic incantation. He didn't recite any ritualistic, sacred prayer. He didn't even know the Dial was in his pocket!

The priest choked and coughed up more foamy blood. His skin had turned pallid, almost colorless. Chris guessed a lung had been punctured.

A voice inside him said, *Believe*.

Chris screwed his eyes shut and focused. What did he think about as he pulled Nigel from the burning car? Nothing—other than wanting to save him, to pull him from the immediate danger. The young boy was innocent, too young to die.

"Stop dawdling, healer."

Chris's teeth ground together as he again pressed against the wound. He mentally pled with whoever could hear his petition: *Please don't let this man die. Please don't let this man die. He is innocent. Please God, through faith I ask, don't let this man die.*

Faith, that's right. Nick had said something about faith.

Focus. Believe.

He concentrated on stopping the blood loss. He pictured the damaged tissues knitting, sealing, healing. He yearned for this innocent man to live. Chris had no idea if the victim was a good man or not, but he *was* a churchwarden, a servant of the Lord. That had to account for something. He sensed the man was compassionate. He didn't deserve to die like this.

Gasping for his own breath, Chris kept the pressure on the wound. The priest groaned again, long and deep, grating, raspy. His skin was now completely ashen; his face was gaunt and flaccid. His breathing had turned shallow, coming in short, wet bursts.

"So you're just going to let him die," Collingswood said, accusingly.

Chris did his best to ignore the imposter. He focused on images of healthy organs, of healed tissue. He tried to believe. He imagined the vicar standing on his rostrum, giving a sermon about brotherly love and forgiveness. Or about false priests and wolves in sheep's clothing.

Like Collingswood.

"Are you going to kill me too?" Chris asked through clenched teeth.

"If I have to," the false priest calmly replied.

"Look, you can have the Dial. I don't want it. I never did."

"Let's wait to see what happens, Vovnik."

"What does that even mean? No—never mind. Please, let me call an ambulance. Before it's too late."

Collingswood didn't answer.

Chris kept an ear cocked for any movement the gunman might make. Suddenly, he felt a sharp pain in his left side—as if he'd been shot. But he hadn't heard the gun fire. Turning his gaze slightly, he saw that Collingswood had taken a step back. The pistol hung loosely at his side.

Turning completely, Chris was confused by the man's demeanor. Collingswood's expression was a twisted amalgam of awe, delight, and astonishment. "You *are* one of the Thirty-Six," he said in a voice hushed with respect.

"What Thirty-Six? What is that?" Chris hissed each sentence with indictment rather than inquiry.

Collingswood slowly returned the gun to his concealed shoulder holster, never taking his eyes from his victim. "Look," he said, nodding.

Chris glanced back at the vicar—and gasped. Father Llewellyn's skin no longer held the curdled pallor of death. Even his hands had regained their pinkish hue. Not only that, his breathing was steady and clear.

"Father? Are you okay? Can you hear me?" Chris asked anxiously.

The vicar was silent, as if in a deep sleep.

Chris carefully smoothed the priest's robes around the wound. He could no longer see any seepage of blood. The area still glistened red with spent plasma, but it appeared to be congealing quickly. Gingerly, he drew down the zipper of the priest's frock. Peeling back the fold, he found the man's white shirt was soaked with blood. But his chest wasn't convulsing; it rose and fell effortlessly with each breath.

Chris glanced back at Collingswood. The man was leaning forward, eager to see the outcome.

"Go on, man. Open his shirt."

Chris unbuttoned the shirt and folded it away from the wound. He blinked then held his eyes closed for a moment before reopening them. The vicar's skin was red and inflamed, but the bullet hole looked like nothing more than a burn scar about the size of a dime. He couldn't believe it. He delicately prodded around the wound. It felt mildly warm but not traumatized or infected. He pressed down on the ribcage, expecting to elicit a moan from the victim; but instead, he got nothing.

"Behold the power of the Dial," Collingswood said in a melodramatic tone, as if he were doing an epic voiceover. He slumped against the table, wiping his brow again with his hankie, as if he'd just completed an exhausting task. "I'll be honest with you, Pendragon. That was better than

I had anticipated. Brilliant! Marvelous! I've seen some remarkable things in my life, my friend, but never a true miracle. May I just say what an honor it is to be in your presence?"

Chris couldn't believe the magnitude of the man's coldhearted apathy toward the priest. He'd just shot the man, for heaven's sake! Didn't he have any remorse? Didn't he have any compunction?

Chris placed his ear to the vicar's chest.

"Oh, he's just fine now, I have no doubt," Collingswood said, primly folding his hankie. "You did it, Vovnik. You healed him."

Chris stood slowly. Making a pretense of wiping his hands on his pants, he spun quickly, slamming his fist into the taller man's jaw. Collingswood fell across the table and rolled off the other side, knocking both marble paperweights to the floor. One cracked in half. Chris shook the sting from his hand and flexed his fingers. He wasn't usually a violent man, but he had to acknowledge the satisfaction he felt in coldcocking the imposter. He quickly rounded the table and pulled the gun from Collingswood's holster.

Returning to the vicar, he picked up his cell phone and dialed 999. As the line rang, he rehearsed what he would say to the operator.

Hello, a man was just shot, but he's okay now.

Hello, I just witnessed a murder, but I healed him.

Hello, there's a priest with a bullet in his abdomen, but he seems to be sleeping it off.

"Emergency services. What is the nature of your call?"

"A man's been shot at the Church of St. Nicholas in Trellech. Come quickly." He hung up and knelt beside the vicar. "Father Llewellyn? Can you hear me?"

There was no response.

He checked the man's pulse and breathing, both of which seemed quite normal.

"Father Llewellyn? Are you okay? Are you in any pain?"

The vicar's eyes began to flutter. His breath caught a couple times before he cleared his throat and smacked his lips. It was then that Chris heard a siren in the distance. Someone else must have heard the gunfire. Emergency services didn't respond *that* quickly.

"Just lie still, Father. You've been shot. Help is on the way." Chris again examined the bullet wound. Using the sleeve of his shirt, he wiped away as much of the blood as he could. The wound now looked almost inconsequential. Sitting back on his heels, he frowned. Everything Nick Tewdrig had said to him came flashing back, but he still refused to believe it. He was *not* a miracle-worker. He was *not* a mystic healer. And he was *not* whatever Collingswood had called him.

As he gently palpated the wound again, something shuffled behind him. He turned just in time to see the Collingswood's pant leg before a hard object slammed against the back of his head.

Chris felt a jolt of white pain before he realized he was falling forward. Then everything went black.

CHAPTER 15

"Sɪʀ? Cᴀɴ ʏᴏᴜ ʜᴇᴀʀ ᴍᴇ, sir?"

The new voice had a classic, rural Welsh quality, in both accent and timbre. Chris tried to respond, but his mouth felt like it was filled with cotton soaked in library paste.

"Jus' take it easy, Mr. Pendragon. No sudden motions, sir, or you'll black out again."

"What . . . ? Who . . . ?"

"Looks like the vicar got in one or two good blows, didn't he."

"The . . . vicar?" he croaked.

"Father Llewellyn. Should be in hospital by now, I should think," the man explained in an accusatory tone. "Hopefully he's still alive—for your sake, that is."

Chris peeled open his eyes. He was still in the back room of St. Nicholas Church. He was sitting on a chair with his hands cuffed behind his back. A length of chord was wrapped around his chest to prevent him from falling. The man in front of him was wearing a police uniform.

Tugging on the restraints, Chris rasped, "Why am I . . . ?"

"You're under arrest, sir."

Chris frowned. He could swear the officer had just said he was under arrest. His head pounded mercilessly. He could tell someone had bandaged his skull; it felt like he was wearing a ten-pound turban. Perhaps the head wrap had muffled what he'd heard.

He blinked several times to focus on the man speaking to him. "Say that again?"

Squatting in front of him, the officer tapped a nightstick in one hand against the opposite palm. He wasn't smiling. "I said you're under arrest, Mr. Pendragon."

Chris swallowed a dry, congealed lump in his throat. "Water. Please."

The constable nodded to someone beyond Chris's view. A glass of water was held in front of him so he could take a drink.

"Thank you," he said when he was finished. Slowly raising his head, each heartbeat boomed in his ears. "Why . . . am I under arrest?"

"Attempted murder, for starters, ay?" the constable said, as if stating the obvious.

"*Attempted*? So the vicar *is* okay?"

"Don't rightly know, now do I, sir?" he said, steadily tapping his baton. "Had emergency services take him to hospital over in Monmouth, didn't we. He was unconscious, jus' like you. But with any luck, he'll live long enough to ID you."

"Good. I *want* him to ID me. He'll tell you I'm not the one who shot him."

"Not the one who—?" the officer gawped. "You were laying across the top of him. You had the gun in your hand, didn't you, sir. Barrel was still warm, wasn't it. Not to mention you're covered with the vicar's blood, ay?"

"I can explain all that. I'm just visiting—"

"Oh, we know quite a bit about you already, Christian Pendragon of Spokane, Washington, USA. What we don't know is why you tried to murder Father Llewellyn."

"But I didn't—" Chris said before pain closed off his voice. The relentless pounding in his head wasn't subsiding fast enough. "I did no such thing," he managed to say, much softer, but no less insistent. "A tall man in a dark, tailored suit shot the vicar. He said his name is Collingswood."

The constable stood and slid his baton into a belt ring. He fished a spiral-bound notepad from one pocket and a pen from another. "Collingswood, you say?" he asked, scribbling. "Can't say as the name rings any bells like. Does he have a first name then?"

"I guess. I don't know." Chris noticed the constable's badge. "Look, Officer Hart, I know how this must look, but I didn't try to kill anyone. I'm visiting from the States to do legend research. I teach at Gonzaga University in Spokane. I came here looking for information about the small stone in my pocket."

"Small stone, you say?" Hart stepped to the table and, using his pen, slid a few objects around. Chris recognized the items as his wallet, passport, keys, cell phone, and a few coins. "Didn't find any small stone in your pockets when we emptied them."

"What? Collingswood must have stolen it. I have to get it back!"

Officer Hart cocked an eyebrow. "Curious he didn't take his own unregistered nine millimeter Ruger covered with the vicar's blood, now isn't it? Care to explain that, sir?"

Chris grimaced against the pounding in his head. "Just check the gun for fingerprints, will you? He wasn't wearing gloves."

"Oh, we'll check it out right proper like, sir. But there was a lot of blood on it. Had to peel it out of your hand, we did. Like glue, it was—the blood. And I'll wager the only prints we'll find on it are the ones *you* left."

Chris cursed under his breath. "Look. You don't understand how important that small stone is."

"More important than the vicar's life?"

This was going nowhere. "So what's going to happen now?"

"The EMTs patched your skull, but it still needs attention. Once they get vicar to hospital they'll be back for you. Couldn't have the gunman riding in the same vehicle with his victim, ay? Until then, we'll keep checking out premises like. So far we haven't seen anyone unusual about . . . except you, of course. Least wise, no 'tall gentleman in a dark, tailored suit,'" Hart quoted, reading from his notepad.

Fighting his rising temper, Chris said, "So you're saying I shot the vicar then laid on top of him and knocked myself unconscious? Does that make sense to you?"

The officer merely shrugged. "I've seen stranger."

"Did you happen to notice there isn't a bullet hole in his abdomen anymore?"

"So you also know precisely where he was shot then, ay? That a mere coincidence, Mr. Pendragon?"

"No. Obviously, I saw Collingswood shoot him."

Officer Hart tipped his hat back and scratched his forehead. "So *you're* saying you saw this Collingswood chap shoot vicar in the breadbasket, but now there *isn't* a bullet hole?"

Chris couldn't very well explain that there *had* been a bullet hole but that he'd healed it. They wouldn't believe it. *He* couldn't believe it. "Okay, look. I know this sounds crazy—"

Chris was cut short by the officer's buzzing cell phone. Hart answered it, mumbled a few words, nodded and grunted a few times, then favored Chris with a grin of triumph.

"Right. We'll be waiting," he said before ending the call. "The EMTs will be taking you to hospital now. They're jus' pulling up outside. We'll get the doctor to check you out like. Then, unless I miss my mark, we'll book you into Monmouth Police Station."

"Is Father Llewellyn still alive?"

"They didn't say." Hart removed the chord around Chris's chest and helped him stand. "But were I you, I'd certainly hope so, ay?"

CHAPTER 16

THE EMTS HELPED CHRIS INTO the back of the ambulance. Officer Hart interrogated him during the entire twenty-minute drive. No matter how many times Chris explained precisely what had happened, the constable continued to pepper him with the same questions, using different angles as if trying to trip him up. Chris found it ludicrous.

Still fettered in handcuffs, Chris sat in an exam cubicle in Monmouth's small community hospital. His head still hurt, as did his abdomen, but it was a strange kind of hurt. There was discomfort but no longer serious pain.

The cubicle was framed by sliding nylon curtains. The table was covered with paper dispensed from a large roll at the head. A bright lamp glared overhead. Wheeled carts with various medical apparatus lined the walls. The small room was functional but rather impersonal—as was the constable standing silently off to one side tapping at his cell phone. The *wheee—crash—smash* sounds suggested the man was playing Angry Birds.

A rap sounded on the room's aluminum framework, and the curtain was pulled aside before Chris had a chance to say, "Come in." Although in no mood to be sociable, he felt himself pleasantly surprised at the woman who entered. The doctor was young, probably in her twenties. Her blonde hair was stylishly short and spikey but not punk; her makeup was minimal and accentuating. She was pretty but didn't appear to flaunt that trait; rather, her conduct was manifestly professional.

"Good afternoon, Mr. Pendragon. My name is Dr. Ingledew. It says here—" She stopped abruptly and scowled at his handcuffs. "What's this nonsense?"

"A misunderstanding," Chris said. He wanted to say *police brutality*.

The doctor turned to Hart and stared, but he was still fixated on his game. Stepping up to him, she grabbed the phone from his hands.

"What the—?"

"This is a hospital, not an arcade, Officer Hart," she lectured. "All unnecessary electronic devices are to be turned off." Shutting his phone off, she thrust it back at him. "There. Now, if you kindly would uncuff my patient, please."

"I can't, ma'am. This man is being detained under authority of the law," he said testily, pocketing his phone.

The young doctor didn't blink. "In this hospital, *I* am the law. Now remove those cuffs so I can properly examine my patient."

"Sorry, ma'am. I—"

"*Doctor*," she cut across.

Hart smiled smugly. "Yes, yes. *Doctor*, then. But if you'll look, it's jus' his head needs tending to, not his wrists."

"Oh, are you a doctor too then? Studied at medical university, did you?" she asked forcefully. Her accent sounded more English than Welsh, yet she used many of the local idioms.

"No, ma'am—Doctor."

"Then do as I say, or I will notify your superiors that you are interfering with and disrupting government-regulated facility operations."

"But he's detained on murder charges, ma'—Doctor. He's a dangerous criminal."

The physician cast her gaze toward Chris. "Who did you kill?"

"No one. I *witnessed* the attempt. The gunman got away."

"He tried to murder the vicar of St. Nicholas Church," Hart said bluntly.

"Father Llewellyn?" she asked.

"The very same."

She glanced between the constable and her patient. "Has Mr. Pendragon been formally charged with murder?"

"Well . . . no, ma'am—Doctor. Not yet."

Noting something on her clipboard, she said, "I can certify that Father Llewellyn is not dead. I've examined him myself. You *will* remove the handcuffs from this patient immediately and exit this cubicle so I can properly examine him, please." When the constable hesitated, she pulled out her cell phone. "Right. Your commander's name and number, please, Officer Hart."

Grudgingly, the constable selected a key from his key caddy and unfastened Chris's handcuffs. Then, putting his face close to Chris's, he said, "I'll be jus' right through those curtains there, ay? No shenanigans. Is that clear?"

"Don't worry. I'm fresh out of shenanigans."

Hart frowned, as if trying to figure out if he'd just been mocked, then gave up, nodded to the doctor, and exited.

As soon as the curtain closed, Dr. Ingledew stood directly in front of Chris and locked eyes with him. "Did you shoot Father Llewellyn?" she asked.

"No. A man named Collingswood did."

"Does he know that?" she asked, tipping her head in the direction of the constable.

"Yes. I gave him a full description and all the details of what happened."

She studied his expression for a long moment then stepped to the curtain and peeked out. Returning, she said, "Since the good father is also a patient of mine, tell me what you told the constable, will you, please?"

Chris laid out the whole scenario, beginning from when he entered the church to the present.

Ingledew took a moment, pondering his tale, then gave a curt nod. "That's settled then. Let's get started, shall we?"

She went through a full cadre of procedures, taking her time to examine every little ache and pain Chris had—which, surprisingly, weren't that many. She spent several silent minutes examining his scalp.

"You said you were bludgeoned just a few hours ago, Mr. Pendragon?" The look on her face clearly showed her bewilderment.

He could imagine her puzzlement when she'd examined a gunshot victim with no bullet hole. "It's Chris. And yes, I was. He used a solid marble paperweight. Felt like he cracked my skull open."

"Oh, I can imagine. You have quite a volume of dried blood on your scalp and in your hair, and I can see some vestige of ecchymosis; but for the life of me, I can't find any laceration or abrasion . . . or even a blunt trauma contusion."

"I assume that means something good?" Chris said in a teasing manner. He knew what the terms meant.

Ignoring his jest, she went on, "Normally I'd suggest an X-ray or CT scan, but you don't exhibit any signs of concussion, ataxia, or swelling of the brain, at least, as far as I can tell."

"There's not much up there to swell," he teased again. She didn't even blink. He wasn't trying to be flirtatious; it just sort of came out that way. "So what's next, Doc?"

"I need to get a blood type," she said, pulling a needle and collection tube from a cart.

"May I ask what for?"

"Yes. Because there's no obvious point of origin, I'm checking to see if the blood on your scalp matches the blood in your circulatory system."

Chris blinked a few times. "Who else's would it be?"

"Only you can answer that, Mr. Pendragon."

It occurred to him that none of the blood on his hands was his own either—but he felt it best not to reveal that tidbit of condemnation just yet. Instead, he tried engaging in some harmless chit-chat. "So, Doc, have you worked here long?"

To his surprise, her reply was filled with defensiveness. "I assure you I am fully qualified, Mr. Pendragon. I graduated fifth in my class and—"

"Whoa, I didn't mean anything by it," Chris cut in with his hands up. "I was just making conversation. Your accent doesn't seem local, is all."

She considered him warily a moment before nodding. "Just to reiterate: You have no headache, ringing in the ears, blurred vision?"

"Correct. I did at first, but it passed shortly before I got here."

"And your scalp is not tender to the touch?"

"Not anymore."

"Can you taste any blood?"

"No. None."

She looked over her notes several times, flipping back and forth between pages, all the while with a knitted brow.

"Got you stumped, huh?" Chris asked.

His question was met with another affronted glare.

"Man, I'm striking out here. Look, I apologize, Dr. Ingledew. I don't mean to be rude or to question your abilities. I'm just as confused as you are. I mean, the guy *did* knock me out. I assumed there'd be a huge goose egg and a nasty cut on my head, but honestly, I feel okay. I'm actually more worried about Father Llewellyn. How's he doing anyway?"

Still leafing through his chart, she replied, "That information is confidential, Mr. Pendragon."

"I am accused of shooting him—which I didn't. I think I have a right to know if I'm going to be arrested on assault or attempted murder charges." He didn't mean to sound so harsh, but he was near his wits' end.

After a brief pause, Ingledew said, "He's lucid and alert. When I examined him, I found no gunshot wound, just some mild bruising on the left side of his abdomen and his back. Yet I know something *had* happened because his clothes were covered with his own blood. We've already typed it to be sure." Her voice wasn't as confident as it was earlier.

Chris felt sorry for the young physician. Something as cut and dry as a gunshot wound usually presented with typical morphology—as did a head wound. But she'd been handed two trauma cases consisting of coherent men covered in blood but in good physical condition.

"I wish I could explain it, Doctor. I really do," he said. "I don't understand it myself. I only know what I saw."

Crestfallen, her expression finally registered defeat. "I just don't know how I'm supposed to write this one up."

"How would you normally do it?"

Scratching her head with her pen, she said, "Standard procedure is to enter what the patient was admitted for, what I found in my examination, and what steps I took to rectify the problem if one is discovered."

"So basically you had two men come in all bloodied up from severe trauma, but you couldn't do anything because they're already healed."

The look of failure in her eyes touched Chris. Being raised in a medical family, he recognized the expression. To a physician, a partial success is often regarded as a complete failure. It was a self-depreciating, impossibly perfectionistic mind-set, but new doctors were sometimes like that. His heart went out to her.

"Hey, but that's okay. I think you've been awesome," he said with a grin. "Very thorough. You did everything by the book and then some. And if I get to fill out one of those patient satisfaction cards, I'll put down that you're a miracle worker."

"Hardly," she said with a scoff . . . and a faint smile. *Progress.*

Chris was about to continue when the curtain parted and in walked the constable accompanied by an intense man wearing a stiff suit and rectangular, black-framed glasses.

"Mr. Pendragon," said the man. "You're under arrest for suspected organized crime activity on British soil."

CHAPTER 17

"WHAT?" CHRIS CRIED.

"Do you mind!" Dr. Ingledew blustered, ignoring the man's shocking allegations. "I'm examining a patient here."

The bespectacled man flashed a badge. "Detective Simon Westcott. MI5."

"Impressive badge, Detective," Ingledew said, "but that doesn't change the fact that you are interfering with a patient's examination. I need you to wait outside until I finish."

"Wait. What's MI5?" Chris asked.

"It's rather like your Homeland Security," Westcott explained as he cocked his head at Hart, indicating that he should exit the room. After the constable left, Westcott continued, "You may finish your examination, Doctor. I promise I will not interfere. But I'm afraid I must remain within sight of the accused for the duration."

She scoffed. "The man he supposedly shot is symptom-free. There's no trace of a gunshot wound or trauma of any kind; therefore, your accusations are unfounded."

Chris was in shock—both from the arrest charge and from the doctor's defense of him. She sounded almost angry. He sat there speechlessly watching the exchange, silently rooting for the doctor but sensing this was just the beginning of something much worse.

"I'm only partially referring to the incident with Trellech's vicar," Westcott explained. "The gun in Mr. Pendragon's possession is unregistered, and therefore, illegal—"

"It's not my gun!" Chris seethed. "I told you guys that already. It belongs to that Collingswood guy."

"Who is not on any records we have at our disposal," Westcott replied snootily. "Curious that, isn't it, Mr. Pendragon? More to the point, ballistics has matched the gun to two previous crimes—both of which are linked to organized crime activity."

"Organized cri— You've got to be kidding!"

"What organized crime activity?" Ingledew asked calmly.

Westcott adjusted his glasses. "I'm afraid that's classified for now, Doctor. Strictly government business and all."

"And *this* is strictly medical business," she shot back, gesturing at Chris. "So if you anticipate locking this man up, it will have to be *after* I have released him from the hospital. Do we understand each other?"

The detective stood fast then glanced at his watch. "I suppose it's a fair compromise. When do you expect that to happen?"

"Tomorrow, at the earliest."

"Tomorrow?" Chris and Westcott said simultaneously.

"My diagnosis is inconclusive. I need to keep him overnight for observation," she said with defiant confidence.

Chris wondered if the detective had overheard their conversation from a moment before, when the doctor was anything *but* confident. He was grateful—and a bit confused—at her delay tactics. He didn't know why she was doing so, but he wasn't going to question her motives.

Westcott glared at Ingledew for a moment before moving to a corner of the small space and removing his phone. "Please, continue your exam, Doctor. Take your time."

"Put away your phone, Detective," she snapped. "They're not allowed in the hospital."

"Oh, that's right. Electronic interference and all. Sorry."

"Just stay there. Don't make a sound; don't move a muscle. I need to concentrate."

Ingledew turned back to Chris and flashed a covert, half-smile of triumph. As she felt the lymph nodes under his ears on along his neck, Chris mouthed, *Why?*

She gave an almost imperceptible shake of her head, meaning, he suspected, *I'll tell you later.*

He didn't have any choice but to trust her.

"Right, Mr. Pendragon," she said. "Let's get you down to X-ray and see what kind of internal damage that blow to your skull did, shall we?"

"I'd like to call my embassy first," he asked hesitantly.

"You'll get that chance," she assured him. "No one's going to haul you off for a while yet. I'll make sure of that."

Chris swallowed the nervous anger welling in him. This had gone from ridiculous to insane. Organized crime? Was the man kidding? Presently, even if he wanted to simply walk away from this whole Nicholas Tewdrig/Dial of Ahaz thing, he couldn't. It'd be considered fleeing justice.

Ignoring the now passive Detective Westcott, Dr. Ingledew pulled the nylon curtain back and grabbed a wheelchair from the hallway. Chris dropped into it gratefully. With his nerves shot, he wasn't sure his legs would support him for very long.

As the doctor wheeled him past the reception counter, Westcott remained step-for-step, uncomfortably close behind her. "Do you mind?" she hissed, backing him off a few paces.

As they were heading down a hallway toward the X-ray department, an orderly came running up. "Dr. Ingledew, a moment, please?"

"Yes?" she said, pausing.

"Father Llewellyn is requesting to see Mr. Pendragon immediately."

"I'm afraid that simply cannot be authorized," Westcott said. "He is a political prisoner and cannot be allowed any public interaction until after interrogation."

"Mr. Pendragon was my patient before he was your suspect," Dr. Ingledew said, narrowing her eyes at him. "If the vicar is feeling up to it, *I* will authorize it."

She obviously had a distaste of authority figures. Chris loved having the pretty physician on his side.

"But, Doctor—"

"No buts, Detective. Mr. Pendragon is accused of shooting Father Llewellyn first and foremost. That gives him precedence. Besides, if the vicar identifies him as the gunman, then you have a solid tie to the unregistered gun, am I correct?"

Westcott paused, thinking. He adjusted his glasses. "I suppose."

"Good. Then let's go see if the father marks Mr. Pendragon as his assailant."

Chris swallowed hard again, wondering if *anyone* was on his side.

CHAPTER 18

FATHER LLEWELLYN WAS IN A private room in the overnight wing. He was sitting up, smiling broadly when Chris was wheeled in. Hooked to a single IV and a blood pressure cuff, the vicar wore only a hospital gown and a simple gold cross on a thin lanyard around his neck. Chris was surprised at the lack of tubes and monitors, but he felt an overwhelming sense of relief that the man was not only alive but seemed to be healthy and happy.

"Christian Pendragon, I assume, yes?" Llewellyn chimed happily. Before Chris could answer, the vicar turned to the doctor and detective. "Thank you, my friends. You may leave us alone now, if you please."

"I'm sorry, Father," Westcott said, showing him his badge. "This man is under arrest and must remain in my sight until he's delivered to the station."

Llewellyn was clearly surprised. "Under arrest, is he? What nonsense is this?"

"That is official government business, Father."

He looked at Chris. "Christian?"

Chris wanted to lash out at how the police had been so quick to falsely accuse him, but his joy from seeing the vicar so well overshadowed his anger. "They have their facts a little mixed up, Father."

"Obviously," Llewellyn said without humor. "Sure about this, are you, constable?"

"Detective. And yes," Westcott replied. "The evidence thus far is very incriminating."

The room settled into an awkward silence. Finally, Llewellyn said, "Well then, an allowance must be made. I asked Mr. Pendragon here to reconcile his confession."

"But I'm not—" Chris stopped short, realizing what the priest was doing. "I'm not sure I'm ready, Father."

"Of course you're not ready, my son," Llewellyn said. "The confession is a sacred confidence, a holy sacrament to be shared only between the penitent and his confessor." Looking at Westcott, he continued, "That is why we *must* have our privacy. A man is allowed his absolution before God prior to facing the executioner, is he not? It is written in the law, yes?"

The look on Westcott's face revealed harsh, inner conflict. He looked to Dr. Ingledew for help. She smiled and said, "Come on, Sherlock. We'll be right outside. This is the only door, and he's not going anywhere with a severe head wound, I can assure you."

With a grunt of annoyance, the detective adjusted his glasses and stepped out of the room. Ingledew followed, gently shutting the door behind her.

Llewellyn motioned for Chris to wheel closer. "How are you, my son?" he asked, keeping his voice low. "Your head looks terrible."

"I'm fine, Father. But I have to tell you I'm not Catholic or Anglican."

"Oh, that," the vicar said, waving the comment away. "The confession was a just ruse, a ploy to get the eavesdroppers to leave, yes?"

"Ah. O-kay," Chris said slowly, wondering why the father wanted to speak to him privately.

"First, I owe you an apology, Christian. Please forgive me for assuming you were with that piece of human debris, Collingswood."

Chris tilted his head to one side. "All right. You're forgiven. But you don't owe me anything. *I'm* sorry you got shot."

The vicar waved away that comment too. "Now, second: I am not comfortable looking down at you in that wheelchair from up here, ay? I feel like a ruddy archangel, which I'm anything but." He patted the edge of his bed. "Please, sit yourself up here, lad."

"O-kay," Chris again said slowly, feeling awkward and still very confused.

"Right, then. My name is Father Benedict Llewellyn," he said, gripping Chris's wrist after he was situated. "I'm head vicar over the Chapel of St. Nicholas, yes? As we were never properly introduced, allow me to get to know thee better, man."

The old vicar was remarkably vibrant for having been shot just a few hours ago. "Sure, Father. What do you want to know?"

"Well, I already know you're an American, so there's no need to rehash that. What else is there to the man who saved my life, is what I want to know."

"There's really not much more," Chris said with a shrug. He didn't want to say anything about the Dial or Nicholas Tewdrig just yet. He wasn't sure he trusted the churchman—or anyone else for that matter.

"Tell me what brought you to my church then." The vicar's warm smile and gentle blue eyes were disarming. There was no mistrust in them, no guile. If anything, they seemed to be looking into his soul.

Chris picked at the dried blood on his hands—probably the vicar's blood—as he rehearsed his reasons for visiting Wales. The more he spoke, the more he opened up. Llewellyn listened patiently, smiling throughout, nodding occasionally.

"Then I came to Trellech to learn more about St. Nicholas Tewdrig." He intentionally used Nick's last name to see if he'd get a reaction from the man. When there wasn't any, he continued: "Since Reverend—I mean, *Mr.*—Collingswood was the only one there, I assumed he was vicar."

"So, you're *not* a doctor of medicine then?" Llewellyn asked, smiling.

"No, sir. Just a student and teacher of history."

"And yet Collingswood called you *healer*. I heard him correctly, did I not?"

Chris shrugged. "He was assuming I'm something I'm not."

"How interesting . . ." The old man reflected, patting the back of Chris's wrist. "So it were pure faith then," he continued, nodding slowly. "You healed me by faith, yes?"

Chris fidgeted a bit before answering. "I don't think so, Father. I'm not much of a churchgoer. My faith is infinitely smaller than a mustard seed," he said with a weak grin. "But I'm glad you're doing well. And I apologize again for trespassing in your study."

"You are forgiven, lad," Llewellyn said, brushing it off. "Besides, Collingswood led you in there under false pretenses, yes? You said so yourself. You didn't go sniffin' around of your own accord like." The vicar patted Chris's wrist once more and finally released it.

"Thank you." Chris paused, glancing at the door and chewing on his lower lip.

"Oh, don't worry about them, my son. This confessional can go on as long as you want. Let 'em wait outside all night, I say." The vicar's eyes crinkled with merriment. The expression confused Chris. He thought for sure the old man would be angry.

"I, um . . . I'm just not sure what to do now. I should probably call the US embassy . . ."

"Nay, lad. You should finish what you came here for," Llewellyn said sternly.

Chris frowned. "Really? You think that's more important than proving my innocence?"

"Aye. That I do. Besides, *I* will vouch for your innocence." The look in his eyes was penetrating. "If you go to the authorities, you will never know your true potential, now will you?"

Chris frowned. "My true potential?"

"Aye. You said you came here to learn about our beloved patron saint, did you not?"

"Ah, yes. Well, honestly, Father, right now I'm more concerned about being arrested for assumed association with the mob."

"You let me worry about that, son," Llewellyn said, again patting his hand. "Now, what is it about St. Nicholas that vexes you?"

Chris cleared his throat. "Well, my questions may sound a little strange, but I mean no offense by them."

"Ask what you like, my son."

Drawing a deep breath, he said, "Are there any records of what he was like? I mean, I know he was a doctor—one of the Physicians of Myddfai—but are there any accounts of what he did after he left the church?"

"Now that *is* a strange query." Llewellyn's brow furrowed as he considered the subject. "The man was never ousted from the church—excommunicated like—if that's what you mean. There *is* the mystery surrounding his passing, but he never *left* the church."

"Okay, what about that? Does anyone know where he's buried?"

Llewellyn smiled softly. "No, son, I think not."

"Are there any accounts of . . . Has anyone claimed to have seen him after his tenure with the church? In this century, I mean?"

"Oh aye," he chuckled. "You could fill a book with 'em, yes?"

Chris lowered his voice. "Have *you* ever seen him?"

With narrowed eyes, Llewellyn looked at Chris askew. "Why do you ask, son?"

He lowered his voice even more. "Because I think I have."

"Aye?"

"Yeah. Twice. A couple days back, at the scene of a car accident and again yesterday."

The vicar slowly folded his arms and considered Chris silently. He nodded almost imperceptibly but never broke eye contact. The intensity of his stare made Chris squirm.

"Look, Father, I'm not here to gather dirt for a tabloid or anything. It's just that . . . well, some strange things have happened the past couple of days, and I'd like to get some answers for my own peace of mind."

After a moment longer, the vicar softly smiled. "I guessed as much. Very well then. It is said that St. Nicholas suddenly turned over the position of head vicar to St. Cwnbran. No warning, no fare-thee-wells or grand doos. He just up and went on a pilgrimage of healing and gift-giving, yes? That's why he's considered one of the possible origins of the Father Christmas you know. Before he left, though, he blessed Trellech's own Virtuous Well so that anyone needing healing could go with faith and be healed."

"Yes. That's what the history books say," Chris agreed, somewhat disappointed. "I was hoping for something more. Something to fill in the blanks . . ." His words drifted off with his thoughts.

With eyes closed, the old priest fingered the crucifix around his neck, as if in prayer. After a long pause, he met Chris's eyes and held them. "Aye, Christian Pendragon. I believe I know what will 'fill in the blanks,' as you say. What's more, I sense it's what you *need* to hear, yes? All signs point to you, don't they, my son. What you seek is the key to your future, yes?"

Chris groaned and massaged his forehead. "Now you sound just like Nicholas Tewdrig."

The vicar grinned widely. "I thank'ee for that comparison, lad. And unless I miss my mark, folks'll be doing the same with you too, yes? Very soon."

"Doing what?"

"Comparing you to the beloved St. Nicholas, my son. Saying *you're* the next healing saint."

"I doubt that," he scoffed.

"I don't. And you won't either, after I show you a secret something that's truly astounding."

CHAPTER 19

A KNOCK SOUNDED AT THE door.

"Father Llewellyn? Is everything okay in there?" It was Westcott's voice.

"Yes, Detective. We're almost finished in here," the vicar said loudly. "Just give us a few more minutes, if you please. I'll be sure to let you know when we're through, now won't I."

Llewellyn reached over to his nightstand, picked up a cell phone, and punched in some numbers. He held up a finger, indicating Chris should wait a moment. "Hello, Michael. Listen fast, son," he said softly. "You know the chippee by the Monnow Bridge? Aye, that's the one. You are to leave immediately. There will be a Yank there."

Chris flinched. *What?* he mouthed.

Llewellyn waved him off. "Aye, right now. You are to collect him and take him back to the rectory, do you understand? Be as obscure as possible. His name is Christian, and he has a very important mission. If anyone asks, tell them he is a ward of the church, yes? But make certain no one asks." A few nods. "Aye. Yes, thank you, Michael." He turned off the phone. "I just love these modern conveniences, don't you?" he said, admiring his cellular.

"What are you doing?" Chris hissed angrily.

"You can't possibly go with the authorities, Christian, can you now. It would be conceding they're right—which they most assuredly are not. Do not let them treat you as a child, my son. Your calling is a much greater one now, is it not? Besides, they are wrong in their assumptions, the police. As with all things, the truth will set you free, yes?"

"Yeah. And until then, I'll be a fugitive."

"Nay, lad. You will be a servant of God, striving to aid your fellow man."

"No," he said, standing. "I have to call my embassy and clear this up before—"

"Before I identify you as the gunman?" the vicar asked. "I can do it, you know."

Chris's jaw dropped. He gawked in disbelief. "What?"

Llewellyn sighed. "Sometimes a parent must do what is best for their child, even if that child cannot see the sense in it, mustn't he."

"You're—you're threatening to—to *lie* to the police so you can get your way? Now who's being childish?"

"You'll thank me later, Christian. Now, go open yon window and hop out before it's too late. I will stall the detective as long as I can, rest assured."

"And just how am I supposed to get there?"

"You have legs, don't you? Now listen up, lad. This facility sits on Monnow Street, yes? Go left toward the old Monnow Bridge. Just before you get there, there's a side street—can't recall the name of it—but just a few doors down you'll find a chippee."

"A what?"

"A fish and chips noshery. Go in and wait. My man Michael will be by presently. He'll be driving an early-model Subaru wagon."

Chris was still gawking. His mind was spinning again. Was this priest actually asking him to break the law? Well, maybe not breaking it directly, but definitely defying it. What would that get him?—except in more trouble. Wasn't it basically resisting arrest? He couldn't do that. He was a law-abiding citizen. He should just head to the door and turn himself in. And yet something inside held him back. It was the same feeling he got when he talked with Nicholas Tewdrig. It's not that he *couldn't* deny what Nick had told him; it was that he *shouldn't*. There was a correctness to it—and to what Llewellyn told him to do. It didn't make sense, but it was the best course of action.

"Time's not on your side, son. It'll be all right," Llewellyn prompted. "You're not guilty of anything untoward—you know it, and I know it; even God knows it. I'll meet you tomorrow at the rectory. Just lay low, and I'll answer all your questions in time, I promise. Now go!" He was almost yelling.

The insistence in the priest's voice stabbed at Chris. He felt compelled to obey.

More knocking.

"Father Llewellyn? I hear shouting. Are you all right? I'm coming in."

"Stop! Do not defile the sanctity of this confession until this man's absolution is finished. It will only be a moment longer, I assure you." He glared at Chris and jerked his head toward the window.

Chris cursed between closed teeth and bolted for the window. It slid open silently; he was outside with minimal effort. Closing the window, he was immediately glad the staff had not replaced his clothing with thin hospital garb. The air was deeply cold. He was also glad that night was almost upon them. The gathering shadows would help mask his escape.

Following the vicar's directions, Chris soon found himself standing in front of a chippee called The Mermaid's Net. Entering, he was assaulted by the heavy odor of cooking grease and fish. At first it was nauseating, but having had nothing to eat since breakfast, Chris found the odor quickly morphing into a mouthwatering scent. Just as well he didn't have time to eat; the heavy grease would undoubtedly land in his stomach like a cannonball.

"Ay up. What's all this? Are you hurt, sir?" asked a middle-aged clerk standing behind the counter.

"I'm sorry?"

"You're covered with blood, mate. Are you okay?"

Chris looked down at his blood-stained shirt and pants. "I, um . . . no. I'm fine. This is . . . I was fishing this afternoon, you see, and got carried away cleaning my catch." He had no idea where that response came from, but he was happy it sounded somewhat plausible.

"Brilliant," the clerk beamed. "Wish I had time to go cast a line, myself. On vacation then, are you, mate?"

"Yeah. From the— From Canada. Calgary."

"Excellent." The friendly man didn't look twice at Chris's blood-stained attire. "Say, if you bring your clutch in here, I can cook 'em up for you. Got my own signature batter, see. Best in the whole UK, I'll wager. Once folks try it, they always come back for more."

"Really? Hey, that sounds great. Maybe I'll run back and grab them," he said, looking out the window for any sign of Llewellyn's assistant. "How late are you open?"

"Till midnight we are. Nothin' beats late-night noshing, eh mate?"

"I agree," he said as a police car zipped past with its lights flashing. *Come on, Michael. Where are you?*

"Would you like to sample a bit of today's catch then, sir?"

"Um . . . sure. Thanks," he said, accepting a shard of golden-battered fillet. It practically melted in his mouth. "Oh my gosh, this is amazing. Where do you get your fish?"

"Cold water, North Atlantic cod is all I serve, mate. None better, I promise you that."

"I'd have to agree," he said, again glancing out the window.

A few seconds later, an old Subaru stopped at the door. *Finally.*

"Gotta run," he told the clerk. "Thanks for the sample. It was delicious."

"Anytime, mate."

Chris exited the shop. Opening the car door, he said, "Michael? I'm Christian."

The man nodded.

Crawling in, he shut the door, turned, and flinched. Llewellyn's assistant was huge. He sat hunched over the steering wheel as if embracing it. His knees brushed the dashboard, even though the seat looked to be all the way back. Chris wondered how he squeezed into the vehicle in the first place. He saw no distinguishing features other than the man's size; Michael wore his hair closely cropped, his clothing simple.

Michael put the car in gear and drove back to the main road. Exiting the town as quickly as possible without drawing attention, they followed a narrow road into the countryside. Both men rode in silence. As the lights of the city faded behind them, the night closed in like a smothering fog.

Chris was a fugitive, fleeing arrest for a crime—*three* crimes—he didn't commit. He should have turned himself in, but he hadn't. He should have never gotten involved with Nicholas Tewdrig, but he had. He didn't know what was going to happen the next week, the next day or hour or minute. The future didn't look promising, and yet, strangely, he knew he was headed in the right direction.

CHAPTER 20

EVEN WITH THE LARGE MAN sitting next to him, Chris felt uncharacteristically alone. Normally, he relished his solitude, especially when things were bothering him. But now, strangely, he felt an overwhelming need to be around people, to be serving them. Nevertheless, being a fugitive, he knew mingling in public was the last place he should be. How long would he have to remain in hiding? How was Father Llewellyn going to help him? *Could* he help? He was just a priest—the churchwarden in a small country parish.

Nerves taut, feeling the need to do *something*, Chris cleared his throat and forced a smile. "Thanks for picking me up, Michael. Hope it wasn't too much trouble."

The hiss of the tires on the wet blacktop was the only reply. The big man stared straight ahead, focusing on the winding road and deepening shadows.

"I'm sorry for what happened to Father Llewellyn. He's a great man. I've only just met him, but I can tell he's very kind and understanding."

Michael glanced in the rearview mirror and slightly increased his speed. Chris turned but couldn't see any car lights behind them. They rode again in silence until it became unbearable.

Guessing that talking about his boss was too sensitive a topic, Chris changed tacks. "So, Michael, are you from Trellech?"

Nothing. And it was too dark to see his face. Was he smiling, frowning, deadpan? Chris sensed he was on edge. Better to keep things light, try to alleviate the tension in the car.

"You a Monmouther then?" Chris guessed.

More nothing.

"Come on, man. Give me something. I'm dying here."

"Porthaethwy," the big guy finally said in a soft, deep voice.

"Porthaethwy? Where's that?"

"Menai Bridge."

"Oh right, right. The Isle of Anglesey. Were you born there?"

He waited for Michael to say more, but nothing came. Chris wished he'd be more loquacious or would at least respond with a nod or something. Michael was acting like a stone statue. *Maybe he's made of alabaster . . .*

Chris ground his teeth and huffed softly. He was so wound up he couldn't sit still. He hated being in this situation; his nerves were short-circuiting like crazy. He found himself talking rapidly, trying to fill the empty space with anything but silence.

"Ah yes, the Menai Bridge. It was the first solid structure to connect Anglesey Island with the mainland. Did you know it was the largest suspension bridge of its kind when it was built?"

More silence.

"This whole country is filled with ancient castles and bridges and cool old buildings. Did you know Monmouth has the last remaining gated stone portcullis bridge of its kind in the UK?"

More nothing.

"It's true," he continued, as if Michael was hanging on every word. "The town of Monmouth was originally a small Roman fort. Later, it became the birthplace of King Henry V. Its bridge, the Monnow Bridge, was completed in the thirteenth century. Man, that's a long time ago. Just imagine how much history it's seen, how many noble men and women have passed between those massive stone lintels."

Road noise. Engine noise.

Apparently Chris's love of history was not shared by his driver. Chris sighed again and stared out the window. It was now very dark outside and apparently very cold. The Subaru's windshield kept fogging up. Michael turned on the noisy defroster full-blast, which would make conversation difficult without shouting. As if there was someone to converse with, Chris thought cynically.

Before long they were in Trellech; a few minutes later, their headlights illuminated the door of the church. Chris's anxiety edged up when he saw yellow police tape barring the entry. If the church was still considered a crime scene, then the police would be snooping around. Did Llewellyn think of that? Was this really the best place to hide? Not knowing anyone else in the area, Chris had no choice.

Michael drove past the church, down a side street, then through an alley to the back of a small cottage. "The rectory," the big man said plainly.

Stepping from the car, Chris felt the cold air bite his skin with icy teeth. The sky was completely clear, offering a spectacular display of northern stars; but without cloud cover, the temperature had plummeted past freezing.

Michael unlocked the cottage door and stooped to enter. Passing through, his shoulders brushed both sides of the doorframe. The man was built like a linebacker: probably around six six and at least 300 pounds—not much of it fluff. And yet, when he turned to beckon Chris inside, he did so with an innocent, childlike expression. "Please come inside, sir."

Passing through a small kitchen with 1940s, enamel-glazed appliances, Chris followed Michael into a dining area which stood at the far end of a narrow, open-beam room. The space itself wasn't more than six hundred square feet. Two wingback chairs, a large fieldstone fireplace, and a bookshelf lining the far wall took up most of the space.

Michael gestured to a chair in front of the hearth then set about starting a fire. The room was cold but not necessarily frigid. Still, Chris welcomed the idea of a cheerful blaze to take the chill from his mood. When the fire was crackling, Michael stood and replaced the brass fireplace implements in a rack on the hearth.

"Coffee or tea?" he asked softly.

"Nothing, thank you," Chris said.

Michael ambled back to the kitchen, leaving Chris to enjoy the fire in the shadowy room. There was something magical about the ambience of a radiant hearth fire, he thought. The same went for the sound of a gurgling brook. Both set the mind at ease, lulling the spectator with tranquil, soothing images and music. The smell of melting pine sap soon filled the room, adding to the fragrance of the open-wood framing and old books. Even with the angst of the day still looming, Chris felt himself relax. He settled snugly into the depths of a large wingback chair and let his mind clear.

Sometime later, he felt his feet lifted onto an ottoman and his shoes removed. A heavy blanket was floated onto him, and a small pillow was guided between his head and the wing of the chair. He wanted to open his eyes to acknowledge his caretaker, but they felt too heavy. Instead, he let himself slip into the blissful embrace of slumber.

CHAPTER 21

WHEN CHRIS OPENED HIS EYES, Father Llewellyn was sitting in the matching wingback chair, reading a book. A low fire continued to hiss and pop in the hearth, still filling the room with radiant warmth and woodsy fragrance; the brass fireplace implements reflected the dancing flames. But the room was no longer dark. The morning sunlight filtered through slatted blinds.

He wrestled himself into a more upright position and ran his fingers through his hair. "Oh. Good morning, Father," Chris said, stifling a yawn. "I'm glad they finally let *you* out on parole."

The old vicar chuckled softly, closing his book. "Good morrow to you, Christian. Not the most comfortable bed, that chair, but I trust you slept well enough. Would you like Michael to freshen your tea?"

Chris noticed a full cup of tea on an end table next to him. He hadn't touched a drop last night. "Yeah, thanks," Chris said, succumbing to a yawn.

Llewellyn called, "Michael, fetch us more tea, if you please."

Chris held his hands to the fire, warming them. Within moments, Michael rolled in two cups of fragrant tea and some delicious-looking scones on a petite, silver teacart. The image of the would-be linebacker pushing a dainty trolley with tea fixings made Chris smile.

"Excellent, excellent. Thank you, Michael," Llewellyn sang. "Help yourself, Christian. Don't be shy."

Chris filled a new cup and cradled it between his hands.

"Now then," Llewellyn began. "I suspect you have a question or two for me, yes?"

"Several, actually," Chris said with a muddled smile.

"Ask away, lad." The vicar seemed totally at ease, as if he hadn't been shot the day before, as if nothing was amiss.

"Okay. First, what's happening with the police?"

Llewellyn cocked his head to one side. "The police?"

"Yeah, you know. What happened after I escaped out the window? Am I still a fugitive of the law?"

The vicar took a measured sip of his tea and placed it on a stand next to him. "The good detective waited another five minutes before insisting that he come in." A smile played across his face. "You can imagine his surprise, can you not? The doctor's too, only she didn't seem as upset like. I think she likes you, Christian, yes?"

Chris snorted. "Hardly. She was just being thorough."

"And stalling the police in the process? She did, you know."

Chris shrugged and sipped his tea.

"Of course they asked where you were," Llewellyn continued. "I told them you decided to take in some night air. The detective ran to the window and called for reinforcements on his radio. He asked where you went; I told him I didn't know exactly."

"You lied to him?"

"Not at all, Christian. I am a vassal of Christ. I do not lie."

He smirked. "But you knew where I was headed."

Llewellyn feigned innocence. "How was I to know you would follow my instructions? You are an accused gunman from a foreign country with connections to organized crime in the UK. Men of your ilk rarely listen to a ward of the church, let alone follow his instructions, now do they? Besides, I didn't remember the name of the chippee, and there are a score of them about Monmouth. You could have ended up at the wrong establishment, yes?"

"So they still think I'm involved with the mob," he said flatly.

"It seems so, yes. I was interrogated by the detective for a time. I told him you were not connected with the mob, but I do not think he believed me. Then he said since I had allowed you to escape I was an accomplice." He paused to select a scone from the cart.

"And . . . ?"

"I told him that I felt threatened like. That my life was in jeopardy and I had no recourse but to allow you to leap from the window."

Chris gawked. "You mean he thinks I threatened to finish what I started, that I'd kill you if you didn't let me escape? Thanks a lot."

"Don't be angry, Christian. I did it for your own good, lad. See, if I was incarcerated like, I wouldn't be able to help you, now would I?" he said with a twinkle in his eyes. "But I also told the detective I would sign an affidavit attesting that you did not shoot me, that it was a Mr. Rafe Collingswood who did. And I hinted that your confessional bore out your innocence, yes?"

"But I didn't confess anything."

Llewellyn took a bite of scone and chewed slowly. "Not in the literal sense, you didn't. But I did glean a great amount about you from our wee conversation, didn't I? Aye, a very great amount."

"So . . . am I still wanted by the police?"

"I would assume so, yes. That Westcott chap asked that I call him immediately if I saw you again. I do not know why. I swore to him you are not a criminal. Whether he accepted that testimony or not, I do not know."

"Great," Chris grumbled.

"Now then," the vicar said sharply, as if the topic of Chris's innocence was closed. "What say you to getting cleaned up, yes? I had Michael purchase fresh clothing for you early this morning at yon haberdashery 'round the corner. Nothing fancy, mind, but they're less conspicuous than the blood-stained rags you're sporting now, yes? Perhaps a shower is in order too, I should think."

Chris couldn't argue. "Sure. Thanks."

"Right. Excellent. Now, if you'll just follow Michael, he'll take care of you. Then we can chat over breakfast, yes?"

"Chat?"

"Of course, lad. About our beloved St. Nicholas."

CHAPTER 22

IT ALWAYS AMAZED CHRIS HOW a hot soak could make him feel human again. He believed that it was long, hot showers, more than the ability to reason, that separated us from the animals.

Linebacker Michael had prepared a spread of poached eggs framed in toast and thick bacon along with some tea. It was delicious.

"Do you think I'm safe here, Father?" Chris asked after finishing his meal.

"Safe from what, son?"

"The police, of course. I'm still a wanted man, and your chapel is still a crime scene. It's likely there'll be investigations done on site. And if they still suspect I shot you—even though you told them I didn't—as long as I'm on the run, they'll assume your life is in danger."

Llewellyn waved the thought away. "Balderdash. Collingswood shot me, pure and simple, yes? But he didn't shoot me out of hatred or to rob me. I don't believe he even intended to kill me. He shot me to make a point, did he not?"

Chris fidgeted in his chair. "Yeah. About that . . ." He rubbed his neck, thinking, not sure where to begin.

After a long silence, the vicar chuckled, "You are an open book, Christian, lad. You should just come out and ask me. You want to know if *you* actually healed me, yes?"

"Okay, yeah. Because I'm not sure I did."

"I've been pondering on that very perplexity, my son. And my answer is yes, you did heal me." He took a sip of tea and smiled. "Next question?"

Frustrated at how quickly that topic was closed, Chris grumbled, "What about Collingswood calling me a Vovnik when I was trying to . . .

um, after he shot you? Could he be referring to the old Jewish legend of the Righteous Thirty-Six?"

Llewellyn set down his cup and interlaced his fingers. "I believe so, yes. 'Twould make sense if you were. Some folk believe St. Nicholas were one of the blessed Thirty-Six, you know."

"Well, yeah, it would make sense *he* was. But not me."

The vicar again smiled softly. "Oh, aye? Let's cogitate on that, shall we? The legend basically says there are thirty-six goodly men who are righteous enough to prevent God from destroying the earth, yes? It's akin to the story of Abraham asking God to spare the wicked city of Sodom if he could find just ten righteous souls there. The Thirty-Six don't necessarily ask for this blessing, but the outcome is the same. It's a Jewish legend for sure an' certain, but being rooted in the Old Testament, it's one that rings true in all religions, does it not?"

"Yeah. But what does it have to do with me? I'm not evil per se, but I certainly don't qualify as someone righteous enough to stay the hand of God," Chris said with a forced chuckle. "And I'm definitely no saint."

"Aye. But then you wouldn't have to be, would you. I believe the legend states there are always thirty-six *compassionate* men; not saints necessarily, nor men who are so righteous they qualify for sainthood, yes? And I know myself, you're a man of deep compassion."

"Really? How?"

"You healed me, Christian—a complete stranger. You gave me another chance at life."

Chris didn't know what to say. He wanted to deny it, but he wasn't sure he could. Something miraculous *had* happened. And whether he admitted it or not, he *had* been part of it. "Did Dr. Ingledew say anything about your gunshot wound?"

Llewellyn laughed. "She said the bullet must have glanced off my belly. Like I'm the ruddy Man of Steel, or some such nonsense." He patted his belly. While not rotund, he did have a solid paunch. "If I do have abs of steel, they're happily insulated under a depth of lard."

"So . . . did it?"

"Glance off my belly? Nay, lad. Collingswood's bullet bore right through the skin, the lard, and the muscle. I know it did," he said, his eyes again filling with gratitude. "I have a frock and shirt covered with my blood to prove it, don't I?"

"But Dr. Ingledew thought otherwise?"

"She called it a 'flesh wound,' yes? Said it cut me but never entered. Said the emergency chaps must have misdiagnosed it when they first called it in."

"So . . . where's the bullet?" Chris wondered aloud.

"Constable Hart took it for evidence. He claimed he found it on the floor of chapel study, right beside where I lay."

"Ah." So maybe it *had* just been a flesh wound, Chris reasoned. Maybe he *hadn't* healed the cleric. Maybe it had caused so much pain that it only *felt* like it'd pierced his belly.

"Which makes it that much more of a miracle, doesn't it now," Llewellyn added with reverence. "Finding the bullet, I mean."

Chris stared blankly at his plate, seeking assurance that seemed impossible to obtain. This whole mess had gone from intriguing to unbelievable to ludicrous. "Father Llewellyn, I appreciate your confidence in me, but please listen: I am no miracle worker. I am very glad you're doing well, that your wound wasn't serious. But I had nothing to do with it, I assure you."

The vicar's gaze bore into him with tempered censure. "My son, whether you think you did or no, *I* believe you did. You laid your hands upon me, and I was made whole. You are destined to follow in the path of St. Nicholas; of that I can testify."

"But I didn't choose this path. What if I don't want it?"

"Don't know as that matters, Christian, does it now? It seems to me the path has chosen you."

That's exactly what Nick said, Chris remembered. It'd frustrated him then too. "And if *I* choose not to follow the path?" he retorted, a little more forcefully than he intended.

A worried frown crossed the vicar's brow, but love still radiated from his eyes. "Do you like the color of your hair, my son?"

Chris blinked hard. "Excuse me?"

"Do you like the color of your hair?" he repeated, patting his own scalp.

"Uh . . . yeah, I guess. It's average, just like me," he said with a lame grin.

"And if you didn't like it?"

He shrugged. "Then I'd color it. Why? I don't understand."

"Aye. You could go blond or black or even purple—like some of the youth nowadays, yes? But would that change its *true* color? Or would it grow back the way God meant it to be?"

Ah. Trick question. Nice. "So what you're saying is that I may not choose to be a healer, but it's what I am, no matter how much I try to deny it." It was more of a statement than a question.

Llewellyn nodded solemnly.

"What if I *opt* not to act on it because *I* don't believe I am supernaturally gifted?"

"Still doesn't matter, son, now does it."

"Somehow I think it does."

The vicar steepled his fingers and thoughtfully tapped them against his lips. "Did you know that engineers have determined that a bumblebee is aerodynamically unable to fly? And yet he flies around anyroad. Now, you have to wonder how, yes?"

More trick questions. Chris gave the vicar a look of open frustration.

"Because he sees a need and just does it," Llewellyn explained. "He doesn't think about it like. He doesn't question his abilities. He just ups and goes about his business when he needs to, yes? It's the same with you, my son. When you saw the accident near Cardigan, you didn't stop and wonder what to do, now did you? Nay; you just *acted.* Same as when the Reaper were calling my name. If you see the need, don't be questioning your abilities, son, just do it."

Not surprisingly, the vicar had talked him into a corner again. Chris stood and shoved his hands into his pockets. "You sound just like Nicholas Tewdrig. He said the same thing to me two days ago. Arguing with you is just like arguing with him."

Showing no indication of surprise, Llewellyn calmly took another sip of tea. "Perhaps that's because I've read his journal."

Chris whipped around in surprise. "His what?"

CHAPTER 23

Without further word, Llewellyn rocked to his feet and stepped into the great room. Sliding the brass fireplace implements to one side, he took a steel letter opener from the mantle, knelt, and began digging along the grout line of a wide, flat stone.

"Do you need some help?" Chris asked, coming up behind him.

"Thank you, no," the vicar said. "I have Michael for that, yes?"

When he had cleared a sufficient amount of grout, he called to his manservant. The big guy rounded the corner almost instantly.

"Yes, Father?"

"Kindly lift this stone from its roost, if you please. There's a good man," he said, settling into his wingback chair.

"Yes, Father."

Michael knelt and wedged his fingers along one side of the stone. They barely fit. With minimal effort he pried the stone from the floor, as if it weighed next to nothing. In a hollow beneath the stone sat a small wooden box. The box was roughly the size of a thick phonebook, secured with a hinged metal clasp. Michael withdrew the box and handed it to the vicar.

"Ah, yes. Thank you, Michael."

The big man stood and, after a quick nod, returned to the kitchen.

"He could have snapped Collingswood in half like a twig. Too bad he wasn't around when we first met in the chapel study," Chris commented.

"Good heavens, no," Llewellyn gasped. "One of the two of them would've ended up dead; if not Michael from Collingswood's bullet, then Collingswood from Michael's hands."

"That I believe."

The vicar used a handkerchief to dust off the box then held it out to Chris. "Be gentle with it, Christian. It is very old, ay?"

Chris gingerly accepted the box. The metal clasp had a locking t-pin where the flange met the hasp. They were cankered with a patina of rust. He twisted the pin until it lined up with the slot then laid back the flange. Opening the lid revealed a rectangular parcel wrapped in yellow oilcloth. Chris removed the parcel and set the box on the floor.

"How old is this?" he asked without taking his eyes from it.

"Hails back to the 1700s . . . maybe even earlier. There are only a few dates mentioned. When the beloved saint wrote, he rarely used annotation like."

Chris carefully unfurled the heavy oilcloth. Inside lay a softbound book filled with thick, time-yellowed pages. The tome was redolent with the smell of leather, vellum, and the dense, acrid odor of India ink.

Looking up, Chris asked, "Are you sure about this, Father?"

Llewellyn nodded. "I've been waiting a long time for you to come, my son. A long time."

Chris marveled at the very words that Nicholas Tewdrig had uttered to him. He wiped his fingers several times before slowly peeling back the thick, gnarled cover. The heavy vellum pages—malleable at one time— now felt dry and in danger of flaking apart. The writing on each page, blotchy and erratic, looked to have been made with a worn quill. Most of the cursive penmanship was nearly illegible.

"You say you've read this?"

"Aye. Many times. It were handed down from headmaster to head-master, time and time again to this very day."

"What's it say?"

"Oh, a great many things," the vicar said, again steepling his fingers. "But the beloved saint was very cunning in his writing. There are some plain verses of text describing villages he ministered to and such like. The account of him blessing Virtuous Well is in there. Most are in the King's English, but some are in Welsh and Cambric, some Latin. He also drew some characters that I have nary a clue about."

"You mean you've never had them translated?" Chris was astonished.

"Nay, lad, nay. Weren't meet for me to do so, were it. And why would I anyroad? Weren't me that was given the stone, now was it."

"The stone," Chris said, swallowing hard. "You know about the Dial?"

Llewellyn grinned. "Aye."

Returning his attention to the ancient manuscript, Chris spoke in hushed tones. "This is absolutely incredible. Look at all this undiscovered history. If it's as old as you say, it really should be in a museum, kept under low oxygen to preserve it."

"I suppose. But that wasn't the charge I was given, now was it."

Chris cocked his head. "Charge?"

"I was told to protect this journal, wasn't I. Was given custody of it, swore a solemn oath not to let it fall into the wrong hands."

"Swore an oath? To whom?"

The vicar gave a wink and tapped the side of his nose.

Chris flattened his palm on the journal. "So *this* is what Collingswood was after?"

"Among other things. Aye."

"I . . . I don't know what to say."

"There's nothing *to* say, lad. It's a pleasure to show it to you. You're free to come study it anytime you like. I will instruct Michael to always allow you access."

Chris looked up sharply. "What—you mean I can't take this with me?"

The vicar's eyes bore a fatherly look of warning. "*I* was given custody, lad, wasn't I. Part of that charge was to never let it leave the churchyard. It never has. And I intend to keep it that way."

Frustration welled inside Chris. "Father Llewellyn, surely you can see the historical significance of such a treasure. I have a PhD in history, in Welsh Mythology to be exact. I know how to care for ancient artifacts and manuscripts. This has inestimable value of a *historical* nature. I'm not going to sell it. I promise."

"No, Christian. I'm sorry, but the answer is no."

"But you said you had something to give to me," Chris cried, knowing he was close to whining.

The vicar sighed heavily. "I said I had som'et to *show* you," he corrected. "And there it is. Examine it all you like, my son."

"Here? Right now? With the police still after me? I can't possibly begin— I don't have my references or notes or—"

"Best return it to the box then, Christian," Llewellyn cut him off gently.

"But—" Chris's rebuttal was again cut off, this time by a large hand on his shoulder. Michael stood directly behind him.

He shrugged it off. "Look, if I truly am this healer you guys keep claiming I am, how am I going to learn how to do it if I can't study the book?"

"I told you, son. My door is always open to you, come rain or shine, snow or blow."

"But I live in the United States. I'm heading back there next week."

"Then you'd best stop yammering and start beavering away at it, yes?"

"Are you kidding? It'll take months to dissect the contents of this manuscript. Perhaps years. And even then, there's no guarantee I'll be able to translate everything."

"Aye, there is that."

"Father?" Michael interrupted. He was now standing by the window, peering between the blinds. Chris hadn't heard him walking away. The big man moved like a ghost.

"Yes, my son?"

"The police are here."

CHAPTER 24

"Take Christian upstairs, will you Michael?"

Michael turned to Chris and gestured toward the kitchen.

Chris lifted the journal. "May I take this with me?"

"Yes. But replace the stone first, if you please."

Chris wrapped the tome in its oilcloth and slid the hearth stone over the hollow, filling the joints with dirt and old grout. He then set the brass implements on the stone and stood.

A knock sounded at the door. Michael gestured again. Chris followed him through the kitchen to a thin door that looked like nothing more than a broom closet. The door opened to a narrow staircase that rose at a steep angle. Michael pointed up the stairs.

"Are you coming up too?" Chris asked.

The big man's shoulders slumped, and his head tilted as if to say, *Are you joking?*

Chris entered and immediately realized the big guy plainly would not fit. Ascending, Chris entered an attic-like space with a plank-wood floor and slanted ceilings. A small, central dormer poked out toward the front of the cottage. It was very cold; Chris's breath plumed in little bursts. He heard voices below. Setting the journal to one side, he placed his ear to the dusty plank floor. He caught only bits of the conversation. It was Detective Westcott's voice.

Did Mr. Pendragon give any clue as to where he was headed?

Did you return directly to the parish after being released from hospital?

Father Llewellyn kept his voice low and gentle; Chris could not make out what he was saying—only that he was answering the questions.

Have you received any threatening phone calls or messages from Mr. Pendragon?

Have you noticed anything missing or awry in the chapel or your cottage?

Has Mr. Pendragon returned for his rental car?

Mind if we have a look around?

Chris crawled over to the dormer. His rental car still sat in a small parking area beside the church. A patrol car was parked next to it; two officers were searching it, inside and out. Chris heard the cottage door open and close and saw Westcott walk toward the two officers. They talked. Heads shook and shoulders shrugged. Westcott glanced back at the cottage—then up at the dormer. Chris jumped back, praying he hadn't been seen. After a few breathless moments, he edged forward and peered out.

The three officers were heading into the chapel.

Chris slumped below the window and drew in a shaky breath. What was he doing here? This was insane. He was not a criminal; he was a university professor. He shouldn't be running from the law. He came here to find direction in his life; to find confirmation, not confrontation; to find clarification, not further confusion.

Outside, the clouds thinned and parted, briefly swiping a slant of pure sunlight across the oilskin parcel, making it glow. Chris sighed and opened it.

The time-yellowed pages crackled when he touched them. He wished he was in a more controlled environment: low oxygen and humidity to preserve the materials, controlled illumination to prevent ink fade, cotton gloves to prevent skin oils from damaging the vellum. He also wished he had language references at his fingertips. His smart phone was still in police custody, as were his wallet and passport. He was so ill-equipped to study the ancient manuscript that he almost gave up before he started. But he felt prompted to go on; strangely, as if his life depended on it. Besides, if he was going to get to the bottom of these bizarre occurrences, he needed to do his research. And he had to admit he loved research!

The markings on the pages were random, haphazard: a few lines here, a block of text there. The pages had no preprinted lines for uniform printing or cursive; it was total freeform penmanship. Along with the obscure segments of writing were rough sketches; examples of mosaic arrays, rune stone tessellations, geometric patterns, Gnostic symbols, uniform arrangements of numbers, and such. It reminded Chris of Da Vinci's sketchbook—the imagery of a brilliant mind constrained to the medieval limitations of quill and ink. Scattered throughout were Bible references—book, chapter, and verse—some with fully quoted text alongside. Very little of the scrawl made sense to Chris, but there was a symmetry about it, a fluidity that implied hidden meaning within. Of note was a passage that repeated at least once on each page—and was always printed in capital letters.

NOBLY THRU WHITE FOG HATH I LED

Thru white fog? This country certainly had more than its share of mist and haze—a form of fog. But why was the sentence repeated so frequently? Was it referencing the weather, or did it have a more metaphorical meaning? And why the abbreviated variant of the word *through*? More importantly, who was doing the leading, and who was being led?

Before long, Chris's eyes began to fatigue, and the writing became harder to read in the low light of the attic. But Chris was loath to set the book aside. With uncommon surety, he knew the answers he sought were written within the ancient leather covers.

Thru white fog? The message had to mean something significant, hence the repetition. But what? Was it a message for Nicholas Tewdrig or for whoever possessed the journal—including Christian Pendragon?

Chris closed his eyes and tried to reason out the meaning on the pages. It felt like he was swimming upstream.

CHAPTER 25

It was close to lunchtime before the police left the chapel. The constables took down the police tape and returned to their patrol car; Westcott headed straight to the rectory. Because the sun was out, Chris felt confident watching from the dormer, certain he could not be seen in the dark attic.

He heard Westcott's knock and the door open, but he couldn't hear the ensuing conversation. He guessed Westcott hadn't entered because the voices remained distant. Soon, the door closed, and he watched the detective return to Chris's rental car and climb in the driver's seat. Chris cursed softly, remembering that his clothing and travel supplies were still in there. The police had confiscated everything he owned.

"Really? You're stealing my car? Now who's the criminal?" he cried softly.

Chris closed the journal and rubbed his eyes. Fatigue and anxiety blurred the edges of his vision. He hadn't gleaned as much from the writing as he would have liked. It was all so disjointed, and there was a ton there. If only he had his reference materials—and a few more months. The information and history in this book alone could earn him a second doctorate. But time and resources were not on his side.

The stairwell door opened, and Michael's gentle voice called up. "Master Pendragon, Father Llewellyn would like a word with you, please."

Chris carefully descended the steep staircase. "Michael, you can call me Chris. And I'm no one's master, even over myself."

A brief smile crossed the big man's face. He had terrible teeth—probably from too much tea—but the sparkle in his eyes more than made up for it. He gestured toward the great room.

Llewellyn was staring out the window, his hands clasped behind his back. "Bless my soul but this sunshine feels wonderful, does it not?"

"Yes, it does. It's a nice change from the constant drizzle."

"Aye, for sure an' certain it is. But the good always balances out the bad. It's the constant drizzle that makes this land so verdant, you see. This is God's country and no mistake."

"As a creationist, don't you believe the whole world is God's country?" Chris teased as he moved the fireplace implements to return the journal to its hiding place.

Llewellyn turned. "No, I do not. The world was left to the whims of nature when our first parents were expelled from the Garden, yes? After that, only chosen locations were fit to be a sanctuary of Jehovah: Mount Sinai, Bethlehem, Jerusalem, and probably a host of other locations we know nothing about. Beyond that, it is up to us to create a place worthy of His dwelling." He paused as if just realizing what Chris was doing. "Nay, lad, don't concern yourself with putting that away. Michael will finish the task. You and I need to talk over more pressing matters, yes? Come. Are you hungry?"

"Starving. But I insist you let me buy you lunch. I owe you. Michael can come too."

The vicar laughed. "Have you looked at the size of the man, Christian?" he said, sweeping his hand at Michael as if presenting a statue. "You'll go broke feeding the likes of him. Besides, you have no money, now do you."

"Oh yeah, I guess not," he replied, patting his empty pockets.

"Not to worry, son. This is just betwixt you and me like, yes? In fact, I find it peculiarly appropriate that you are in this situation."

"Really," Chris said without enthusiasm.

"Yes, of course," he said, opening the door. "Come on then, lad. I'm rather peckish, and there's a great pub just around the corner, if you've no objections."

Chris stopped at the doorway to accept a patchwork tam from Michael. The big man pantomimed tugging it low over his brow. Chris followed suit. If that's the way the locals wore them, best to blend in as much as possible.

Walking down a busy street, people passed by them as if nothing remarkable had happened to their spiritual leader or their ancient chapel. Some of the townsfolk stopped to wish the vicar a good day. Father Llewellyn was obviously a well-liked person. One man across the street paused to holler, "You'll have chapel up and running again soon I trust, Father?"

"Yes, Jonas. Never you fear."

"Aye. If you say so. Good day to you, Father."

"Godspeed, my son."

Chris followed the vicar into a tavern called the Sow's Ear. Llewellyn paused just inside the doorway and made the sign of the cross. "God bless all in this house."

The dozen or so patrons in the establishment raised their mugs, toasting his blessing. A number of them responded with: "God bless *you*, Father."

"Why thank you, Father," a young woman said from behind the bar. "Your post is open."

"Excellent, Bambi," Llewellyn said, leading Chris to a small circular table beside a massive brownstone hearth.

"Bambi?"

"Aye. That's her given name and true."

Barmaid Bambi was instantly at their side. She was in her late twenties, stocky, with thick arms and spiked hair highlighted the same color turquoise as her eye shadow. She wore a red, teardrop jewel at the corner of one eye, and a snake tattoo coiled several times around her neck. She boasted a lower lip stud shaped like a thin serpent's tongue, which bobbed anxiously when she spoke. She looked like she took guff from no one.

"Is it the usual then, Father?"

"Yes, Bambi. And the same for my new friend here. Name's Christian Pendragon, esquire. He's a professor of history, from America no less."

Chris flinched at the open use of his name, knowing the police were still after him. "Hi," he said with a forced smile, offering his hand.

The barmaid glared suspiciously at his hand. "Pendragon, is it? A history professor from America, ay? Come home to pull Excalibur from the stone, have you? Gonna reign o'er us with the same totalitarian autocracy your Pendragon forefathers did, ay? Expect us poor folk to grovel an' beg for your table scraps, do you?" Her tone was simultaneously harsh and lyrical. "Well you'll get none of that rubbish here, mind you. That servile codswallop went out with the Magna Carta in 1215, don'cha know."

His smile vanished. "Yes, ma'am—I mean, no, ma'am," Chris said defensively. "I'm just visiting. Honest."

She tipped her head back and laughed uproariously. Her volume made him flinch. "No need to get your knickers in a twist, professor. I's a'jestin' and a'teasin' you is all. Jus' having a go 'round with ya like. Ain't that right, Father?" Before he could answer, she leaned in close and added, "Unless you think you *are* better than us poor country Welshfolk. Then I'll really give you what for, if you get my meaning, ay?"

Chris was speechless. He nodded quickly.

With another boisterous laugh, she smacked him on the shoulder and returned to the bar.

Llewellyn was grinning from ear to ear. "Hard to believe she's still single, isn't it, Christian?"

"Very. She certainly knows her history," he answered, daubing his brow with a napkin.

"Aye, that she does; that she does indeed." The vicar leaned forward and winked. "And she's not hard on the eyes, neither—except for her hair, yes? Changes color every month, it does. You get used to it though. But raise her ire, and she'll pluck your tonsils for harp strings."

"Yeah, I caught that."

Bambi returned with two mugs of frothy draft ale. "There you are, gents. Sup up."

Chris stared at the mug and fidgeted.

"Ay up. Som'et wrong with me ale?" Bambi asked, placing her fists on her hips.

"May I just have some water, please?" Chris asked in his friendliest tone, thinking, *Here we go again*. "I need to keep a clear head."

"Water?" Her look was one of sheer disgust. She turned to the vicar. "And here I thought you finally brought me a man's man, Father. Good-looking, appears to have some muscle on his bones. Smart too, ay? A history professor at a big Yankee university and all? Bet he has more'n two bob a'clickin' in his pocket, I'll wager." She gave Chris a bald-face examination from head to toe. "But no. No, I'm sorry, Father. I just can't trust a man who don't drink proper Welsh draft in me own house."

Without awaiting an answer, she walked away and began talking loudly with some men at another table.

"I think I just made another friend," Chris said dryly.

"Nay, don't you worry, Christian. She likes you well enough." He took a long pull from his flagon and smacked his lips. "Now then. Did you learn anything from St. Nicolas's journal?"

Chris opened his mouth, but he wasn't sure what to ask or where to even start. There were so many questions! "May I be perfectly frank with you, Father?"

"Of course. But if this is going to be a soul-bearing confessional, perhaps we should adjourn to the chapel, yes?"

Chris snorted. "No. Well, maybe. I'm not so concerned about my past actions as I am with future responsibilities."

"Oh aye?"

"Yeah. With me, with Nicholas Tewdrig and the Dial, and . . . and with everything. See, to be honest, I didn't really get much of anything from the journal."

"Perhaps you weren't reading it right."

He leaned back. "How was I supposed to read it?"

"With an open heart, lad." Llewellyn took another pull at his ale and wiped his mouth on his sleeve. "The tall and short of it is I believe you *are* the next Physician of Myddfai. I believe the calling has fallen to your shoulders and that the Beloved Saint has passed the mantle of healing to you. That is why I have protected you from the authorities. That is why I showed you his journal."

Chris stared blankly at the tabletop. The vicar had confirmed what he least wanted to hear. "I was afraid of that."

"Why, son? 'Tis a noble calling, for sure an' certain."

"Because I don't want it, okay? That's what I tried to tell Nick. But he said he'd already passed the mantle to me." Chris then rehearsed what had transpired during that awful incident on the moors—the churning fog, the dead mother, the fire, Nigel Madsen. He described tugging at the boy's ankles. "Then Nicholas Tewdrig showed up out of nowhere, slipped the Dial in my pocket, and mumbled something to me."

"What did he say—the Beloved Saint?"

"I can't remember. It was in Welsh, which I know only a little of. And I was so worked up I didn't catch much of it. Maybe it was his strong accent."

"Ay, what's wrong with our strong accents now?" Bambi spat.

Chris hadn't seen her approach. She was holding two wooden platters bearing sandwiches stacked with so much sliced beef, it probably took a whole cow to make them.

"Um, nothing, nothing. I like it, when I can understand it," he said with an open smile, trying to be charming.

It didn't work.

"Well at least we don't talk through our bloomin' noses." She set the platters down none too gently. "I suppose you don't eat meat either, ay?"

"Oh, I'm not a vegetarian. I love beef."

"Good. Chew it nice and slow like," she said, jabbing a finger at the sandwich. "Wouldn't want you to choke on it." She stormed away, cursing under her breath.

"Ay, laddie, I warned you not to mess with that one," Llewellyn hissed.

Chris shivered. "I see what you mean."

"Aye. Now let's get wedged into this lot," he said, indicating their meal. "I'm famished."

Chris gnawed out a mouthful of sandwich before he noticed Llewellyn's hands clasped in prayer. He set the sandwich on the platter, bowed his head, and chewed as inconspicuously as possible. When the vicar said amen, Chris swallowed and echoed his benediction. The sandwich was delicious. The beef practically melted in his mouth, and the bread tasted freshly baked. The sandwich had the ideal amount of Worcestershire, horseradish, and au jus. It was ambrosia.

The priest took a huge bite and chomped noisily through an equally huge smile. After forcing a swallow, he said, "Now then. Can you recall any of what St. Nicholas said to you?"

"Only a little bit. When I asked about it later, he said it was Welsh, but he never told me what it meant. He was good at never giving me a straight answer."

The priest chuckled and took another bite.

Chris continued, "It was something like *pasio chia puer ewella*."

Llewellyn nodded slowly and swallowed. "That's Welsh, for sure an' certain," he confirmed. "But your pronunciation is dreadful, did you know?"

"Yeah, I know. You'd think a man who studies Welsh mythology could do better. But I'm only quoting what I *thought* I heard."

"I suspected as much. Happen to start with *Rwy'n*, did he?"

Chris nodded enthusiastically. "Yes, that's right. It was *Rwy'n pasio chi* . . . something."

"*Rwy'n pasio i chi y pŵer i gwella*?"

"Bingo," he said, slapping the table. "That's it! Do you know what it means, Father?"

"Aye. It means I was bang on."

CHAPTER 26

"Bang on? So you think I *am* a Vovnik healer?"

"More to the point, what do you think?"

As delicious as his sandwich was, Chris's appetite quickly vanished. "I don't know. I wish I did. See, I have a career, a whole life back in the States."

"Aye. But are you happy in it?"

Chris felt like he'd been slapped. *Was* he happy? "It's a good life," he waffled. "I can't just throw it all away to go on some crusade I don't really understand. I mean, in a way I want to believe it's possible, but . . . *ugh*! I don't know." Frustrated, Chris grabbed the mug of beer and took a generous gulp, forgetting how strong English ale was. He gagged and heaved, barely keeping down the heavy malt beverage. He remembered why he never drank the stuff.

"Are you all right, son?"

Chris coughed and sputtered until his throat was clear. "Fine. I'm not usually this indeterminate. It's just that I've had these strange feelings, these assurances that this is all true. It's like, even if I wanted to deny it, I couldn't."

"It's the Holy Spirit testifying to you, my son."

"Is it? I'm not so sure." Chris tugged a sliver of beef from his sandwich and nibbled on it. "So what *did* Nicholas say when he helped me pull the boy from the wreck?"

"*Rwy'n pasio i chi y pŵer i gwella?* It in essence means, 'I pass to you the power to heal.'"

Chris scooted his platter to one side, removed his cap, and placed his forehead on the tabletop. He feared it was something like that. The passing of a mantle of authority, of some kind of holy power. Once again, the same armada of questions assaulted him, and once again he found himself defenseless against the seige. True, he had hoped to "discover himself" on this trip. But he wasn't sure he liked what he'd found thus far.

"Ay, what's wrong with him?" Bambi asked, again startling Chris with her stealth. "You sick or som'et, mate?"

Chris decided to not respond. *Keep your head down and stay perfectly still. Maybe she'll think you're dead.* He heard her place a glass next to him.

"Poor lad's in a quandary, yes?" Llewellyn said sympathetically.

"A quandary, is it? Lady troubles, is it? A fine specimen like him? Bah. If he's in need of womanly comfort, I'm off at eleven."

"No, my child. He's confused about his future."

"His future, ay? Out of work, is he? Aye, many a chap's in same quandary 'round here." She gave Chris's arm a playful squeeze that really hurt. Her grip was viselike. "You're not alone there, mate. Lots of fellers are on the dole these days, ay?"

When he didn't respond, she punched his shoulder good-naturedly but hard. "Ay, Yankeeman. Come on, lad, buck up. Life's not all that bad if ya take it one day a time like."

"Just leave him be, Bambi, lass. He'll come 'round soon enough, if you just give him time."

"Oh aye? Well, if you say so, Father. Oh—you wouldn't per chance be holding services tomorrow, would you, Father? If so, you might want to block out some time for my confession. I've got a list I'm bringing long as your arm." She walked away laughing loudly.

Without sneeking a peak, Chris whispered, "Is she gone?"

"Yes, she's gone," he chuckled. Then, "You know, son, what she said makes sense. There's no need for you to feel like you have to take on the whole world like. One day at a time, Chris, lad. You'll know when you should use your gift and when you shouldn't. No need to fret over it."

Chris sat up and saw that Bambi had left him a tall glass of water. He drank the whole thing without pause. "You sound like you know everything about being a Vovnik."

"Just about." He took another gluttonous bite from his sandwich and chewed loudly.

"But what if I mess up? What if I'm not worthy?"

"St. Luke 6:43. 'A good tree bringeth not forth corrupt fruit; neither doth a corrupt tree bringeth forth good fruit.' You are *not* a corrupt tree,

Christian. You are a good man, a compassionate man. You will use the Dial only for good. I know it for sure an' certain."

Once again, he felt backed into a corner. "Any other Bible verses you care to throw at me?"

"Thousands, but the ones you really need to read are in the Gospel of St. Luke."

"Why him?"

"Because, lad, he was a physician, now wasn't he. St. Luke followed Jesus and the Apostles to learn their secrets of healing. Of course, he was converted in the process. Stuck with them after that too, even after the crucifixion of our Lord, yes? Wrote the book of Acts, he did, in addition to his own Gospel no less."

"But again, I'm not an Apostle."

"Neither was Luke."

"Nor do I have the faith of Jesus Christ."

Llewellyn sternly folded his arms and huffed. "Don't be twp, son. No one on earth has that kind of faith. If we did, we'd all be perfect, yes? You simply have to believe in yourself enough to keep trying."

Chris scoffed. "And therein lies the quandary."

"Nay, lad. There's no quandary there. Do you remember what St. Luke had to say about *how* the Lord healed the sick?"

"No."

"St. Luke 6:19. 'And the whole multitude sought to touch him; for there went virtue out of him, and healed them all.'"

"Virtue went out of him? Really? You're saying Jesus was less virtuous after he healed someone?"

The vicar palmed his forehead and sighed. "You're the historian, Christian, yes? You know translations often have different meanings. In Hebrew, they pronounce the word *seh-goo-lah*. It translates to both *virtue* and *power*. Power went out of our Lord. The power to heal, lad, now wasn't it? Just as Hezekiah was healed and the Lord showed him the sign on the Dial of Ahaz. You now hold a piece of that Dial, yes? And St. Nicholas Tewdrig passed the sacred mantle on to you. Like it or not, believe it or not, you have the power to heal those who need it, those who are worthy of it."

The fervency with which the vicar spoke rocked Chris's soul. Even if he wanted to argue or ignore what the churchman had said, he knew he couldn't. But there was still one major snag. "I, um . . . What if I don't have the Dial anymore?"

Llewellyn's expression was a dreadful mix of shock and disbelief. "Nay, lad," he breathed hoarsely. "Say it isn't thus."

"I'm afraid it's true. Collingswood took it."

With sorrow in his eyes, the vicar leaned across the small table and made the sign of the cross on Chris's forehead and chest. "God help you, my son. God help us all."

CHAPTER 27

Suddenly Chris felt as pale as Father Llewellyn looked. "What do you mean? What's wrong?"

"What's wrong?" Llewellyn echoed in disbelief, clasping his small crucifix in both hands. "Not only have you lost the Dial, son, it's in the hands of a madman."

Chris frowned. "Can he use it? I mean, Nick said the Dial doesn't give power *to* the holder, it gets it *from* him. Unless Collingswood is a Vovnik, it'll be useless, right? Is that what you're saying—that he's a Vovnik?"

The vicar finished off his flagon and shakily wiped his mouth. "No, thank the Good Lord. That—that uncivilized man only wants it for his own power and glory. He cares not for his fellow man—only for his fellow man's money."

"What will happen when he tries to use it?"

The vicar shrugged. "I cannot say for sure. Maybe nothing. He has not the mantle or the authority to call upon its power. But one never knows when dealing with sacred things, does one."

Chris aimlessly played with a chip that had come with his sandwich. "I'm sorry about losing it, Father. I had no idea—"

"Nay, you did not lose it, my son. It was taken from you." The vicar swallowed nervously. "But you must do all you can to get it back."

"Why?"

"Because without it you will die sooner than you think."

Instead of fear, frustration again surged in Chris. "Really. Well here's a news flash: I'm mortal. I'm going to die anyway. We all are. So why should I care about a piece of rock?"

"Because it is your *calling*, my son. It is what the Lord wants of you, yes? For want of a better term, it is your destiny."

Chris stared at the fire in the hearth and sighed. "My destiny. One I didn't choose."

"Who *does* choose their own destiny, ay?"

"True, but . . . well, I'm still not sure what this calling is all about. Even if I got the Dial back, I don't know how to use it."

Llewellyn smiled warmly and patted the area of his former gunshot wound. "I believe you do, lad."

"I think *that* was just dumb luck. Look, you've read Nick's journal, same as me. I saw nothing in there about *how* to do this job." He snorted derisively. "There's an understatement! I've only had the Dial for two days, and I've already lost it. Now I'm on the run from the police. I have no ID, no money, no means of getting back home, and now you're telling me I'm going to die prematurely. Some Vovnik I turned out to be! I've only just started, and already I've hit rock bottom."

"Aye, maybe so. But what a firm foundation from which to start a new life, yes?"

"Excuse me?"

"Rock bottom, son. The wise man built his house upon a rock, did he not? You were given a precious relic, a curious stone with sacred power. It gave you a new life and a new name. Like the white stones in the book of Revelation whereon is written the new name. Yes, yes," he said, holding up a hand to stop the anticipated objection. "I know the Dial didn't give you a new *name*, but it did give you a new *title*. You're still Christian Pendragon, but you are also a Physician of Myddfai, one of the Righteous Thirty-Six, a Lamed Vovnik."

Chris stared blankly at his unfinished sandwich. Not only had his appetite vanished, he now felt a bit queasy. How did this happen to him? Yes, he'd come to Wales seeking many answers. Yes, he wanted to find out who he was, perhaps even discover a destiny that would bring him true happiness. But he certainly didn't expect a calling from God.

He stared into the utter kindness of the vicar's eyes. The priest seemed to understand exactly what he was going through. "You feel you have not the faith required to fulfill your calling, yes?"

Chris nodded.

Llewellyn wiped his mouth with a napkin then folded his arms. He looked at Chris from under heavy, gray eyebrows. The expression held mild reprimand. "Christian Pendragon. Faith comes in many forms. My faith, though strong enough to die for, is not the kind to hold the mantle you now carry, is it. Yours is a noble calling for sure an' certain, a faith of pure compassion, but it is a faith that must be exercised, just like a muscle, yes?"

"And if I don't?"

"Faith not used withers and dies . . . as will you."

"Which will be sooner than later because I don't have the Dial," he said, as if deciding to give up right there. Then, tapping his finger on the tabletop, he said, "Yeah, and another thing. Even if I *did* have the Dial, how would I know who to heal and who to ignore? There are millions of sick people on this planet. I can't possibly heal them all."

"Through the spirit of discernment, of course. Listen to the still, small voice, yes?"

"Great; another foggy answer," he huffed. "We've come full circle and accomplished nothing."

Father Llewellyn looked sad and somewhat offended. "Have I not answered all your questions, just as I promised?"

Chris bit his lip. He wasn't angry with the vicar. If anything, he was angry with himself.

Llewellyn leaned forward and took ahold of Chris's wrist. His gaze bore straight into Chris's soul. "Trust in yourself, lad, and trust in the Lord. He'll nobly lead you through whatever fog you encounter. It's up to you to follow. Only then will His will be done."

Chris flinched and sat up. In a whisper he said, "Nobly thru white fog hath I led."

The vicar smiled warmly and leaned back. "Aye, lad. Now you're beginning to see."

He flinched again when he noticed Bambi was standing next to him. How could someone so large and boisterous be so stealthy? She was glaring at his half-eaten sandwich.

Quickly, Chris said, "I'm glad you're here, Bambi. I want to tell you, this has got to be the best roast beef sandwich I've ever had. Only, it's just so big I can't finish it right now. May I have a container to carry the leftovers, please? I do not want to waste a single bite."

The praise seemed to work. Bambi's expression softened a bit. She turned her gaze to the vicar. "And how were your doings, Father? Hit the spot, did they?"

"Bambi, my child. If I were the marrying kind, I'd have asked for your hand an age ago. Any lass who can cook like this is one I'd like to spend the rest of my days with."

She tipped her head back and belted out a guffaw that loosened dust from the rafters. "Father, you ought not to say such things, ay? You'll make me blush in front of the professor. Besides, it were our Seth who made your sandwich. Maybe you should propose to him." She slapped Chris on the back and walked away roaring with delight.

Llewellyn winked at Chris. "I knew who made our doings. I just like to make her laugh. She's got a whimsy that reaches to the heavens, does she not?"

Chris wished he could laugh right now. Instead, the seriousness of his situation weighed down on him like an elephant on his shoulders. What would he do now? Where would he go? How would he find Collingswood and the Dial while avoiding the police?

The answer came with the buzzing of Llewellyn's phone. It was the hospital in Monmouth.

CHAPTER 28

"Forgive me, Christian, while I take this," he said, tapping a key. "Hello? Oh hello, Doctor. How are—" He paused, listening. "Really? Yes. Yes, he's here with me. Yes, I will tell him. Excellent. Until then, Doctor. Godspeed to you."

Chris opened his palms in question.

"Feel like going for a drive, Christian?"

"Where?"

"Back to the hospital, of course. That was Dr. Ingledew. She wants to see you straight away." His quirky smile suggested more to the story than a simple meeting.

"What about the police?"

Llewellyn shrugged. "I don't believe the good physician wants to turn you over to the authorities. I'm confident she believes in your innocence. And as I said, I think she likes you."

"Hardly," he scoffed. "No. I'm pretty sure she thinks I'm an idiot."

"Nonetheless, she has someone there you will be interested in meeting, I should think. Come along then, we need to make haste," he said, standing.

Chris was at the door before he realized he'd left his sandwich. Seeing Bambi heading toward their table with a paper bag in hand, he hastily pulled his cap low on his brow and exited the tavern.

The sunny morning had morphed into a dull afternoon blanketed with gray overcast. It didn't help his somber mood. Michael opened the rectory door before they were on the stoop.

"Ah, Michael. We'll be needing the car for a time, yes? No need to accompany us. Please watch over the chapel in my absence will you? There's a good lad."

Clearly not liking the decision, the big man gave a slight bow.

Llewellyn lifted the keys from a peg in the kitchen and handed them to Chris.

"I don't have my license, remember?"

"Neither do I, lad. But you are a young man, and I'm not. I trust your driving more than I trust my own, so there's an end to it."

Figuring he didn't have much more to lose, Chris accepted the keys and settled behind the steering wheel. Once on the road, he asked, "So, are you going to tell me what's going on?"

"In all honesty, I'm not sure myself. The good doctor said she has a man named Collingswood in her hospital. She wants us to identify him before she calls the authorities."

"What's wrong with him?"

"Now, how should I know? The doctor didn't tell me, and I didn't ask, now did I."

Chris frowned. "Do you think it's the same guy?"

"I do," he said without pause.

"Great," Chris replied with little enthusiasm. While it was imperative to ID the man who shot the vicar, Chris had another concern gnawing at him. If he got back the Dial, would he be expected to continue learning to be a Vovnik healer? Would he have to give up his teaching position to go on a pilgrimage of healing the sick and infirm? Is that really what was expected of him? "Great," he said again, just under his breath.

* * *

Llewellyn told Chris to park in the staff lot behind the hospital. He pulled out his phone and hit the callback function.

"Hello, Doctor. Father Llewellyn ringing. We're here now. Yes, I have him with me. Is it safe to come in then? Excellent. Thank you."

As they neared the door, Ingledew opened it from inside. She didn't look happy. "Thank you for coming so quickly, gentlemen. I—" She stopped abruptly and took in Chris's attire. "You look like a true Welshman, Mr. Pendragon. It suits you," she said with the hint of a smile. Then, sobering, "Even so, I must warn you that I will have to report your presence here. We have cameras in every corridor that record everything. Your visit here is irrefutable, but I can delay that report if need be."

"I understand," Chris said. "Thank you."

She nodded curtly. "Follow me then."

The doctor led them to the same room Llewellyn had occupied the previous day. The irony was not lost on Chris.

Collingswood lay in the bed, unconscious. Dressed only in a hospital gown, he was hooked to a pulse-ox monitor and an IV. Llewellyn walked to his side and gently placed one hand on the crown of his head. Gripping his crucifix in his other hand, he closed his eyes and began a quiet prayer.

"Is this the man?" Ingledew asked quietly.

"Definitely. What happened to him?" Chris replied, equally quiet.

"We don't know. He was brought in unconscious about two hours ago."

"How's he doing?"

"Not so good. Those are his effects," she said, indicating a plastic tote on the counter. "His billfold contains no less than three IDs, all with the same photograph but different names."

Chris looked in the tote and felt a rush of elation. On top of a folded set of clothing sat a collection of items: a wallet, a cell phone, a set of keys, and the Dial of Ahaz. Instinctively, Chris picked up the Dial and held it to his chest. An indescribable comfort immediately ebbed through him. He felt his anxieties begin to seep away. He almost wished it wasn't so. Yet he could not deny a powerful impression of correctness filling his soul. He drew a deep breath and let it out slowly, then pocketed the relic.

"Where was he brought in from?" Llewellyn asked. Chris turned quickly, unaware the vicar had finished his benediction.

"A public park not far from here. A transient named Kip asked a couple of pensioners to hail the EMTs."

"A transient?" Chris asked.

"Yes. Apparently he had some interaction with Mr. Collingswood in the park. He's very distraught over the whole affair. I have him stabilized in the next room." She gave a quick shake of her head. "The man has a remarkable story to tell the police when they get here."

"What? I thought you said you haven't called them yet."

"I haven't, Mr. Pendragon. They undoubtedly know the EMTs brought Collingswood in, but they won't come until after I call with an assessment. It's standard procedure for a small facility like ours."

Chris breathed a little easier.

Ingledew continued: "When I recognized Mr. Collingswood's name on one of his IDs, I thought you might like a chance to come clear your name."

"Thanks," Chris said then frowned in confusion. "Wait. How did you know I was with Father Llewellyn?"

She glanced at the vicar.

"I confess, before leaving hospital, I told the good doctor I'd know how to contact you if Collingswood showed up here."

Now Chris was really perplexed. "And how did you know Collingswood might show up here?"

"Oh, I had a hunch like. I knew he couldn't resist trying to use the Dial for his own ill-gotten gain, yes?"

"But . . . but you said nothing would happen if he tried to use it."

"Aye, that's right. Nothing happened to the person he was trying to heal."

Chris looked to the doctor.

She shrugged. "I have no idea what you gentlemen are referring to."

"Perhaps we could have a moment of time with Mr. Kip, please?" Llewellyn asked.

Ingledew thought for a moment then nodded. "Only a moment. Although, you might not believe what he has to say."

CHAPTER 29

THE SCRAWNY MAN IN THE next room was also dressed in a hospital gown and had an IV running into his arm and a pulse-ox monitor attached to his finger. Sporting a scruffy growth of beard and long, oily hair, Kip looked like a typical vagrant. His rheumy eyes stared off at nothing in particular; his lower lip quivered incessantly.

"Kip. This is Father Llewellyn and Christian Pendragon. Can you tell them what happened in the park?"

One of Kip's eyes slowly looked in their direction; the other one remained staring off at an obscure angle. Amblyopia, thought Chris. A friend of his had it as a youth.

"Hello, Kip, lad," the priest said tenderly. "I'm Father Llewellyn, vicar of the St. Nicholas chapel in Trellech. Can you hear me, son?"

The stray eye slowly began aligning with the other one.

"Son, can you tell us what happened in the park, please? There's a good fellow."

Kip's mouth moved, but no sound came out.

"Louder please, Kip," Ingledew said.

"Tried . . . ta heal me like."

"He tried to heal you? Did you ask to be healed, my son?"

A shake of the head. "He just . . . came up and said . . . he could . . . make me whole."

"Are you ill?" Chris asked.

The eye wandered away again. "The bottle done it."

"Terminal liver cirrhosis," the doctor interpreted with regret. "I found his records on the National Health Service database."

"How would Collingswood know that?" Chris whispered.

Ingledew shrugged.

"Tell us what happened, my son. It's all right. You are under no condemnation from the Lord or the church."

The transient coughed and closed his eyes. "He said he were a priest. He said he could . . . make me whole . . . make it so I never touch a drop again."

"Then what happened? Can you describe what he did, son?"

Kip swallowed. It looked painful. "He placed hands . . . on me head like, and said . . . said some words I didn't understand, you know? Then he . . . he . . ." Kip's head drooped to his chest, and he began to sob. Tears darkened his hospital gown.

"Hush now, son. No need for that. Go on and tell us what happened next," Llewellyn prompted. "It's okay; God is with thee."

"Please, Kip. This is very important," Chris joined in.

He gradually regained his composure and looked up. Both bloodshot eyes slowly focused on Chris. "He screamed. The priest screamed like he were in agony. Out of nowhere an' for no reason. I don't know why, I swear it. He just up and screams, like a banshee he did. Then he—he just dropped. Dead as a doornail. Just like that," he said, trying to snap his gnarled fingers.

Chris didn't know what to think or say. He glanced at the doctor. She shrugged again. "He's not dead, but close enough."

Kip closed his eyes again and let out a raspy sigh, as if telling the tale had sapped all his strength. His lower lip quivered relentlessly, flicking bits of spittle across his chest.

"Like Uzzah of old," the vicar said in quiet awe. When the others turned to him, he explained: "Come, come now. In the Old Testament, remember? Second Samuel, sixth chapter, I believe. Only the Levite priests were allowed to touch the ark of the covenant, yes? So when one of the priests stumbled, poor Uzzah reached out his hand to steady the ark, and God instantly struck him dead, just like that."

"Ah," Chris said. "But how is this . . . ?"

"Is this not the same story, Christian? Collingswood is not allowed to use the Dial, is he. He knows this. He knows the legend of the Lamed Vovnik better than most. And yet he did so anyway, did it just to see if he could. He tried to call upon the power of the Dial without the proper authority, and the Good Lord, in all His infinite wisdom, struck him down."

Chris shared a puzzled glance with the doctor. She held up her hands in bewilderment. "If the vicar says so. I failed out of parochial school."

"And Kip? How's his liver?" Chris asked.

With an expression of regret, she discreetly shook her head. "Haven't run a biopsy yet, but blood analysis doesn't look good."

"'Tis a shame and no mistake," Llewellyn offered. "But his fate is far better than that piece of rubbish in the other room, yes?" When both Chris and Ingledew raised their eyebrows in question, the vicar waved them into a corner so they could speak privately. "Neither man is long for this world, truth be told, yes?"

The doctor nodded.

"So even though our man Kip hasn't lived a saintly life, his sins are not as grievous to be borne as the imposter next door, yes? That reprobate Collingswood, his fate in the hereafter is sealed for sure an' certain, and it's not pretty. That's why I administered his last rites."

"You gave Collingswood his last rites?" Chris asked, astonished.

"Aye. He offended God, and God chose to—"

Suddenly an alarm sounded from Collingswood's room.

"That's his heart monitor," Ingledew said, sprinting from the room. Chris and Llewellyn followed close behind.

CHAPTER 30

THE DOCTOR SILENCED THE ALARM and began assessing the patient. Collingswood's skin was the color of old milk. His eyes stared wildly. Foam dribbled from his mouth. He wheezed loudly, his heart thumping heavily at 138 beats per minute, pulse-ox 85 percent. His eyes darted to and fro frantically until they locked on Chris. "Y-y-you!" he stammered hoarsely.

Chris said nothing.

"Help me, Pendragon. P-Please."

"Help? After you shot the Father and nearly cracked my skull open?"

"I'm s-sorry," he cried. "I had to know. You *are* one of the Thirty-Six." Turning to Llewellyn, he said, "P-please, Father. Hear my confession. Absolve me of my sins."

"I'm afraid your sins are the kind I cannot absolve."

The heart monitor jumped to 156 bpm.

"How—how c-can you say that? You haven't heard m-me."

"I've heard enough from you over the past year to last a lifetime, haven't I. I know men of your ilk. You are an affront to God, sir. You have caused grief and misery in many a chapel throughout this country with your treasure hunting. You're a thief and a liar and, for all I know, a murderer too. God will be your judge, not I."

Collingswood's skin blanched a shade whiter. "But—but look what I've discovered," he balked, his eyes snapping to Chris. "A true Vovni—" He gasped and began coughing.

"You have *discovered* nothing, sir," the vicar said steadily. "You have *uncovered* your true nature. And now you are paying the price."

"I—I am not the first. And I won't be the last," he wheezed. "They know who you are, Vovnik," he said to Chris. "I told them, and—" His words cut off as he began coughing convulsively.

"May God have mercy on your soul," Llewellyn said, stepping away from the bed while making the sign of the cross.

Ingledew tried to coax her patient to sit up so he wouldn't aspirate. His paroxysms turned convulsive. Between fits, he sucked in rasping gulps of air. A nurse joined the fray.

"Lean forward and breathe lightly, Mr. Collingswood," the nurse coached.

His pallor was now cadaverous. His eyes bolted back and forth with frenzied randomness. His fist clenched wildly at his chest.

"Calm down and breathe, Mr. Collingswood."

Chris stepped up to help but was unsure what to do.

"Heart rate 198; he's getting no oxygen. Give him six megs adenosine, STAT. Prepare to intubate."

Suddenly, Collingswood's hand shot out and grabbed Chris's shirt; their eyes locked. "Heal—me," he wheezed.

Chris looked to the vicar, feeling completely helpless. Llewellyn lowered his eyes, giving him no assistance.

"Step back, Mr. Pendragon," Ingledew yelled.

Collingswood clung to Chris's shirt. "Heal—me!"

Chris's hand instinctively went to his pocket and encircled the Dial. He sensed its power; he knew he could do it. But he also felt . . . constrained? With sincere compassion, he whispered, "I'm sorry."

Suddenly, a massive convulsion slammed Collingswood's skull back into the headboard. Blood-tinged sputum blew from his mouth, misting into the air. The heart monitor flat-lined.

Ingledew punched a large red button on the wall, triggering an alarm. "Beginning chest compressions! Get the crash cart in here!"

Within seconds, two orderlies entered the room pushing a red cart. Chris staggered back and tore some paper towels from a dispenser at the sink. He scrubbed desperately at the flecks of blood on his shirt. The doctor ripped Collingswood's hospital gown open and prepped the AED paddles.

"Charging . . . Clear!"

An electronic shock contracted Collingswood's muscles. He arched from the bed then collapsed back down with a *thud*. A nurse bagged him and began synchronized respirations. More chest compressions.

"Charging . . . Clear!"

More respirations. More compressions. Another shock.

The flat-line continued to sing its monotone death knell. The cycle continued for a full five minutes before Ingledew dropped the AED paddles and stepped back. "I'm calling it. Time of death: 16:45 Greenwich Mean Time."

As the nurses began cleaning up, Ingledew had Chris accompany her to her office. Father Llewellyn opted to stay with Kip to offer him solace.

"Please sit down, Mr. Pendragon," the doctor said, gesturing to a chair in her office. He did. "Did you get any blood on your skin?"

"I don't think so. Just my shirt."

"One can never be too cautious. You may use the hospital laundry and the shower in the doctor's lounge if you like. I strongly recommend cleaning up as soon as possible."

"Okay," he said, not understanding why she'd brought him to her office to give him such basic advice.

Sitting behind her desk, she opened a steno pad and clicked a pen. "Okay, here's the thing, Mr. Pendragon. I want some answers, and I don't want any backtalk or messing about, is that understood?"

"O-kay," he said again.

"There are a number of issues that are . . . well, irritating me. I can't seem to figure them out, and I hate not being able to figure things out."

"I know that feeling."

The young doctor wasn't smiling. In fact, if anything, she looked agitated. "What exactly is going on here?"

Chris frowned. "I'm not sure what you mean."

She considered him silently for a few moments. "How about this? I know for a fact that Father Llewellyn was shot in the abdomen with a nine millimeter slug. The bullet entered just under his ribcage, two centimeters from midline, and pierced his left lung. He should be dead, but he's not because of something you did. I want to know what it was."

"Something *I* did?"

"Don't play coy to me. Father Llewellyn swore to that fact, and I know he does not lie. So tell me what's going on right now, or I *will* turn you over to the authorities."

CHAPTER 31

CHRIS SWALLOWED HARD, FEELING LIKE a child caught with his hand in the cookie jar. "May I ask how you know Father Llewellyn was shot?"

"The EMTs reported a GSW—a gunshot wound—upper left abdomen, so that's what I looked for when they brought him in. But I found nothing but a blood-stained shirt and a small bruise. So later I took an MRI and found something very interesting . . . and very confusing."

"Welcome to my world," Chris snorted cynically. "What did it show?"

"Channeling. You see, there is a distinct channel bored into the tissue when a bullet goes through it—a pathway, if you will. It's typical of most all GSWs. It's rather like a scar; it shows where an injury has occurred, the angle at which it occurred, depth of penetration, and so forth. Eventually it does turn into a scar. Father Llewellyn's MRI showed fresh channeling—which confuses me because there was no bullet *hole*—no entry or exit wound—nor was there a bullet at the end of the channel. Police say they found it next to his body, covered with his blood. So I scheduled a second MRI the following morning, and guess what I found?"

"Scarring?"

"Precisely. Fully formed, pliable scarring—which is impossible just ten hours later. Now how does *that* happen, Mr. Pendragon?"

Chris shrugged, feeling backed into a corner. "I wish I knew."

"I think you *do* know. The vicar *had* been shot, but there was no *external* evidence—as I said, no entry or exit wounds. I want to know how. No excuses. No shillyshallying. Just the truth, if you please."

Chris didn't know what to say. He couldn't simply come out and say he'd healed the vicar with positive thinking and a magic rock. He knew the kind of response he'd get. And yet, that was precisely what *had* happened.

It was really quite simple, and yet he couldn't explain it in simple terms. She wouldn't believe it. He was just beginning to believe it himself.

"Listen, doc. I'm the one who's confused here. I can tell you what I've gone through the past few days by way of explanation, but I'm pretty sure you'd think I was mocking you. That, or that I'm just plain crazy. There are a couple of things I still need to check out before I decide if *I* believe what has happened."

She considered him with cold gray eyes. "What things?"

Chris slipped his hand in his pocket and encircled the Dial. It brought undeniable comfort. Feeling his tensions ease, he asked, "How much time do you have?"

"Why?"

"Because the full explanation may take a while."

She consulted her wristwatch. "My shift ends at seven. That gives you the generous side of two hours to get cleaned up and hone your story. I expect nothing but the truth, Mr. Pendragon. Do we understand each other?"

Despite the vehemence with which she spoke, Chris felt an inexplicable measure of joy knowing he would open up to her. It was as if he finally had a chance to resolve his own doubts, one intellectual to another.

Emboldened, he said, "I understand you perfectly, Doctor, and I will try my best to reason this out with you. But I must make one stipulation first."

She cocked an eyebrow. "Which is . . . ?"

"Please stop calling me Mr. Pendragon. It makes me sound so old. Dr. Pendragon won't do either. That was my dad. I prefer Chris." She blinked, as if caught off guard. Then her eyes softened, and dropping her gaze, she smiled. "Okay. Chris."

"And while I give your title the utmost respect and admiration, I would like to call you by your first name, if you don't mind."

Her cheeks colored slightly as she doodled on her notepad. "Kathryn."

"Kathryn. With a C or a K?"

"A K," she said firmly. "But please, no Kate or Katie or Kat."

"A family name?"

"Yes, it is. My great-grandmum's. Yours?"

"Dad named me after Christiaan Barnard, the first doctor to perform a heart transplant, in hopes that I'd follow in his footsteps."

"A tad quixotic, don't you think?"

"Definitely. May I call you Kathryn then? It has a certain sense of nobility and . . . dignity, very befitting a brilliant doctor of medicine."

The shy smile returned. Chris noticed dimples he hadn't seen before. He liked them.

"I don't know about brilliant," she hedged, "but you may call me Kathryn."

Progress.

Chris was led to the hospital laundry, where he borrowed a gown then stripped down to get his clothes washed. Father Llewellyn stopped by to say that he was returning to Trellech. Chris told the vicar that he'd promised Dr. Ingledew a full explanation.

"Besides, I don't want it to look like I am running away again."

"Not a bad idea, my son. Well, good evening for now. Call me if you need anything."

"Count on it," Chris said, shaking the priest's hand.

* * *

"Would you care for something to drink?" Kathryn asked, entering her office some two hours later.

"No, thank you."

"Very well," she said, pouring herself a cup of tea before settling behind her desk. "Now then, let me hear this from beginning to end."

He sat up straight and cleared his throat. "Okay. So I've been touring the country for just over a week now, checking out castles, studying some history and such. Then three days ago, I was driving north, just outside of Cardigan, when this four-door sedan zipped past me, missed a turn, and flipped over onto the moor." Chris did his best to recount each detail of each event as it actually happened: Nigel Madsen's broken ankles, Nicholas Tewdrig and his peculiarities, the Dial of Ahaz, the Physicians of Myddfai legend, the call from Mary McKenzie, the Church of St. Nicholas, Collingswood's deception, Father Llewellyn. The gun shot. The healing.

"I swear to you I'm not making this up. I've never been an overly religious person, so I'm having a hard time wrapping my head around this. I'm an academic, like you. I hold a doctorate in history. I scrutinize everything, study everything. I thrive on research. That's why I feel the need to check a few more things out before I draw any final conclusions."

He paused, searching her face for any signs of anger. All he saw was a flat stare from expressionless eyes.

"But you still feel there's a spiritual element to it," she said without emotion.

"Yes, I do. Look, you know as well as I do that Collingswood shot Father Llewellyn. How he healed so quickly is still up to debate—as is how Nigel Madsen's ankles healed. But I cannot deny what happened, what *I saw* happen in both cases. And somehow it all revolves around this," he said, pulling the Dial from his pocket.

Setting the relic on her desk, he stood and walked to her window. Outside, the cold evening air was heavy with mist. Below, blurry halos pulsed around the tall parking lot lamps like pale, spherical ghosts. Chris sighed. Unloading the past had lifted some of the burden from him, but it also left an empty feeling inside. He wished he'd had a more rational story to tell, but that simply wasn't the case.

Kathryn was silent for a long time. He could guess what she was thinking. And it wasn't good. He heard her tapping a few computer keys.

"So . . . do you believe me?" he asked without turning.

"I'm not . . ." She hesitated. "I have a hard time believing in miracles, Chris; but that's not to say I *don't* believe in them. I guess I lack faith at this point in time. Your story . . . well, let's just say it stretches plausibility *and* credibility, shall we? I think what you said earlier makes sense though: You need to confirm that the bauble is what you say it is."

"I agree. But therein lies the problem," he said, turning. "How am I going to do that? I'm not exactly at liberty to come and go as I please with the police still looking for me."

"True. There is that," she said, focusing on her monitor, still pecking away at the keyboard. If she heard the accusation in his voice, she didn't acknowledge it.

After another moment of awkward silence, Chris asked, "What are you looking for?"

"Confirmation, of course."

CHAPTER 32

"CONFIRMATION?" HE ASKED.

She held up an index finger, asking for another minute. Then, after a couple more keystrokes, she said, "Now, that *is* curious."

"What?"

"I've accessed NHS records. Carmarthen Hospital confirms that Nigel Madsen appears to have broken his ankles in a traffic accident precisely when you said, but there is no mention of reparative surgery or casting or physical therapy of any kind. They admitted him, confirmed he'd broken his ankles, and released him with a writ of full health, all in one day. It's almost as if they intentionally left something out."

"Or they didn't know *how* to write it up," Chris suggested, referring to Kathryn's angst on how to write up Llewellyn's injury.

Her eyes darted up, filled with affirmation. "Precisely."

When she refocused on her computer, Chris busied himself by perusing her bookcase. There was the usual assortment of medical books and journals, but he also noticed a number of fictional works, particularly those of Emily Brontë, Jane Austin, Elizabeth Browning, and Sarah Eden. "I see you like classical romance."

He smiled at the color tinting her cheeks.

"It's a harmless distraction," she said, not making eye contact.

Chris pulled out a thick tome entitled *Pharmacopoeia of Wales* and flipped to the index. Under the letter *M*, he found the subheading: "Myddfai, Physicians of, p. 102." Turning to that page, he read the text. It rehearsed history Chris was already familiar with but then added a single paragraph on the fourth son.

In addition to the three Physicians of Myddfai, there are numerous citations of a fourth son (or sons). It is said that the original fourth son was called by the second son to carry on the charge of healing. This calling was considered sacred and transferred with it an exhortation of altruism and anonymity. This adoption into the family of Myddfai physicians is said to bestow the inheritor with certain bequests, including uncommon longevity, the gift of discernment, and the ability to heal all manner of infirmity. The office may only be passed on by the current title holder to a person of uncommon compassion (typically a male) and is traditionally done shortly before the retirement (death) of the current title holder. It is assumed that the calling of Fourth Son of Myddfai continues to the present day.

Although "Christian Pendragon" wasn't printed (neither was "Nicholas Tewdrig"), Chris felt the information had his name written all over it. "Son of a gun," he whispered.

"Find something of interest?" Kathryn asked, her eyes still fixated on her computer screen.

"Sort of."

"Well, I have," she said with a smug grin. "Turns out Cardiff University has staff that specialize in geology, anthropology, and ancient languages. I'd say a trip to the capital is in order, wouldn't you?"

"What—just go there, let them examine the Dial, pick it apart, perhaps even confiscate it?" Despite his distrust of the man, Collingswood's warnings raged in his head.

"Have you a better idea?"

"No. I guess not. I'm just afraid of losing it again."

"Seems to me it wasn't lost; it was stolen, right?"

He nodded. "Even so, I doubt the university will offer much help to a foreigner."

"Not so. They love visiting luminaries. Just tell them who you are; they'll give you preferential treatment as a university fellow, I'm sure of it."

"Yeah," he scoffed. "I'll just walk in and say I'm the man wanted by the government for international terrorist activity. Hey, but if you have a second, could you tell me about this chunk of rock?"

Rather than take offense, Kathryn smirked. "Do you really think the authorities have issued a criminal watch on you? You have a suspected link to mob activity, not international terrorism. You don't fit the terrorist profile, with your auburn hair and cobalt eyes—" She stopped abruptly and returned to her computer. Chris could almost feel heat from her face.

"I guess not," he said with a shrug, letting her comments about her attraction to him slip slide. "But I have no ID. I suppose I could print duplicates of my driver's license and university ID from the Internet, but they might not accept copies."

"It's unlikely they'll even ask. Just act like you know what you're doing. Be stuffy and insistent."

Chris doubted that would work, but he wasn't in the mood to argue. Something he'd just read was pricking the back of his mind. He opened the pharmacopeia again and reread the pages. Just before he got to the paragraph about the fourth son, Kathryn gave a soft gasp.

"What is it?" he asked.

"More confirmation. I think." Instead of excitement in her voice, Chris heard a twinge of remorse.

"Of . . . ?"

"Nicholas Tewdrig. Or in this case: John Doe."

Chris frowned.

"I truly hope I'm wrong, Chris, but your description of Nicholas Tewdrig exactly matches a John Doe that was delivered to Cardiff Hospital just this morning."

Chris's mouth was open, but he was afraid to voice any words. He felt his stomach twist into a knot.

"I can't . . . be sure," she said hesitantly, "but it's probably something we should look into, just in case, you know?"

Still speechless, Chris's gaze dropped back to the open book in his hands. There in the penultimate sentence was the item that had bothered him moments before.

> The office may only be passed on by the current title holder to a person of uncommon compassion (typically a male), and is traditionally done shortly before the retirement (death) of the current title holder.

Death. Nicholas Tewdrig's death.

I am not afraid to meet my Creator.

I have fought the good fight. My time is short.

I need to teach you som'et before I go.

All the clues Tewdrig had given flooded Chris's mind. Nick *knew* he was dying. He'd lost the protective mantle of the Dial, and his body was rapidly experiencing the mortal burden of more than two hundred years.

"He's dead?" he mumbled in a whisper.

"I'm so sorry, Chris. I could arrange for you to identify him privately, if you like," Kathryn offered. "It may be someone else. Let's not give up hope just yet."

Chris nodded, feeling a hot tear course down one cheek. But he already knew it was Nick: the man he'd declined to learn from, the man he'd booted from his hotel room, the man who'd had such tremendous faith in him. His mentor. He swallowed hard. "When?"

"Tonight would be best. While the university likely doesn't have a bulletin out on you, I'm certain the hospital does. You know, just in case you show up . . . as a patient."

"Or a corpse," he said bitterly.

"Yes, of course. That too."

CHAPTER 33

AFTER A QUICK PHONE CALL to Cardiff Hospital, Kathryn led Chris through a service door to a side parking lot. At that late hour, only a handful of vehicles were still there. Kathryn depressed a button on her key fob, and a utilitarian-looking Range Rover growled to life. Equipped with wide tires, multiple fog lamps, and a winch, it looked like something the military might issue, only much more elegant.

"Whoa," Chris exclaimed.

"The winters here get unreasonably harsh—snow and ice mostly, but the wind can whip across the moor with frightening velocity. I need something dependable." She climbed into the driver's seat. "It takes a little over an hour to drive to University Hospital, weather permitting."

Chris nodded, still feeling emotionally hollow. He was just beginning to allow the possibility of a new calling, a new destiny, and now the one man who could teach him all he needed to know was dead. Maybe. But he sensed it was the truth. Self-condemnation encircled his heart with caustic fetters. He'd missed the chance to learn because of his own apathy and bullheadedness. *Idiot!*

When Kathryn turned on her sound system, a soothing electronic voice announced the time and temperature. "No wonder I'm ravenous," Kathryn said, pulling Chris from his denigrating reflections. "It's well past suppertime. Are you hungry?"

"Not really."

"Well, you have to eat something to keep up your energy, right? I have a feeling you're going to need it. Doctor's orders now. What do you like?"

"Whatever you like," he said, staring out the window.

Kathryn pulled into a drive-through and ordered some tacos and Cokes. "I know this isn't the healthiest fare, but it's all we have time for just now. Besides, it's what I usually eat when I'm melancholy. Thought it might help you too."

Accepting his meal, Chris asked, "Why are *you* melancholy?"

He saw her jaw clench in the glow of the dashboard as she pulled back on the road and checked her mirrors several times—an obvious tactic to delay her response. "Let's just say I have my reasons, shall we?"

In other words, don't ask.

Chris munched on the greasy taco with little interest in its taste. He needed to focus on something else, anything else; anything that would make him less miserable company to be with. Forcing a smile, he said, "Okay. New topic. Tell me all about the brilliant Dr. Kathryn Ingledew. What makes her tick?"

"Oh, there's not much to tell, I'm afraid."

"Where were you born?"

"Ettington, England."

"Siblings?"

"None."

"Father?"

Her voice softened. "Deceased. About two years back. He was a banker for thirty-three years. He was two years away from retirement when he died of a massive heart attack."

"I'm so sorry, Kathryn. I lost my dad a year ago. Same reason," he said, shoving his hands deep in his coat pockets. "Dad was a workaholic, thoracic surgeon. He was in decent shape, so I'm pretty sure stress did him in."

Kathryn nodded. "My da worked hard too, but he didn't watch after his health. His favorite place in the world was behind a tall mug and a bowl of crisps. But he was a good father."

Chris detected the strain in her voice. It was still a delicate topic. "He sounds like a great man."

"He was. He loved foreign food, especially tacos. It's why I eat them when I'm feeling down; to remind me of him, you know?"

"I see. And your mom?"

"She's not doing so well. She's on bed rest at home. I have a nurse watching her 'round the clock. She's—" Her voice caught, and she took a generous sip of her soda to avoid talking.

"My mother considers me the black sheep of the family," he jumped in, "because I chose teaching history over practicing medicine." He snorted.

"And now look at me: a wanted criminal in a foreign country. Guess I should have followed mom's advice."

She smiled graciously then reached forward and clicked on her stereo. Conversation time was over, Chris assumed.

Bittersweet music filled the cabin. Chris recognized it as Ralph Vaughan Williams, *Fantasia on a Theme by Thomas Tallis*. "Good choice," he said. "Although I prefer his *Five Variants of Dives and Lazarus*."

Her smile was genuine this time. "I'm impressed."

"Hey, you can't be a lover of history without classical music being a part of your world."

"Truly."

Chris leaned back, absorbing the music while gazing out at the dark landscape whizzing by. He wanted to keep talking, if only to keep his mind off the upcoming task, but he sensed Kathryn was still fighting some inner battle of her own. He was confused at why she'd threatened to turn him over to the police—twice now—and then seemed so intent on bending over backwards to help him. It was just one more mystery to add to the list.

Traffic stayed light. The remaining distance to Cardiff took about forty minutes to cover, during which time not a single additional word was exchanged.

* * *

Kathryn pulled into a parking area reserved for doctors. She opened the glove box and took out a plastic placard to hang from her rearview mirror. "It designates me as a physician," she explained.

The city air felt warmer to Chris. That was usually the case in metropolitan areas. *Urban warming*, he'd heard it described. Whatever the case, he welcomed the respite from the chill.

"Let me do the talking," she said quickly, entering the emergency room doors.

"Good evening, Doctor," one of the nurses greeted.

"Good evening," Kathryn replied with a neutral smile.

Chris passively ignored them.

At an elevator, Kathryn pressed the call button. "I hope we're not too late. If it's a slow night, the coroner sometimes closes early."

"How can you close a morgue?" Chris asked with a grin. "You never know when a body will come in."

"There's a repository in the basement; the coroner's office is where they do the autopsies."

"Ah." Chris wasn't squeamish, but he felt himself blanch. The fact that he'd grown up surrounded by doctors had calloused his gag reflex. Conversations at the dinner table were not for the faint of heart. But that didn't mean he liked the sight of dead bodies. Or the blood. Or the smells.

The elevator doors opened to a tall, lanky, middle-aged man with a weak chin and a weaker comb-over. His eyes were sad and brooding.

"Oh. Good evening, Percy," Kathryn said in surprise. "We're not too late, I trust?"

"Well hello, Kathryn. I was beginning to think you weren't going to make it," he said with a forced smile.

"This is Dr. Christian," she said by way of introduction. It wasn't a complete lie. "Dr. Christian, meet Dr. Blackham."

They shook hands.

"Please tell me you're not closed up yet," Kathryn fairly pled. "As I mentioned over the line, we really need to see the Doe you're holding from this morning."

Blackham gave Chris a snooty once-over. "Are you a friend, Dr. Christian?"

Chris almost said yes. Keeping his tone even, he said, "Good question. But I won't know until I see the body, will I?"

The coroner's brow lifted haughtily. "I meant of Dr. Ingledew's."

Kathryn said no at the same time Chris said yes.

One eyebrow moved a fraction higher.

"He may be a friend of the Doe's family," Kathryn explained. "He simply needs to ID the body, Percy. It may give us a clue as to his origin."

"From America, are you, Doctor?"

"Canada. Calgary."

The coroner's eyes narrowed. "Indeed. Then how is it you may be a friend of the deceased?"

Crap! "I, um, have cousins throughout the area. I visit as often as I can."

Blackham pulled a thin chain running into his vest pocket and withdrew a brass watch. Flipping open its lid, he frowned at the face. It was five minutes to ten. "Well, since it's not *technically* closing time, I suppose a quick peek is not out of order."

They followed him down a dimly lit corridor to a double-door marked *Morgue*. Unlocking one side, Blackham said, "Please do be brief. I have a date."

Chris bit his tongue and followed Kathryn inside. She flipped on the lights and paused.

"Number four," the lanky doctor said, pointing.

They walked along an embankment of stainless steel doors to number four. Chris struggled to put one foot in front of the other. His stomach was still in knots. More apprehensive than he could ever remember being, Chris hoped his tight, shallow breathing wasn't noticeable.

Kathryn opened the latch and pulled out the table. A blue shroud covered the body. She took hold of the sheet then looked up at Chris. "Sure about this, are you?"

He nodded. "It's all right. Let's do it."

CHAPTER 34

PALE BUT NOT GHOSTLY, NICHOLAS Tewdrig lay stripped of his clothing on the polished steel tray. Except for a small incision on his neck, he looked just like he did before. Chris had always scoffed at people who said the dead looked peaceful. To him they always looked . . . well, dead. There was no energy or glow in the deceased, no verve. And yet, Nick Tewdrig did not bear any of the sallow, empty characteristics of a corpse. He literally looked like he was resting, as if blissfully asleep. There was even the slightest hint of a grin on his lips. He appeared . . . *happy*.

Kathryn flashed Chris a glance of inquiry mixed with sympathy.

"He looks remarkably well," he heard himself whisper.

"So this *is* him?" she asked.

"Yes," Chris said, resisting the urge to place his hand gently on Nick's shoulder.

"Are you certain?"

"Yes, 100 percent. This is Nicholas Tewdrig from Trellech."

She nodded. "Anything appear out of the ordinary or amiss?"

Chris looked closely at the peaceful old man. "I don't remember this wound," he said pointing to the neck sutures.

"It's where they drain the blood during embalming," she explained.

"*Doctor* Christian?" Blackham asked, his voice filled with suspicion. "Is that a real title?"

"Yes," Chris said, glaring at him. "From the University of Calgary. Graduated with honors, class of twenty ten. I teach at the academy there." He marched to a wall phone and yanked the handset free. "Would you like to call and verify my credentials? I believe it's just past lunchtime there."

"No, no, that is not necessary," Blackham fairly blustered, pulling out his pocket watch again. "Will there be anything else then, Doctors?"

"No," Kathryn said.

"Yes," Chris countered. "Did my friend have any personal effects with him? A walking staff with an alabaster crown perhaps?" While he tried to keep his voice filled with accusation, he could not mask his overall sadness.

Blackham looked like a cat caught with canary feathers protruding from its mouth. He walked over to a door with his name on it and unlocked it.

"Your friend's clothing and effects are held in storage next door. They will be cremated along with his body if unclaimed within two weeks. Standard procedure and all, you understand."

"As it is back home," Chris said evenly.

Blackham entered without switching on the lights and returned with Nick's cane. He handed it to Chris. "It seemed a shame to destroy such an elegant piece of craftsmanship," he said without meeting Chris's eyes.

The sight of the alabaster knob and polished wood filled Chris with an unexpected rush of emotion. His throat tightened, and unbidden tears stung his eyes. He drew several sharp, shallow breaths. Then, steeling himself, he turned to Kathryn. "This is his cane."

"Yes, I recognize it from your description."

Blackham cleared his throat. "Dr. Christian. I wish to apologize for this regrettable misunderstanding. I had no idea the deceased had any relations around here. He had no identification or any NHS records we could locate. Rest assured he has been handled with the utmost respect. You are welcome to take this walking staff and his other effects if you wish. And I extend the sincere condolences of the hospital."

Chris held the cane to his chest, feeling Nick's presence as he did. The rich timbre of the old man's voice filled his mind; the memory of his penetrating gaze pierced Chris's heart. He gathered solace from it, as if it radiated an aura of serenity.

"Thank you," he managed to say.

Blackham cleared his throat again. "Very good. Will that be all then?"

Chris nodded and returned to Nick's lifeless form. He smiled and gently placed his hand on the top of the old man's head. "Good-bye, my friend," he whispered. "Be at peace. You fought the good fight. Rest eternal now."

After a minute or two of silence, Blackham cleared his throat a third time.

Chris looked up. "You said his other effects are next door? May I see them, please?"

The coroner led them to a narrow room lined with cubby nooks. Without a word, he pulled out a plastic tote numbered FOUR and set it on a countertop. Inside were a few coins, a wad of banknotes folded in a brass clip, a wrinkled handkerchief, and a pocket-sized copy of the New Testament.

"This was all that was on him?" Chris asked.

"Yes," Blackham said, again glancing at his watch.

As Chris began to fill his pockets with Nick's effects, the coroner grabbed a clipboard with a pen attached. "You'll need to sign for the items, Doctor."

"Of course."

"Thank you, Percy," Kathryn said as Chris scribbled his name. "You've been very helpful."

"Not at all," he said, accepting back the clipboard.

"Yes, thank you," Chris echoed. "We won't take any more of your time."

Silently, the three doctors left the morgue and hailed the elevator.

Stepping into the cab, Chris offered his hand and said, "Sorry for my short temper, Doctor. I appreciated the opportunity to say good-bye to my friend. It meant a lot to me."

The coroner took his hand in a brief shake. "My pleasure, Dr. Christian."

"I hope we didn't make you too late for your date."

"Not to worry," he said arrogantly. "I'm sure she'll understand."

CHAPTER 35

AFTER SETTLING INTO KATHRYN'S RANGE Rover, Chris asked, "Is there any way of confirming what Nick died from?"

"Yes, of course. I can access the files as soon as they're posted, but that may take a few days. The preliminary finding is 'of natural causes,' but the autopsy has yet to be performed. All aspects of healthcare move dreadfully slow in the UK, especially in the shires."

"The shires?"

"Pretty much anywhere that's not England proper. Wales is a very old country, as you know, but that doesn't mean it gets seniority or special consideration. Socialized healthcare carries with it a slog of bureaucracy and paperwork, which typically makes a sticky hash of everything."

"But he will be autopsied, right?"

"Most definitely, yes. All unexplained or unwitnessed deaths are autopsied. It's the same in your country, is it not?"

"I really don't know," he said, once again wishing he had a little more information.

As Kathryn maneuvered out of the city and back onto the country roads, Chris felt crushed under a weight of despondency. He couldn't believe how much he missed a man he'd barely met. Curiously, it felt as if he'd lost his father again: the same emptiness, the same remorse, the same pangs of guilt.

"I am truly sorry about your friend," she offered sincerely.

"Thank you," he said, forcing himself to think rationally. "In truth, I really didn't know that much about him. Well—let me rephrase that: I know *about* him, I just never got to know *him*."

"I understand precisely," she said. "I've felt the same about many of my patients."

They rode for a long time without talking. Kathryn turned on her sound system and selected some Delius. The music was as soothing as the Vaughan Williams. And just as melancholy.

Chris held the walking staff in his fingers, turning it as Nick had when he'd visited. The old man's words came back, haunting Chris as if a voice of warning. The mantle had fallen to him. It didn't matter that he didn't believe in it; the power was now his to heal the sick. The fact he'd openly denied that mantle the past few days encumbered Chris with shame. His was a gift to be shared, not horded, not hidden. How many opportunities had already passed him by because of his denial? How many people *could* he have helped had he accepted the call in the first place? And yet, could he honestly accept such a calling, such a burden, if he still had doubts?

Slowly rotating, the spherical head of the cane picked up the glow from the dashboard and passing traffic, reflecting bands of muted color like a subtle aurora borealis rippling across its milky surface. It was beautiful. He couldn't blame Dr. Blackham for wanting it.

Chris searched his pocket and pulled out Nick's relic, the Dial of Ahaz. Next to the orb, it looked like the same material but with different marbling and a slightly lighter hue. Collingswood desperately wanted the Dial, so much so that he was willing to kill for it. Only, he hadn't wanted it for its beauty; he'd wanted it for its power. The charlatan sought after the fame and glory and wealth it could bring, but that was not how it was to be used. Nick had issued a warning never to lose the Dial, saying the consequences could be deadly.

Chris frowned, pondering the edict. Would the deadly consequences be to himself, to the Dial, or to those that weren't supposed to possess it? Would the same thing that happened to Collingswood happen to anyone who misused the sacred artifact?

Chris then noticed Kathryn glancing at the Dial. Sensing her curiosity and her confusion, he said, "It looks like the same kind of stone, don't you think?"

"There is a definite similarity in them."

"Maybe I *should* follow your advice."

"My advice?"

"Yeah. Go to the university and ask about the stone and these markings. Find out if they really are what Nick claimed."

"And if they are, what then?" she asked. "Does that prove they're imbued with supernatural powers?"

"I . . . I really don't know. But Collingswood thought so. So does Father Llewellyn."

"Is that the reason he shot the father?"

"Partly," Chris said then hesitated. "I think he wanted to see it in action. That's why he didn't just simply steal it."

He thought he heard a subdued huff. The good doctor was having as much difficulty accepting this as he was.

"Look, I'm fishing for answers too. There's a force at work here that I'm not familiar with. It frightens me because it requires belief in . . . well, in *spiritual* matters. And that's something I'm just not comfortable with."

"Like faith healing," she stated.

"Perhaps. Maybe. I'm not sure."

She frowned. "So you're not sure if *you* healed Father Llewellyn or if your magic rock did, is that it?"

He sighed. "Yes and no. My head is telling me no, but my heart is saying yes. I wish I had a definitive answer because all I have right now are assumptions and guesses."

"And a gut feeling," she added.

"Yeah. A strong one."

She glanced at the Dial again. Chris thought he saw in her expression a desire to believe. But it passed just as quickly as it had come.

"Look, Kathryn, I've been struggling with this ever since the car accident. I still have a hard time believing it, but I've seen it happen twice now. I've seen—for want of a better word—*miraculous* healings that I was—again for want of a better word—an *instrument* in. I don't know how, and I don't know why. I just know what I've seen."

"Because of that bit of rock."

"Maybe not completely, but yes, I believe it is."

She was pensive for a long while. Chris occasionally caught slight indications of body language: her head shaking no then nodding yes, and an occasional shrug. Then, finally, she said, "I don't know, Chris. I believe in God and miracles. I truly do. I've seen things in my practice that defy explanation. But what you're suggesting is miracles *on command* with that, that talisman."

"I know. As a man of logic and history, I think it's a ridiculous notion. And yet something else is going on here that *is* undeniable. That's why I want to check everything out as soon as I can."

"I understand," she said, with little emotion. "Where to now?"

"Your office, if it's okay. I'd like to use the Internet."

"Why?"

He absently rubbed his neck. "It's a place to start."

They again rode in silence. The music helped fill in the emptiness. As a light mist began to hiss against the windshield, Kathryn turned on her fog lamps and wipers. All too soon, they were back at the hospital—and all too soon Chris's problems started up again.

Two police cars sat out front with their lights flashing.

"Should we run?" Chris asked, slumping down in his seat.

"Too late," she said, slowing to a stop. "They've already seen my car."

CHAPTER 36

Detective Westcott tapped on Kathryn's window. She rolled it down. "Yes?"

"Out for a leisurely midnight drive then, Doctor?" he asked with an edge of suspicion.

"No. I was deep sea fishing. Why do you ask?"

"Sure you haven't been aiding and abetting a mob affiliate wanted by MI5?"

She barked a short guffaw. "Since I don't know anyone who fits that category, I should think not."

"Come, come now, Dr. Ingledew. We both know I'm talking about Christian Pendragon. The hospital staff says he was here not long ago. Do you know his current whereabouts?"

"Haven't the foggiest."

Lying under a sheet of blue plastic in the cargo hold of the Rover, Chris couldn't see Westcott's expression, but he could guess what it might be.

"Who have you been with since you left work just before eight o'clock this evening?"

"None of your business, Detective."

"Actually, ma'am—"

"Doctor."

He scoffed. "Yes, yes, I forgot. Actually, *Doctor*, it is in point of fact precisely my business."

"Well, I haven't been with any criminals, I can tell you that," she said firmly. "And I don't appreciate being called on the carpet in front of my place of employment in the middle of the night. If you'd like to question me, please make an appointment with my nurse."

"Actually, I was thinking of calling the hospital director and telling him one of his physicians is being uncooperative with an official MI5 investigation that involves his facility. Tell me, Doctor, how do you think he'd respond to such a call in the middle of the night, hmm?"

"Oh, he'd probably feel the same about you as I do," she said evenly.

Westcott forced a brief chuckle. "Charming to the last."

"Listen, Detective," Kathryn continued. "I shouldn't be blocking the drive like this, and my interior is getting soaked. Come on inside where it's warm and dry, and we'll discuss this like civilized people, shall we?"

There was a lapse in the conversation. Chris saw the flash of a torch beam pass over the thin plastic. He hoped he'd done a good enough job wriggling between the boxes and materials back there. With luck, he'd look like nothing more than a bundle of old clothing.

"If you prefer," Westcott finally said.

Chris heard her window roll up and felt the forward motion of the Rover.

"Stay down," she said softly. "This shouldn't take long."

"Should I run?" he whispered.

"Absolutely not. They will be watching the area closely now that I've returned, won't they. And if you take my Rover, they'll add auto theft to your list of charges, you can wager."

He didn't reply. What could he say?

"Not to worry, Chris. You've got me curious about your trinket and your newfound abilities. I'm not saying I believe you. But I'd like to see you get some answers."

The Range Rover pulled to a stop, and he heard the ratcheting of the parking brake.

"Kathryn?"

"Yes?"

"Thank you."

All was still. Chris heard nothing but the soft hiss of the light rain and the ticking of the drivetrain cooling. Then, "Don't thank me yet, Chris. As I said, I'm not sure where I stand on all this, but I'd like some answers too." There was a slight pause. "I don't see Father Llewellyn's car here, so I assume he's gone back to the rectory. Frankly, I'm surprised Detective Westcott is still pestering you. Surely the father's affidavit of your innocence would remove the focus from you."

"My thoughts exactly."

"Well. Never you fear. I'll sort things out soon enough, then we'll find a place for you to stay for the night."

"Thanks, Kathryn. I owe you."

"Yes, you do—"

A loud knock on the window interrupted Kathryn. She let out a chirping scream as her door was yanked open.

"Is there a problem in here?" Westcott's voice came through.

"Good heavens, Detective," Kathryn said breathlessly. "You gave me a fright. No, there's no problem. Come, let's get inside. It's freezing."

"Just one minute, please," the detective said. "I'd like to have an officer search your vehicle."

"Yes, of course. Be my guest," she said without pause. "But I'm going inside where it's dry. Oh, and you might want to warn them not to disturb anything. It's all very delicate and highly contagious."

"What is?" Westcott asked.

"The materials in the boot, of course. Don't you recognize the biohazard emblem on that plastic sheet back there?" she said as if talking to a five-year-old. "Unless your men have respirators or bio-containment suits, I suggest they not jostle things too much."

What?! Chris almost screamed.

"And just what is a highly contagious substance doing in your car?"

"Honestly now, Detective. What kind of a crime sleuth are you, anyway? I am a doctor of medicine, am I not? I transport substances to and from the lab in Cardiff Hospital all the time. If you'd like to call Cardiff, they'll tell you I was there just this evening. Now let's get inside before we freeze to death, shall we?"

The car door closed and locked. Chris heard muffled conversation and fading footfalls. Then there was just his coarse breathing under the thin plastic. And a sour chemical odor he hadn't noticed before.

CHAPTER 37

FLASHLIGHTS CONTINUED TO SCAN THE interior of the Rover, but no one tried to open the doors. Kathryn's deception had worked for now—at least he hoped it was a deception. *She wouldn't really hide me with a bunch of bio-hazardous materials . . . would she?*

A second thought occurred to him moments later. Would his breath fog the windows of the car—proving someone was inside? He opted not to worry about things he could not change, but he still caught himself holding his breath intermittently.

Instead, he tried to focus on why Kathryn was helping him. Yes, she said she'd like some answers, but why? How would *she* benefit from his calling, if in fact she accepted it as true? He hoped it wasn't for the same reasons as Collingswood. She was a doctor; her practice could definitely gain prestige from something as amazing as the Dial. With all her questions and willingness to help, was she secretly maneuvering to benefit from the relic? Father Llewellyn had mentioned Collingswood was one of *many* treasure seekers. Even Collingswood had said he wouldn't be the last person seeking the Dial. Others knew about it. Like those searching for the Holy Grail, there could be countless Dial hunters combing England for such a priceless possession. Was the pretty Dr. Kathryn Ingledew the next thief in line?

Chris scolded himself for such a thought. If that'd been the case, he'd be in police custody right now. Maybe she was sincere in her intent—just as Chris was. After all, why wouldn't she be?

More scattered thoughts, rationales, and assumptions raced through Chris's mind as he lay awaiting Kathryn's return. What was he going to do? How would he handle something as life-altering as this, if it turned out to be factual? *Is it real? Is it true?* The minute that question entered his mind, an inner rebuttal resoundingly confronted it: *You know it is.*

The battle in his mind raged on. He never came to any solid conclusions. Just as he didn't know exactly when it was he fell asleep.

* * *

The car door opened, jarring him from his slumber.

"Must you breathe so heavily?" Kathryn asked, shutting her door. "The windows are so fogged up it looks like a couple of high-schoolers are making out in here."

"What was I supposed to do, hold my breath?"

"Why not? I wasn't gone *that* long."

Chris couldn't tell if she was teasing or angry. "So is it safe to come out?"

"Yes. The authorities have gone."

He pushed back the plastic tarp and sat up. His muscles were knotted and stiff, and his head ached from the noxious chemical smell.

"Please tell me you didn't hide me next to hazardous substances just for fun," he said, crawling into the front seat.

"Don't be a bore, Chris," she said, starting the engine. "I acquired that tarp back in college as a lark. It has a bio-hazard insignia on it, but it was never used as such."

"Then what is that smell back there?"

"Turpentine, most likely. I like to paint. Oils, you know?"

"Ah. Good. What time is it, anyway?" he asked, rubbing his hands briskly. It was bitterly cold in the car and ghostly dark outside. The spectral glow around the parking lot lamps still pulsated eerily.

"Half past one o'clock. I'd invite you in, but I'm afraid letting you use my office computer at this hour would raise questions. Here's a coffee to help warm you," she said, handing him a Styrofoam cup.

"Thanks." He took a sip. "So you talked with Westcott for over an hour?"

"Of course not. I can't stand that man."

"Oh. Is there some bad history behind that statement?" he asked with a smile.

"More or less. Now, let's get you to a hotel, shall we?"

"But I haven't got any money."

"Yes, you have. How much is in that bundle of Mr. Tewdrig's?"

He'd forgotten about that. He pulled the bill clip from his pocket and leafed through the British pounds. "Wow. A lot more than I thought."

"That's what I suspected," she said, putting her Rover in gear.

The Riverside Hotel was not far from the hospital. Using Chris's money, Kathryn secured a room, returned to the Rover, and handed Chris the key. "I booked you a cozy room. Nothing fancy, mind, but you'll be comfortable. Get some sleep, Chris. I'll be by to collect you in the morning."

"Okay. Then what?"

"Then we'll look into authenticating that bit of stone you put so much faith into."

He rolled his eyes. "If I had faith, I wouldn't feel the need to authenticate it."

She smiled as if he'd just made a joke, but he was deadly serious. He was not the kind of person to blindly accept things he didn't understand. That included Kathryn's involvement.

"Listen, I know I've asked this already, but why are you doing this?"

She stared vacantly at her fingers as they fiddled with her keys. "Get some sleep, Chris. We'll talk in the morning, ay?"

Not knowing what else to say, he nodded and stepped out of the Rover. Kathryn drove off in a swirl of mist. Chris looked across the river at the Monnow Bridge. The ancient stone edifice, barely visible through the thick drizzle, was an engineering marvel—especially considering when it was constructed. Everything was done by hand; all the massive stones were moved by human muscle, ropes, and beasts of burden. The task must have seemed insurmountable, but the builders didn't balk simply because it appeared difficult, if not impossible. They saw what was required and just did it. It was very much like the task that now lay before him.

Chris found his room, removed his coat and shoes, and collapsed on the bed. His thoughts were still spinning with tornado-like velocity. He wasn't sure he could get back to sleep even if he wanted to. His body screamed for rest, while his mind demanded answers.

Sitting up, he removed the Dial from his pocket. Holding it in the light of his nightstand, he compared it to the orb on Nick's cane. It wasn't from the same quarry, but the characteristics were very similar.

Then Chris noticed something peculiar at the base of the alabaster sphere: there was a thin seam where a fine metal band separated the stone and wooden staff. Taking hold, he cautiously twisted the stone counterclockwise. It didn't budge. When he applied more force, it finally gave way and turned in a screw-like fashion. The male end of the cane entered the stone about a half inch. Removing the cane, he tipped the orb on end and saw that it was hollow—but not empty. Inside was a tiny scroll.

Gingerly extracting the scroll, he discovered it was a piece of thick parchment. Luckily, it hadn't dried out or rotted with mildew over the years. He paused, wondering just how many years that amounted to. The parchment was stiff but pliable.

Taking exquisite care, he slowly unrolled the tiny scroll. Written on it were seven words in Roman characters, all capitals:

NOBLY THRU WHITE FOG HATH I LED.

CHAPTER 38

A KNOCK ON CHRIS'S DOOR awoke him. When his eyes focused, he saw it was 9:16. Cursing softly, he stumbled to the door and opened it. Kathryn stood outside, frowning.

"Please tell me you're not still asleep."

"Not anymore," he said, matting down his bed-hair. "Sorry. I guess I forgot to set my alarm."

"Set your alarm? For nine o'clock in the morning? Do you usually sleep this late?"

"No, I'm usually an early riser. It was a late night, remember?"

Her frown softened. "Okay, I'll give you that," she said. "I suppose I'm simply used to odd hours."

"Thanks. Give me ten minutes, okay?"

"Right."

Chris washed his face and shaved; then he dressed and met her in the lobby. They walked to a coffee shop on the corner and purchased some cream-filled pastries that were so rich they must have been a thousand calories each. Kathryn ordered Earl Gray tea; Chris opted for Oolong.

"So about last night. What happened with Westcott?" Chris wondered.

"He asked a bunch of inane questions and such. Oh, I know he's just doing his job, but does he have to be so priggish about it? Some folk can't get even a little authority without it going straight to their head."

"Is that why you're helping me? Because you have a dislike of authority figures?"

She sipped her tea and cast her gaze out the shop window. "Partly. But that's unimportant right now, okay? After Westcott left, I sent some e-mails."

"At one in the morning?" Chris asked after swallowing a bite of pastry decadence.

"Yes, of course," she said as if it wasn't a big deal. "I checked this morning and secured a visiting professor pass for you at Cardiff University. It'll allow you to roam the campus freely . . . under an assumed name, you understand."

"That's probably for the best. Am I still on Westcott's 'most wanted' list?"

"Regrettably, yes. He has Father Llewellyn's deposition in your behalf, but he also has the handgun with both yours and Collingswood's fingerprints on it. I told him about Collingswood's death. He can get fingerprints from the body, but he says he still needs yours."

"Mine are on file with US customs, I'm certain."

"Yes, but he wants them from you. He said anyone can falsify public records."

"So now I'm suspected of forgery too. Anything else?"

"Well, he knows you didn't shoot Father Llewellyn, but because your prints are on the weapon and you ran away, he still believes you may be involved in organized crime."

Chris set down his pastry and rubbed his puffy eyes. "Great."

"Don't worry about that. Let's focus on one issue at a time, the first being authentication of that holy relic."

He smiled at her description that the Dial was holy. That meant she didn't consider it a complete hoax. Strangely, the fact that she hadn't automatically written it off was encouraging. Perhaps even faith-promoting.

After breakfast, they climbed into her Rover and headed south. Traffic was about what Chris expected for a Friday. Luckily, he saw no police cars along the way.

Kathryn cued her stereo to play Maurice Ravel.

"Did you know Vaughan Williams was a student of Ravel's?" Chris said with a nerdy grin—at least it felt nerdy to him.

She glanced his way. "Truly?"

"Yep. I can't remember how many years he studied with him, just that he did."

She smiled as if he'd just done something cute.

Chris felt pretty foolish, not because he couldn't remember the history of Ralph Vaughan Williams, but because he hated sounding like a know-it-all.

As they passed a turnoff for a town called Glenelg, Kathryn announced, "The palindrome province."

He turned to her. "Excuse me?"

"Glenelg. It's a palindrome; it reads the same forward and backward."

"Oh yeah," he said, remembering. "Like 'radar.'"

She rolled her eyes playfully. "Honestly. I expected a man with a doctorate in history to do better than *radar*. Haven't you ever read the *Poisonwood Bible*? Barbara Kingsolver?"

"I'm afraid not."

"You know history and music but not literature? That strikes me as queer."

"Meaning 'odd,' right?"

She frowned in confusion.

"Never mind. Trust me, I've read my fair share of lit, classic and contemporary. A lot of history comes from stories and journals and such, but I don't remember many employing palindromes."

"I adore such word play, especially palindromes that make up entire sentences. Like: 'A Santa dog lived as a devil god at NASA.'"

He scribbled the sentence in the air, trying to visualize it. "Wow. That's pretty cool."

But her reference to Santa brought back the purpose of visiting the university in Cardiff. Santa. St. Nick. St. Nicholas the Giver, the Healer. It also brought to mind the cryptic message he'd found in Nick's cane.

"So you like word games, huh? How good are you?"

"Very. You don't want to challenge me at Scrabble. Why?"

"I have a sentence for you. It doesn't really mean anything to me just yet, but I think it has a lot to do with what's going on. I found it in Nick's journal and again in a compartment in his walking staff."

"Okay."

"It's 'Nobly thru white fog hath I led.' That mean anything to you?"

"Well, it's not a palindrome," she said straight off. "But . . ."

Her brows knitted in concentration while keeping her eyes on the road. Her lips moved, silently voicing the sentence over and over. The music played softly as she contemplated the riddle. Chris watched the countryside pass by, again marveling at how green everything was, even with summer not fully in swing.

She was still working out the sentence when she took the exit to Cardiff. "I think you've got me, Chris. Could it possibly be an anagram?"

Astonished, he said, "I hadn't considered that."

"Well, while you're learning about your stone tile, I'll grab some paper and start working out variables. 'Nobly through white fog hath I led'?" she repeated, just to make sure.

"Yes. But *through* is shortened to t-h-r-u."

"Ah. Good to know."

They pulled into a parking slot reserved for visitors at the administration building and headed inside. Kathryn again did most of the talking. He signed for his pass using the name printed on the reservation: Professor Chris Ingledew.

"I told them you were relation," she explained quietly.

Chris was handed a pamphlet-sized map of the campus and his ID badge.

"Do you want to walk around first or go right to it?" she asked as they exited the building. It was a beautiful day with only a few clouds in the sky.

"Let's get right to it, if you don't mind. I think I'll go to the geology department to find out what kind of stone this is."

"I thought you said it was alabaster."

"Nick said it was alabaster. I just want to make sure. Then I'll find the language arts department to see if anyone can decipher the markings."

She nodded and glanced over the map with Chris.

"I'll be in the library," she said, pointing at the map. "Let's meet there at say . . . one o'clock, shall we?"

"Sounds good."

Chris had to admit to an abundance of giddiness whisking through him. He hadn't felt this happy or excited since he'd landed in this country. He felt like he truly had direction again.

Yes, he was still under investigation, a fugitive from the law, but once he knew more about the Dial, he'd be able to make sense of the rest of this mystery. More importantly, he'd then be able to decide once and for all what to do about it.

"I hope you find what you're looking for," Kathryn said before walking briskly toward the library.

"So do I," he sighed.

CHAPTER 39

CHRIS ENTERED THE FOYER OF the geology department and caught the attention of a pretty girl with copper-red hair. "Can I help you, sir?" Her accent was decidedly Scottish.

"Yes. I'm Professor Ingledew, visiting from the United States. While touring the countryside, I was given a curious stone that I'd like to get an opinion on." He'd rehearsed what he was going to say while walking.

"Have you now? A curious rock, you say?" Her Rs rolled mellifluously.

Chris pulled it from his pocket and held it out just as a lean, middle-aged man in a beige cardigan passed behind the girl. He cast a quick glance at the Dial and stopped in his tracks.

"Nice bit of alabaster you have there, my good man," he said. "Might I inquire as to how you came by it?"

"A friend gave it to me," Chris answered simply.

The man stepped closer and drew a pair of reading glasses from his breast pocket. Donning them, he asked, "Was this gentleman a world traveler?"

"That's highly probable. But he was from Wales originally."

"Was?" the man asked, looking over the rim of his spectacles.

"Regrettably, yes. He passed away day before yesterday."

The girl gasped softly. "Oh, I am so sorry, sir. It must be a terrible loss for you."

"Yes. It was quite unexpected."

The man extended his hand. "Professor Keogh, department head, geology."

Chris shook it. "Chris Ingledew, history professor, Gonzaga University."

"A pleasure, Professor Ingledew," Keogh said, again peering at the stone. "Might I?"

Chris handed him the Dial.

Keogh pulled a small magnifying glass from his other pocket and moved to a window to examine the stone in natural light. "Marvelous. Simply marvelous."

"I'm curious why you asked if my friend was a world traveler?"

"Simple deduction, Professor. This is quite an exquisite piece of Mesopotamian alabaster."

Chris wasn't surprised. Nick had claimed it was from that region. "How can you tell?"

"Come look," he beckoned. Chris rounded the desk at which the redhead sat and stepped beside the professor. "You can see the striations just under the polished surface, here?" he said, pointing with the nail of his little finger. "And here . . . and here again?"

"I think so."

"Please, use this," Keogh said, handing Chris his small magnifier.

Chris examined the stone more closely, still unsure what he was looking for. "Um, okay, yeah, I think I see them."

"Beautiful, is it not?" the professor crooned.

"It's lovely, but I'm afraid I don't see the significance."

"The twinning, Professor, the polysynthetic calcite twinning. You see, common alabaster—that is to say, the alabaster used in medieval Europe— is mostly of gypsum composition. But alabaster from the Middle East and Asia, that was almost exclusively calcite. And because this twinning is so dense, I conclude it is Mesopotamian in origin."

Very little of what Keogh said made sense to Chris, but he took the expert's word for it. "And why would a person use calcite alabaster as opposed to gypsum?"

"This specimen was most likely used outdoors, perhaps in a mosaic fresco or a mural. Gypsum is too soft and washes away in continued exposure. If you'd like, we can take this to the lab and test it to be certain."

"Test it how?"

"With hydrochloric acid."

The impassioned warning of Collingswood suddenly came to mind. *They'll defile it. They'll destroy it.* He cleared his throat. "Acid?"

"Yes, yes. We take a small fragment, a millimeter or so, and drop hydrochloric acid on it. If it effervesces, it's calcite alabaster; if not, it's gypsum."

Chris tactfully took the Dial from Keogh's hand. "I'm sorry, Professor, but I can't allow even a millimeter of this to be damaged. It . . . has sentimental value, you see."

"Yes, of course. I understand. But may I be permitted to snap a photograph or two?"

Red flags flashed through Chris's mind. A picture would ID the Dial to treasure hunters, perhaps some as despicable as Collingswood. And that might lead them to him.

"I'm sorry, but I'd rather not."

"I beg of you, Professor Ingledew. Just one snapshot. It won't damage the artifact, I promise you that."

Chris hesitated.

"Oh, go on, Professor," the young receptionist said. "One wee picture won't turn it into a golem."

"It's not that," Chris backpedaled. "It's just that I want to keep its existence secret until I can learn more about it."

"Learn what, precisely?" Keogh asked.

"Well, like these engravings, for instance. I'd like to find out what they say."

"Ah." The professor stepped to a desk phone and punched in a number. He waited just a moment before speaking. "Reggie, Abel. Listen, I have a chap here who has in his possession a shard of Mesopotamian alabaster with some very curious markings on it." He paused, listening. "Yes, yes, I'm quite certain it's Mesopotamian." Pause. "Yes, of course. Listen, do me a favor, old chum, and take a look at it, will you? He can come right—" He paused again, being interrupted. "I see. A lecture. Oh very well, then. Can he meet with you afterward? Splendid. Thanks, Reggie. Let me know what you find, will you? Fine—what's that? Oh. He's an American; Chris Ingledew, professor of history." A final pause. "Yes, but this chap's not as irregular as all that. I think you'll find his specimen rather interesting. Right-o. Thank you."

Keogh hung up and turned to Chris. "You're all set, Professor. Go to the linguistics department and ask to meet Dr. Reginald Smart. And please don't make jokes about his name. He's very sensitive, you understand—although the man *is* nothing short of brilliant, to say the least. He's the best man I know in Middle Eastern languages. Unless I miss my hunch, those markings are Babylonian."

"Not Aramaic?" Chris wondered.

"Aramaic? No, no, I don't believe so; but I'm not a linguist, either. Aramaic would mean this specimen came from an ancient temple site, which would make it a national heirloom, which might indicate that it was obtained illegally—" He stopped short and took a step back. "And . . . you do not want any pictures taken . . ."

Chris bristled at the inference. "I assure you I did not steal it, nor did my friend. In fact, someone has already tried to steal it from *me*. That's why I don't want anyone to know I have it."

Keogh gave Chris a dubious look. He pulled an unlit pipe from his cardigan and noisily chomped down on the stem. It was supposed to be an act of defiance; to Chris it seemed somewhat over-the-top.

"Let me explain, Dr. Keogh. I *am* a legitimate professor of history," he said, showing his temporary ID. "I know the importance of protecting national treasures and ancient artifacts from looters and sycophants. I promise that once I find out what this really is, I will return it to its proper owner—even if I have to fly to Turkey or wherever it belongs."

Keogh chewed on the pipe stem while examining the ID card, then handed it back. "Very well then, Professor Ingledew. You'll find Dr. Smart in the linguistics department of the humanities building. He can meet with you in about an hour."

"Thank you," Chris said with a sincere smile. "I appreciate your help."

"Good luck, Professor Ingledew. Not a name one easily forgets, is it?" Keogh said, lightly tapping the side of his temple with his pipe stem. "Ingledew."

The message was clear: if there was any mention of a missing piece of Mesopotamian alabaster with Middle Eastern markings, Keogh would know where to send the authorities.

Chris nodded his understanding and left the office.

CHAPTER 40

THE HUMANITIES BUILDING WAS ON the opposite side of the library. Chris was tempted to peek in on Kathryn but decided against it. She was undoubtedly focused on unscrambling the message found in the orb and would disdain any interruption. Secretly, he hoped she'd unscramble something that would disqualify him as the Dial-bearer. If not, maybe the foreign words scrawled on the Dial would spell out how to negate the burden. Knowing his luck, both messages would only seal it.

Pausing at a large water feature, Chris referenced his map of the campus. There were scores of old buildings he could explore, including a history museum that looked like it'd been constructed during Arthurian times. Tempting, but he knew himself well enough not to go there. He'd be stuck the rest of the day.

Instead, he grabbed a soda from a vending machine and took a leisurely stroll, enjoying the uncharacteristically pleasant weather and sunshine. The students he saw were clean cut and well-mannered. There was the occasional rebel with purple hair and five pounds of metal studs in his face, but for the most part, everyone looked cultured and, well, classically Welsh. He was glad his local clothing helped him blend in.

The humanities building was an old four-story, brownstone structure. English ivy crept tenaciously up one side and along half the building's front façade. Pigeons cooed happily, perched on the many stone window sills, and sparrows flitted and chirped in and out of hollows in the ivy.

Inside, the reception desk was manned by a young student who looked like he'd barely graduated from prep school.

"Good morning, sir," the kid greeted cheerily.

"Morning," said Chris. "I'm here to see Dr. Smart."

"Yes, sir. His office is at the end of the corridor, door on the right. Would you like me to escort you, sir?"

"No, thank you. I'll find it."

Chris headed down the hall, admiring the old-style architecture of the building. Posters and fliers lined the walls between office doors—publicizing upcoming lectures, performances, and events—along with a collage of typical college minutia: study group announcements, roommates wanted, tutors available, etc.

Dr. Smart's office was clearly marked. Chris knocked on the door.

"Come."

He entered a room that looked like the aftermath of an earthquake. Stacks of papers rose from the floor like stalagmites. Books were scattered helter-skelter. A small couch offered no place to sit due to piles of debris strewn across the cushions. Dr. Smart sat behind a desktop that probably hadn't seen daylight in many fortnights. He was a portly man in his late sixties. He wore a tweed blazer and a mismatched bow tie. His thin brown hair was impeccably plastered in place; his eyebrows resembled two large, wooly caterpillars perched just above deep eye sockets.

He stood, offering his hand. "*Doctor* Ingledew, is it?"

"Yes. I have a PhD in history. But I prefer to be called Chris."

"Oh, my," the man flustered, as if embarrassed by the informality. "I'll call you Professor, if it's all the same, *hmm*? Please, take a seat. Shall I call for some tea or coffee perhaps?"

"None for me, thank you," he said, searching for a nonexistent empty spot.

"Oh, just push the *hmm* papers to the floor. There's a good sport."

Chris gingerly moved a stack of files from a folding chair to the floor and sat. "Professor Keogh suggested you might know the origin of the inscription on a piece of alabaster I've obtained."

Smart's expression was close to one of offense, but it quickly changed to a smirk of superiority. "You Yanks do have a reputation for dispensing formalities and getting straight to the point, *hmm*?" He chuckled warmly—with a healthy dose of condescension. "Very well then, let's see what you brought me, shall we?"

Chris set the Dial on Smart's desk blotter. The professor retrieved a magnifying glass from a desk drawer. He bent to examine the specimen, turning it slowly, taking in every angle, humming softly as he did.

"Might I ask where you acquired such a unique sample?"

"A friend gave it to me. He never mentioned where he got it. Can you read the inscriptions?"

"Yes, *hmm* yes, I believe so."

Of everyone Chris had shown the Dial to, this man seemed the least enthusiastic. Or perhaps he was simply too old or too smug to display such novice excitement.

"And . . ." Chris prompted.

"Patience, Professor Ingledew," Smart said without looking up. "As a doctor of history, you will agree that the most *hmm* reliable records we possess of all things ancient are the ones patient enough to stand the test of time, *hmm*?"

"Yes, I would agree," Chris said, even though he knew it was impossible for an inanimate object to possess patience.

After listening to another three minutes of meaningless hums, Chris stood and made his way to a bookshelf overflowing with texts. There, he found several references on Middle Eastern languages. He pulled out one on Aramaic and began thumbing through the pages.

"A lucky guess, Professor," Smart said, seeing the book in his hand. "I too believe this is a form of Aramaic script. Regrettably, it contains only two short sentences; one of which is *hmm* incomplete."

Chris reshelved the book and retook his seat. "What do they say?"

"This appears to be Hebraic Aramaic. It's *hmm* one of the many dialects of the ancient tongue, of which over forty have been identified. It is the most commonly used language in *hmm* pre-Christian religious ceremonies."

"And architecture?"

Smart's bushy eyebrows inched upward irrespective of each other. "Indeed. There are few remaining examples from this epoch, but I've seen a remnant or two from digs believed to be *hmm* former temple sites." He held up the Dial to catch a slant of sunlight coming through his office window. "If that is what this is, it is truly a remarkable find, to be sure. Have you had it *hmm* dated yet then?"

"No. That's probably my next step. But I'd like to know what you can interpret from the markings, if you don't mind."

"Yes, of course. I believe this larger inscription says, *hmm*, 'Praise Yahweh, for He is in all.'" He pointed with the tip of a pencil. "And this smaller writing says, 'He dwells,'—or lives or resides, *hmm* depending on your interpretation—'in you for . . .' and that's where the inscription breaks off, yes?"

"Ah." Chris didn't know why he felt so disappointed. Was he really expecting to have a secret code revealed, some cryptic phrase that would grant him all the powers of the universe? If the artifact *was* a piece from *the* Dial of Ahaz, those who frequented the temple would've seen it every time they ascended the stairs. Of course it would say something like *Praise Yahweh*, the Hebrew name for God. It wouldn't say, *To cure leprosy mix two parts hyssop with one part jackal spleen and apply to rotted flesh.* It might contain prayer words or commandments, but nothing more revealing than that. Still, it was encouraging knowing the script was the temple language used at the time of Hezekiah and Isaiah.

"Well, thank you for your expertise, Dr. Smart. I appreciate your help."

He reached for the Dial, but Smart drew it away. "Professor Ingledew, a moment, please, *hmm*? If this *is* authentic, it has inestimable value in the fields of archeology, religious and secular history, linguistics, etymology— the list is exhaustive, *hmm*? You really must leave it with us for further study. It really *is* for the best."

Chris didn't like the condescending manner with which the linguist spoke. "I recognize its importance, Professor, and I fully intend to investigate it until I'm satisfied with its authenticity." He remained fixed with his hand extended, palm open.

Smart hesitated, his eyes darting between Chris's palm and the artifact in his own hand. After a heavy sigh, he placed the Dial in Chris's hand.

"*Hmm* thank you for giving me the opportunity of examining this intriguing relic, Professor Ingledew," he said, trying to maintain a professional demeanor.

"You're welcome," Chris said, pocketing the shard. "I promise to forward you any information of linguistic significance that I find on this piece."

The portly man leaned back in his chair with a discontented clearing of his throat. He pulled out a pipe and lodged it between his teeth—just like Dr. Keogh had done. Chris wondered if it was the way every British professor dealt with frustration and disappointment.

"Well, thanks again, sir," Chris offered with a smile.

"A pleasure, Professor Ingledew. Do come again when you're *hmm* in Wales or England, will you?"

Chris nodded and left, feeling even less confident that he'd find a loophole releasing him from the burden of the Dial.

CHAPTER 41

CHRIS FOUND KATHRYN SITTING ON the steps of the library, soaking in the rare sunshine. Her purse lay casually to one side. He noted how well she fit in with the students, in both appearance and manner. She had one of those faces that seemed to never age.

"Gee, Doc. Aren't you worried about melanoma?" Chris teased.

"Of course," she said frankly. "But I'm also concerned about my cholecalciferol and endorphin levels, both of which are enhanced by a little natural sunlight." She closed her eyes and tipped her head back. "More to the point, it *feels* wonderful, doesn't it?"

"Oh, I totally agree," Chris chuckled. "Plus it gives you a great-looking tan."

She peered at him with mild umbrage. "That's the least of my concerns."

Chris shifted his weight, unsure of how to respond.

"So did you find what you needed?" she continued, again closing her eyes to the sun.

"Yes. Well, yes and no. How about you?"

"Of course. I told you I'm brilliant with word puzzles. Do you want to know what your secret message really says?"

"Definite—" He stopped short, reconsidering. "I don't know. Do I?"

She offered a lopsided smile. "As with any information, you can choose to take it or leave it. It doesn't do much for me, but you'll find it helpful, I think."

He sat beside her. "Okay. What'd you find?"

"Hang on a tick. Not so fast," she said, sitting up. "What do I get out of it?"

Chris's head cocked to one side. "Excuse me?"

"What's it worth to you?" Her insistent bartering belied a dubious ulterior motive.

Just then the campus belfry chimed the noon hour. "How about lunch?"

"Lunch?"

"Well, yeah . . . to start with." He wasn't sure what he was supposed to offer. He doubted she was after money. Was it the Dial? Was this the beginning of a ploy to obtain it?

She considered him with narrowed eyes. "All right then."

They walked to the college commons and found a café. They ordered sandwiches and flavored waters, and ate under a huge horse chestnut tree. Above them, a soft breeze fluttered the silky leaves as birds frolicked cheerily amongst the branches.

"First, tell me what you discovered," Kathryn said, after one bite.

Chris fished the Dial from his pocket. "It's made of Mesopotamian alabaster; the geologist had no doubt. The linguist said the top inscription reads: 'Praise Yahweh, for He is in all,' and this smaller writing starts with 'He dwells in you for—', and that's where the stone breaks off."

Chewing slowly, she considered the words pensively. Chris ate his sandwich while trying to act uncaring. Inside, he was dying.

"Yahweh is God, correct?" she asked.

"His Hebrew name, yes. The Old Testament was written in Hebrew, but most translations use 'God' or 'Jehovah' instead of the proper noun Yahweh for various reasons."

"Interesting."

He waited for more, but she didn't offer any. "Interesting how?" he pressed. "To me, it's pretty common phraseology."

She shrugged. "Depends on your perspective. If you're of a religious inclination, it reiterates that God is everywhere, in everything, including you, correct?"

"Yes, but the second sentence is what intrigues me. 'He dwells in you for . . .' For what?"

Kathryn pulled a slip of paper from her pocket and unfolded it. "Maybe this will help. If your hidden sentence *is* an anagram, there are a number of permutations that come from it, but only a few make sense. Considering the message on your piece of alabaster, I'd say one corollary in particular is too remarkable to be mere coincidence. In fact, it's really quite brilliant."

There was that word again: *coincidence*. Was all this just some unique alignment of happenstance? Or was God trying to tell him something? Had Nick been telling the truth all along?

With a knot in his chest, he said, "I'm almost afraid to ask."

Showing him her renderings, she said, "'Nobly thru white fog hath I led' rearranges to 'Through faith thy will be done.' Only 'through' is not truncated as it is in the first example; it's the full word. It's brilliant how the two messages relate to each other," she said, becoming more excited as she progressed. "Although both 'through's are synonymous, in the first instance, 'thru' is used as an adjective—as in 'moving from one side to another,' see? But in the anagram, it's used as a preposition—as in 'by' or 'via.'"

Chris felt like he'd been punched in the gut. He could barely breathe. All at once, the whirling scraps of information lined up. His mind compared, matched, correlated, and confirmed their meanings. One word was the synonym of another; one term meant something different when translated with a different emphasis, while also corroborating the original meaning.

"I wonder if your friend Nicholas knew about this," she pondered aloud.

"I'm certain he did," he said in little more than a breath.

"What do you suppose the 'white fog' represents?"

Chris stared blankly at the ground in front of him. The pleasant textures of the day faded from his perception. It was as if everything had focused to a single pinpoint of truth. Softly, he whispered, "My life."

Kathryn stared at Chris as if expecting more, but he had none to offer. His mind again spun trying to find rationalizations, loopholes, any excuse by which he could refute their discoveries. But there were none. He could no longer deny the combination of facts they'd uncovered. The message was clear: Through faith *thy* will be done. It wasn't a petition, it was instructions. Not only did the word 'through' have two meanings, so did the word 'thy.' 'Thy will' meant God's will as well as Chris's will. Through faith, *he* had the power to perform miracles, if it was *God's* will they be performed.

The Dial doesn't give you power. You give it power.

Suddenly, crystal-clear understanding burst upon him, not in abrupt comprehension, but in an absolute, perfect epiphany. He felt the stoking of an all-consuming fire—one that didn't burn but was just as intense, unquenchable, and unequivocal in its fullness. Even if he wanted to deny it, he knew he couldn't. Something marvelous had happened to him—*was still* happening to him. It was true revelation. And, just as Nick had said, it was all due to the Dial.

His mouth moved, forming soft, sure words. "He dwells in you, for . . . by faith thy will be done."

"What was that?" Kathryn asked, leaning closer.

"*Thy* will." Chris continued to stare blankly ahead. "*My* will."

Kathryn waved her hand in his field of vision, breaking his trance. "Chris? Are you all right?"

He nodded slowly; his eyes wide with excitement. "It's instructions. For healing. Healing . . . with faith."

"Healing with faith?" she sighed despondently. "I was afraid of that." She no longer sounded enthused; instead, she sounded disappointed, almost resentful. "That's it then? You hold the stone in one hand and smack someone on the forehead with the other? Is that how it works? And if they don't get better, it's what?—because they didn't have enough faith?"

Chris didn't answer. In fact, he could barely hear her. Although he now believed in the Dial, his mind was again whirling. There was one last connection he was missing—*his* connection.

"I need to get back to Trellech," he said, standing. "As soon as possible."

CHAPTER 42

"WHAT'S IN TRELLECH?" KATHRYN ASKED.

"Nicholas Tewdrig's journal."

"His journal? And in it you'll find all the secret chants and rituals needed to use your magical rock; is that it?"

Chris was saddened by her swift change in demeanor. Her remark stuck him as somewhat childish. But her mockery of the Dial assailed him on a much more personal level.

"What's wrong? You sound angry."

She looked away. "I don't know. Part of me was hoping we'd find something more than that, something more substantial. 'Through faith' seems a little too passé, don't you think?"

Chris had to admit that stating miracles work through faith did come across as rather simplistic; but *this* passage went much deeper than that. He knew what it meant; he just wasn't sure it meant *him*.

"Please don't be upset," he said. "We accomplished what we came here for. The Dial *is* authentic; I know that now. As far as the anagram goes, I believe you nailed it."

Her response was a less-than-conciliatory smile.

"What I hope to find in the journal is its relevance to me."

She huffed, clearly not as enthused as before. "Come on then."

On the drive back, the beautiful day quickly palled with overcast. The threatening storm muted the bucolic vistas to somber shades of gray. It wasn't very uplifting. Chris hoped it wasn't a foreshadowing of things to come—especially with Kathryn. She hadn't spoken a word since exiting the university parking lot.

Gathering his courage, he turned down the music and shifted to face her. "Look, Kathryn, I'm really sorry about all this. Believe me when I say I'm just as confused as you are."

"So now you can read minds too?"

He flinched. "No, of course not. You just seem . . . I don't know, disappointed maybe? Like the answers we found weren't the ones you were hoping for?"

He watched her jaw clench a few times, but nothing was said.

"To be honest, I wasn't sure what I was looking for. It definitely wasn't the answer I got," he said through a forced chuckle.

Kathryn drew in a long breath and blew it out slowly. "I'm sorry too, Chris. You're right: I'm not sure what I was hoping for. Just not something as cowardly as faith."

"Cowardly?"

She closed her eyes for a second. "My apologies again. Bad word choice. How about 'convenient'? 'Failsafe'? It's what religionists always fall back on, isn't it: faith?"

"Agreed," he said with a contemplative tilt of his head. "I've thought that too. But the validity of the Dial and the solving of the scroll have made everything more plausible. As fanciful as this seems, it could actually be real."

She sighed. "You truly believe that."

"Yes. But I still don't see *my* connection in all this," he said, gazing out at the lowering sky. "Why did this fall to me? How was it passed? I'm . . . I'm close to seeing it . . . but it's just not coming. It's like the hazy fog you have here all the time. When you come up to something, you first sense it's there, then you can kind of see a vague outline taking shape. But it's only if you continue forward that it becomes clear, and it's only when you make contact that you know for sure."

"Okay . . . ?"

"It's the same with history. I can tell you exactly what transpired on a specific date, but I can't always tell you why. Sometimes it makes sense; sometimes it doesn't. It depends on who recorded the event."

She gave a brief smile. "Believe it or not, I do understand. I see it in medicine quite often. A number of drugs come with the manufacturer's statement: 'Although the exact mechanism of action is unknown, we *think* this drug works in this manner . . .' and so on. Not very reassuring, is it. What they're saying is that they know the drug works, they're just not sure how or why."

He nodded rapidly. "Yes! Exactly."

"So you want to find out if you really *are* one of those Vovnik healers."

"It's more like a need."

She nodded but said no more. They traveled in silence for a time, each wrapped in their own thoughts. The soft music lulled them through the presently lackluster countryside. After a few more minutes, Kathryn cleared her throat. "I owe you an apology," she said softly. "I shouldn't have made light of your quest."

"My *quest*?" He couldn't help but grin. "I like that. But instead of the Holy Grail, it's the Dial of Ahaz."

Her grin matched his. "And you're not from Camelot."

"Spokane, Washington," he chuckled. "Gonzaga University. Not nearly as romantic sounding, is it."

"Indeed. *Gonzaga* sounds like a sexually transmitted disease."

Chris burst out laughing. "You apparently don't know it's a private *Catholic* university."

"Does that matter?" she argued innocently. "It all comes down to direct contact, not religious upbringing."

Chris froze. He stared at her wide-eyed. "Say that again?"

She frowned in confusion. "It all comes down to physical contact, not religious upbringing?"

He felt the air drain from his lungs.

"What?"

He gazed at her in awe. "Once again, you've said exactly what I didn't want to hear—the *right* thing." He rubbed his forehead forcefully. "It all comes down to direct contact."

"I'm afraid I'm not following you."

Chris thought hard for a moment. "Okay, I'm still working this out myself, but I think I know *how* Nick Tewdrig passed this on to me. You remember I told you about pulling Nigel Madsen from the car? When Nick grabbed my legs, he said something in Welsh: *Rwy'n pasio i chi y pŵer i gwella.* Father Llewellyn told me it means, 'I pass to you the power to heal.' That's also when Nick put the Dial in my pocket—at the same time I grabbed Nigel's broken ankles. I didn't chant any Druidic prayers or Latin phrases, but I did make direct contact with Nigel while Nick made direct contact with me."

"Okay. But what about Father Llewellyn?"

"Well, I had the mantle then—the authority—and the Dial . . ." His words drifted off as he wrestled with the memory.

"You prayed over him; you told me so," she reminded him.

"Yes, but I can't remember what I said."

Kathryn's eyes darted in his direction. Somewhere behind their gray depths rose an inner turmoil. It was as if she wanted to believe him but couldn't bring herself to do so. "I see. You're not sure if you *can* heal again. Is that what you're saying? Will it come down to an abundance or absence of faith again? Or is it more of a personal preference of who to help?" The mocking in her voice was sharpened with frustration.

Quite unexpectedly, Chris felt the back of his eyes burn. Why her comment drew out his emotions, he didn't know. He'd always had tender feelings and a compassionate heart, but he'd always been able to keep them in check. Kathryn's questions felt like a personal insult. And worse, they instilled doubt in him. *Could* he heal again—"on command," as she'd said?

"I'm really not sure," he admitted weakly.

After a lengthy pause, she said, "Then neither am I."

"Not sure? About what?"

She reached in her purse and lifted out an electronic device that resembled a small cell phone. A tiny green LED indicated it was on. "About this recording."

Chris blinked a few times. "Why are you recording us?"

"MI5 orders. Detective Westcott threatened an injunction against me and the hospital if I didn't."

"What?"

Kathryn flipped on her turn signal as they approached the road to Trellech. "I'm sorry, Chris. He had no authority over me in the hospital, but outside? He could bring me in for questioning without so much as a by-your-leave—especially if he caught me with you."

"But . . . when did . . . ?"

"When you were hiding in the boot. Detective Westcott followed me into the hospital, right? He had a subpoena to search all records dealing with you, Father Llewellyn, and Rafe Collingswood. He insisted he would search my apartment and my mother's house if I didn't give him information as to your whereabouts. So I told him you were with me and explained what we were going to do. I convinced him to let you finish your research because it might turn up more clues as to your involvement with the mob. I also promised to get him your fingerprints. Remember that coffee cup I handed you that night? He has it now. Anyway, he gave me this device and ordered me to record everything you said to and from Cardiff."

"Wait. So he knew where I was staying last night?"

"Without a doubt. Believe it or not, we've had an unmarked car following us the whole time."

Chris whipped around in his seat. It was darker now, and most vehicles had their headlights on. He really couldn't tell who was behind them.

"So why didn't he just pick me up there?"

She shrugged. "Like I said, he knows you didn't shoot Father Llewellyn, but he still wanted to know what you were up to—just to be sure you weren't contacting any known mob affiliates in Cardiff."

Chris was dumbfounded and appalled. He'd trusted her completely. He thought she was helping him. Well—actually she *had* helped him. Immensely. But he also remembered she'd never told him why. "So now what?" he asked ruefully.

"I'll drop you off at the vicar's, and I'll give this to Detective Westcott."

"And he'll come arrest me?"

She clicked off the recorder and pushed it back in her purse. "I'm not privy to his agenda. I'll ask him to give you another day if possible, but I can't promise anything. Remember, Chris, you have the sanctuary of the church. I'm sure whoever is following us will report that you're here. Whether you'll be arrested or not, I don't know, but my guess is he'll simply lay low and continue to watch what you do."

"Great," he grumbled.

Stopping in front of the Church of St. Nicholas, Chris felt a knot of fresh anxiety twisting in his gut. The shadowy parking lot had just a few vehicles, none of which looked like police cars. He looked up at the church's tall steeple. It bespoke reverence. That was good. He needed to feel safe again, to feel hope and assurance. He prayed Father Llewellyn was in the rectory and willing to listen. Unless . . . unless the vicar was in on this too. "Maybe I should just forget this whole thing and turn myself in."

Kathryn turned to him. "No. You have to see this thing through, Chris. It's important."

His head was pounding again. Kathryn wasn't making sense. Whose side was she on? "Didn't you just get through saying this was a bunch of hogwash?"

A look of effrontery crossed her face. "I said no such thing. I merely stated that I have my reasons for distrusting the police *and* for questioning religious ambiguities. Both are purely selfish reasons, I admit, but they are also very private, so please don't ask."

"So you want me to just accept how you feel when you can't—or won't—accept how I'm feeling? Yeah, that seems real fair."

"Life isn't fair."

Chris grumbled, "Now you sound like my parents."

Kathryn's eyes abruptly filled with anguish. Tears pooled and escaped. She hastily wiped them away and pulled out a tissue. Her chin trembled. "Please get out. Now."

Sudden understanding filled Chris's mind. He knew what Kathryn wasn't able to say. Her private feelings and anxieties centered around *her* parents.

He sighed, opened the door, and stepped out. Thunder grumbled in the distance. It sounded as lonely and forlorn as he felt. A light rain began to fall. Leaning down, he retrieved Nick's cane. "Will I see you again?"

She swallowed hard but didn't look up. "I wish you luck, Chris. You're a good man with a good heart. You care about people. I can sense that."

"Thank you," he said flatly. "So . . . good-bye then."

Kathryn finally met his eyes. She appeared heartbroken. She tried to force a smile that didn't quite come. Chris closed the door, and she drove off into the darkness.

CHAPTER 43

MICHAEL OPENED THE DOOR ON Chris's first knock. "Come in, please."

He directed Chris to sit by the hearth then stirred the slumbering coals into a small fire and added more wood.

"Tea?" he asked, standing.

"Yes, please. Is Father Llewellyn around?"

"In chapel, holding evening mass."

The homey warmth of the cottage was a welcome sight, but neither the soft patter of the rain nor the cracking of the fire did much to soothe Chris's nerves. Strangely, he felt angst from his certain knowledge of the Dial's validity. Its authenticity meant that the things connected to it must also be real, including the legend of the Lamed Vovniks . . . and Chris's part in the legend. But that didn't mean it made sense. That's what frustrated him most. He leaned forward and held his palms to the fire. The sizzle and pop of sap caused a mote of glowing ember to tumble from the firebox. It came to rest next to the brass fireplace implements, directly over the hidden journal.

Michael wheeled in the dainty tea cart and parked it next to Chris. On it sat a steaming pot, an empty cup, and an assortment of pastries. Chris's stomach gurgled. It was only then he realized he hadn't eaten since lunchtime.

"Can I bring you anything more?" asked Michael.

"I'm very hungry, but I hate to impose," Chris answered sheepishly.

The big man walked back to the kitchen without further word. Chris sipped his tea, considering his options. Not only was he worried about his future, thoughts of Kathryn kept filling his mind. Had she been working for MI5 the whole time? She was obviously struggling with issues of her own. He wished he could help her; he owed her that much. But she seemed intent on working out her challenges by herself. He couldn't fault her for that. His search for answers had brought with it a host of startling occurrences: two miraculous healings (three, if he counted himself), one bizarre death, and one pretty doctor with personal turmoils that made him deeply sad.

Michael returned with a plate on which sat a thick plank of cheese between two slices of bread and a pickle on the side. He set the plate on the tea cart and went back to the kitchen.

Roughly an hour later, Father Llewellyn came in the back door mumbling soft blasphemies about the weather. Chris heard Michael say something about a visitor.

When the vicar turned the corner, an instant smile stretched across his face. "Christian! I'm so glad to see you, lad."

"And I you, Father."

He gave Chris a quick embrace and a hearty slap on the back before settling in the opposite wingback. He vigorously rubbed his hands in front of the fire. "I wish summer would stop lollygagging about and just get here, yes?"

Michael followed right behind with a steaming cup of tea. "Ah, thank you, Michael."

When the manservant left, Llewellyn withdrew a silver flask from a pouch on the side of his chair and poured a bit into his cup. He blew on the tea and took a sip. "Ay now, that's just the thing to take the damp from a man's bones, isn't it."

"I bet," Chris chuckled softly.

"Would you care for a wee dram?" the vicar asked, holding out the flask.

"No, thanks." Simply being in the man's presence helped settle Chris's feelings of unease and despondency. Llewellyn was old and frail but still full of a zest for life. He had an indomitable spirit Chris envied. "So how are you feeling, Father?"

"Not bad, my son. Oh, this miserable weather makes my rheumatics act up something awful like, but at least I'm not dead, ay?" he said with a wink. "Now then, what did you and the good doctor discover after leaving me praying over Collingswood's eternally damned soul?"

Chris pulled the Dial from his pocket. "I found out this is the real thing. It's real alabaster, likely from the Middle East, and these markings say, 'Praise Yahweh, for He is in all,' and 'He dwells in you for—' and that's where the stone breaks off."

Llewellyn held out his hand. "May I?"

Chris handed him the stone.

"Bless my soul," he whispered reverently. "You can almost feel the holiness radiating from it, can you not?" He took his small crucifix in one hand and the Dial in the other and pantomimed weighing the two objects, as if comparing them. He then gently placed them together, closed his eyes, and brought them to his lips. Chris marveled at the sacredness of the simple act.

"I am a blessed man," the vicar quietly said. "Thank you, Christian Pendragon, for coming into my life."

He kissed the Dial again and, with his crucifix, made the sign of the cross against his chest. Reluctantly, Chris accepted back the relic when Llewellyn handed it to him. He felt unworthy to hold it, to be its keeper. The humble churchwarden should hang on to it. The faith of the man was pure, without question. Chris wondered if he'd ever be as believing as Father Llewellyn.

After a long sip and a contemplative stare into the fire, the vicar asked, "What else did you learn, my son?"

Chris leaned over the opposite side of his chair and picked up Nick's cane.

"Bless my soul," Llewellyn gasped again. "Is that . . . ?"

"Yes. But me having it also means that . . . Nicholas Tewdrig is dead," he said tenderly.

"Well, of course," the vicar said with surprisingly little remorse. "He's been dead for over two hundred years, yes?" he added, winking again. "The proof is in his cane, yes?"

"Yes, but how do you know it's the same cane?" Chris asked.

The churchman sighed. "The beloved saint passed the mantle of healing onto you, did he not? You are the next in line, lad. I know that for sure an' certain as fervently as I know you're sitting next to me now. You hold the Dial of Ahaz, yes? It's only fitting you carry the cane too."

Llewellyn stood and searched for a title in his bookcase. Finding it, he returned to his chair and flipped through the pages until he located a specific entry. "Come look, son."

Chris rose to see what he'd found—and drew in a sharp breath. On the page was the same photograph he'd seen inside the Black Boar, the one of Nicholas Tewdrig standing with five other clergymen. Below the old photo the same caption read, *The clergy of St. Nicholas Church, April 1880.*

"This is the only known photograph of the beloved St. Nicholas. There are paintings and lithographs aplenty of him, yes, but no other photographs. Look'ee here, Christian," he said, pointing at the cane in the photo. "This proves you now hold Nicholas Tewdrig's walking staff, wouldn't you say?"

"Yeah," he sighed. "I guess it does. I got it from the coroner who did Nick's embalming in Cardiff. But it's not just a walking staff. Did you know about this?" he asked, unscrewing the alabaster knob.

"Of course. Did I not just say proof is *in* the cane?"

Chris pulled out the slip of parchment and handed it to the priest. "What about this?"

"'Nobly thru white fog hath I led,'" Llewellyn read aloud. "Aye, now that is a phrase with which I am well familiar. Know you the meaning of it, Christian?" he asked with a twinkle in his eye.

"It's an anagram. The letters rearrange to say, 'Through faith thy will be done.' The two sentences basically are saying the same thing—that if the holder of the Dial has enough faith, he will be led to where his desires will be done."

"Aye." The vicar's eyes shone with tears of joy. "Christian Pendragon, I have so much to thank thee for. I thank thee for sharing these marvelous omens with me. You've no idea how I've longed to witness them for myself. I thank thee for saving my life. I thank thee for bringing me closer to our beloved St. Nicholas. And I thank thee for allowing me to befriend one of the Righteous Thirty-Six."

Chris was humbled and frustrated. He didn't feel exceptionally righteous. He'd always been rather ambivalent about religion. He'd simply been in the wrong place at the wrong time. "Father, I am no one special. Please don't—"

"Stop! Do not take this from me, I beg of you," Llewellyn cut across angrily. "And do not take it from yourself. Regardless of what you think, this calling, this mantle has fallen to you. You *are* one of the Righteous Thirty-Six, Christian. Just as you have come to learn of the truth of the Dial, you will also come to know of your place in this legend."

His place in this legend. *His* place. Chris was utterly dumbfounded that he'd been studying legends all his life and yet had not seen his potential role in one of those legends. The thought made him smile. Was he destined to be a legend?

"I don't know what to say about that, Father," he said in humble exasperation. "I was hoping to look at Nick's journal again . . . to see if there are any more clues about . . . well, about me. I know my name isn't written in it, but maybe there's some other clue that will at least point to *me.*"

"There are clues aplenty, Christian, my son. You just need faith to see them."

CHAPTER 44

CHRIS SPENT THE EVENING READING Nick's journal in the narrow study behind the chapel chancel. He referenced other volumes and papers in the room but found it difficult to focus on the task at hand rather than the blood stains on the floor. The irony of searching for secular verification in the same room where spiritual confirmation had occurred was not lost on him. But he could not bring himself to accept what Father Llewellyn had said. He simply could not be a Vovnik. No way.

By three a.m. he'd found nothing new. Rather than returning to the rectory, he located a robe room with a cushioned bench and, covering himself with several choir frocks, stretched out on it. But sleep refused to come. After a restless half hour, he rolled onto his knees and offered a fervent prayer.

Still, sleep was fitful at best. Dreams and images plagued him. He was restless when he tried to apply analytical explanations to his experiences, happy when he remembered the joy of healing others, and serene when he relived the epiphany he'd had about the Dial. Mostly, the deep trust of Father Llewellyn battled his vacillating distrust in himself. In the end, he determined what he needed was one more chance to test his newfound calling. But he dreaded that chance more than anything.

* * *

A strong hand jostled Chris's shoulder. "Master Pendragon. There's a call for you."

He awoke to see Michael looming over him. The big man stood with a woolen Mack ready for Chris to slip into. Chris crawled from the bench, accepted the overcoat, then followed the manservant back to the rectory.

Llewellyn sat at the kitchen table behind a steaming pot of tea, a plate of kippers, and a Bible. He was speaking consolingly into his cell phone.

"Good morning, my son," he said, handing him the phone. "Be gentle."

Chris accepted it warily. He heard what sounded like the strained breaths that accompany crying. "Hello?"

"Chris? It's Kathryn."

"Oh, hi. Are you okay?" he asked, shocked that she'd called. He hadn't expected to hear from her ever again.

"Mostly yes, thank you." She sounded sincere but also extremely distraught. "Listen, Chris. I know all you're doing is trying to solve a personal mystery. I want to apologize for last night. I shouldn't have been such a troll."

Any animosity he'd held for her abruptly vanished. "Now *you* listen, Doc. I have a PhD in Welsh mythology. And I've *never* read about any troll as pretty as you. Or as intelligent. Or—"

"Okay stop. You'll give me a big head." she said, her tone definitely lighter.

"Well, I mean it."

He heard a scoff then a sniffle. "Thank you, Chris."

"You're welcome. Now, can you tell me what this is all about?"

"I, um . . . I need to talk to you. In private."

"Okay."

"This morning, if possible. In my office at the hospital."

"Um, sure." He hesitated. "Is this another setup with the police?"

"No, of course not!" she cried. "That was so stupid of me. I played the fool, and I'm terribly embarrassed by it. Please accept my humble apology."

He sighed. "Accepted."

"Thank you, Chris. Now come quickly, please, before I change my mind."

She disconnected before Chris could say good-bye. *Before I change my mind?*

"I guess I'm headed back to Monmouth. Any chance I can borrow your car?"

The priest smiled broadly. "But of course, me lad. Anything for a chance to pave the path of true love."

He winced. "Hardly."

Llewellyn shrugged and sipped his tea. "If it doesn't work out with the doctor, there's always Bambi, yes?"

Chris left without comment, cleaned himself up, then returned for a quick cup of tea and a scone. He tactfully opted out of the smelly kippers.

Outside, it was misting heavily. He hopped in the vicar's Subaru and headed south along a now very familiar road.

* * *

He pulled in next to Kathryn's Range Rover in the staff lot. There were no police vehicles in sight. She was waiting at the side entrance. When he entered, she immediately wrapped him in a big hug. He was shocked but had little problem returning the embrace.

"Um, it's good to see you too," he said with an awkward chuckle.

"Come with me," Kathryn said, leading him to her office. Drawing the curtains closed, she told him to shut the door. "Sit." She pointed to a chair.

She wheeled her desk chair around and sat across from him. After wringing her hands a few times, she looked up. Her expression held a strong aura of defeat.

"Okay, here's the in and out of it," she said. "I don't know what's going on with all this Dial of Ahaz stuff. I'm not real big on things I can't explain, and lately there's been a lot of that where you're concerned. Maybe there's nothing to it; maybe there is. And, with that in mind, we need to be totally up front about it. Can we be honest with each other?"

"Yes. I'd like that."

"Excellent. Did you find out how it works? The healing?"

"You mean beyond having faith? No. Your anagram is key, but I don't know if it's a code phrase or just basic guidelines."

She stared at her hands. "Forgive me, Chris, but that seems rather anticlimactic."

"Yeah, my feelings exactly. I've told you I've never been a spiritual guy, Kathryn. I'm like you—pretty grounded in facts. But the fact is that there *is* something to it. Father Llewellyn told me to trust my instincts. He said the Dial isn't some kind of divining rod that leads me to the sick. As you well know, the sick are all around us. He said it's up to me to discern when to use it. But I'm still not sure *how*."

"Can anyone use the Dial?" she asked studiously.

"No. You saw what happened to Collingswood when he tried."

She nodded. "Complete cardiac failure. His heart just shut down for no apparent reason. Never seen anything like it."

"But *I can* use it. Don't ask me why, because I don't know." He snorted in frustration. "Nick said it was because the Dial and I had bonded—whatever that means."

She stared silently at Chris for almost a full minute. He tried to discern the mental battles raging behind her steely eyes. There was a brutal contest going on, one that he too was waging. *Trust your mind and your heart*, the priest had said. Okay, but what if the two conflicted? His mind had volumes of facts substantiating its conclusions; his heart had a driving, intuitive assertion that he *was* the next Myddfain physician in line.

Finally, Chris broke eye contact and huffed. "I'm sorry for not having a clearer answer, Kathryn. As you can tell, I'm still trying to accept my place in it." He walked to the window and parted the curtains to look at the weather. No change.

"And those are your honest feelings?"

He made his way back to his chair. "Yes. I can no longer deny the validity of the Dial—even if it doesn't make sense."

Her voice was unusually soft. "Thank you, Chris."

"Sure. Is that the reason you wanted to speak to me in private?"

"Yes. I wanted to be sure you truly believed it."

"I do. Why?"

Tears filled her eyes and traced down her cheeks. She didn't bother to wipe them away. "Because I want you to heal my mother."

CHAPTER 45

CHRIS SCOOTED CLOSER AND GENTLY cupped Kathryn's hands. "Your mother is worse?"

She sniffled and nodded.

"And you've undoubtedly pursued every avenue of care?"

"Yes, of course," she said, pulling a hand free and using a tissue to wipe her face. "Mom's got stage IV-A pancreatic cancer. That means she has numerous large tumors that've spread to the blood vessels surrounding the pancreas, the lymph nodes too. They've confirmed it's metastasized to other organs—her lungs, liver, stomach, maybe even her bone marrow."

"And it's untreatable?"

"They've basically said they can't afford to try anymore." The look in her eyes was beyond hopeless; it was complete surrender. "She's classified as inoperable. I've tried everything. I've even gotten experimental drug clearance with NHS. Nothing has worked. Now she's on fentanyl, morphine, and midazolam pretty much around the clock just to keep her comfortable."

"I'm so sorry, Kathryn. I wish there was something I could do," he said automatically, without thinking.

She locked eyes with him. "But there is."

Panic sliced through him. "Whoa, Kathryn, wait. I told you, I'm not even sure how it works. What if I can't? What if—"

"What if you don't even try? Then she's guaranteed to die, right? Her cancer is insidious and—" She choked on a sob and paused to swallow her emotions. "I got a call last night after dropping you off. Her live-in nurse says Mom's vital signs are giving out. Her organs are shutting down. She's in constant, unbearable pain—even with the meds. Please, Chris. You're my last hope."

Chris stood and returned to the window. Doubt flooded his mind, inundated his soul. Could he do it again? How *had* he healed Nigel Madsen and Father Llewellyn?

Or had he?

Of course you did. Stop doubting yourself. You can *help ease her suffering.*

"You said you believe, Chris. I want to believe too. As you said, perhaps that's all it takes." Kathryn was pleading now. "She's suffering. I won't blame you if nothing happens. I've done all I can and have gotten nowhere, haven't I. You might as well try."

He felt sick to his stomach. He knew he needed another chance to prove himself, but nothing this personal. He turned from the window. Kathryn was staring at him with wide, puffy eyes. Her lower lip trembled.

It's your calling. How can you say no?

Swallowing his trepidation, he asked, "How long will it take to get there?"

She leapt from her chair and in one step had her arms wrapped around him, squeezing tightly. Over and over, she whispered words into his neck. They sounded like 'thank you,' but he wasn't sure. It didn't matter.

Chris stood watching the rain clouds march toward the east, leaving a moist haze of sunshine in their wake. Kathryn was on the phone asking a colleague to cover the rest of her shift. She had a family emergency.

"My apartment is just up the street," she told Chris. "You can come with me while I change. Then we'll go from there."

Chris cleared his throat. "If it's that close, I'd rather wait here, if you don't mind. I need some time to . . . to think before we do this."

She smiled in a way that melted his heart. "I'll be right back then," she said, exiting her office.

Chris closed her door and turned off the lights. Kneeling with his back to the window, he clasped the Dial in his hands and bowed his head. He wasn't accustomed to praying, but thankfully, it didn't feel hypocritical. He knew this was what he was supposed to be doing. The biggest problem was that he wasn't sure what to say. If anything, he knew he should ask for God's guidance and companionship. There was no way he could do this by himself. Nor did he want to.

He knelt for some time, aware time was passing but not really concerned about it. He cleared his mind and awaited inspiration. It didn't take long—and he couldn't help but smile at the warmth washing through him.

He softly cleared his throat and whispered, "Nobly, thru white fog, hath you led me to this calling. I still don't know why, but I trust in you. Lord, I ask that you lead me now. Through faith thy will be done. Amen."

CHAPTER 46

CHRIS SAT FOR SOME TIME just waiting. He couldn't imagine what was taking Kathryn so long. He perused her bookshelf again, looking for anything out of the ordinary—and found it. On the bottom tier, far right, sat a King James Bible. He smiled, not surprised that she owned one, but that it would be in her office. He opened to the book of St. Luke—the only Gospel not written by an Apostle, Llewellyn had said. Maybe Chris could relate to this guy.

He began reading. The words had a familiar timbre. Chapter two was the Christmas story. Childhood memories flooded his mind, warming his heart. He continued reading. The stories were strangely recognizable. He'd rarely paid attention in Sunday school, but something must have sunk in. Then one story in particular stood out. Llewellyn had referenced it. Jesus was being thronged by the masses. A woman with a blood disorder touched the hem of his garment to be healed. And she was. Instantly. Jesus hadn't said a blessing or a prayer, hadn't commanded her to be whole, hadn't really done anything except be there. But he felt virtue—*power*, according to the priest—flow from him. Jesus turned to the woman and said her faith had made her whole. *Her* faith.

Perhaps that was the answer Chris had been seeking. He didn't need any magic words, any holy recitation. He simply had to believe he had the gift—which he did. If the person receiving the healing also had faith, then it would happen.

He was almost through the first half of Luke when he heard a noise in the hallway.

The doorknob turned, and the door opened. "Chris. Is everything all right?"

"Sure. I was just reading."

Kathryn entered wearing a tan, button-down blouse untucked over shapely blue jeans. A wide leather belt around her midriff emphasized her trim figure. Her makeup and hair were flawless.

"Wow. You look gorgeous," he said through a wide smile.

A blush danced across her cheeks. "Thank you. Sorry I'm late."

"No problem," he said, following her out of the room.

The storm had all but passed, leaving a day promised with plenty of sunshine. Only a few wispy clouds now dotted the horizon in all directions. Chris took it as a good sign.

"So what were you reading?" Kathryn asked after turning onto the highway to Ettington.

"The King James Bible."

She flashed him a questioning glance. "Really? Why?"

He shrugged. "Seemed appropriate."

"Huh. So what's a history professor's take on the Bible?"

Chris snorted. "You know, if you'd asked me that question last week, I'd have given you my pat answer: It's a handpicked history compiled by a pagan-worshiping dictator trying to appease the Christian masses."

"Really?"

"Yep. The Council at Nicaea, 325 AD. Emperor Constantine? It was then they created the Bible from various epistles and journals. And therein lies a major red flag. You see, the trouble with most histories is that they're written by the victors. You can't help but have some bias. And Constantine made sure the Bible said only what he wanted it to say."

"Truly? Um, okay. And *now* what do you think?"

"Now I'm not so cynical. There's some interesting verbiage in there. I'm seeing things I never knew about. I'm not talking about being born again or seeing a bright light or anything," he said, flicking away an imaginary rebuttal. "It's more like, before, I was reading with an expectation of holier-than-thou biased historical fiction. But looking at it as containing accurate history and being crammed with hidden spiritual truths—kind of like the hidden message you helped me decipher—then all sorts of lessons can be learned. So yeah, it's historical, but it's also spiritual, educational, and . . ."

"And?"

"Instructional?" He glanced at her, as if seeking approval. "But not in a how-to, DIY kind of way, you know? More of a 'this is simply how it is' manner of speech. So even though it was compiled by man, the Lord definitely had His hand in it."

She considered his words with a tilt of her head. After a minute, she gave a quick nod. "Okay," was all she said. But her tone held little enthusiasm.

Chris knew she was wrestling with many of the same issues he was. They were both highly educated people. Their secular learning had basically done away with the need for religious influences. The "wise men" of the day had sequestered God to the realm of legends. And yet, there was definitely still a need for Him in the world.

Chris sighed deeply, knowing that *his* personal need for God would soon be put to the test.

CHAPTER 47

AN HOUR LATER, THEY PULLED up to a small whitewashed house in the suburbs. The tiny yard was prim and orderly but in need of some attention. A moss- and lichen-dappled field-stone fence surrounded the parcel. Perennials bloomed in random beds; hummingbirds flitted from flower to flower. Life surrounded the old home; but to Chris, a sense of barrenness permeated the scene.

Kathryn led him up the short walk and into the house. A middle-aged nurse sat reading a paperback on the living room sofa. She looked up in surprise. "Oh. Good afternoon, Dr. Ingledew," she said, standing. "I'm so glad you came today."

"Hi, Beatrix. How is Mom?"

Despondency clouded the nurse's face. "Not so good, I'm afraid. As I mentioned yesterday, her organs seem to be shutting down. I'm so very sorry."

Kathryn nodded. Chris could tell she was struggling to remain professional and stoic, but he sensed debilitating sorrow emanating from body language and face.

"This is Dr. Pendragon, from the United States," Kathryn offered.

"Pleased to meet you," Chris said, extending his hand to the nurse.

Beatrix was of average build and health for a middle-aged woman, but her tired eyes bespoke years of serving the terminally ill. He could tell she liked being a nurse, liked helping people, but it was taking its toll on her.

"The pleasure is mine, Doctor."

"Is Mom awake?" Kathryn asked.

"She was up for her morning medicines, but she's sleeping now."

Kathryn removed her coat and tossed it on a chair. Chris did the same.

"Can I make you some tea?" the nurse asked pleasantly.

"That would be excellent. Thank you, Beatrix. We'll just pop in and check on her, okay?"

Beatrix gave a slight nod before scooting into the kitchen.

Chris followed Kathryn into a small bedroom. Her mother lay motionless on a hospital bed. With her head slightly raised, the seventy-year-old was hooked to an IV drip and a med-stats monitor. Chris saw a definite family resemblance to Kathryn—their bone structure was identical—but Mrs. Ingledew was painfully frail and gaunt. Her cancer had taken everything but her life, and that was clearly next on the list.

Kathryn drew a stuttering breath and wiped at her cheeks. Even though she'd spent her life around the infirm and injured, she clearly had difficulty seeing her own mother in such a weakened state.

"She looks serene," Chris whispered.

"It's the drugs," Kathryn said flatly. She checked the stats on the monitors and read the chart notes. "She's losing kidney function. I don't know if it's the cancer or if her body is just giving up." Her voice was dry and strained.

Chris felt a welling compassion for both women. The woman on the bed looked very close to death. Chris guessed it was probably the machines keeping her alive. He stepped to the bed and touched her hand.

"What's her name?" he asked tenderly.

"Lona—short for Moelona. Moelona Jones was the penname of Elizabeth Mary Jones, a Welsh children's novelist that my grandmother adored."

"I see."

He picked up Lona's hand and held it while gazing at her face. Even pallid and drawn, her face had a certain angelic quality. She looked calm but challenged, like she was waging an inner battle she refused to let surface. That seemed a fair simile.

Chris didn't know what he was supposed to do at this point, but he trusted it would come to him. Moving more by instinct than logic, he sat on the edge of the bed and closed his eyes. Still holding Lona's hand, he tried to clear his mind and sought inspiration. Except for the soft beeping of the monitor, the room was silent. He knew Kathryn was there, watching, but he forced himself to focus on the patient.

After a moment, he felt a strong urge to place his hand on Lona's head, which he did. He concentrated on this cherished woman and how much her daughter needed her. They were everything to each other.

Kathryn loved her mother with all her heart—that was obvious. She was devastated at the prospect of losing her. But for some reason, Chris didn't feel a prompt to heal her.

He readjusted his hand and tried again. He thought of tissues healing, of tumors shrinking and vanishing, of the laughter and love between mother and daughter. He experienced the bond between them. It was rich, complete, seamless. There was trust and caring . . . and heartache. But he felt no sensation of repair, no indication that the Dial was doing anything other than confirming the love between Kathryn and her mother.

Chris clenched his jaw. He knew he was failing.

Please, God. I sense his woman is an innocent soul. Please let me help her. Through faith, thy will be done.

He reflected back on the healings of Nigel Madsen and Father Llewellyn. What had he done then? What had he thought or said? He remembered feeling intense compassion for each before a sharp pain surged in the area that needed healing. With Nigel, his ankles had throbbed; with Father Llewellyn, his torso seized. Presently, he expected to experience pain in the area of his liver, perhaps some aching across his belly. But there was nothing. He perceived this woman was worthy of healing. She was a victim, an innocent soul afflicted with a grievous malady through no fault of her own. She didn't *deserve* to die.

Concentrating, Chris repeatedly centered on the command to "come back." Was that how she'd recover—by "coming back" to full health?

Come back.

He opened his eyes when he heard Lona take a long, raspy breath, but there'd been no transference of pain, no indication that he'd succeeded.

Kathryn was instantly by her side. "Mum?"

Lona's eyes fluttered open. She glanced at Chris then fixed her gaze on Kathryn. "My pet," she wheezed.

"Mum, this is Chris. He's going to heal you. He's going to make you all better." Her voice was strained with desperation.

Lona's eyes fluttered again. A slight smile spread across her lips. "Oh, my sweet pet. No."

Tears coursed unrestrained down Kathryn's cheeks. "Yes, Mum. Please. I don't know how, but I know he can heal you." To Chris, she begged, "Please, Chris. Tell her. Tell her about the Dial. Tell her you can heal her."

Chris didn't know what to say. The feelings he received were so different from what he'd experienced before. He certainly wasn't an expert at this, but he knew something here wasn't right—like he was traveling down a one-way street in the wrong direction. He knew he *could* do it, but he now wondered if he was *supposed* to do it.

With a fractional shake of his head, Chris gave Kathryn a sympathetic, heartfelt look of remorse and apology.

"No!" she yelled.

Lona shushed her softly. With her eyes straining to remain open, she turned her head toward her daughter. "It's all right, pet. Walter is here."

Chris looked up.

"My dad," Kathryn forced past a sob.

Seeing his friend so grief-stricken nearly tore Chris's heart in two. He couldn't let this happen—if only for her sake. But he couldn't go against the wishes of the patient either. Or of God.

He bent close to Lona's head. "Mrs. Ingledew, I believe I can heal you," Chris explained, "but only if you want me to."

Without acknowledging him, Lona reached for Kathryn's hand. It was as if he wasn't even there. The woman swallowed several times before whispering, "Not heal. Release."

Kathryn crumpled onto the bed. She held Lona's hand to her cheek and cried, "No, Mum. He's going to heal you—aren't you, Chris?" She was almost yelling the words now, forcing them between gasps and sobs. "He's going to heal you, and you're going to live many more years, and we're going to do so many things togeth—" Her voice broke off. She buried her face in her mother's chest.

Chris felt awkward with his hand still on Lona's head, but he didn't lift it. His work was not done. He didn't know how he knew that; he merely perceived it—but in a way that was set and irrefutable.

Key words blazed crystal clear in his mind. *Thy will be done.*

That was it. This was *God's* will, not his. He knew what he had to do.

"Kathryn," he said tenderly. "Sometimes healing doesn't mean curing. Sometimes it means letting go of whatever afflicts us."

Chris moved his free hand to gently stroke Kathryn's hair. She was shuddering, taking short gasps of air.

"Kathryn—"

"No!" she snapped, sitting up. "She promised to be here for me. Mother, you promised!"

Chris had never experienced anything like this before. Even with the death of his father, which was undeniably a sad occasion, he'd never felt such a crippling depth of loss. He knew Kathryn was terrified of letting her mother go. He also knew Lona was just as reluctant to leave. Yet at the same time, there was an all-encompassing correctness to what was transpiring. Emotive compassion and love permeated the air. Lona had said her husband was there. Was it *their* love he was feeling—the love between Lona and Walter Ingledew?

Chris's voice was surprisingly calm. "Kathryn. Your mother loves you very much. There's no question about that. But she needs to go."

"No! You said you'd try to heal her. You said you'd use the Dial and whatever power it holds to cure her."

"I'm so sorry. But it wouldn't be right. She'd only suffer more. You wouldn't want that, and neither does she."

Kathryn's mouth continued to move, but no words came out. Her eyes were red and puffy, her face strained and frightened. Denial overpowered her, possessed her. She stood abruptly and stepped back. Bitter anger flashed from her eyes; her clenched fists blanched and trembled.

"You promised you'd try." Her tone was dark and level, filled with accusation and venom.

"Yes. And I did try. I really did. But it isn't meant to be."

She rolled her eyes and let fly an expletive that shocked Chris. "Typical. That's just so typical of all you religious types. When things don't go your way, you always fall back on 'it wasn't meant to be,' or 'it wasn't God's will,'" she said scathingly. "What a load of rubbish."

Lona reached out again. Kathryn rushed to her bed and cradled the frail hand next to her heart. Lona's lips moved, but only faint wisps escaped. Kathryn leaned in close, as did Chris.

"He's right. Please, let me go." Her strained, thin voice sounded like a breath of wind passing through a rusty screen.

"No," Kathryn wept, again burying her face in her mother's chest.

Chris said nothing. He knew this was right. It made perfect sense. He *was* a healer, but this time he was supposed to heal someone from the ignominy and pain of life with cancer. He closed his eyes and thought of the love between Lona and Walter. A voice in his mind softly repeated the words, *Go now. You're free.*

"Kathryn, it's time," Chris said quietly.

Slowly regaining some composure, Kathryn sat up. She wiped her face repeatedly, swallowed several times, then leaned forward and kissed her mother on the cheek.

"Farewell, Mum. I love you."

Chris gave a slight nod and whispered, "I release you."

The tender smile remained on Lona's face as she issued a long, final sigh.

The monitor immediately flat-lined.

Kathryn stumbled from the room. Chris followed, turning off the lights as he did.

Beatrix came running, but Chris stopped her. "There's nothing we can do," he explained.

"But she's flat-lining. We should resuscitate."

"No," Kathryn said from the living room sofa. "It's time to . . . let her go."

Her voice sounded stronger, but Chris could tell it was done at a cost. Her willpower was spent. She'd just made the most difficult decision of her life.

"So you're giving the order *not* to resuscitate?" Beatrix asked her.

"Yes," Kathryn rasped with a nod.

The nurse nodded in return, entered the bedroom, and switched off the monitor.

Chris sat beside Kathryn. "I'm so very sorry, Kathryn. I know it doesn't make sense. Like I said, I still don't understand it. But it *was* her time. I don't know how else to explain it beyond that."

She sniffled, wiped her nose with a tissue then threw her arms around his neck.

With her face on his shoulder, she muttered, "I know."

Then, breaking the embrace, Kathryn folded her arms tightly against her stomach and rocked back and forth. She was battling the reality of what just happened. And although Chris knew he'd done the right thing, he still could not ignore the pangs of guilt buffeting his soul. So much for his first attempt to *knowingly* heal someone. Seeing Kathryn withdraw into herself only amplified his feelings of utter failure.

CHAPTER 48

NURSE BEATRIX CALLED THE HOSPITAL. An ambulance came, along with a mortician. Chris gave a brief statement to a technician, saying he and Kathryn were in the room when Mrs. Ingledew died. Nothing unusual or untoward had occurred; she simply slipped away. Kathryn confirmed and notarized the statement. The rest of the paperwork could be handled later.

The drive back to Monmouth was deeply quiet—no conversation, no music. He was desperate to talk about what had just happened—if only to settle his own conscience—but he didn't want to pressure Kathryn. She'd open up when the time was right.

Strangely, he felt . . . *fulfilled* by the event. He *had* relieved someone's suffering. It wasn't a pleasant experience, but it *was* the right thing to do. Moelona Ingledew was *supposed* to pass on. She was happier now, happier to be with her husband, happier to be pain-free. Chris was sure of that. Only, he wished he could somehow make Kathryn happy too.

* * *

The Range Rover came to a stop next to the vicar's Subaru. Kathryn and Chris sat silently for a while, numbly watching the afternoon sun become obscured by a fleet of dark clouds. Chris sensed it was warmer outside the vehicle than inside.

"Thank you for trying," Kathryn said evenly, finally breaking the silence.

"I'm sorry for your loss. I wish I could have done more," he said genuinely.

"I know."

A full minute of silence passed before Chris said, "I don't know what to say."

She nodded.

"Is there anything I can do for you?"

"Not anymore." Her voice had a sharp finality that cut him deeply.

"Well, if there ever is . . ."

Silence reigned again. Deep-purple shadows began to creep up the facility walls. Kathryn sat motionless, as if her muscles were wound as tight as bridge cables, ready to snap.

Gathering his nerve, he reached over and took her hand. "Please believe me that . . . well, this may sound trite, but that your mother is happy now. I truly believe she is."

Kathryn remained static, rigid. Tears again filled her eyes. "It'll take some time to accept that," she said, pulling her hand away. "To accept . . . what happened." Her tone was cold, distant.

He gave a slight nod. "I, um . . . I guess I better get going then."

She scoffed in bitter frustration. "Perhaps you'd better. There are lots of sick and dying who need help to the grave."

He stared at his empty hands. "That's not fair," he said quietly.

The tears spilled down her cheeks. She refused to meet his eyes. She was like a statue, staring straight out the windshield. "What happened wasn't fair." Using her sleeve, she angrily wiped away the tears. "I put my trust in you, Chris. I went way out of my way, put my professional standing on the line to help you. I even lied to the police. I believed you even when I didn't want to. I did it because it was the last chance I had to save my mom. I was grasping at straws—and you took the last straw away."

"Kathryn. I only did what I was prompted to do."

"Then I'm sorry, Chris. I must now do what *I'm* prompted to do." Removing a handkerchief from her purse, she stuck it out the car window and waved it back and forth. Within seconds, a car pulled up on the passenger side, and another blocked them from behind. Four men dressed in plain black business suits got out and approached the Rover. One of them was Detective Westcott. Although his pistol wasn't drawn, the other three officers' were.

He rapped on Chris's window and motioned for him to roll it down.

When Chris complied, Westcott adjusted his glasses and smiled. "Hello again, Mr. Pendragon. Long time, no see, ay? Please step out of the car slowly, and put your hands on the roof."

CHAPTER 49

CHRIS GAWKED AT KATHRYN. "WHAT'S going on?"

"I should think that is obvious," she said, not meeting his gaze.

"Out of the car, sir," Westcott repeated.

"Because I didn't heal your mom?"

She continued to stare forward, not moving, not speaking. Tears spilled down her cheeks.

"And if I had? What then?" Chris did not hide the anger he felt from her duplicitous betrayal. "You'd give me a new car? A trip to Hawaii? She was dying, Kathryn. She was suffering. I did what *she* wanted. You heard her."

Westcott opened the door.

"I'm coming," Chris grumbled, unfastening his seat belt. He climbed out and slammed the door shut. The detective pulled Chris's arms behind him and cuffed his wrists. As he was being led away, Kathryn cried out, "Wait."

She scrambled out, rounded the car, and threw her arms around Chris. In a voice hoarse with sadness, she whispered, "I'm sorry." She then turned and walked briskly away and through the hospital entrance.

Westcott joined Chris in the rear seat of the MI5 sedan. He switched on a recording device and placed it in a cup holder between them, making sure Chris saw and recognized it.

"Anything you wish to declare, Mr. Pendragon?"

"Yeah. Never trust women."

The driver burst out laughing then quickly sobered to a snigger.

Westcott gave a courtesy chuckle and adjusted his glasses. "When referring to the good Dr. Ingledew, I'd have to agree with you. Did she tell you she blames His Majesty's police force for the death of her father?"

Chris looked up quickly. "She said her dad died of heart failure."

"Oh, he did. A massive heart attack, as I understand it. She claims it was brought on by an embezzlement investigation against him."

"I see. Did he do it?"

Westcott removed his glasses and wiped them with his tie. "No."

"But by then it was too late," Chris intuited. "Right?"

"Regrettably, yes," he said, replacing his glasses. "Dr. Ingledew is a woman who knows how to carry a grudge, Mr. Pendragon, but she does recognize right from wrong. That's why she arranged this little rendezvous, you see. She knew we've been following the two of you. She said she'd signal if she needed help. Care to tell me why you wanted to visit her mother in Ettington?"

Chris clenched his teeth. He was angry and confused and very alone. He wanted to scream but held it in. What should he tell the detective? That he'd tried to heal Kathryn's mother with the power of a holy relic, but it didn't work? That he now had a spiritual gift by which he could cure all manner of sickness, but he needed practice? How much of the truth should he share, and how much should he keep secret? Both Nicholas Tewdrig and Father Llewellyn had said not to flaunt his gift, not to seek fame or glory, to remain anonymous. Did that exclude explaining it to the police?

"Mr. Pendragon, I promise it will go easier on you if you cooperate."

"Am I under arrest?"

"Yes, you are, sir."

"On what charges?"

"Let's see, there's suspected involvement with organized crime and resisting arrest for starters."

"I think I should have a lawyer present. I'd like to call my embassy."

Westcott gave a closed-lip chuckle. "All in good time, Mr. Pendragon." He patted the driver on the shoulder. "Let's go, Charles."

Charles started up the car and headed out of the parking lot. Chris had never felt so despondent in his life. The fact that Kathryn had led him along then handed him over to the police was unthinkable. Why would she do that? He truly felt sorry for the loss of her mother. He wished the whole event had gone differently. But it hadn't—and there was nothing he could do to change that. He took a steadying breath and tried to organize his thoughts. He was innocent; he had to keep that foremost in his mind.

"Okay, look. I don't know what Dr. Ingledew told you, but *she* called *me* and asked that I go with her to her mother's home."

"She called you?"

"Yes."

"And how, pray tell, did that take place? We have your mobile back at HQ."

"At Fa—" he stopped short, wondering if he should involve Father Llewellyn. He'd hate to be responsible for getting the vicar in trouble with the authorities.

"What was that, Mr. Pendragon?"

Just tell the truth, he told himself.

The truth shall set you free, another voice said.

"I'd gone to see Father Llewellyn in Trellech. Since he knew the truth about what happened in the chapel, I figured he'd be the best person to get help from. Dr. Ingledew must have assumed the same thing because that's where she called me."

"How did you get to Trellech?"

"I hitched a ride." Admitting that the vicar had prearranged the pickup would be too incriminating.

"So she called you and asked that you steal the vicar's car to meet her in Ettington?"

Chris frowned. He knew the detective was asking leading, partial-truth questions to trip him up. "Of course not. When I explained what was happening, Father Llewellyn loaned me his car. I drove here as per Kathryn's request. You can call and ask him."

"Driving without a license . . ." Westcott said thoughtfully, as if adding it to Chris's rap sheet.

"Yes, because *you* took my license and my passport! You also—" He stopped and shook his head. "Never mind that. Look, Kathryn asked me to try and help her mother. Lona Ingledew was terminally ill, and Kathryn was hoping there was something I could do to help."

"Practicing medicine without a license . . ."

"Stop it, will you? I don't intimidate easily, so you might as well knock off the lame TV cop mimicry."

Westcott raised an eyebrow. "Don't intimidate, you say? Then why did you jump out of the hospital window and make a run for it?"

Chris clenched his teeth so hard this time his jaw hurt. *Just tell the truth*. "Father Llewellyn told me to."

The detective's other eyebrow joined the first over his glasses. "So a respected Anglican priest told you to intentionally break the law. I'm pretty sure that goes contrary to their holy vows, don't you think?"

"He said he was going to talk to you and convince you I had nothing to do with his attempted murder."

"Oh, he did, he did."

"Good. And did you know Rafe Collingswood, the man who *did* shoot him, is dead?"

"Yes, of course. I've already inspected the body."

"Did they show you his empty shoulder holster?"

Westcott tipped his head. "How is it you know about that, sir?"

"Because I saw him draw his gun from it, Sherlock. That clearly proves the gun was his, not mine."

"Actually, it proves very little, Mr. Pendragon," he said, again cleaning his glasses, ignoring the insult. "What we *do* know is that the gun is unregistered, that it has been positively matched with mob activity, and that it has your fingerprints on it."

"Because I took it from him," he hissed. This was going nowhere, and he knew it. "I'm not answering any more questions until I speak with my embassy."

"As you wish, Mr. Pendragon. Only, your embassy is closed now and won't open again until nine o'clock Monday morning."

"Great. Does that mean I'm going to jail for the weekend?"

"Don't be absurd," he said with a supercilious grin. "They can only keep perpetrators for one night in Monmouth's tiny jail. Bureaucratic nonsense about inadequate extended accommodations and all that. Besides, you're a known flight risk. No, our prison in Cardiff is just the ticket, I should think. Better security."

Chris gawked at the man, totally speechless.

"Tell me, Mr. Pendragon, do you like pottage for breakfast? I've heard theirs is quite hardy stuff. It's what HMP Cardiff always serves terrorists these days, isn't that so, Charles?"

The driver nodded. "Yes, sir, it is."

CHAPTER 50

BY THE TIME CHRIS WAS processed into Cardiff prison and placed in a cell, night had fallen. The barred door rolled shut with gut-wrenching finality.

There were two cots in the darkened cell; one was occupied by a gray-haired black man facing the wall. Chris sat heavily on the empty cot and put his face in his hands. He refused to be depressed. He knew he was innocent. Everything would be okay . . . eventually.

After a moment of silence, his cellmate quietly asked, "What'd you do, man?"

"Nothing," Chris assured him.

A deep, rumbling chuckle rose from the old man's chest as he rolled over. "Man, you gonna fit right in. No one in here never done nothin' wrong. They all innocent."

Chris was still in a state of shock and rage. The last thing he wanted to do was strike up a conversation with the man. He simply wanted to get through the night with whatever sleep was possible, survive the weekend, and have the embassy collect him Monday morning. Some vacation this had turned out to be! He was just beginning to feel good about meeting Nicolas Tewdrig and accepting the daunting responsibility of being a Vovnik healer. So why was all this other tribulation happening?

"You from 'round here, son?"

"Nope," he said, hoping his short answer would discourage further questions.

"Then where you from, chum? You from the States? 'Cause you sound like you from the States."

"Look, buddy, I'm not in the mood for chitchat. I just want to get some sleep, okay?"

"It's cool, man. It's cool. Jus' gettin' acquainted is all."

"Sorry. Maybe later. It's been a rough day."

The man chuckled again. "'Course it has, son. You in here, ain't ya?" He turned his back to Chris and continued to chuckle to the wall.

Darkness settled on Chris like a smothering, opaque fog. Ambient prison noises slowly drifted away until the only sound remaining was his cellmate's soft snoring and the faint buzzing of fluorescent lamps in the airy concourse. Chris tossed and fussed, never able to get physically comfortable because mentally he was in misery. Remembrances wrestled with regrets; excuses clashed with convictions. He had no idea why any of this was happening to him. He was a history teacher, for heaven's sake! He'd lived a life of decency and respect. No, he wasn't perfect. But he tried to be understanding and helpful. He rarely judged anyone.

His father used to say you never know a person's full backstory. A happy little girl could come from a seemingly loving home, but at night she hid under her bed, cowering from an abusive father. A respected business owner could donate thousands to his church and spend three times that much on hits of heroin. A single mom could appear to have her life perfectly in order, but at night she scrounged through Dumpsters to feed her kids and sold her body to pay the rent. An unkempt vagrant could be a former executive, now destitute because he'd lost his job and spent his life savings trying to pay for his wife's terminal cancer treatments.

Terminal cancer. Like Moelona Ingledew. Why couldn't Chris save her? Because she wasn't meant to be saved? She wanted to move on. She wanted to be free from bodily pain and reunited with her husband. Chris *had* done the right thing. He knew it as profoundly as he knew the Dial was real. If only Kathryn could experience that same assurance.

Kathryn! He still couldn't believe she'd turned him in. He'd thought that, though she was far from believing him, she was beginning to *understand* him. He was shocked at how quickly she'd turned. Or . . . had she? Was she planning on handing him over all along?

Chris stared up at the pale, gray cement ceiling. He needed answers. He needed comfort. He needed . . . a miracle. More than anything, he wished he still had the Dial with him. The admissions officer had placed it in a manila envelope with Chris's name on it. He'd been given prison garb—in exchange for his civilian clothes—and a small toiletry kit, even though he'd yet to be convicted or sentenced.

He turned on his side and faced the cold, stark wall. What if the American embassy didn't offer to bail him out? What if they complied with MI5 demands and let Chris rot in jail while Westcott slandered his name on one trumped-up charge after another?

Chris didn't know how long he lay there battling his doubts and fears; he didn't know when it was he'd rolled off his cot and knelt on the cold cement floor, but he unexpectedly found himself on his knees, pouring out his soul to God. Much to his chagrin, he realized praying was what he should have done in the first place. The thought made him frown. But immediately after feeling remorse for his lack of faith, a soul-warming upwelling of succor and forgiveness began to wash over him. It felt as though a thick comforter, fresh from the drier, had been draped across his shoulders. He reveled in it, embraced it, accepted it. And the more he talked with God, the greater that feeling became.

Sometime early the next morning, he remembered to crawl back into bed.

CHAPTER 51

A LOUD BUZZER OUTSIDE THE cell jolted Chris awake. He heard the metal casters squeal as the door rolled open.

"Man, you one righteous dude or what?"

Chris rubbed his eyes. Bright sunshine glared through skylights over the concourse. His roommate was sitting on his bunk, elbows on his knees, watching Chris.

"What makes you say that?" Chris asked, sitting up and slowly flexing his sore knees.

"Ain't seen no one pray that long before. Son, you was on your bones of supplication nearly most of the night. What you do out there, kill someone?"

Vigorously scratching his head with both hands, Chris said, "No; I saved someone's life, actually."

"You don't say. Now they arresting people for being good?" His cellmate gave a low whistle. "Lord, have mercy. What's this world coming to?"

"I wish I knew."

"So whose life you save, man?"

"A priest."

The old man's eyebrows almost rose off his forehead. He tipped back his head and roared with laughter. "Man, this jus' keeps gettin' better an' better. I knew you's a natural-born liar when they brought you in, sure as I live an' breathe." He extended an arthritic hand across the space between them. "Name's Ezekiel Athens, son. Folks call me E.Z. It's a real pleasure."

"Chris Pendragon," he said, shaking the hand. It was then that he noticed a thick, bluish-white mottling over the man's left eye, visibly rendering the eye useless. The old wound looked hideous and painful.

"Ain't seen a thing out this eye some twenty-five year now," E.Z. said, seeing Chris's repulsed reaction. "Boys in here call it a devil's eye."

"Sorry. Didn't mean to stare. A cataract?"

"Stupidity."

Chris blinked. "Excuse me?"

"Stupidity, plain and simple, son. Got a whopping great dose of pepper spray from an old pensioner I was tryin' to rob. Point blank, man, right in the eye, God bless her." Strangely, his words were said with a large measure of love and respect.

"You sound grateful," Chris said with a crooked smile.

"'Course I'm grateful, ya dummy. I was jus' a stupid kid back then. Most nineteen-year-old boys are though, aren't they. Been paying for my stupidity ever since."

"So you're what now—fifty-five-ish? That's not that old."

"Look much older though, don't I?" E.Z. said with a weak smile. "Feel older too. It's not the years or the miles, son; it's how you walk the miles."

Chris frowned and rubbed his neck. "Wow. Twenty-plus years for attempted robbery, huh? That seems rather harsh."

Old E.Z. lowered his eyes and thoughtfully wrung his crooked hands. His voice was soft, full of humiliation. "Twenty-plus years for blindly takin' a swing at the sweet old gal after she sprayed my eye. Accidently sent her down a flight of stairs. Snapped her neck like it was a toothpick, man. Didn't mean to, I swears it. It was a reflex, is all; from the pain, you know? Should'a been manslaughter; instead I got second-degree murder." He shrugged ruefully. "Could'a been worse, I suppose."

Chris felt compassion for the old man. He could sense E.Z.'s remorse, his utter shame at the foolish act committed a quarter century ago as an impertinent young man. But he also felt for the family of the old woman he'd accidentally killed. And for what—a few dollars?

"What did you need the money for?" he asked.

"To help my mum. See, Pop walked out on her jus' after my kid brother was born. An' she already supportin' two kids from a previous loser. We'd been strugglin' ever since. I just tryin' to help is all, man. Don't do no drugs, no gamblin', no scorin', or whorin' neither. Ain't never been that way, anyhow. We just . . . tryin' to live, ya know?"

"I'm sorry," Chris offered, not knowing what else to say.

Ezekiel waved the condolence away. "Nah, man. I got what I deserved. Lost an eye for the attempted robbery and sentenced to thirty years a' my life for all a' hers. It's more'n a fair cop, don't you think?"

"Yeah. Thirty years is more than a fair cop," Chris said as he turned his attention to the prisoners passing by their cell. Regardless of age, the men jostled each other and swapped vulgar expletives like a bunch of rowdy teenagers without a care in the world. "I have a feeling not many in here feel the same about their sentences. But they should."

E.Z. smiled a deplorably discolored smile. "See, I knew you was different, Pendragon. Any man who prays like you can see clean into the hearts of men, be they black or white, sinners or saints, am I right?"

Chris didn't share the fact that he'd simply fallen asleep on his knees—that he hadn't been praying all night long. So he just shrugged. "I don't know about that."

"Well I do." Ezekiel groaned to his feet and cocked his head. "Come on, son. Let's get some of His Majesty's famous home cookin', eh?"

Following his cellmate down a flight of stairs, Chris noticed that E.Z. walked with a pronounced limp. The other prisoners flowed roughly past them, not caring that they nearly knocked the old man off his feet several times. Many of them called him names, most included hateful, degrading references to his bad eye. Chris sidled up to E.Z. and took his arm to prevent him from falling.

Entering the cafeteria, Chris held a tray and a plastic fork and spoon for his cellmate. The room was noisy and overcrowded. Profanity abounded. Worse, the place smelled like a locker room. It ruined what little appetite Chris had. He felt hundreds of mistrusting, hate-filled eyes on them as he followed E.Z. through the food line. With his stomach so knotted up, he selected only a small bowl of thick mush and a box of milk.

Standing his spoon upright in the dense porridge, he asked his cellmate, "Is this food or wallpaper paste?"

E.Z. chuckled warmly. "Well they calls it food, but you might want to get two or three more milks and a bottle of water, eh? That there stuff is stodgy enough to clog a storm drain, man. Jus' think what it do to *your* plumbing."

Carrying both trays, Chris followed E.Z. to a table in the corner. Two men already there got up, scowling, and left. Right as Chris and E.Z. sat down, two large guards approached at a brisk pace.

"Christian Pendragon?" asked one of them.

"Yes?"

"Warden wants to see you."

Chris glanced at E.Z. The old man was focused on his food tray, clearly not wanting to get involved. It was probably wise in a place like this. Chris rose, leaving his food behind, and followed the guards out of the cafeteria, down a corridor, through several electronic gates, and finally to an office marked: J. D. Flanders, Warden.

Flanders was a big-boned man with a shaved head and a look that said, "Don't test my patience." Wearing narrow reading glasses, he was perusing some official-looking papers. Behind him, a framed cross-stitch read: *God's law is higher than man's law*. Without looking up, he motioned to a chair in front of his desk. "Sit."

Chris did. Along the wall to his right was a bank of monitors displaying images of various locations in the prison, including the cafeteria. E.Z. was still sitting alone in the corner.

"I'm not sure why you're here, Mr. Pendragon," the warden said, scanning the papers with a deep frown. "MI5 seems to think you may have organized crime connections in the UK, but I just don't see it."

"Neither do I," Chris agreed.

"Please, do not speak unless I ask you a direct question. Is that understood?" Flanders said in an even tone, still reading.

"Yes, sir."

He spent another two or three minutes reading the documents before conversing again. "Normally, you'd be processed through the local police station and held there, considering the minor infractions listed here, but since there's a possible connection with the mob in the UK—and since you are a foreigner and a flight risk—I suppose we'll just have to accommodate you for the time being." Looking up over his reading glasses, his frown deepened. "Are you a mobster, Mr. Pendragon?"

"No, sir."

"What do you do for a living?"

"I'm a history teacher."

The warden snorted and shook his head. Then, removing his reading glasses, he tapped the sides of the papers into a neat stack. Giving Chris a patronizing once-over, he sniggered, "A history teacher is just about what I would've pegged you as."

Chris ignored the jibe.

"What do you make of the embroidered message behind me, Mr. Pendragon?"

"God's law trumps man's law."

The warden nodded. "True, but to what degree?"

"Sir?"

"Most men in here interpret the phrase as meaning they can get away with whatever they like so long as it's done in God's name. I like to read it as meaning, as long as you obey God's laws, you'll do just fine with man's laws too."

Chris thought for a moment. "Yes, I'd have to agree with that."

"Excellent. Now, as a foreigner, I assume you'd like to contact your consulate pretty soon, is that right?"

"Yes, please. I believe the American embassy is located somewhere in London, but I don't know the number."

Flanders fastened the papers with a clip and slid them into a folder. "I am well aware of where your embassy is, Mr. Pendragon, and I happen to have their telephone number too. I will allow one brief call to them at this time. If they wish to address any change in your venue or any other legal considerations, please have them contact MI5 directly, not this facility. I have more pressing issues to deal with than how some wayward history teacher was in the wrong place at the wrong time."

"Thanks," Chris said, wondering why his situation was blatantly obvious to this man but not to Detective Westcott. "But isn't the embassy closed?"

"Closed? No. It's an embassy; it never closes unless there's a terrorist threat. Why would you think that?"

"Never mind," he sighed bitterly.

CHAPTER 52

"YES, MR. PENDRAGON, WE DO understand the gravity of your situation," the female voice said with strained patience over the phone, "but we don't have an office in Cardiff, and it'll take at least twenty-four hours to verify your passport and assign a researcher to your case. And being the weekend, it may well be Monday afternoon before you hear anything."

"In other words, it'll be two or three days before the United States embassy even *starts* to look into helping one of its citizens," Chris spat, failing at quelling his rising temper. "Gee, thanks."

"I'm sorry, sir, but the wheels of justice turn as slowly here as they do back home."

"Yeah. Makes me proud to be an American."

"We'll be sure to confirm fair and humane treatment of you while you're incarcerated. You have nothing to fear as long as you obey the rules, okay? Is there anything else I can do for you, sir?"

"Yes. Please contact Gonzaga University in Spokane, Washington. I'm scheduled to resume teaching next Thursday. Tell them I may be unavoidably and indefinitely detained because the wheels of justice are mired in ludicrous bureaucracy and shoddy administration."

There was a bitter feel to the pause on the line. Chris looked up at Warden Flanders. The large man sat reclined in his desk chair, arms folded, eyes expressionless as he chewed on the stem of his reading glasses.

"I'll see what I can do, sir. Thank you for calling. Good-bye." *Click.*

It took all Chris's willpower not to slam down the handset.

"A soft answer turneth away wrath," Flanders said.

Chris frowned. "Excuse me?"

"Proverbs 15:1. It's better not to stir up ill will in a situation like yours with insolent remarks. 'Grievous words stir up anger,' the Good Book says. Your 'ludicrous bureaucracy and shoddy administration' comments probably didn't help your case, eh, Mr. Pendragon?"

Chris swallowed his pride and nodded. "No, sir." He sighed. "It's been a rough week."

Flanders rocked forward and tapped the folder containing his papers. "So I've read." He set his glasses on the desk and interlaced his fingers. Chris squirmed uncomfortably under the calm, steely gaze. Finally, the warden said, "I tell you what, Mr. Pendragon. I can put you in a single cell for now; keep you away from the riffraff of our facility if you like."

Chris almost jumped at the chance, but his mind went to Ezekiel Athens, alone again in his cell. Twenty-five years ago the man was guilty of a stupid crime, but he was innocent in intent. He didn't mean to kill or even hurt the woman whose money he wanted. Her death was an accident. But it *was* a crime, and E.Z. was willing to fulfill his penance for committing it. What Chris really wanted was to feel the comfort of the Dial again. Perhaps he could share some of that comfort . . .

"I don't mind bunking with Mr. Athens. He seems harmless enough. But I would like to ask one favor, if I may."

Flanders tilted his head to one side. "Bold. Unwise. But I'm willing to entertain your request."

"When I was brought in, I had in my pocket a small piece of alabaster with some writing on it. It's a religious token and too small to be a danger to anyone. May I please have it back? It would be a great comfort to me."

"Yes, I saw that. Is it a Mezuzah?" Flanders asked, referring to the sacred marker Jewish practitioners place on the lintel of their front door.

"No, sir, but it has the same intent. It reminds me of responsibilities and promises important to me."

The warden resumed chewing on the stem of his reading glasses. "It seems to me Mr. Athens wears a small crucifix and has a picture of the Christ by his bed."

Chris hadn't noticed those things, but he wasn't surprised.

Flanders nodded. "Okay. I'll agree to that. But no one, including Americans, gets special consideration in my prison without earning it."

"Thanks," he said, then paused. "But . . . may I ask *how* I earned it?"

The warden indicated the bank of TV monitors along his wall with a tilt of his head. "I've watched how considerate you've been to an old man you just met. That rates high in my book."

"Ah. Well, thank you, sir."

With the Dial in hand, Chris was escorted back to his cell. E.Z. was on his cot reading a book on Japanese gardening.

"What'd Warden Flanders want?" E.Z. asked, looking up.

"Just to introduce himself. Nice guy."

E.Z.'s rumbling chuckle ensued. "Now, that proves you a natural-born liar."

"No, seriously," Chris laughed. "He's strict, but he seems to have a good head on his shoulders. I get the feeling he doesn't take much guff."

"You got that right, son. Man thumps the Bible harder than most preachers hereabouts."

Chris sat and pointed at the book in E.Z.'s hands. "Where'd you get the reading material?"

"Prison library, ya dummy. Where you think, man?"

"Nice. What else is there to do around here?"

"You could work out in the gym with half the inmates or get beat up playing rugby outside with the other half. Or I could show you the way to the library, where you can exercise your brain, if'n you have one."

Chris rolled his eyes. "Why don't you just tell me how to get there, old man. I don't want you overdoing it on my account."

* * *

By the time Chris got back from the library, E.Z. was fast asleep on his cot. It being lunchtime, Chris considered waking him but decided simply to bring him back something from the cafeteria. Lunch offered only two choices: some kind of pale, pasty meat stew or grilled cheese sandwiches swimming in grease. Chris opted for the stew, regretted it, then slipped two rolls into his pockets and returned to his cell. E.Z. was sitting up, reading again.

"I brought you a couple rolls."

"Thanks, man. I catnap a lot and miss a meal now and then."

"You should eat to keep up your strength."

"Yeah? What you know about it?"

"I come from a family of doctors," he said as if wasn't a big deal.

Ezekiel scrutinized Chris with his one good eye. "You a doctor?"

"In a way. I have a PhD and I . . . um . . ."

"And you what, man?"

Chris sighed. "And that's about it. Now you eat. I'm going to catch a nap myself."

Because he hadn't slept well the night before, Chris dropped off quickly and slept deeply until three o'clock.

When he got up, he encouraged his cellmate to go for a walk in the yard. "Exercise is good for your joints as long as you take it easy," he said, helping E.Z. downstairs and through the outer doors. "Besides, we both could use a little sunshine. It's good for the mood."

They casually strolled the inside perimeter of the fence a few times. Even though the sun was shining, it was cold enough for both men to opt for sweaters. Chris lost track of time, but it didn't matter. He wasn't expecting to get out of there anytime soon.

They returned to their cell at a leisurely pace. Neither man was in a big hurry, knowing they had nowhere else to go.

E.Z. talked about his life before prison. He'd been a high school dropout, but since entering HMP Cardiff, he'd earned his GED. After that, he lost interest in education. "Never been the scholarly type," he said without remorse. He was content to simply read and bide his time. He'd been offered early parole nine times but had turned it down each time, much to the chagrin of his family. He was determined to serve the full sentence for his stupidity. Chris explained how the system was meant to help the accused understand the social and moral implications of their wrongdoings. After they'd learned their lesson, they were eligible to leave. E.Z. had learned his lesson long ago, but he still felt compelled to finish his sentence. He'd spent half his life behind those walls. What was a few more years compared to a lady who'd lost all of hers?

At close to nine o'clock that evening, Chris looked up to see Warden Flanders standing at his cell door. Ezekiel was already asleep—or pretending to be. The warden motioned with a tip of his head for Chris to approach.

"Yes, sir?" Chris whispered.

"You have visitors," Flanders said quietly.

"Who?"

"Best come with me," he answered cryptically. "And grab your things. You won't be coming back."

Chris glanced back into the cell. "Can I say good-bye first?"

A nod. "Do so quietly."

He returned to slip on his sweater and confirmed that the Dial was still in his pocket. The warden watched intently, but Chris didn't care. He knelt beside Ezekiel's cot. "Good-bye, my friend. You have more than paid for your stupid mistake."

An unexpected rush of compassion engulfed Chris. Instantly, he knew what he must do next. It was the right thing. He removed the Dial and gently placed his other hand over his cellmate's forehead and bad eye. Focusing on Ezekiel's damaged eye, he imagined the scar tissue dissolving, the iris and lens healing, and his eyesight being restored to normal. He prayed with all his heart that forgiveness and healing would come to this kind old man. "Yours is not the devil's eye; it is the eye of the penitent," he said reverently, barely above a whisper. "Be healed, Ezekiel. Through faith thy will be done."

Chris felt an intense, sharp burning in his left eye. He recoiled and covered the eye with his palm, trying not to cry out. Then, as quickly as it came, it passed. He stood and moved carefully to the cell door, feeling inexplicably unsure of his balance. Flanders opened the bars just enough for Chris to exit then closed them again.

Moving down the dimly lit causeway, Flanders glanced at Chris and frowned. "Did you contract pinkeye or take a punch out in the yard?"

"Neither. Why?"

"Your left eye looks very painful. It's all red and swollen like."

Chris shrugged. "It'll pass."

CHAPTER 53

CHRIS DID A DOUBLE-TAKE WHEN he saw Father Llewellyn and Michael sitting in the warden's office.

"Christian, my lad," Llewellyn sang, standing. "Bless my soul, you sure do find the strangest places to land, don't you, son. I never know where I'm going to find you next."

"It's good to see you, Father. You too, Michael."

The linebacker smiled briefly.

"Did you enjoy your stay in His Majesty's prison?" Llewellyn asked dubiously.

Chris glanced at Flanders, unsure of what to say. "'Enjoy' isn't the first word that comes to mind, but, um, I guess it was okay. Food could be better."

"So I've heard," Llewellyn laughed. "Right then: change out of those silly pajamas, and gather your belongings. It's late, and we've a long journey home, yes?"

Chris looked to Flanders again, this time for instruction.

"He's correct, Mr. Pendragon. You're free to go."

"Okay, um . . . thanks," he said in confusion.

The warden folded his arms and offered a weak smile. "It seems the good Father here has been beating the halls of justice in your behalf. He contacted the head magistrate, the Right Honorable Lord Wellington, and asked him to review the case."

"Which he was more than pleased to do," Llewellyn interjected.

"Quite. Anyway," the warden continued, "Lord Wellington has ruled that you do not pose an imminent threat to the public's safety. He has rescinded all warrants for your detention and has nullified all existing investigations except one."

"Really? Which one?" Chris wondered.

"Suspicion of connection with organized crime in the UK."

"That's ridiculous. I—"

Flanders extended a palm, stopping the tirade before it ran amuck. "I would accept the Right Honorable Judge's good graces and not make a fuss over it if I were you, Mr. Pendragon. Being suspected of mob connections is not a crime in and of itself, but it does carry with it a burden of civil obedience above and beyond the mark, if you get my meaning."

He understood perfectly. As long as he was in Wales, he would be watched like a hawk day and night. "Yes, I see," he said backing off, tempering his anger.

"Excellent. The investigation will continue, of course, so do not be surprised to hear from MI5 again. They can be . . . tenacious," he said with a knowing tilt of the head.

Chris nodded.

"Good. Now, one last thing: please explain to me what all that falderal was when you were saying good-bye to Mr. Athens."

"Nothing. I just whispered good-bye."

The warden's eyes narrowed slightly. It was clear he didn't believe Chris. "Very well," he said after a moment. "Since there's nothing more to discuss, you'll find your personal effects in the admittance office. You may change into your civilian clothing there."

"What personal effects?"

"Your watch, your wallet and mobile phone, your passport and some money, I should think. There's also your luggage and a satchel of some sort the constables confiscated from your rental car. Oh, and a very nice walking staff, I'm led to understand."

Chris couldn't believe his ears. He nodded with a blank stare.

"Traditionally, I give departing inmates a stern lecture about the purpose for laws and civil obedience; of being a benefit to society rather than a burden, and so forth. But I trust you understand these principles of common decency," Flanders said, nodding toward the stitched saying behind his desk. "Suffice it to say I will be greatly disappointed if you return here as a ward of the crown, Mr. Pendragon."

"Yes, sir," he replied sincerely. "So will I."

Flanders offered his hand. "It was a pleasure to meet you, Mr. Pendragon. I know Mr. Athens will miss your company."

Chris returned the brief shake. "He's a good man."

Flanders moved to his office door and opened it. "Stay a good man yourself, Christian. And as a word of personal advice, stick to your chosen calling. You're not much good at being a criminal."

A guard escorted Chris, Llewellyn, and Michael to the admittance office. Chris's civilian clothing had been cleaned and pressed. He changed in an exam room, feeling instantly freer being out of prison garb. At the processing counter, a clerk handed Chris a Release of Property form. Chris compared what was listed on the form with the items on the counter. It was all there. He reverently took Nick's staff with both hands. It was more beautiful than he remembered. Holding the cane snuggly against his chest, he felt a tide of serenity wash through him. Although he knew the cane held no spiritual powers or magical faculties, he nonetheless sensed virtue surrounding it. Closing his eyes, he offered a quick, silent prayer of thanks.

As Chris handed back the completed form, the clerk slid a form toward Michael. The big man frowned.

"What's all this then?" Llewellyn asked, craning his neck to look at the paperwork.

"Employment application, Father," the clerk said. "We need blokes his size in here, ya? I'm only five foot six, see. Inmates won't give me time of day like, but they'd do whatever he says without batting an eye."

CHAPTER 54

"How'd you know I was in there?" Chris asked, settling in the backseat of the Subaru.

Llewellyn sat next to Chris, and Michael squeezed into the driver's seat. "Dr. Ingledew told me, of course. She called to say my car was still at hospital and someone needed to collect it. She said you'd been arrested. So, naturally, I called the authorities in Monmouth straight away. The detective with the spectacles—"

"Westcott."

"Yes, yes, of course. Detective Westcott explained that he'd transferred you directly to His Majesty's Prison in Cardiff. It's a bit out of the ordinary, yes? But he claimed some obscure precedent allowed for it. He was in fear for the public's safety, bless his soul."

"Yeah, I'm a real menace to society," Chris said, staring out the window, taking in Cardiff's weekend nightlife. "Did Kathryn say anything else?"

"Kathryn? Oh yes, Dr. Ingledew. No, she merely passed on the news of your arrest by Detective Westcott."

"When did she call?"

"Oh, long about suppertime, I should think. She did not sound happy, Christian, if that's what you're fishing for. She was concerned. I heard tears over the line, for sure an' certain, I did."

Chris scoffed loudly. "I take it she neglected to tell you *she* was the one who turned me in."

Llewellyn frowned. "Oh aye? No, that crumb of information was left out, I'm afraid."

As Michael turned east onto the M4, the weekend traffic thickened. The night was clear and dry, but the big man clenched the steering wheel as if driving through a blizzard. He was visibly anxiety-ridden by big-city driving. Chris considered offering to take the wheel, but he was too preoccupied with his own distracting thoughts.

Forcing thoughts about Kathryn aside, Chris asked, "So how *did* you get me out?"

"Ah yes, that. I tried calling the prison directly after I received no help from Detective Westcott, but they wouldn't patch me through to anyone in authority. So rather than continuing to beat around the bush, I got on the horn to Alfred."

"Alfred?"

"Yes, the Right Honorable Lord Alfred Wellington. I didn't always minister in Trellech, my son," he said, patting Chris on the knee. "Before I was assigned to the Church of St. Nicholas, I was an assistant churchwarden under the Archbishop of Wales in Llandaff Cathedral. There, I became good friends with Judge Wellington, as that is his place of worship, yes? He's quite the man's man, I must say." With a lopsided grin, he cocked his head to one side and chuffed. "It's a good thing I've vowed to uphold the secrecy of the confessional. As God is my witness, some of the sins I absolved would make a sailor blush. May God forgive the man his weaknesses," he whispered, still grinning, crossing himself twice. "Anyroad, Alfred felt he owed me a few favors—which he didn't—but I cashed one in nonetheless."

"Ah. Well, I'm glad you did," Chris said, returning his attention to the night scenery. He watched the passing cars and cities with veiled interest. The brightly lit industrial and urban sprawl of this part of the country was impressive but somewhat disheartening. While much of the local history and lore was preserved, Chris felt it couldn't compare to the placid, bucolic nature of rural Wales. He was certain Father Llewellyn felt the same way.

"I take it you didn't care for the big city? Is that why you moved to the Church of St. Nicholas?"

Sudden glistening shone in the vicar's eyes. He drew a quick breath to compose himself and released it slowly with a warm, soft smile. When he spoke, his words were mellowed with deeply rooted emotion. "No, my son. I requested the transfer because I too have been blessed to have met the Beloved Saint."

"Wait—you've met Nicholas Tewdrig? But I thought you hadn't."

"Never said the like, now did I? He came to me once, many, many years ago. The long and short of it is that he cured me of a vexation that was sure to take my life."

"What vexation?"

Llewellyn gave him a look of fatherly admonition. "That's between St. Nicholas and myself, isn't it now, Christian."

"Sorry," he said, duly chastened. "So in essence, he . . . healed you?"

"Aye. He showed up when I needed him most, laid his hands upon me, and then left. I've never seen him since, though I've spent myriad hours searching for him." He scoffed derisively. "I am truly ashamed of the number of days—nay, *years*—I've wasted that could have been used in the Lord's service. In truth, I hoped he might someday return to his chapel so I could thank him properly; but, alas, he never came—leastwise, not that I know of. But I did learn many wonderful things about the man, yes? He was a saint, called of God, for sure an' certain, I can tell thee. Oh, the stories I could share . . ." He drifted off as if daydreaming.

After a moment or two, Chris prompted, "And . . . ?"

Llewellyn wiped a tear from his cheek. "And then I met you, my son; which I consider the next best thing, if you'll take no offense to the notion."

"Of course not," he said, wanting a more detailed story but sensing now was not the time to ask. "So . . . what happens next?"

"Next I suggest you take a good night's rest then be on your way, lad, yes?"

"On my way?"

"Yes, of course. You may stay the night in the rectory loft again, but in the morning you'll need to act sharp in order to catch your flight."

"But my flight doesn't leave until Tuesday."

"Forget about that flight, lad. We booked you a new flight under the church's purview."

Chris blinked. "Excuse me?"

"Christian, my son. While you now bear a high and holy calling, yours will not be a life of leisure or bliss. I've come to believe that those with the greatest blessings are often those with the greatest challenges. For the present, it would be prudent for you to leave Wales as quickly and as quietly as possible, yes?"

"But why? The judge said I was cleared of all charges. Besides, aren't I meant to serve as a healer here?"

"The calling of healer—indeed, as one of the Physicians of Myddfai—is not necessarily an indigenous one. The world is full of good people in need of your gift, son, but you should always give it anonymously. Go whenever and wherever you're prompted to go. As a Vovnik, you'll soon learn how."

He frowned. "Then why leave in such a rush? Am I in danger here?"

"Yes, I believe you are. I fear word of your doings has already gotten out. There have been a few strange men visiting the chapel, sitting long hours in their cars, and the like. You may soon be set upon by treasure hunters seeking the Dial of Ahaz and its power. I've little doubt Collingswood told his associates about you and his acquisition of the Dial, yes? You need to vanish, as it were, for a time."

"Vanish to where?"

"To the United States, of course. You'll blend in easier there than anywhere else, won't you now? You'll probably want to assume a new name and such. And try not to stay in one location for very long."

Chris couldn't believe what he was hearing. He'd finally accepted his calling as a healer, but he had no indication that would require him to become a phantom from society. What about his job? What about his family? What about a life of his own—a future with a wife and kids? Was he meant to be a vagabond the next two hundred plus years?

"You know, Christian, that Warden Flanders chap is a wise man," the vicar continued. "He hit the peg squarely on the head about you, for sure an' certain. You *do* need to get on with your calling."

"My *calling*? It's beginning to seem more like a burden."

"Perhaps. But you and I both know it is a sacred gift passed on to *you* by our Beloved St. Nicholas because no one else but you could carry it, yes?"

Trapped again. If Chris answered yes, he'd be ensnared in the commitment forever. But if he answered no, he'd be discarding a sacred trust. *Not much of a choice*, he groused silently.

He sat in a stupor the rest of the trip, wondering for the umpteenth time why he'd decided to come to Wales in the first place.

Michael pulled up to the old cottage just before midnight. Chris was desperately fatigued, but he doubted he could sleep. His head hurt from thinking, from speculating on what a lonely future his would be. Exiting the Subaru, he numbly followed the priest and his manservant inside and slowly climbed the stairs to the loft. His luggage was still in the car, but he was too tired to care.

Kneeling, he offered up his soul to God, asking for guidance and wisdom, but mostly for confidence that he would finally understand why he'd been chosen for this life-altering mission.

CHAPTER 55

"St. Pendragon, sir. It's time to get up." The voice from below belonged to Michael.

Chris realized his head was filled with morning cobwebs, but he could swear the big man had just referred to him as "Saint." He wondered what that meant but knew he'd get scant explanation from the quiet giant.

He trudged down the stairs and sat at the breakfast table. So many uncertainties filled his head it was hard to focus on any single issue. More than anything he felt . . . directionless.

"Why the long face, Christian?" Father Llewellyn asked, pulling up a chair opposite him.

"Just feeling a little overwhelmed," he admitted.

"A little? As God is my witness, lad, I'd be completely beside myself and would have to spend the entire day in the water closet were I in your breeches."

Chris smiled at the vicar's attempt to lighten his mood.

"What are your concerns, my son? Let me be a balm to your troubled soul."

He thought for a moment. "Okay. What do I do about my teaching job back home?"

"Tenure your resignation."

He blinked hard. "Then how will I make money? I still have to eat and sleep somewhere, not to mention getting around from place to place."

"Luke 22:35."

Chris cupped his head between his hands and massaged his temples. "I should have known you'd answer with something like that. Okay, what does that verse say?"

Llewellyn cleared his throat. "'And he said unto them, When I sent you without purse, and scrip, and shoes, lacked ye anything? And they said, Nothing.' It were the Apostles Jesus was speaking to just then, yes? You're not an Apostle, but you do have a sacred and holy calling, same as the Apostles, do you not? The Lord will provide, son. Trust in him."

"That's going to take a much higher level of faith than I have. Money makes the world go 'round, or haven't you heard?"

"Oh aye. I'm well aware of that. But money for your *needs* will always be there; it's the money for *wants* that people spend their lives chasing."

He couldn't argue with that.

"Father?" Michael said, pointing to his watch.

"Right," Llewellyn chirped, slapping the table. "Time to gird up your loins, Christian. We said adieu once before, and I found you in prison the next day."

"It was two days," Chris argued lightly.

"Whatever. Please try to do better this time," he said with a wink—but also with a catch in his voice. His attempts at jovialness failed to pierce the profound sadness of this good-bye.

They stood and embraced warmly. "I thank'ee for complicating my life, lad. It's brought me more joy than you can ever comprehend."

"Same to you, Father." Feeling his throat tighten, Chris asked, "Will I ever see you again?"

The vicar's eyes pooled with tears. "I would love that more than all things. But you must only come if you feel so prompted by the Holy Spirit."

"You mean I can't simply stop by for a quick hello?" he said, forcing a grin.

The tears fell. "No, my son."

"Why?"

"Twice I've been graced by a Vovnik healer, yes? It is prideful of me to desire the gift a third time . . . and it would be wrong for you to offer."

Duly chastened but accepting the admonition, Chris felt as if his heart would rip in two. Swallowing hard, he whispered, "Good-bye then, Father."

Llewellyn nodded, unable to voice his last farewell.

As they drove away, Chris glanced back at the Church of St. Nicholas and the small cottage beside it. Father Llewellyn stood in the rectory doorway, solemnly making the sign of the cross while weeping like a child.

Michael drove Chris straight to Cardiff International Airport. It was the third time Chris made the trip from Trellech to the Welsh Capital, but it was not any easier. He wrestled tear-filled eyes and a lump in his throat the entire way. Michael softly hummed church hymns, as if trying to soothe Chris's raw emotions. The man was completely tone deaf, but Chris appreciated the effort. He held the Dial in his hands and let his mind fill with fond memories rather than future ambiguities. It was his only comfort.

* * *

Chris packed Nick's walking staff in a box with bubble wrap he bought at a FedEx kiosk in the airport, and he checked the package in with his luggage. He paid for it with money still in his wallet. Curiously, he didn't remember having so much in there. The Dial rested in his pocket. He continued to wonder when and how he'd be prompted to use it. He hoped it'd be obvious. Subtle hints were never his forte; a brick to the side of the head was more to his liking. Nick had said something about a *still, small voice*. The adage was in the Old Testament somewhere. The voice of the Lord isn't always in a rushing wind, a trembling earthquake, or a billowing fire. Quite often it's merely a still, small voice.

Would he be in tune enough to hear it?

Michael walked him to the airline counter and showed the attendant a reservation slip. The woman processed the boarding pass without pause, verifying the name on it with Chris's passport. No problem.

After they stepped away from the counter, Michael offered Chris a crushing handshake, turned, and left him standing alone in the terminal.

"Good-bye," Chris said to the quiet man's back.

Chris quickly located his gate and sought out a vending machine. One of the selections was Day's Pale Dry Ginger Ale. He chuckled to himself, thinking back to the owners of the Black Boar pub. If they only knew what the Dial—a rune stone and a talisman, they'd called it—actually did.

Waiting for his flight to board, Chris felt his phone buzz. The ID read HMP Cardiff.

"Hello?"

"Mr. Pendragon? This is Warden Flanders speaking. Have I caught you at a bad time?"

"No, sir. What can I do for you?"

"There's something I just can't stop wondering about. Your eye, sir. How is it? The left one that was so inflamed last night."

Chris's brows pulled together. "Fine, thank you. Why do you ask?"

"Because so is Ezekiel Athens's eye—the one that's been useless for twenty-five years now. There's no longer any scarring or discoloration, and his vision is 20-20. Curious that, isn't it?" His tone was frank and only mildly accusatory.

Chris knew he'd been discovered, but he didn't feel threatened by it. Flanders seemed more inquisitive than judgmental, and Chris was pretty certain he only wanted clarification. "Yes, that is curious. But it's great news too, don't you think?"

"Oh, it's downright *miraculous* news, if you take my meaning. Care to enlighten me on what really happened in that cell?"

Chris hesitated, unsure of what—if anything—to say. There was no question the warden suspected he had somehow healed E.Z.'s bad eye. Still, Chris couldn't just brazenly admit to that. Part of his charge as a Vovnik was to remain anonymous. "I'm not sure what you—"

"I saw you put your hand on Mr. Athens's head that night. Then I saw you whisper something to him. Why did you do that, Mr. Pendragon?"

Chris shied from the answer. Why *did* he do it? The old man hadn't asked to be healed. He accepted his injury as punishment for his wrong deed. And yet Chris had felt justified—even prompted—to heal him because he had shown true, humble, sincere repentance. Perhaps it was merely a way of showing compassion.

"I just said good-bye."

"No, I can't accept that. You did more than say good-bye, sir. Was it some kind of witchcraft—some black magic of some sort?"

Chris took a deep breath. "Okay, look. You believe in spiritual gifts, don't you, Mr. Flanders? You quoted scripture to me, and your wall plaque indicates you're a spiritual man."

There was pensive hesitation on the other end of the line. Then, "Yes, I believe in gifts of the Spirit."

"So do you really think it was witchcraft that healed Ezekiel Athens?"

A longer, deeper silence prevailed this time. Chris waited patiently until he heard his flight number announced over the loudspeakers. "I'm sorry, Mr. Flanders, but my flight's just been called. Thank you for updating me on E.Z.'s condition. I'm very happy for him. You have a nice day, sir."

"Wait! Please. Who—who are you?" the warden nearly begged.

"I'm just a man, Mr. Flanders. A man with a gift he suddenly found himself burdened with, a gift that even he can't explain. I hope to be able to someday, but until that time, I wish to remain anonymous, if it's all the same to you."

Chris heard the warden draw a stuttering breath and let it out slowly. "I understand," he said. "Thank you, Christian. Thank you for strengthening my faith in mankind. That's not easy to do, considering the people I deal with daily."

"It's been my pleasure."

He ended the call with an unexpected realization: It *had* been his pleasure to heal Ezekiel. A real joy, in fact. Like a second epiphany, the insight lifted him from his chair with surprising exuberance. His melancholy and self-doubt seemed to vanish like a puff of murky smoke. This calling, this destiny of his wasn't the burden he'd previously thought it was. His gift could not only help others, it could actually bring him true happiness too.

He started laughing giddily. Waiting passengers cast concerned and amused glances his way—which made him laugh even more. He was making a spectacle of himself, but he didn't care. Suddenly, all was right in his life.

CHAPTER 56

CHRIS'S FLIGHT ACROSS THE ATLANTIC was fraught with a bizarre mix of wistfulness and happiness. He was happy about the epiphany he'd received. His confidence was high; it buoyed him up tremendously. But he was reticent to be leaving a country he truly loved. He regretted not being able to spend more time exploring castles, researching legends, and unearthing genealogy. But those were desires from a former life, a life that now seemed decades old, a life he could never go back to.

As he waited for his connecting flight at LaGuardia, Chris casually watched the throngs of passengers coming and going. How many had sicknesses he could heal? How many were worthy of healing? Should he heal those people who suffered from self-inflicted ailments, such as lung cancer from smoking, drug addiction from illegal consumption or prescription abuse, or a sexually transmitted disease from a rash act driven by desire? Did they deserve the gift? It seemed more of a judgment call, but then thoughts of Ezekiel Athens filled his mind. The man deserved what he got; however, his case was unique because he was truly penitent. He recognized his sin and was willing to pay the full price for it.

In the end, Chris didn't feel prompted to heal anyone in the airport. He heard no still, small voice. Perhaps he was too tired. Although his body felt strong and ready to climb mountains, emotionally he was shattered. Secretly, he hoped he wouldn't be called on to heal anyone until after he got home and had a chance to rest and reflect, to plan and prepare.

He scoffed noisily. Plan for what? Prepare for when? In certain ways, his life was now as fanciful as the legends and myths he had studied. Legends were generally embellishments or misinterpretations of actual events. And yet there was no misinterpreting what Chris had experienced. He had a shard from *the* Dial of Ahaz. He knew what it was and what it did. He still wasn't sure *how* it worked, but that no longer seemed to matter. He had been adopted into the family of Myddfai. He could heal, just as many of the Righteous Thirty-Six before him. The question that continually plagued him was, Why him? Maybe someday that would become clear too. Maybe.

After Chris had his boarding pass scanned, he entered the plane. Finding his seat in coach, he settled in next to the window. As a number of passengers jostled by, a young boy stood staring at him from the aisle. The kid looked to be about eight or nine—the same age as Nigel—but with brown eyes and closely-shorn hair. He wore a light-blue T-shirt with a big pink boxing glove pictured on it. A caption read: *I'm going to beat it!*

"Hi," the boy said with a disarming smile.

"Hey," Chris responded.

"That's my seat," he said, pointing to the center chair in the row of three.

Only then did Chris realize his satchel was still sitting there. "Oops, sorry," he said, quickly removing it and storing it under the seat in front of him.

As the boy took his seat, a woman—undoubtedly the boy's mother—sat in the aisle seat next to him. She looked to be in her late thirties, attractive, but with dark circles poorly hidden under makeup around her eyes.

"My name is Kaylee," the child said. "What's yours?"

Wait, Chris thought. *She's not a boy?* Only then did he notice tiny, flower-capped posts in each ear. The mom seemed fairly traditional—loosely styled hair, conservative clothes. He wondered why she would allow her daughter to buzz her hair. And then it came to him. His heart immediately went out to her.

"My name's Chris. I'm very pleased to meet you."

"This is my mom," the girl said cheerily. "Her name is Kristen."

Chris gave a friendly half-wave. "Hi."

Kristen smiled and said hi. She had a lovely smile pinched by fatigue. Kaylee's smile was impish and full of life, but it too held traces of an inner conflict.

The backstory was clear. They were traveling to or from some cancer treatment center. Chris recognized the small bump beneath the neck of Kaylee's tee as a medication port.

As the plane sealed up and prepared for departure, fresh pangs of remorse assaulted Chris. He'd been unable to save Kathryn's mother from cancer. The little girl beside him would be a constant reminder of that failure the entire flight.

When they were at cruising altitude and allowed to unfasten their seat belts, Kaylee leaned over the armrest to see out the window. Chris smiled and shifted to allow her a better view. Poor girl—

It hit him suddenly—a surge of compassion that nearly took his breath away. Its intensity and clarity were overwhelming. He knew what he must do, but the bitter memory of Lona Ingledew caused doubt to encircle his heart. He knew he should do it, but *could* he?

Nobly thru white fog hath I led. It was a test of faith. It would *always* be a test of faith. Father Llewellyn had said faith was like a muscle; it needed exercise to be strong. *So be it*, Chris thought, again feeling a surge of affirmation.

"Excuse me, Kristen?" he said, adopting his best smile. "Would you mind if I switched seats with Kaylee during the flight so she can see out the window?"

The mother seemed surprised that he would offer such a consideration.

"Oh yes, Mom, please oh please oh please?"

"Okay, okay," she chuckled. "That's very kind of you, Chris. Are you sure you don't mind?"

"Not at all," he said.

They all stood and moved into the aisle then reentered with Kaylee at the window and Chris in the middle. After buckling in again, Kristen said, "Thank you. That's very generous."

He waved it away. "My pleasure. I remember being a kid. The window seat is a make-or-break deal."

She rolled her eyes. "Don't I know it. I have to book these flights on a last-minute basis, and window seats are usually the first ones to go."

"Last minute?" he asked with a tilt of his head. He was trying to assess the extent of Kaylee's cancer without asking directly.

"Bone marrow transplant," Kristen said softly, nodding toward her daughter. "We're fighting leukemia. Matching bone marrows is not as easy as matching blood types. When a compatible one shows up, they call us for immediate transfusion. It hasn't worked yet, but we keep going back. This was number four."

Her eyes moistened as she spoke. Chris could tell it wasn't easy for her to remain stoic. The woman was at her breaking point, which meant Kaylee's prognosis wasn't good. His heart filled with compassion for both of them.

"So . . . to or from this time?"

"From. Back to Salt Lake from Johns Hopkins."

"Well, she's a brave girl, a fighter."

"Thank you, Chris. You're very kind. But she's a tornado. I can't keep up with her. She's not afraid to try anything. Says she wants to be a doctor." Her forced cheerfulness didn't fully cover her grief. She looked away and quickly wiped at her eyes. "Do you have children?"

"Oh no," he chuckled. "Haven't found a woman crazy enough to marry me yet."

She smiled appropriately. "Well, it won't be long, I'm sure. You're attractive and very kind. What do you do for a living?"

"I, um . . . I teach history at Gonzaga University. That's what repels women. I'm clinically boring."

She tipped her head back and laughed. "And you have a great sense of humor."

"Thanks. Hey listen, I know this is very sensitive and personal, but mind if I ask about the therapy? I come from a medical family."

"With AML? It's pretty brutal. We've done several rounds of chemo and radiation, and three previous rounds of bone marrow infusion. I—" Her voice caught. She turned away again.

"It's okay," Chris said. "I'm sorry. I shouldn't have asked."

"No. I'm sorry," she said, touching his wrist. "I should be used to this by now."

"Hard thing to get used to. Was this your first trip to Johns Hopkins?"

"Yes. The first bone marrow was done at the Huntsman Center in Salt Lake, one at Seattle Children's Hospital, and one at the Mayo Clinic in Rochester."

"Well," he said, stretching his arms forward with a groan. "I've heard they're very good at Johns Hopkins. I bet it'll take this time. You should rest. I'll let you know if Kaylee wants to try skydiving or asks to fly the plane."

She chuckled again and tipped her seat back. "You don't have to tell me twice."

Within minutes, Chris could hear the deep breathing signifying sleep from Kristen. Kaylee was still glued to the window. The sky was clear and offered a gorgeous view of the Great Lakes.

"Hey, Kaylee. Do you know what lake that is?"

"Um, Michigan?"

"Yes, good job," he praised. "So what's that big city along the shore?"

"Um . . . I don't know."

"Do you think it could be Chicago?"

"Yeah, probably."

Chris shifted so he could point at landmarks out the window—and put his hand across the nape of her neck. "You know the tallest building in America is in Chicago?"

"Cooool," she said.

"Tell me if you can see it when we pass over."

He closed his eyes and cleared his mind of all things except this innocent little girl with terminal cancer. His empathy swelled for her. She had so much to get out of life and so much to give. Holding the Dial in his other hand, he concentrated on leukemia—all he knew about it anyway, which sadly wasn't much. It affected the white blood cells; something about the bone marrow producing too many immature cells that destroy the mature ones. He imagined Kaylee's bone marrow developing properly and functioning exactly the way it was supposed to. He pictured her immune system strengthening, her muscles regaining tonicity, her ultra-short, auburn hair becoming as full as her mother's. Then he silently repeated the words: *Through faith thy will be done.*

The hand on her neck began to tingle. Then a sudden, intense wash of pain coursed through him. His joints ached and burned. His muscles twinged and seized. Unbelievable weakness inundated his body, making him glad he was sitting. He fought a welling urge to throw up, but he kept on imagining Kaylee in full health, silently repeating, *Please God, heal this child. Through faith thy will be done.* Then, finally, the pain began to subside.

He sat back and reclined his seat. After catching his breath, he said, "If you don't mind, I'm gonna follow your mom's example and take a nap, okay?"

"Okay," she said, still gazing out the window.

"How do you feel?" he asked hesitantly.

"Fine."

A typical nine-year-old response. But Chris didn't need any more confirmation than that. Kaylee *was* fine. He knew it. She'd remain "fine" and cancer-free the rest of her life. And that thought made him smile.

CHAPTER 57

KAYLEE AND CHRIS SWITCHED SEATS again when the captain flashed the *fasten-your-seat-belt* sign. Kristen asked her daughter all kinds of questions about what she'd seen, and Kaylee was only too happy to supply the answers.

"Chris said we flew past the tallest building in America," she chimed. "But we must have flown *over* it, because I didn't see it at all."

"Well, it's not *that* tall," her mother laughed. She then smiled at Chris and mouthed *thank you*.

He grinned and nodded. *You have no idea.*

Chris felt immense satisfaction, knowing what he'd done. Remarkably, the last thing he wanted was to gloat or seek glory. His was a gift to be shared, not hoarded or used for personal gain. Plus, *he* really hadn't done anything; a higher power had healed the young girl. He was merely a means to an end. And he was perfectly fine with that.

They landed in Salt Lake City to a clear blue sky. Chris had an hour layover before boarding his flight to Spokane. He said good-bye to Kristen and Kaylee, receiving a light hug from both before they headed off to their gate. He bit his tongue, wanting to ask to keep in touch so he could hear their reaction when they learned Kaylee's leukemia was gone. *No. Let it be their time for rejoicing*, he told himself.

He pulled the Dial from his pocket and kissed it. He didn't know why. Maybe as a thank you? He certainly knew venerating and worshipping a piece of alabaster wouldn't do anything. He was simply . . . happy.

Instead of heading to his gate, Chris wandered the concourses of the large airport, feeling the need to stretch his legs. Expecting to experience some jetlag, he was instead curiously restless.

Salt Lake International boasted hundreds of shops and kiosks from which travelers could purchase snacks, meals, drinks, and souvenirs. He passed by a Cinnabon outlet and stopped in his tracks at the aromas wafting from it: cinnamon, buttercream glaze, coffee, yeast. To allow such tempting scents into the general public seemed downright criminal. And even if it wasn't, it was definitely conniving.

Stepping up to the counter, he ordered a cinnamon roll and a carton of milk. The roll was almost the size of a baseball glove. He hoped he could take the leftovers on the plane. There was little chance he could eat the whole thing in less than an hour.

Sitting at a small, raised table near the causeway, he watched the tidal crowds ebb and flow. Again, he wondered if any of the passersby had ailments he could heal. The temptation to wield his power with reckless abandon was strong, but he knew he'd only be miserable doing so. Plus, it would draw too much attention. More than anything, he wished for some direction on *how* to run his new life.

Sipping his milk, he noticed an old man making a beeline toward him. The senior citizen was average height and weight, but he carried himself as if he were in tip-top condition. He had thick, silvery hair and deep, gray-green eyes.

"Christian Pendragon. Have you got a minute?"

Be careful what you wish for, Chris thought behind a smirk. Curiously, he wasn't surprised the old man knew his name. "Sure," he said, licking buttercream icing from his fingers.

"I know you have a flight in an hour."

"Of course you do."

"And you're anxious to get back to Spokane. But if you could indulge me, there's someone who desperately needs your abilities."

Chris wiped his fingers on a napkin and cautiously glanced around. He wasn't sure why; he simply felt like this conversation needed to be private, guarded. Leaning forward, he whispered, "For how long?"

"No need to whisper, Christian," the man said, with a sympathetic smile. "You'll miss your flight, but I can assure you another will be available at no extra cost when we return."

The man was so assertive and yet so non-threatening that Chris had no trouble believing him. Still, his bold, omniscient approach made Chris feel like a CIA operative. The man obviously knew of his abilities. Did that mean he was also . . .

"Are you a Vovnik?"

The man smiled warmly. "As are you."

Chris nodded and glanced at the half cinnamon roll on his plate. Sadly, his appetite was gone. "So, is this pretty much what my life will be like from now on: my personal freedom's a thing of the past?"

"No, Christian. You need only respond when you feel it is right. There are times you'll be prompted, but it is up to you whether to heed that prompt. You will not be judged one way or the other for your decision. As you well know, your gift is not to be flaunted, but it is also not to be hoarded or ignored. I'm asking this time as a favor. There is a woman—a single mother—who was strangled so severely, her throat was crushed. It's limited the oxygen to her brain. She's in critical condition, on life-support as we speak. She doesn't have much time."

"Where?" Chris asked through a sigh of resignation.

"Cody, Wyoming. West Park Hospital."

"Never heard of it."

"Does that matter?" the man asked, brazenly tearing a coil from the cinnamon roll.

"I guess not. How will I get there?"

"I have a light plane that can take us there directly. But we need to leave now, Christian. As I said, time is of the essence."

"Of course it is."

He didn't know why he was being flippant. The whole scenario was beyond belief. And yet every time he'd followed through on the unbelievable, he'd had a positive outcome. Well—almost every time. There was Kathryn's mother. He shook off his negative thoughts and stood. "I'd really rather you called me Chris. I prefer informality."

The man chuckled warmly. "Of course. And you may call me John."

Chris reached into his pocket and gripped the Dial. He closed his eyes and cleared his mind and, in doing so, immediately felt the validity of what this man was telling him. More importantly, he felt intensely drawn to the woman, knowing only he could save her.

CHAPTER 58

SITTING ON THE TARMAC, THE twin-engine Cessna was primed and ready to go. John instructed Chris to take the copilot's seat then rounded the plane and settled into the captain's chair. Chris followed his example by buckling in and donning a headset.

John started the props, checked his gauges, radioed the tower, and asked for clearance. They taxied to a runway away from the big jetliners and took to the sky.

"So, do you have a last name?" Chris asked once they leveled out.

"Oh. My apologies. I should have formally introduced myself. My name is John Aquila."

"Christian Pendragon—although you already know that."

John smiled. "I suppose you have many questions for me?"

Chris looked out the window at the peaks of the Wasatch mountain range. "Thousands. But whenever I asked Nicholas Tewdrig a question, he answered it with two of his own. I always got behind and forgot my original question. That's not a Vovnik training exercise of some kind, is it?"

John burst out with a resounding chortle. "No, it's not. But that sounds like good old Nicholas."

"You knew him?" That surprised Chris.

Sobering, John said, "It was my great privilege to meet him on several occasions."

"Then . . . I suppose you know he's dead."

"He passed the Dial to you, did he not?"

"So?"

"He would only do that because he reached the end of his calling." John blinked rapidly a few times. "I shall miss him dearly."

"Yeah. I miss him too."

They flew in silence for a short time. Chris *did* have many questions, but none that seemed pressing. He'd grown weary of trying to categorize, explain, and reason through the events of the past week. Simply believing them was much easier.

"So have you been a pilot long?" he asked casually.

"Ever since the aeroplane was invented."

"Really? So are you as old as Nick was?"

"A great many years older," he said, turning his deep, gray-green eyes to Chris.

"And I take it you're *not* a healer; otherwise you'd be doing this yourself."

"That is correct. Although I hold the authority and *can* heal, I'm more of an overseer, if you will. I instruct and help when I can."

"I see."

John smiled again. There was so much depth in his eyes, so much compassion and understanding in his countenance. But older than two hundred plus years? Chris didn't dare ask. He was confident this man had seen a significant span of earth's history come and go.

The two-hour flight passed quickly as they talked easily of current events and the path Chris took to get his doctorate in history. He studiously avoided topics dealing with his future, his abilities as a Vovnik healer, or the chance that he'd outlive his own grandchildren. In truth, he was afraid of the answers. It'd be like living history before it actually happened, which could alter true history from its intended course.

Then one thing came to mind that had never quite connected. "How much did you know about Nick Tewdrig and his calling?"

"All I needed to know. Nothing more."

"He said I was an adopted Physician of Myddfai through transference of the Dial of Ahaz. Are all Vovnik healers Myddfaian sons? I assume there's more than one of me, other pieces of the Dial."

"The simple answer is no. You hold the only Dial shard I know of. As far as the legend of Myddfai goes, being a man of history, you recognize that identical legends are often found in multiple cultures, regardless of geography."

Chris nodded. "Sure."

"Almost every civilization on earth has a Great Flood tale, a record of great destruction around the time of the crucifixion, and legends of divine visitation—even in non-Christian nations. The events actually occurred but were recorded according to local understanding. With that in mind, let me ask: what happens when different scribes record the same event in different locations or at different times?"

"The story gets embellished to favor the writer and the writer's culture."

"Precisely. It's true: the fourth Myddfaian son was a Vovnik healer, but so was the second. And so were others throughout the UK and Europe. Only those from Wales and Southern England take the added name of Myddfai."

"But I'm not from there."

"Your ancestry is, Dr. *Pendragon.*"

"So the fourth son doesn't *have* to be a Welshman, right?"

"No. It all depends on who possesses the Dial *and* who has the proper authority to call upon its power."

"Because the power comes from the bearer, not the Dial itself."

John nodded. "Nicholas taught you well."

Chris rubbed the back of his neck. "I still don't understand why, but I'm trying to. I guess I still have a boatload to learn."

John laughed again. "I'll never get used to Americans and their strange turns of phrase. Exactly what volume is a 'boatload'?"

"A lot," Chris laughed with him. "More than *I* want, anyway."

A few minutes later, John radioed for permission to land. The plane touched down as if it were a feather landing on a pillow. The old man had clearly flown for a very long time. A rental car awaited them. The weather in the mountain state was a pleasant change from the nearly perpetually overcast skies of Wales and Spokane.

"I could get used to springtime here," Chris commented. "It's beautiful."

"Spring has always been my favorite time of year," John concurred. "It represents new birth. It's when our Savior was born and when He gave His life so we could live again."

Chris smiled and nodded. The straightforward talk of this man struck a chord within him that resonated truth. He felt as if he could—and *should*—believe everything he said.

The drive to West Park Hospital took only minutes.

"I sense we are not too late, but we must hurry," John said, stepping from the car.

"Who is the patient?"

"Her name is Mandie Griffs. She and her son were attacked by her ex-husband. He almost succeeded in killing her. The son is okay, but she's in a coma."

"Is she under guard?"

"Not really. No police; but the place—a critical care unit—does have a secured entrance." He then grinned. "Not to worry. Just *act* like you know what you're doing."

Chris chuffed. "Story of my life."

They went directly to the elevator.

"It is best if no one has a chance to question you," John said, pressing the call button. "Mandie is on the second floor, room five in the CCU."

"Wait—you're coming with me, right?"

"I'll be there, Chris, but this is something *you* must attend to. It is *your* gift. I am not the Dial-bearer."

"Just moral support, then?"

John smiled. "Of course. But I am also here to meet someone. He is ready to learn the true nature of *his* gift."

"Another Lamed Vovnik?" Chris asked, intrigued.

"Yes. He is here for Mandie, but he is not a healer like you. His interest in her is more on a personal level."

"Ah."

The elevator door opened, and the two men stepped in. Chris drew a deep breath and let it out slowly. There was no question what he sensed. "I feel as if Mandie is calling me."

Still smiling, John reached over and pressed the button for the second floor.

CHAPTER 59

CRITICAL CARE TOOK UP A good portion of the second floor. The CCU was just off the waiting area. A prominent sign read that unauthorized persons were not allowed inside. When Chris pointed to the sign, John said, "Your authorization comes from God."

He had no argument for that.

As they approached the glass door, a nurse on the other side swiped a pass card across the lock, triggering a buzzer. In a frenzied rush, she pushed the door open and scooted down the adjacent hallway. Chris grabbed the handle just before the door fully closed.

Entering the CCU, the two men slipped past the nurses' station to Mandie's room. No one seemed to notice them.

"You go ahead. I'll keep watch out here. But please make haste."

Chris nodded and entered.

Mandie Griffs was hooked to more machines than Kathryn's mother had been. That worried him. Doubt crept in on his confidence. This young woman looked worse than Lona Ingledew had—and he hadn't been able to save her.

He clenched his jaw and silently chastised his insecurity. He reminded himself that Kathryn's mother was *supposed* to pass on. He'd felt that impression strongly. But that didn't mean Mandie was.

Stepping up to the bed, Chris drew a deep breath then placed his right hand on her neck and the Dial in his left. He focused on blocking out all ambient noises and concentrated on what he perceived beyond his hands. There was fear there. And pain. But even more, he felt anger, irrational jealousy, and betrayal. Her wounds had been caused by someone rife with such emotions. Ignoring that, he fixated on the healing of physical substance, the repairing of damaged tissue. Boney cartilage and punctured tracheal tissue required mending in her throat; blood vessels and nerve fibers needed to reform in her brain. She'd lost so much life-sustaining cerebral matter. He could feel confusion within her body—as if it *wanted* to repair itself but didn't have the wherewithal to do so.

He'd learned from John that this woman was a good person; her wounds were caused by a hateful soul bent on inflicting pain and suffering. She was without blame. This shouldn't have happened.

Father, this is an innocent soul. Please repair these injuries that should have never come to her. Through faith thy will be done.

Chris's hands and arms immediately began to tingle with prickly heat. The sensation grew, then surged. Then, as if someone took a baseball bat to his head, pain filled his skull, so intense his knees buckled. His throat went raw, like it was on fire and he was given gasoline with which to quench it. Breathing coarsely, bracing his trembling knees against the bedframe, he managed to keep his hands in place.

Nobly thru white fog thou hast led me here. Through faith thy will be done. Please, God, let Thy will be to heal this sweet woman.

Suddenly Mandie gasped. It was dry and scratchy. She let it out and gasped again. When her eyes began to twitch and blink, Chris removed his hand from her throat.

"It's okay, Mandie. You're going to be all right," he whispered in her ear.

She jerked in and out of consciousness, her eyes fluttered, and her head moved back and forth. When Chris felt the tingling in his hand fade, he removed it from her head.

"Well done, Chris," John said from the doorway. "Now, let's go. The nurse is coming back."

"But . . ." He paused and looked back at Mandie. "I want to see if she's okay."

"She is. Have faith in your abilities, son." The chastisement was said in a friendly tone.

Chris briefly squeezed Mandie's hand and whispered, "Go with God."

The two men exited the CCU, pushing past the nurse as she returned through the secured entrance. She called after them, but they didn't heed her. Entering a stairwell, they descended to the first floor.

John handed Chris his keys. "Please wait in the car. I'll be there presently."

Chris nodded and headed to the rental. Once there, he was hit with a jolt of fatigue. He unlocked the door and fell into the passenger seat. His thoughts kept going back to the anger he felt from Mandie's wounds and the severity of damage that anger caused. Her ex must have truly hated her.

When John returned, Chris revealed, "Man, that was brutal. She was really messed up inside. Is it always like this?"

"It depends on the severity of the ailment and what caused it—or so I'm told. Nicholas claimed to experience similar reactions when he began his calling. You'll get used to it."

"Mandie is a fighter. I felt every bit of damage as well as the bitterness of her ex, but I also sensed a strong will to live."

John cocked his head and smiled. "I envy you that. Not in a jealous way; rather, in the depth by which you heal. What a miraculous thing to experience."

"What—you've never done this?"

"Oh, I've given my share of blessings, some with truly miraculous results. But I don't *experience* healing like you. That cherished gift is reserved for the bearer of the Dial of Ahaz."

"It's a gift for sure; I'm not sure if I cherish it yet."

"You will, my friend," the old man said with a chuckle. "And you will be cherished for it. Regrettably, you will never be able to bask in that adoration."

"That's okay," he said, stretching forcefully. "I never was one for blowing hot air up my own skirt."

John guffawed. "There's another one. Why would anyone want to do that in the first place? I tell you, I love this country of yours. Peculiar experiences happen around every corner."

"Great. I can't wait," Chris said with unmasked cynicism.

The flight back to Salt Lake International was made mostly in silence. Chris's head and throat still bore remnants of discomfort, but no real pain. And there was still a curious, mild soreness in his liver and bones. *Kaylee,* he thought with a smile. *That* healing was actually fun. No one was expecting a thing, so there was no pressure on him to succeed. Perhaps that's why he'd been so sure, so confident that the little girl was healed. Oh how he wished he could be at her next oncology appointment—if only to see the bewildered look on her physician's face and the sheer joy on her mother's.

Chris wondered to what extend he'd be able to heal. Mandie had been near death; the machines in the CCU were basically keeping her alive. But he experienced everything she'd gone through. Is that why Nicholas said he couldn't bring someone back from the dead? Because to do so would mean he'd have to die? The thought intrigued him . . . and scared him. What if he was prompted to raise someone from the dead? Did he have that level of faith, that level of compassion? Would he willingly give his life for someone else to live?

True to John's word, a new ticket awaited Chris at the airline counter. First class. Nice. According to the receptionist, his luggage was already en route to Spokane. It'd be waiting for him in the Flight Club.

"You must have great connections," Chris said to John.

The old man gave a long wink. "I travel the world. Connections come in handy."

"I bet. Will I see you again?"

John shrugged. "When it is necessary. If you feel you have need, call me."

"On what? Do you have a global cell phone or something?"

"Yes, as a matter of fact, I do," he said, pointing a finger toward the heavens.

"Ah. Never mind."

"You know, I feel Nicholas Tewdrig made an excellent choice," John said, patting Chris on the shoulder. "Godspeed, my friend." The silver-haired man then blended into an ebbing tide of people and disappeared.

"Godspeed," Chris echoed softly to himself.

CHAPTER 60

By the time Chris got back to his apartment in Spokane, it was well past midnight. Rain cascaded from the heavens. Wet and emotionally exhausted, he tossed his suitcase in a corner, his satchel on his desk, and stood the box containing Nick's cane next to his bed. He then removed his shoes, socks, and shirt, and fell backward, letting his body completely relax. The downpour beat a steady, quieting pattern against the window. The temperature in his room was perfect. His bed offered a familiar comfort that seemed to envelop him in assurance and peace. The sounds and smells and feel of his apartment were calming, soothing. He was finally home, but sadly, he recognized he would not be able to stay here. He needed to keep moving.

Though his body craved sleep, he knew he'd get little. His mind was as active as ever—and as pessimistic. Could he really live this new life, this unpetitioned calling? It seemed so chaotic. On the other hand, the prospect of such an unpredictable life was incredibly exciting. The whole healing process fascinated him. He suspected he'd never fully understand the exact mechanism of *how* he healed, and that disappointed him.

Flopping an arm over his eyes, he inhaled deeply. He then reached into his pocket and pulled out the Dial. An unprecedented miracle occurred on the face of this very stone. The earth had changed its rotation or shifted on its axis to the point that a shadow appeared to move backward. It was a sign; a sign brought about by the faithful actions of King Hezekiah.

The faithful *actions* of Hezekiah!

Chris sat up quickly. Was that it? Was it Chris's *actions* that channeled the power of the Dial?

The Dial doesn't give you power; you give it power.

He thought back to what Nicholas said about the Apostle James's teachings on faith and works. If faith without works is dead, then it made sense that works without faith is also dead. To fulfill his destiny, he not only had to *have* faith, he had to *act* on that faith, to exercise it, like a muscle. *That* was how the Dial gained its power!

Chris lay in the dark, awash in solace as an inner sense of correctness and affirmation filled him from head to toe. It was all crystal clear. He didn't need to worry about tomorrow. Tomorrow was another day. Yes, he still had to tenure his resignation with the university. That wouldn't go over well. And he'd have to move, leaving no forwarding address. He would cash out his 401K and other investments and put it all in a single bank account under a new name. That should last him for a while. He wondered about telling his family of his resolution but decided to put off crossing that slippery bridge until later. Right now, he simply wanted to drift away, to feel the presence of the Dial, and to listen for a still, small voice telling him his actions were acceptable to God.

With his eyes closed, he held the Dial to his chest and let his mind fill with the tranquil voice of the rain. A warm smile crossed his lips. Finally, for the first time in his life, he felt truly happy.

AFTERWORD

Although this book is a work of fiction, the legends and locations are authentic. The weaving of one legend with another was solely the work of the author.

For readers interested in learning more about the legends and locations used in this novel, please visit the sites referenced below:

Lady of the Lake. en.wikipedia.org/wiki/Llyn_y_Fan_Fach

Physicians of Myddfai. en.wikipedia.org/wiki/Myddfai

St. Anne's Well/The Virturous Well (prayer ribbons, maiden bubbles). en.wikipedia.org/wiki/Trellech

Gatehouse on Monnow Bridge. en.wikipedia.org/wiki/Monnow_Bridge; en.wikipedia.org/wiki/Monmouth

The Menai Bridge. www.anglesey-history.co.uk/places/bridges

The Church of St. Nicholas. en.wikipedia.org/wiki/Trellech; http://www.churchinwales.org.uk/?s=trellech&submit.x=0&submit.y=0

The Dial of Ahaz. 2 Kings 20:5-11; www.bible-history.com/isbe/D/DIAL+OF+AHAZ

Lamed Vovniks/ Righteous Thirty-Six. en.wikipedia.org/wiki/Tzadikim_Nistarim; www.lamed-vav.com

Thirty-Six, **by Daron Fraley**. www.daronfraley.com and www.lamed-vav.com.

ABOUT THE AUTHOR

GREGG R. LUKE, RPH, WAS born in Bakersfield, California, but spent the majority of his childhood and young adult life in Santa Barbara, California. He served an LDS mission in Wisconsin then pursued his education in natural sciences at SBCC, UCSB, and BYU. He completed his schooling at the University of Utah, College of Pharmacy.

Gregg currently practices pharmacy in Logan, Utah. He is a voracious reader and has been writing stories since childhood. He has been published in *Skin Diver* magazine, *The Oceanographic Letter*, *Destiny* magazine, and the *New Era* magazine. His fiction includes *The Survivors*, *Do No Harm*, *Altered State*, *Blink of an Eye*, *Bloodborne*, *Deadly Undertakings*, and *Twisted Fate*, five of which were Whitney Award finalists.

Find out more about Gregg's novels at www.greggluke.com